PENGUIN MODERN CLASSICS

A Clockwork Orange

Anthony Burgess was born in Manchester in 1917 and educated at Xaverian College and Manchester University. He
spent six years in the British Army before becoming a schoolmaster and colonial education officer in Malaya and Brunei.
After the success of his *Malayan Trilogy*, he became a full-time
writer in 1959.

He achieved a worldwide reputation as one of the leading
novelists of his day, and one of the most versatile. He wrote
criticism, stage plays, translations and a Broadway musical,
and he composed more than 150 musical works, including a
piano concerto, a violin concerto for Yehudi Menuhin, and
a symphony. His books have been published all over the
world, and they include *The Complete Enderby*, *Nothing Like
the Sun*, *Napoleon Symphony*, *Tremor of Intent*, *Earthly Powers*
and *A Dead Man in Deptford*. Anthony Burgess died in London
in 1993.

Andrew Biswell is the Professor of Modern Literature at
Manchester Metropolitan University and the Director of the
International Anthony Burgess Foundation. His publications
include a biography, *The Real Life of Anthony Burgess*, which
won the Portico Prize in 2006. He is currently editing the
letters and short stories of Anthony Burgess.

ANTHONY BURGESS

A Clockwork Orange
The Restored Edition

Edited with an Introduction and Notes by Andrew Biswell
Foreword by Martin Amis

PENGUIN BOOKS

PENGUIN CLASSICS

Published by the Penguin Group

Penguin Books Ltd, 80 Strand, London WC2R ORL, England

Penguin Group (USA) Inc., 375 Hudson Street, New York, New York 10014, USA

Penguin Group (Canada), 90 Eglinton Avenue East, Suite 700, Toronto, Ontario, Canada M4P 2Y3
(a division of Pearson Penguin Canada Inc.)

Penguin Ireland, 25 St Stephen's Green, Dublin 2, Ireland (a division of Penguin Books Ltd)

Penguin Group (Australia), 707 Collins Street, Melbourne, Victoria 3008, Australia
(a division of Pearson Australia Group Pty Ltd)

Penguin Books India Pvt Ltd, 11 Community Centre, Panchsheel Park, New Delhi – 110 017, India

Penguin Group (NZ), 67 Apollo Drive, Rosedale, Auckland 0632, New Zealand
(a division of Pearson New Zealand Ltd)

Penguin Books (South Africa) (Pty) Ltd, Block D, Rosebank Office Park,
181 Jan Smuts Avenue, Parktown North, Gauteng 2193, South Africa

Penguin Books Ltd, Registered Offices: 80 Strand, London WC2R ORL, England

www.penguin.com

First published in Great Britain by William Heinemann 1962
This edition published by William Heinemann 2012
Published in Penguin Classics 2013
003

Penguin Books is committed to a sustainable
future for our business, our readers and our planet.
This book is made from Forest Stewardship
Council™ certified paper.

Contents

FOREWORD by Martin Amis   vii

INTRODUCTION by Andrew Biswell   xv

A CLOCKWORK ORANGE   1

  ONE
  Page   5

  TWO
  Page   83

  THREE
  Page   141

NOTES   207

NADSAT GLOSSARY   215

PROLOGUE to *A Clockwork Orange:*
A Play with Music by Anthony Burgess   219

EPILOGUE: 'A Malenky Govoreet about the
Molodoy' by Anthony Burgess   227

ESSAYS, ARTICLES AND REVIEWS   235

'The Human Russians' by Anthony Burgess   237

'Clockwork Marmalade' by Anthony Burgess   245

Extract from an Unpublished Interview
  with Anthony Burgess   253

Programme Note for *A Clockwork Orange
2004* by Anthony Burgess   259

'Ludwig Van', a review of *Beethoven* by
  Maynard Solomon by Anthony Burgess   263

'Gash Gold-Vermillion' by Anthony Burgess   267

'*A Clockwork Orange*' by Kingsley Amis   275

'New Novels' by Malcolm Bradbury   277

'Horror Show' by Christopher Ricks   279

'All Life is One: *The Clockwork Testament,
  or Enderby's End*' by A. S. Byatt   293

Afterword by Stanley Edgar Hyman   297

A Last Word on Violence by Anthony Burgess   305

ANNOTATED PAGES from Anthony Burgess's
1961 Typescript of *A Clockwork Orange*   307

FOREWORD
Martin Amis

The day-to-day business of writing a novel often seems to consist of nothing but decisions – decisions, decisions, decisions. Should this paragraph go here? Or should it go there? Can that chunk of exposition be diversified by dialogue? At what point does this information need to be revealed? Ought I to use a different adjective and a different adverb in that sentence? Or no adverb and no adjective? Comma or semicolon? Colon or dash? And so on.

These decisions are minor, clearly enough, and they are processed more or less rationally by the conscious mind. All the major decisions, by contrast, have been reached before you sit down at your desk; and they involve not a moment's thought. The major decisions are inherent in the original frisson – in the enabling throb or whisper (a whisper that says, *Here is a novel you may be able to write*). Very mysteriously, it is the unconscious mind that does the heavy lifting. No one knows how it happens. This is why Norman Mailer called his (excellent) book on fiction *The Spooky Art*.

When, in 1960, Anthony Burgess sat down to write *A Clockwork Orange*, we may be pretty sure that he had a handful of certainties about what lay ahead of him. He knew that the novel would be set in the near future (and that it would take the standard science-fictional route, developing, and fiercely exaggerating, current tendencies). He knew that his vicious anti-hero, Alex, would narrate, and that he would do so in an argot or idiolect that the world had never heard before (he eventually settled on an unfailingly delightful blend of Russian, Romany, and rhyming slang). He knew that it would have something to do with Good and Bad, and Free Will. And he knew, crucially, that Alex would harbour a highly implausible passion: an ecstatic love of classical music.

We see the wayward brilliance of that last decision when we reacquaint ourselves, after half a century, with Burgess's leering, sneering, sniggering, snivelling young sociopath (a type unimprovably caught by Malcolm McDowell in Stanley Kubrick's uneven but justly celebrated film). 'It wasn't me, brother,' Alex whines at his social worker (who has hurried to the local jailhouse): 'Speak up for me, sir, for I'm not so bad.' But Alex *is* so bad; and he knows it. The opening chapters of *A Clockwork Orange* still deliver the shock of the new: they form a red streak of gleeful evil.

On their first night on the town Alex and his *droogs* (or partners in crime) waylay a schoolmaster, rip up the books he is carrying, strip off his clothes, and stomp on his dentures; they rob and belabour a shopkeeper and his wife ('a fair tap with a crowbar'); they give a drunken bum a kicking ('we cracked into him lovely'); and they have a ruck with a rival gang, using the knife, the chain, the straight razor: this 'would be real, this would be proper, this would be the nozh, the oozy, the britva, not just fisties and boots . . . and there I was dancing about with my britva like I might be a barber on board a ship on a very rough sea'.

Next, they steal a car ('zigzagging after cats and that'), cursorily savage a courting couple, break into a cottage owned by 'another intelligent type bookman type like that we'd fillied [messed] with some hours back', destroy the typescript of his work in progress, and gangrape his wife:

> Then there was like quiet and we were full of like hate, so [we] smashed what was left to be smashed – typewriter, lamp, chairs – and Dim, it was typical old Dim, watered the fire out and was going to dung on the carpet, there being plenty of paper, but I said no. 'Out out out out,' I howled. The writer veck and his zheena were not really there, bloody and torn and making noises. But they'd live.

And all this has been accomplished by the end of chapter 2.

Before Part 1 ends with Alex in a *rozz-shop* smelling 'of like sick and lavatories and beery rots [mouths] and disinfectant', our 'Humble Narrator' drugs and ravishes two ten-year-olds, slices up Dim with his britva, and robs and murders an elderly spinster:

> . . . but this baboochka . . . like scratched my litso [face]. So then I screeched: 'You filthy old soomka [woman]', and upped with the little malenky [little] like silver statue and cracked her a fine fair tolchock [blow] on the gulliver [head] and that shut her up real horrorshow [good] and lovely.

In the brief hiatus between these two storms of 'ultra-violence' (the novel's day one and day two), Alex goes home – to Municipal Flatblock 18A. And here, for a change, he does nothing worse than keep his parents awake by playing the multi-speaker stereo in his room. First he listens to a new violin concerto, before moving on to Mozart and Bach. Burgess evokes Alex's sensations in a bravura passage which owes less to *nadsat*, or teenage pidgin, and more to the modulations of *Ulysses*:

> The trombones crunched redgold under my bed, and behind my gulliver the trumpets three-wise silver-flamed, and there by the door the timps rolling through my guts and out again crunched like candy thunder. Oh, it was wonder of wonders. And then, a bird of like rarest spun heavenmetal, or like silvery wine flowing in a spaceship, gravity all nonsense now, came the violin solo above all the other strings, and those strings were like a cage of silk round my bed.

Here we feel the power of that enabling throb or whisper – the authorial insistence that the Beast would be susceptible to Beauty. At a stroke, and without sentimentality, Alex is decisively realigned. He has now been equipped with a soul, and even a suspicion of innocence – a suspicion confirmed by the deft disclosure in the final sentences of Part 1: 'That was everything. I'd done the lot, now. And me still only fifteen.'

In the late 1950s, when *A Clockwork Orange* was just a twinkle in the author's eye, the daily newspapers were monotonously bewailing the rise of mass delinquency, as the post-war Teddy Boys diverged and multiplied into the Mods and the Rockers (who would later devolve into the Hippies and the Skinheads). Meanwhile, the literary weeklies were much concerned with the various aftershocks of World War II – in particular, the supposedly startling coexistence, in the Third

Reich, of industrialised barbarism and High Culture. This is a debate that the novel boldly joins.

Lying naked on his bed, and thrilling to Mozart and Bach, Alex fondly recalls his achievements, earlier that night, with the maimed writer and his ravaged wife:

> . . . and I thought, slooshying [listening] away to the brown gorgeousness of the starry [old] German master, that I would like to have tolchocked them both harder and ripped them to ribbons on their own floor.

Thus Burgess is airing the sinister but not implausible suggestion that Beethoven and Birkenau didn't merely coexist. They combined and colluded, inspiring mad dreams of supremacism and omnipotence.

In Part 2, violence comes, not from below, but from above: it is the 'clean' and focused violence of the state. Having served two years of his sentence, the entirely incorrigible Alex is selected for Reclamation Treatment (using 'Ludovico's Technique'). This turns out to be a crash course of aversion therapy. Each morning he is injected with a strong emetic and wheeled into a screening room, where his head is clamped in a brace and his eyes pinned wide open; and then the lights go down.

At first Alex is obliged to watch familiar scenes of recreational mayhem (tolchocking malchicks, creeching devotchkas, and the like). We then move on to lingering mutilations, Japanese tortures ('you even viddied a gulliver being sliced off a soldier'), and finally a newsreel, with eagles and swastikas, firing squads, naked corpses. The soundtrack of the last clip is Beethoven's Fifth. 'Grahzny bratchnies [filthy bastards],' whimpers Alex when it's over:

'Using Ludwig van like that. He did no harm to anyone. He just wrote music.' And then I was really sick and they had to bring a bowl that was in the shape of like a kidney . . . 'It can't be helped,' said Dr Branom. 'Each man kills the thing he loves, as the poet-prisoner said. Here's the punishment element, perhaps. The Governor ought to be pleased.'

From now on Alex will feel intense nausea, not only when he contemplates violence, but also when he hears Ludwig van and the other starry masters. His soul, such as it was, has been excised.

We now embark on the curious apologetics of Part 3. 'Nothing odd will do long,' said Dr Johnson – meaning that the reader's appetite for weirdness is very quickly surfeited. Burgess (unlike, say, Franz Kafka) is sensitive to this near-infallible law; but there's a case for saying that *A Clockwork Orange* ought to be even shorter than its 196 pages. It was in fact published with two different endings. The American edition omits the final chapter (this is the version used by Kubrick), and closes with Alex recovering from what proves to be a cathartic suicide attempt. He is listening to Beethoven's Ninth:

When it came to the Scherzo I could viddy myself very clear running and running on very light and mysterious nogas [feet], carving the whole litso of the creeching world with my cut-throat britva. And there was the slow movement and the lovely last singing movement still to come. I was cured all right.

This is the 'dark' ending. In the official version, though, Alex is afforded full redemption. He simply – and bathetically – 'outgrows' the atavisms of youth, and starts itching to get married and settle down; his musical tastes turn to 'what they call *Lieder*, just a goloss [voice] and a piano, very quiet and like yearny'; and he carries around with him a photo, scissored out of the newspaper, of a plump baby – 'a baby gurgling goo goo goo'. So we are asked to accept that Alex has turned all soft and broody – at the age of eighteen.

It feels like a startling loss of nerve on Burgess's part, or a recrudescence (we recall that he was an Augustinian Catholic) of self-punitive religious guilt. Horrified by its own transgressive energy, the novel submits to a Reclamation Treatment sternly supplied by its author. Burgess knew that something was wrong: 'a work too didactic to be artistic', he half-conceded, 'pure art dragged into the arena of morality'. And he shouldn't have worried: Alex may be a teenager, but readers are grown-ups, and are perfectly at peace with the unregenerate. Besides, *A Clockwork Orange* is in essence a black comedy. Confronted by evil, comedy feels no need to punish or correct. It answers with corrosive laughter.

In his book on Joyce, *Joysprick* (1973), Burgess made a provocative distinction between what he calls the 'A' novelist and the 'B' novelist: the A novelist is interested in plot, character, and psychological insight, whereas the B novelist is interested, above all, in the play of words. The most famous B novel is *Finnegans Wake*, which Nabokov aptly described as 'a cold pudding of a book, a snore in the next room'; and the same might be said of *Ada: A Family Chronicle*, by far the most B-inclined of Nabokov's nineteen fictions. Anyway, the B novel, as a genre, is now utterly defunct; and *A Clockwork Orange* may be its only long-term survivor. It is a book that can still be read with steady pleasure, continuous amusement, and – at times – incredulous admiration. Anthony Burgess, then, is not 'a minor B novelist', as he described himself; he is the *only* B novelist. I think he would have settled for that.

INTRODUCTION
Andrew Biswell

In 1994, less than a year after Anthony Burgess had died at the age of seventy-six, BBC Scotland commissioned the novelist William Boyd to write a radio play in celebration of his life and work. This was broadcast during the Edinburgh Festival on 21 August 1994, along with a concert performance of Burgess's music and a recording of his *Glasgow Overture*. The programme was called 'An Airful of Burgess', with the actor John Sessions playing the parts of both Burgess and his fictional alter ego, the poet F. X. Enderby. On the same day, the *Sunday Times* ran a front-page story about the same radio play under the headline 'BBC in Row Over Festival Play's Violent Rape Scene'. The newspaper claimed that the broadcast would feature 'a live re-enactment of a rape scene based on the controversial Anthony Burgess work, *A Clockwork Orange*.' Stanley Kubrick's film, which was said in the article to have been 'blamed for carbon-copy crimes', was also criticised for its 'explicit depiction of gratuitous rape, violence and murder.' Yet anyone who tuned into the radio broadcast hoping to receive the kind of indecent gratification promised by the *Sunday Times* would have been severely disappointed. William Boyd's play, which featured less than two minutes of material derived from *A Clockwork Orange*, was a dignified tribute to Burgess's long life of musical and literary creativity. Even in death, it seemed, Burgess (who had often parodied the style of no-nonsense, right-wing columnists in his fiction) could not escape being the subject of under-informed and apocalyptic journalism.

To understand the development of the controversy which has come to surround *A Clockwork Orange* in its various manifestations, we must go back more than fifty years to 1960, when Anthony Burgess was planning a series of novels about imaginary futures. In the earliest surviving plan for *A Clockwork Orange*, he outlined a book of around 200 pages, to be divided into three sections of seventy pages and set in the year 1980. The anti-hero of this novel, whose working titles included 'The Plank in Your Eye' and 'A Maggot in the Cherry', was a criminal named Fred Verity. Part one was to deal with his crimes and eventual conviction. In the second part, the imprisoned Fred would undergo a new brainwashing technique and be released from jail. Part three would consider the agitation of liberal politicians who were concerned about freedom and churches concerned about sin. At the novel's conclusion Fred, cured of the treatment, would return to his life of crime.

The other novel Burgess was planning at this time was 'Let Copulation Thrive' (published in October 1962 as *The Wanting Seed*), another futuristic fable about an over-populated future in which religion is outlawed and homo-sexuality has become the norm, officially promoted by government policies to control the birth-rate. In Burgess's imaginary future, men are press-ganged into the armed forces to take part in war games. The true purpose of these conflicts is to turn the bodies of the dead into tinned meat to feed a hungry population. What *The Wanting Seed* and

A Clockwork Orange share is an underpinning idea of politics as a constantly swinging pendulum, with the governments in both novels alternating between authoritarian discipline and liberal *laissez-faire*. Despite his gifts as a comic novelist, and the cultural optimism he had shown during his years as a school-teacher, Burgess was an Augustinian Catholic at heart, and he could not altogether shake off the belief in original sin (the tendency of humankind to do evil rather than good) which had been drilled into him by the Manchester Xaverian Brothers when he was a schoolboy. A similar fascination with evil is found in the works of his friend and co-religionist Graham Greene, whose novel *Brighton Rock* (1938) presents a comparable blend of social decay and teenage delinquency.

Before Burgess came to write dystopian novels of his own, he had spent nearly thirty years reading other examples of the genre. In his critical study *The Novel Now* (published as a pamphlet in 1967 and expanded to book-length in 1971), he devoted a chapter to fictional utopias and dystopias. Twentieth-century literary writers, he argued, had on the whole rejected the socialist utopianism of H. G. Wells, who denied original sin and put his faith in scientific rationalism. Burgess was far more interested in the anti-utopian tradition of Aldous Huxley, who challenged the progressive assumption that scientific progress would automatically bring happiness in speculative novels such as *Brave New World* (1932) and *After Many a Summer* (1939). He was no less impressed by the political dystopianism of Sinclair Lewis's novel *It Can't Happen Here* (1935), a gloomy prophecy about the rise of a right-wing dictatorship in America, or by *The Aerodrome* (1941), Rex Warner's wartime fable about the appeal of handsome young pilots with fascist inclinations. Burgess had read George Orwell's

Nineteen Eighty-Four shortly after publication (the title page of his diary for 1952 is headed: 'Down with Big Brother'), but he tended to disparage Orwell's novel as a dying man's prophecy, which was unduly pessimistic about the capacity of working people to resist their ideological oppressors. In his hybrid novel/critical book *1985*, Burgess suggested that Orwell had simply been caricaturing tendencies that he saw around him in 1948. 'Perhaps every dystopian vision is a figure of the present,' Burgess wrote, 'with certain features sharpened and exaggerated to point a moral and a warning.'

British dystopian fiction was enjoying a minor renaissance in the early 1960s, and Burgess, who was reviewing new novels for the *Times Literary Supplement* and the *Yorkshire Post*, was well placed to notice this phenomenon and respond to it in his own imaginative writing. In 1960 he read *Facial Justice* by L. P. Hartley and *When the Kissing Had to Stop* by Constantine Fitzgibbon. But the novel which caught his attention more than any other was *The Unsleep* (1961) by Diana and Meir Gillon, a husband-and-wife writing team who also worked together on a number of political non-fiction books. Reviewing this book in the *Yorkshire Post* on 6 April 1961, Burgess wrote:

> [*The Unsleep* is] much to my taste, a piece of FF (futfic or future fiction) which, in that post-Orwellian manner which is really a reversion to *Brave New World* Unrevisited, terrifies not with the ultimate totalitarian nightmare but with a dream of liberalism going mad. In this perhaps-not-so-remote Gillon-England, with its stability (no war, no crime) ensured by advanced psychological techniques, life is for living. Life's biggest enemy is sleep; sleep, therefore, must be

liquidated. A couple of jabs of Sta-Wake and you reclaim thirty years from the darkness.

But things don't go quite as expected. There's too much wakeful leisure: crime and delinquency ensue and there have to be police. Then comes an epidemic of unconsciousness, believed at first to be caused by a virus from Mars. Nature reacts violently to Sta-Wake and warns man, as she's warned him before, against excessive naughtiness or liberalism.

The other book Burgess read while he was preparing to write *A Clockwork Orange* was *Brave New World Revisited* (1959), Huxley's non-fiction sequel to his earlier novel. From Huxley he learned about the emerging technologies of behaviour modification, brainwashing and chemical persuasion. There is no evidence to suggest that Burgess had read *Science and Human Behaviour* by the psychologist B. F. Skinner, but he found a summary of Skinner's theories in the pages of Huxley's book:

And even today we find a distinguished psychologist, Professor B. F. Skinner of Harvard University, insisting that, 'as scientific explanation becomes more and more comprehensive, the contribution which may be claimed by the individual himself appears to approach zero. Man's vaunted creative powers, his achievements in art, science and morals, his capacity to choose and our right to hold him responsible for the consequences of his choice – none of these is conspicuous in the new scientific self-portrait.'

As Jonathan Meades has observed, 'Skinner would be completely forgotten today were it not for Burgess's hatred of him,' which he articulated in fictional form through the character of Professor Balaglas in *The Clockwork Testament* (1974). In his day, Skinner was well known for his utopian novel *Walden Two* (1948), in which he imagined a bright technocratic future of teetotal conformity, communal child-rearing (the words 'mother' and 'father' have become meaningless), utilitarian clothing, and harmonious living in single-sex dormitories. The bright lights and garish posters of advertising have been abolished in Skinner's ideal community, and history is no longer thought to be worth studying. In *Science and Human Behaviour*, he dismisses genetics, culture, environment and individual freedom of choice as insignificant factors when it comes to determining human personality. To Burgess, who believed in the primacy of free will (and whose public persona was almost entirely self-created), this was the most revolting kind of nonsense. One of the purposes of his own dystopian novel was to offer a counter-argument to the mechanistic determinism of Skinner and his followers. The prison chaplain in *A Clockwork Orange* sums up Burgess's position very concisely: 'When a man cannot choose, he ceases to be a man.'

Burgess was a talented linguist who had studied Malay to degree standard and made translations of literary works written in French, Russian and Ancient Greek. It was his interest in Russian language and literature rather than politics which took him to Leningrad (now known as St Petersburg) for a working holiday in June and July 1961. He had been sent there by his publisher, William Heinemann, who hoped that he might write a travel book about Soviet Russia. He taught himself the basics of Russian by acquiring copies of *Getting Along in Russian* by Mario Pei, *Teach Yourself Russian* by Maximilian

Fourman, and *The Penguin Russian Course*. Yet the intended non-fiction project was soon put aside when a different kind of book began to take shape. Before leaving England, Burgess had contemplated writing his novel about teenage hoodlums using British slang of the early 1960s, but he was worried that the language would be out of date before the book was published. Outside the Metropole Hotel in Leningrad, Burgess and his wife witnessed gangs of violent, well-dressed youths who reminded him of the Teddy Boys back home in England. He claimed in his memoirs that this was the moment at which he decided to devise a new language for his novel based on Russian, to be called 'Nadsat' (this being the Russian suffix meaning 'teen'). The urban location of the novel 'could be anywhere,' he wrote later, 'but I visualised it as a sort of compound of my native Manchester, Leningrad and New York.' For Burgess, the important idea was that dandified, lawless youth is an international phenomenon, equally visible on both sides of the Iron Curtain.

Burgess's literary agent, Peter Janson-Smith, submitted the typescript of *A Clockwork Orange* to Heinemann in London on 5 September 1961, with a covering letter explaining that he had been too busy to read it. Heinemann's chief fiction reader, Maire Lynd, wrote a cautious report, and she noted that 'Everything hangs on whether the reader can get into the book quickly enough [. . .] Once in, it becomes hard to stop. But the language difficulty, though fun to wrestle with, is great. With luck the book will be a big success and give the teenagers a new language. But it might be an enormous flop. Certainly nothing in between.'

James Michie, Burgess's editor, circulated a memo on 5 October, in which he described the novel as 'one of the oddest publishing problems imaginable.' He was worried about how to promote the book, which was very different in genre from Burgess's previous comic novels about Malaya and England. Michie was confident that the invented language would not be too forbidding for most readers, but he identified a risk that certain episodes of sexual violence in *A Clockwork Orange* might lead to a prosecution under the 1959 Obscene Publications Act. 'The author can plead artistic justification,' Michie wrote, 'but a delicate-minded critic could convincingly accuse him of indulging in sadistic fantasies.' One of Michie's suggestions was that the possible damage to Burgess's reputation could be limited by publishing the novel with Peter Davies (an imprint of Heinemann) and under a pseudonym. It is unlikely that Burgess knew anything about these flutters of nervousness among his publishers. By 4 February 1962 he was corresponding with William Holden, Heinemann's publicity director, about a glossary of Nadsat to be circulated to the travelling bookshop reps.

One other publishing difficulty was created by Burgess himself. At the end of Part 3, Chapter 6, the typescript contains a note in Burgess's handwriting: 'Should we end here? An optional "epilogue" follows.' James Michie decided to include the epilogue (sometimes referred to as the twenty-first chapter) in the UK edition. When the novel was published in New York by W. W. Norton in 1963, the American editor, Eric Swenson, arrived at a different answer to Burgess's editorial question ('Should we end here?'). Looking back on these events more than twenty years later, Swenson wrote: 'What I remember is that he responded to my comments by telling me that I was right, that he had added the twenty-first upbeat chapter because his British publisher wanted a happy ending. My memory also claims that he urged me to publish an

American edition without that last chapter, which was, again as I remember it, how he had originally ended the novel. We did just that.' Burgess came to regret having allowed two different versions of his novel to circulate in different territories. In 1986 he wrote: 'People wrote to me about this – indeed much of my later life has been expended on Xeroxing statements of intention and the frustration of intention.' Yet it is clear from the 1961 typescript that Burgess's intentions about the ending of his novel were ambiguous from the start.

A Clockwork Orange was published by Heinemann on 14 May 1962 in an edition of 6,000 copies. The book sold poorly, despite having been praised by critics such as Julian Mitchell in the *Spectator* and Kingsley Amis in the *Observer*. A memorandum in the publisher's archive notes that only 3,872 copies had been sold by the mid-1960s. The tone of many early reviews was one of bafflement and distaste for the novel's linguistic experiments. Writing in the *Times Literary Supplement*, John Garrett described *A Clockwork Orange* as 'a viscous verbiage which is the swag-bellied offspring of decay.' Robert Taubman in the *New Statesman* said that it was 'a great strain to read.' Diana Josselson, writing in the *Kenyon Review*, compared *A Clockwork Orange* unfavourably with *The Inheritors*, William Golding's novel about Neanderthals: 'How much one cares for these hairy creatures, how much one hates their successor, Man.' Malcolm Bradbury, whose more encouraging review appeared in *Punch*, claimed that the novel was a 'modern' work in the sense that it dealt with 'our indirection and our indifference, our violence and our sexual exploitation of one another, our rebellion and our protest.'

Despite these mixed responses from the mainstream press, *A Clockwork Orange* soon began to gather an underground following. William S. Burroughs, the author of *The Naked Lunch* (published in Paris in 1959), wrote an enthusiastic recommendation for the Ballantine paperback edition in the United States: 'I do not know of any other writer who has done as much with language as Mr Burgess has done here – the fact that this is also a very funny book may pass unnoticed.' In 1965 Andy Warhol and his regular collaborator Ronald Tavel made a low-budget 16mm black-and-white film, *Vinyl*, based very loosely on Burgess's novel and starring Gerard Malanga and Edie Sedgwick. Described even by its admirers as sixty-six minutes of torture, *Vinyl* is composed of four shots and apparently improvised dialogue. The film was first shown at the New York Cinematheque on 4 June 1965 and, according to Warhol's memoir, *POPism*, it was subsequently projected at least twice in 1966, forming a series of background images for the Velvet Underground's concerts in New York and at Rutgers University. In April 1966, Christopher Isherwood noted in his diary that Brian Hutton (who went on to direct *Where Eagles Dare* in 1978) had asked him to write a film script based on *A Clockwork Orange*. In May of the following year, Terry Southern and Michael Cooper, who proposed to cast Mick Jagger in the leading role, submitted their draft script to the British Board of Film Censors, but this version was rejected as 'an unrelieved diet of hooliganism by teenagers [. . .] not only undesirable but also dangerous.' Burgess himself was asked to write another script in January 1969, but nobody could be persuaded to film it. By January 1970 Stanley Kubrick was corresponding with Si Litvinoff and Max Raab, who sold the film rights to Warner Brothers shortly afterwards. In retrospect it is clear that, from its first appearance in print, Burgess's story had always been waiting to find a wider audience.

Kubrick's cinematic adaptation was released in New York in December 1971 and in London in January 1972. Kubrick said that he had been attracted to Burgess's novel because of the 'wonderful plot, strong characters and clear philosophy,' and Burgess repaid the compliment by describing the film as 'a radical reworking of my own novel.' Forced by the constraints of his visual medium to abandon a good deal of the invented language, Kubrick as director does his best to imply the first-person perspective by playing one of the fight scenes in slow motion (with a soundtrack by Rossini) and shooting the orgy scene at ten times normal speed. But the realism of film inevitably makes the violence of the first forty-five minutes more immediate, which may be one reason why Kubrick chose to omit the second murder in the prison, and to raise the age of the ten-year-old girls who are sexually abused by Alex (they become consenting adults in the film).

It is clear from Burgess's correspondence with his agent that Kubrick was aware of both of the novel's possible endings, and that his decision to follow the shorter US version of the book was reached only after careful thought. Speaking to Michel Ciment in 1980, Kubrick said: '[The] extra chapter depicts the rehabilitation of Alex. But it is, as far as I am concerned, unconvincing and inconsistent with the style and intent of the book [. . .] I certainly never gave any serious consideration to using it.'

Although Burgess reviewed the film enthusiastically on its first release in 1972, he changed his mind about Kubrick when the director published his own illustrated book, under the title *Stanley Kubrick's A Clockwork Orange*. Burgess, infuriated by the idea that Kubrick was presenting himself as the sole author of the cultural artefact known as *A Clockwork Orange*, reviewed this book-of-the-film for the *Library Journal* (on 1 May 1973) in persona as Alex, deploying some new items of Nadsat vocabulary which had not appeared in the novel itself:

Our starry droog Kubrick the sinny veck has, my brothers, like brought forth from his like bounty and all that cal this kniggiwig, which is like all real horror-show lomticks from his Great Masterpiece which would make any fine upstanding young malchick smeck from his yarbles and keeshkas. What it like is is lashings of ultraviolence and the old in-out in-out, but not in slovos except where the chellovecks are govoreeting but in veshches you can viddy and not have to send the old Gulliver to spatchka with like being bored when you are on your sharries in a biblio.

And you can like viddy as well that the Great Purpose in his jeezny for this veck Kubrick or Zubrick (that being the Arab eemya for a grahzny veshch) which is like now at last being made flesh and all that cal, was to have a Book. And now he has a Book. A Book he doth have, O my malenky brothers, verily he doth. Righty right. It was a book he did wish to like make, and he hath done it, Kubrick or Zubrick the Bookmaker.

But, brothers, what makes me smeck like bezoomny is that this like Book will tolchock out into the dark-mans the book what there like previously was, the one by F. Alexander or Sturgess or some such eemya, because who would have slovos when he could viddy real jeezny with his nagoy glazzies?

And so it is like that. Righty right. And real horror-show. And lashings of deng for the carmans of Zubrick. And for your malenky droog not none no more. So gromky shooms of lip-music brrrrrr to thee and thine. And all that cal. – Alex.

The other point to note about Kubrick's film is that it overlooks the prominence of drugs within the subculture of the novel. In Burgess's unpublished screenplay, which had been rejected by Kubrick, Alex's bedroom closet contains various horrors, including a child's skull and hypodermic syringes. In the novel, immediately before Alex rapes the young girls, he injects himself with a drug to increase his potency. And in the Korova Milkbar ('korova' being Russian for 'cow'), where Alex and his droogs gather to plan their crimes, the milk is spiked with an assortment of drugs, such as 'synthemesc' (mescaline) and 'knives' (amphetamines).

Burgess, who had frequently smoked hashish and opium in Malaya in the 1950s, was sometimes said to be one of the pioneers of the literary drug movement. His reputation in this area must have arisen purely from the novel version of *A Clockwork Orange*, since drugs are almost entirely absent from Kubrick's film. Anyone who had read the novel with attention in or shortly after 1962 would have been able to make the connections between teenage gang culture, fashion, music and the casual use of drugs, and it is likely that these elements were instrumental in spreading the novel's countercultural reputation. In many ways it looks like a book which might have been calculated to appeal both to the hallucinogenic flower people of the late 1960s and to the more aggressive skinhead and punk subcultures which followed throughout the 1970s. Burgess, who was vociferous in his hatred of hippies ('bearded louts') and pop music, was appalled by many of the cultural shifts which his novel had anticipated.

It would be difficult to overestimate the significance of *A Clockwork Orange* in terms of its influence on popular culture. On a simple level, we might point to a number of bands whose names are drawn directly from the novel: Heaven 17, Moloko, The Devotchkas and Campag Velocet are merely the most obvious examples. Julian Cope, the front man of the Liverpool band The Teardrop Explodes, recalls in his autobiography that he decided to learn Russian after reading Burgess's novel while he was at school. The drummer of the Sex Pistols claimed that he had only ever read two books: a biography of the Kray Twins and *A Clockwork Orange*. The Rolling Stones wrote the sleeve-notes to one of their albums in Nadsat. Blur dressed up as droogs for the video of their song 'The Universal'. The décor of Kubrick's Korova Milkbar is replicated in the nightclub scene in Danny Boyle's film version of *Trainspotting*. Even Kylie Minogue put on a white jumpsuit, black bowler hat and false eyelash during the stadium tour of her *Fever* album in 2002.

Beyond all this, there is an abiding sense that Burgess's novel opened up new linguistic possibilities for subsequent generations of British novelists. Martin Amis, J. G. Ballard, Will Self, William Boyd, A. S. Byatt and Blake Morrison are among the more established literary writers who have acknowledged its influence on their work.

Burgess, who was a prolific amateur composer in addition to his work as a linguist and novelist, made two separate musical stage adaptations of *A Clockwork Orange* in 1986 and 1990. One of these (with the futuristic title *A Clockwork Orange 2004*) was performed by the Royal Shakespeare Company at the Barbican Theatre in London in 1990. On this occasion the music was provided by Bono and The Edge from the Irish band U2. Reviewing this 'blandly inoffensive' RSC production, directed by Ron Daniels, in the *Sunday Times*, John Peter wrote: 'The violence is obviously mimed: it creates a sense of balletic hysteria rather than terror. The acting is coarse, hard and impersonal, but only partly because the script has no room for anything as finicky as character. Alex (Phil Daniels) is yukky but never frightening, and he narrates the events as he goes along, which makes the story come across like a bizarre anecdote. I know that the novel is a first-person narrative too; but there is a vital difference between the implied drama of the printed text and the open drama of the live stage.' Burgess's theatrical version of the play has been revived on many subsequent occasions – most recently in London and Edinburgh – but at the time of writing (spring 2012) there has been only one complete performance of his *Clockwork Orange* music.

In the final scene of Burgess's stage version, 'a man bearded like Stanley Kubrick' enters, playing *Singin' in the Rain* on a trumpet. He is kicked off the stage by the other actors. Burgess's determination to regain control over his own text is readily apparent in this musical joke. But perhaps his anxiety about authorship was misplaced. Among the younger generation of readers which has come to maturity since his death in 1993, there is little doubt about whose version of *A Clockwork Orange* is more likely to last.

A Note on the Restored Edition

Readers of this fiftieth anniversary edition will notice that, among other additions, it includes the Prologue and Epilogue written by Burgess in the 1980s. These paratexts have not previously been published alongside the text of the novel. Both of them were written around the time that he was making the first of his stage adaptations, published as *A Clockwork Orange: A Play with Music* in 1987, and they illustrate some of the ways in which he revisited his own novel and entered into dialogue with it. I have restored the music for the prisoners' hymn in Part 2, Chapter 1, as it appears in the typescript. The likely reason for its omission in the 1962 Heinemann and 1963 Norton editions is that the cost of reproducing music would have been very high before the introduction of cheap offset lithography.

The 1961 typescript has formed the basis of this restored text, and I have compared each line with the published Heinemann and Norton texts. My principle has been to include as much Nadsat as possible, and on occasion this has involved restoring words and passages which were cancelled in the typescript. Some of Burgess's handwritten amendments to the 1961 typescript are ambiguous, but in general I have preferred a 'lost' Nadsat word (such as 'bugatty', meaning 'rich') to the standard English equivalent as it appeared in the earliest published editions. The 1973 Caedmon audio LP, *Anthony Burgess Reads A Clockwork Orange*, differs in some respects from the printed texts, and I have preferred 'boorjoyce' from the LP to 'bourgeois' as it appears in the typescript. Burgess was not always a careful typist or proofreader, and he was inconsistent in his spelling of 'otchkies' (sometimes 'ochkies') and 'kupetting' (sometimes 'koopeeting'). I have done my best to bring order to the text, but I have been mindful of what Burgess wrote to James Michie (in a letter of 25 February 1962) on the subject of Nadsat spelling: 'One has to remember that it's a spoken language and is bound to be orthographically a bit vague. But I think it's spelt like proper now.'

The 1963 Norton edition and the subsequent Ballantine paperbacks included an afterword by the literary critic Stanley Edgar Hyman (included here because it is part of the history of Burgess's book) and a glossary of Nadsat terms. The expanded glossary in this edition has been compiled with reference to Burgess's letters to his editors in the Heinemann archive. I am grateful to Tom Avery and Jean Rose for bringing these to my attention.

One of the pleasures of annotating Burgess's novel is that the breadth of his allusions has become fully apparent for the first time. Those who are familiar with Burgess's critical writings about Shakespeare and T. S. Eliot will not be surprised to find these authors being quoted in the text. But nobody has previously commented on the extent to which Burgess, who was fascinated by the dark corners of slang, was indebted to Eric Partridge's *Dictionary of Slang and Unconventional English*. Burgess's two copies of this work, which are now part of the book collection at the International Anthony Burgess Foundation, have been read so heavily that they are almost falling apart. The embedded quotations from the poems and plays of Gerard Manley Hopkins have not been noticed before, and I have included one of the essays on Hopkins from *Urgent Copy* to give a sense of the importance of Hopkins to Burgess's formation as a writer. No doubt there are one or two allusions that I have missed; but I should like the notes to be read.

A Clockwork Orange is unique among Burgess's novels in carrying no dedication. The text of this book is not mine to dedicate, but my part in it could not have been accomplished without the help and encouragement of Dr Katherine Adamson, Mr Yves Buelens and Mr William Dixon, to whom I offer grateful thanks.

A CLOCKWORK ORANGE

SHEPHERD: I would that there were no age between ten and three-and-twenty, or that youth would sleep out the rest; for there is nothing in the between but getting wenches with child, wronging the ancientry, stealing, fighting—

Shakespeare, *The Winter's Tale*, Act III, Scene 3

1

'WHAT'S it going to be then, eh?'

1

There was me, that is Alex, and my three droogs, that is Pete, Georgie, and Dim, Dim being really dim, and we sat in the Korova Milkbar making up our rassoo-docks what to do with the evening, a flip dark chill winter bastard though dry. The Korova Milkbar was a milk-plus mesto, and you may, O my brothers, have forgotten what these mestos were like, things changing so skorry these days and everybody very quick to forget, newspapers not being much read neither. Well, what they sold there was milk plus something else. They had no licence for selling liquor, but there was no law yet against prodding some of the new veshches which they used to put into the old moloko, so you could peet it with vellocet or synthemesc or drencrom or one or two other veshches which would give you a nice quiet horrorshow fifteen minutes admiring Bog And All His Holy Angels And Saints in your left shoe with lights bursting all over your mozg. Or you could peet milk with knives in it, as we used to say, and this would sharpen you up and make you ready for a bit of dirty twenty-to-one, and that was what we were peeting this evening I'm starting off the story with.

Our pockets were full of deng, so there was no real need from the point of view of crasting any more pretty polly to tolchock some old veck in an alley and viddy him swim in his blood while we counted the takings and divided by four, nor to do the ultra-violent on some shivering starry grey-haired ptitsa in a shop and go smecking off with the till's guts. But, as they say, money isn't everything.

The four of us were dressed in the heighth of fashion, which in those days was a pair of black very tight tights with the old jelly mould, as we called it, fitting on the crutch underneath the tights, this being to protect and also a sort of a design you could viddy clear enough in a certain light, so that I had one in the shape of a spider, Pete had a rooker (a hand, that is), Georgie had a very fancy one of a flower, and poor old Dim had a very hound-and-horny one of a clown's litso (face, that is), Dim not ever having much of an idea of things and being, beyond all shadow of a doubting thomas, the dimmest of we four. Then we wore waisty jackets without lapels but with these very big built-up shoulders ('pletchoes' we called them) which were a kind of mockery of having real shoulders like that. Then, my brothers, we had these off-white cravats which looked like whipped-up kartoffel or spud with a sort of a design made on it with a fork. We wore our hair not too long and we had flip horrorshow boots for kicking.

'What's it going to be then, eh?'

There were three devotchkas sitting at the counter all together, but there were four of us malchicks and it was usually like one for all and all for one. These sharps were dressed in the heighth of fashion too, with purple and green and orange wigs on their gullivers, each one not costing less than three or four weeks of those sharps' wages, I should reckon, and make-up to match (rainbows round the glazzies, that is, and the rot painted very wide). Then they had long black very straight dresses, and on the groody

8

part of them they had little badges of like silver with different malchicks' names on them – Joe and Mike and suchlike. These were supposed to be the names of the different malchicks they'd spatted with before they were fourteen. They kept looking our way and I nearly felt like saying the three of us (out of the corner of my rot, that is) should go off for a bit of pol and leave poor old Dim behind, because it would be just a matter of kupetting Dim a demi-litre of white but this time with a dollop of synthemesc in it, but that wouldn't really have been playing like the game. Dim was very very ugly and like his name, but he was a horrorshow filthy fighter and very handy with the boot.

'What's it going to be then, eh?'

The chelloveck sitting next to me, there being this long big plushy seat that ran round three walls, was well away with his glazzies glazed and sort of burbling slovos like 'Aristotle wishy washy works outing cyclamen get forficulate smartish.' He was in the land all right, well away, in orbit, and I knew what it was like, having tried it like everybody else had done, but at this time I'd got to thinking it was a cowardly sort of a veshch, O my brothers. You'd lay there after you'd drunk the old moloko and then you got the messel that everything all round you was sort of in the past. You could viddy it all right, all of it, very clear – tables, the stereo, the lights, the sharps and the malchicks – but it was like some veshch that used to be there but was not there not no more. And you were sort of hypnotised by your boot or shoe or a finger-nail as it might be, and at the same time you were sort of picked up by the old scruff and shook like it might be a cat. You got shook and shook till there was nothing left. You lost your name and your body and your self and you just didn't care, and

9

you waited till your boot or your finger-nail got yellow, then yellower and yellower all the time. Then the lights started cracking like atomics and the boot or finger-nail or, as it might be, a bit of dirt on your trouser-bottom turned into a big big big mesto, bigger than the whole world, and you were just going to get introduced to old Bog or God when it was all over. You came back to here and now whimpering sort of, with your rot all squaring up for a boohoohoo. Now, that's very nice but very cowardly. You were not put on this earth just to get in touch with God. That sort of thing could sap all the strength and the goodness out of a chelloveck.

'What's it going to be then, eh?'

The stereo was on and you got the idea that the singer's goloss was moving from one part of the bar to another, flying up to the ceiling and then swooping down again and whizzing from wall to wall. It was Berti Laski rasping a real starry oldie called 'You Blister My Paint.' One of the three ptitsas at the counter, the one with the green wig, kept pushing her belly out and pulling it in in time to what they called the music. I could feel the knives in the old moloko starting to prick, and now I was ready for a bit of twenty-to-one. So I yelped, 'Out out out out!' like a doggie, and then I cracked this veck who was sitting next to me and well away and burbling a horrorshow crack on the ooko or earhole, but he didn't feel it and went on with his 'Telephonic hardware and when the farfarculule gets rubadubdub.' He'd feel it all right when he came to, out of the land.

'Where out?' said Georgie.

'Oh, just to keep walking,' I said, 'and viddy what turns up, O my little brothers.'

So we scatted out into the big winter nochy and walked

down Marghanita Boulevard and then turned into Boothby Avenue, and there we found what we were pretty well looking for, a malenky jest to start off the evening with. There was a doddery starry schoolmaster type veck, glasses on and his rot open to the cold nochy air. He had books under his arm and a crappy umbrella and was coming round the corner from the Public Biblio, which not many lewdies used those days. You never really saw many of the older boorjoyce type out after nightfall those days, what with the shortage of police and we fine young malchicki-wicks about, and this prof type chelloveck was the only one walking in the whole of the street. So we goolied up to him, very polite, and I said, 'Pardon me, brother.'

He looked a malenky bit poogly when he viddied the four of us like that, coming up so quiet and polite and smiling, but he said, 'Yes? What is it?' in a very loud teacher-type goloss, as if he was trying to show us he wasn't poogly. I said:

'I see you have them books under your arm, brother. It is indeed a rare pleasure these days to come across some-body that still reads, brother.'

'Oh,' he said, all shaky. 'Is it? Oh, I see.' And he kept looking from one to the other of we four, finding himself now in the middle of a very smiling and polite square.

'Yes,' I said. 'It would interest me greatly, brother, if you would kindly allow me to see what books those are that you have under your arm. I like nothing better in this world than a good clean book, brother.'

'Clean,' he said. 'Clean, eh?' And then Pete skvatted these three books from him and handed them round real skorry. Being three, we all had one each to viddy at except for Dim. The one I had was called *Elementary Crystallography*, so I opened it up and said, 'Excellent,

11

really first-class,' keeping turning the pages. Then I said in a very shocked type goloss, 'But what is this here? What is this filthy slovo? I blush to look at this word. You disappoint me, brother, you do really.'

'But,' he tried, 'but, but.'

'Now,' said Georgie, 'here is what I should call real dirt. There's one slovo beginning with an f and another with a c.' He had a book called *The Miracle of the Snowflake*.

'Oh,' said poor old Dim, smotting over Pete's shoulder and going too far, like he always did, 'it says here what he done to her, and there's a picture and all. Why,' he said, 'you're nothing but a filthy-minded old skitebird.'

'An old man of your age, brother,' I said, and I started to rip up the book I'd got, and the others did the same with the ones they had, Dim and Pete doing a tug-of-war with *The Rhombohedral System*. The starry prof type began to creech: 'But those are not mine, those are the property of the municipality, this is sheer wantonness and vandal work,' or some such slovos. And he tried to sort of wrest the books back off of us, which was like pathetic. 'You deserve to be taught a lesson, brother,' I said, 'that you do.' This crystal book I had was very tough-bound and hard to razrez to bits, being real starry and made in the days when things were made to last like, but I managed to rip the pages up and chuck them in handfuls of like snowflakes, though big, all over this creeching old veck, and then the others did the same with theirs, old Dim just dancing about like the clown he was. 'There you are,' said Pete. 'There's the mackerel of the cornflake for you, you dirty reader of filth and nastiness.'

'You naughty old veck, you,' I said, and then we began to filly about with him. Pete held his rookers and Georgie sort of hooked his rot wide open for him and Dim yanked out his false zoobies, upper and lower. He threw these down on the pavement and then I treated them to the old boot-crush, though they were hard bastards like, being made of some new horrorshow plastic stuff. The old veck began to make sort of chumbling shooms – 'wuf waf wof' – so Georgie let go of holding his goobers apart and just let him have one in the toothless rot with his ringy fist, and that made the old veck start moaning a lot then, then out comes the blood, my brothers, real beautiful. So all we did then was to pull his outer platties off, stripping him down to his vest and long underpants (very starry; Dim smecked his head off near), and then Pete kicks him lovely in his pot, and we let him go. He went sort of staggering off, it not having been too hard of a tolchock really, going 'Oh oh oh', not knowing where or what was what really, and we had a snigger at him and then riffled through his pockets, Dim dancing round with his crappy umbrella meanwhile, but there wasn't much in them. There were a few starry letters, some of them dating right back to 1960, with 'My dearest dearest' in them and all that chepooka, and a keyring and a starry leaky pen. Old Dim gave up his umbrella dance and of course had to start reading one of the letters out loud, like to show the empty street he could read. 'My darling one,' he recited, in this very high type goloss, 'I shall be thinking of you while you are away and hope you will remember to wrap up warm when you go out at night.' Then he let out a very shoomny smeck – 'Ho ho ho' – pretending to start wiping his yahma with it. 'All right,' I said. 'Let it go, O my brothers.' In the trousers of this starry veck there was only a malenky bit of cutter (money, that is) – not more than three gollies – so we gave all his messy little coin the scatter treatment, it being hen-korm to the amount of pretty polly we had on us already. Then we smashed the umbrella and razrezzed his platties and gave them to the blowing winds, my brothers, and then we'd finished with the starry teacher type veck. We hadn't done much, I know, but that was only like the start of the evening and I make no appy polly loggies to thee or thine for that. The knives in the milk-plus were stabbing away nice and horrorshow now.

The next thing was to do the sammy act, which was one way to unload some of our cutter so we'd have more of an incentive like for some shop-crasting, as well as it being a way of buying an alibi in advance, so we went into the Duke of New York on Amis Avenue and sure enough in the snug there were three or four old baboochkas peeting their black and suds on SA (State Aid). Now we were the very good malchicks, smiling good evening to one and all, though these wrinkled old lighters started to get all shook, their veiny old rookers trembling round their glasses and making the suds spill on the table. 'Leave us be, lads,' said one of them, her face all mappy with being a thousand years old, 'we're only poor old women.' But we just made with the zoobies, flash flash flash, sat down, rang the bell, and waited for the boy to come. When he came, all nervous and rubbing his rookers on his grazzy apron, we ordered us four veterans – a veteran being rum and cherry brandy mixed, which was popular just then, some liking a dash of lime in it, that being the Canadian variation. Then I said to the boy:

'Give these poor old baboochkas over there a nourishing something. Large Scotchmen all round and something to take away.' And I poured my pocket of deng all over the table, and the other three did likewise, O my brothers. So double firegolds were brought in for the scared starry lighters, and they knew not what to do or say. One of

14

them got out 'Thanks, lads,' but you could see they thought there was something dirty like coming. Anyway, they were each given a bottle of Yank General, cognac that is, to take away, and I gave money for them to be delivered each a dozen of black and suds that following morning, they to leave their stinking old cheenas' addresses at the counter. Then with the cutter that was left over we did purchase, my brothers, all the meat pies, pretzels, cheese-snacks, crisps and chocbars in that mesto, and those too were for the old sharps. Then we said, 'Back in a minoota,' and the old ptitsas were still saying, 'Thanks, lads,' and 'God bless you, boys,' and we were going out without one cent of cutter in our carmans.

'Makes you feel real dobby, that does,' said Pete. You could viddy that poor old Dim the dim didn't quite pony all that, but he said nothing for fear of being called gloopy and a domeless wonderboy. Well, we went off now round the corner to Attlee Avenue, and there was this sweets and cancers shop still open. We'd left them alone near three months now and the whole district had been very quiet on the whole, so the armed millicents or rozz patrols weren't round there much, being more north of the river these days. We put our maskies on – new jobs these were, real horrorshow, wonderfully done, really; they were like faces of historical personalities (they gave you the name when you bought) and I had Disraeli, Pete had Elvis Presley, Georgie had Henry VIII and poor old Dim had a poet veck called Peebee Shelley; they were a real like disguise, hair and all, and they were some very special plastic veshch so you could roll up when you'd done with it and hide it in your boot – then the three of us went in, Pete keeping chasso without, not that there was anything to worry about out there. As soon as we launched on the shop we went for Slouse who ran it, a big portwine jelly of a veck who viddied at once what was coming and made straight for the inside where the telephone was and perhaps his well-oiled pooshka, complete with six dirty rounds. Dim was round that counter skorry as a bird, sending packets of snoutie flying and cracking over a big cut-out showing a sharp with all her zoobies going flash at the customers and her groodies near hanging out to advertise some new brand of cancers. What you could viddy then was a sort of a big ball rolling into the inside of the shop behind the curtain, this being old Dim and Slouse sort of locked in a death struggle. Then you could slooshy panting and snorting and kicking behind the curtain and veshches falling over and swearing and then glass going smash smash smash. Mother Slouse, the wife, was sort of froze behind the counter. We could tell she would creech murder given one chance, so I was round that counter very skorry and had a hold of her, and a horrorshow big lump she was too, all nuking of scent and with flipflop big bobbing groodies on her. I'd got my rooker round her rot to stop her belting out death and destruction to the four winds of heaven, but this lady doggie gave me a large foul big bite on it and it was me that did the creeching, and then she opened up beautiful with a flip yell for the millicents. Well, then she had to be tolchocked proper with one of the weights for the scales, and then a fair tap with a crowbar they had for opening cases, and that brought the red out like an old friend. So we had her down on the floor and a rip of her platties for fun and a gentle bit of the boot to stop her moaning. And, viddying her lying there with her groodies on show, I wondered should I or not, but that was for later on in the evening. Then we cleaned the till, and there was flip horrorshow takings that nochy, and we had a few packs of the very best top cancers apiece, then off we went, my brothers.

'A real big heavy great bastard he was,' Dim kept saying. I didn't like the look of Dim; he looked dirty and untidy, like a veck who'd been in a fight, which he had been, of course, but you should never *look* as though you have been. His cravat was like someone had trampled on it, his maskie had been pulled off and he had floor-dirt on his litso, so we got him in an alleyway and tidied him up a malenky bit, soaking our tashtooks in spit to cheest the dirt off. The things we did for old Dim. We were back in the Duke of New York very skorry, and I reckoned by my watch we hadn't been more than ten minutes away. The starry old baboochkas were still there on the black and suds and Scotchmen we'd bought them, and we said, 'Hallo there, girlies, what's it going to be?' They started on the old 'Very kind, lads, God bless you, boys,' and so we rang the collocoll and brought a different waiter in this time and we ordered beers with rum in, being sore athirst, my brothers, and whatever the old ptitsas wanted. Then I said to the old baboochkas: 'We haven't been out of here, have we? Been here all the time, haven't we?' They all caught on real skorry and said:

'That's right, lads. Not been out of our sight, you haven't. God bless you, boys,' drinking.

Not that it mattered much, really. About half an hour went by before there was any sign of life among the millicents, and then it was only two very young rozzes that came in, very pink under their big copper's shlemmies. One said:

'You lot know anything about the happenings at Slouse's shop this night?'

'Us?' I said, innocent. 'Why, what happened?'

17

'Stealing and roughing. Two hospitalisations. Where've you lot been this evening?'

'I don't go for that nasty tone,' I said. 'I don't care much for these nasty insinuations. A very suspicious nature all this betokeneth, my little brothers.'

'They've been in here all night, lads,' the old sharps started to creech out. 'God bless them, there's no better lot of boys living for kindness and generosity. Been here all the time they have. Not seen them move we haven't.'

'We're only asking,' said the other young millicent. 'We've got our job to do like anyone else.' But they gave us the nasty warning look before they went out. As they were going out we handed them a bit of lip-music: brrrr-zzzzrrrr. But, myself, I couldn't help a bit of disappointment at things as they were those days. Nothing to fight against really. Everything as easy as kiss-my-sharries. Still, the night was still very young.

2 WHEN we got outside of the Duke of New York we viddied, by the main bar's long lighted window, a burbling old pyahnitsa or drunkie, howling away at the filthy songs of his fathers and going blerp blerp in between as it might be a filthy old orchestra in his stinking rotten guts. One veshch I could never stand was that. I could never stand to see a moodge all filthy and rolling and burping and drunk, whatever his age might be, but more especially when he was real starry like this one was. He was sort of flattened to the wall and his platties were a disgrace, all creased and untidy and covered in cal and mud and filth and stuff. So we got hold of him and cracked him with a few good horror-show tolchocks, but he still went on singing. The song went:

> And I will go back to my darling, my darling,
> When you, my darling, are gone.

But when Dim fisted him a few times on his filthy drunkard's rot he shut up singing and started to creech: 'Go on, do me in, you bastard cowards, I don't want to live anyway, not in a stinking world like this one.' I told Dim to lay off a bit then, because it used to interest me sometimes to slooshy what some of these starry decreps had to say about life and the world. I said:

'Oh. And what's stinking about it?' He cried out:

'It's a stinking world because it lets the young get on to the old like you done, and there's no law nor order no more.' He was creeching out loud and waving his rookers and making real horrorshow with the slovos, only the odd blurp blurp coming from his keeshkas, like something was orbiting within, or like some very rude interrupting sort of a moodge making a shoom, so that this old veck kept sort of threatening it with his fists, shouting: 'It's no world for an old man any longer, and that means that I'm not one bit scared of you, my boyos, because I'm too drunk to feel the pain if you hit me, and if you kill me I'll be glad to be dead.' We smecked and then grinned but said nothing, and then he said: 'What sort of a world is it at all? Men on the moon and men spinning round the earth like it might be midges round a lamp, and there's not no attention paid to earthly law nor order no more. So your worst you may do, you filthy cowardly hooligans.' Then he gave us some lip-music – 'Prrrrzzzzrrrr' – like we'd done to those young millicents, and then he started singing again:

O dear dear land, I fought for thee
And brought thee peace and victory –

So we cracked into him lovely, grinning all over our litsos, but he still went on singing. Then we tripped him so he laid down flat and heavy and a bucketload of beer-vomit came whooshing out. That was disgusting so we gave him the boot, one go each, and then it was blood, not song nor vomit, that came out of his filthy old rot. Then we went on our way.

It was round by the Municipal Power Plant that we came across Billyboy and his five droogs. Now in those days, my brothers, the teaming up was mostly by fours or fives, these being like auto-teams, four being a comfy number for an auto, and six being the outside limit for gang-size. Sometimes gangs would gang up so as to make like malenky armies for big night-war, but mostly it was best to roam in these like small numbers. Billyboy was something that made me want to sick just to viddy his fat grinning litso, and he always had this von of very stale oil that's been used for frying over and over, even when he was dressed in his best platties, like now. They viddied us just as we viddied them, and there was like a very quiet kind of watching each other now. This would be real, this would be proper, this would be the nozh, the oozy, the britva, not just fisties and boots. Billyboy and his droogs stopped what they were doing, which was just getting ready to perform something on a weepy young devotchka they had there, not more than ten, she creeching away but with her platties still on, Billyboy holding her by one rooker and his number-one, Leo, holding the other. They'd probably just been doing the dirty slovo part of the act before getting down to a malenky bit of ultra-violence. When they viddied us a-coming they let go of this boo-hooing little ptitsa, there being plenty more where she came from, and she ran with her thin white legs flashing through the dark, still going 'Oh oh oh.' I said, smiling very wide and droogie, 'Well, if it isn't fat stinking billygoat Billyboy in poison. How art thou, thou globby bottle of cheap stinking chip-oil? Come and get one in the yarbles, if you have any yarbles, you eunuch jelly, thou.' And then we started.

There were four of us to six of them, like I have already

indicated, but poor old Dim, for all his dimness, was worth three of the others in sheer madness and dirty fighting. Dim had a real horrorshow length of oozy or chain round his waist, twice wound round, and he unwound this and began to swing it beautiful in the eyes or glazzies. Pete and Georgie had good sharp nozhes, but I for my own part had a fine starry horrorshow cut-throat britva which, at that time, I could flash and shine artistic. So there we were dratsing away in the dark, the old Luna with men on it just coming up, the stars stabbing away as it might be knives anxious to join in the dratsing. With my britva I managed to slit right down the front of one of Billyboy's droog's platties, very very neat and not even touching the plott under the cloth. Then in the dratsing this droog of Billyboy's suddenly found himself all opened up like a peapod, with his belly bare and his poor old yarbles showing, and then he got very very razdraz, waving and screaming and losing his guard and letting in old Dim with his chain snaking whisssssh-hhhhhhhh, so that old Dim chained him right in the glazzies, and this droog of Billyboy's went tottering off and howling his heart out. We were doing very horrorshow, and soon we had Billyboy's number-one down underfoot, blinded with old Dim's chain and crawling and howling about like an animal, but with one fair boot on the gulliver he was out and out and out.

Of the four of us Dim, as usual, came out the worst in point of looks, that is to say his litso was all bloodied and his platties a dirty mess, but the others of us were still cool and whole. It was stinking fatty Billyboy I wanted now, and there I was dancing about with my britva like I might be a barber on board a ship on a very rough sea, trying to get in at him with a few fair slashes on his unclean oily litso. Billyboy had a nozh, a long flick-type, but he was a malenky bit too slow and heavy in his movements to vred anyone really bad. And, my brothers, it was real satisfaction to me to waltz – left two three, right two three – and carve left cheeky and right cheeky, so that like two curtains of blood seemed to pour out at the same time, one on either side of his fat filthy oily snout in the winter starlight. Down this blood poured in like red curtains, but you could viddy Billyboy felt not a thing, and he went lumbering on like a filthy fatty bear, poking at me with his nozh.

Then we slooshied the sirens and knew the millicents were coming with pooshkas pushing out of the police-auto-windows at the ready. That little weepy devotchka had told them, no doubt, there being a box for calling the rozzes not too far behind the Muni Power Plant. 'Get you soon, fear not,' I called, 'stinking billygoat. I'll have your yarbles off lovely.' Then off they ran, slow and panting, except for Number One Leo out snoring on the ground, away north towards the river, and we went the other way. Just round the next turning was an alley, dark and empty and open at both ends, and we rested there, panting fast then slower, then breathing like normal. It was like resting between the feet of two terrific and very enormous mountains, these being the flatblocks, and in the windows of all of the flats you could viddy like blue dancing light. This would be the telly. Tonight was what they called a worldcast, meaning that the same programme was being viddied by everybody in the world that wanted to, that being mostly the middle-aged middle-class lewdies. There would be some big famous stupid comic chelloveck or black singer, and it was all being bounced off the special telly satellites in outer space, my brothers. We waited panting, and we could slooshy the sirening millicents going

23

east, so we knew we were all right now. But poor old Dim kept looking up at the stars and planets and the Luna with his rot wide open like a kid who'd never viddied any such thing before, and he said:

'What's on them, I wonder. What would be up there on things like that?'

I nudged him hard, saying: 'Come, gloopy bastard as thou art. Think thou not on them. There'll be life like down here most likely, with some getting knifed and others doing the knifing. And now, with the nochy still molodoy, let us be on our way, O my brothers.' The others smecked at this, but poor old Dim looked at me serious, then up again at the stars and the Luna. So we went on our way down the alley, with the worldcast blueing on on either side. What we needed now was an auto, so we turned left coming out of the alley, knowing right away we were in Priestley Place as soon as we viddied the big bronze statue of some starry poet with an apey upper lip and a pipe stuck in a droopy old rot. Going north we came to the filthy old Filmdrome, peeling and dropping to bits through nobody going there much except malchicks like me and my droogs, and then only for a yell or a razrez or a bit of in-out-in-out in the dark. We could viddy from the poster on the Filmdrome's face, a couple of fly-dirted spots trained on it, that there was the usual cowboy riot, with the arch-angels on the side of the US marshal six-shooting at the rustlers out of hell's fighting legions, the kind of hound-and-horny veshch put out by Statefilm in those days. The autos parked by the sinny weren't all that horrorshow, crappy starry veshches most of them, but there was a newish Durango 95 that I thought might do. Georgie had one of these polyclefs, as they called them, on his keyring, so we were soon aboard – Dim and Pete at the back, puffing away lordly at their cancers – and I turned on the ignition and started her up and she grumbled away real horrorshow, a nice warm vibraty feeling grumbling all through your guttiwuts. Then I made with the noga, and we backed out lovely, and nobody viddied us take off.

We fillied round what was called the backtown for a bit, scaring old vecks and cheenas that were crossing the roads and zigzagging after cats and that. Then we took the road west. There wasn't much traffic about, so I kept pushing the old noga through the floorboards near, and the Durango 95 ate up the road like spaghetti. Soon it was winter trees and dark, my brothers, with a country dark, and at one place I ran over something big with a snarling toothy rot in the headlamps, then it screamed and squelched under and old Dim at the back near laughed his gulliver off – 'Ho ho ho' – at that. Then we saw one young malchick with his sharp, lubbilubbing under a tree, so we stopped and cheered at them, then we bashed into them both with a couple of half-hearted tolchocks, making them cry, and on we went. What we were after now was the old surprise visit. That was a real kick and good for smecks and lashings of the ultra-violent. We came at last to a sort of a village, and just outside this village was a small sort of a cottage on its own with a bit of a garden. The Luna was well up now, and we could viddy this cottage fine and clear as I eased up and put the brake on, the other three giggling like bezoomny, and we could viddy the name on the gate of this cottage veshch was HOME, a gloopy sort of a name. I got out of the auto, ordering my droogs to shush their giggles and act like serious, and I opened this malenky gate and walked up to the front door. I knocked nice and gentle and nobody came, so I knocked a bit more and this time I could slooshy somebody coming, then a bolt drawn, then the door inched open an inch or so, then I could viddy this one glaz looking out at me and the door was on a chain. 'Yes? Who is it?' It was a sharp's goloss, a youngish devotchka by her sound, so I said in a very refined manner of speech, a real gentleman's goloss:

'Pardon, madam, most sorry to disturb you, but my friend and me were out for a walk, and my friend has taken bad all of a sudden with a very troublesome turn, and he is out there on the road dead out and groaning. Would you have the goodness to let me use your telephone to telephone for an ambulance?'

'We haven't a telephone,' said this devotchka. 'I'm sorry, but we haven't. You'll have to go somewhere else.' From inside this malenky cottage I could slooshy the clack clack clacky clack clack clackity clackclack of some veck typing away, and then the typing stopped and there was this chelloveck's goloss calling: 'What is it, dear?'

'Well,' I said, 'could you of your goodness please let him have a cup of water? It's like a faint, you see. It seems as though he's passed out in a sort of a fainting fit.'

The devotchka sort of hesitated and then said: 'Wait.' Then she went off, and my three droogs had got out of the auto quiet and crept up horrorshow stealthy, putting their maskies on now, then I put mine on, then it was only a matter of me putting in the old rooker and undoing the chain, me having softened up this devotchka with my gent's goloss, so that she hadn't shut the door like she should have done, us being strangers of the night. The four of us then went roaring in, old Dim playing the shoot as usual with his jumping up and down and singing out dirty slovos, and it was a nice malenky cottage, I'll say that. We all went smecking into the room with a light on, and there was this devotchka sort of cowering, a young pretty bit of sharp with real horrorshow groodies on her, and with her was this chelloveck who was her moodge, youngish too with horn-rimmed otchkies on him, and on a table was a typewriter and all papers scattered everywhere, but there was one little pile of paper like that must have been what he'd already typed, so here was another intelligent type bookman type like that we'd fillied with some hours back, but this one was a writer not a reader. Anyway he said:

'What is this? Who are you? How dare you enter my house without permission.' And all the time his goloss was trembling and his rookers too. So I said:

'Never fear. If fear thou hast in thy heart, O brother, pray banish it forthwith.' Then Georgie and Pete went out to find the kitchen, while old Dim waited for orders, standing next to me with his rot wide open. 'What is this, then?' I said, picking up the pile like of typing from off of the table, and the horn-rimmed moodge said, dithering:

'That's just what I want to know. What *is* this? What do you want? Get out at once before I throw you out.' So poor old Dim, masked like Peebee Shelley, had a good loud smeck at that, roaring like some animal.

'It's a book,' I said. 'It's a book what you are writing.' I made the old goloss very coarse. 'I have always had the strongest admiration for them as can write books.' Then I looked at its top sheet, and there was the name – A CLOCKWORK ORANGE – and I said, 'That's a fair gloopy title. Who ever heard of a clockwork orange?' Then I read a malenky bit out loud in a sort of very high type preaching goloss: '– The attempt to impose upon man, a creature of growth and capable of sweetness, to ooze juicily at the last round the bearded lips of God, to attempt to impose, I say, laws and conditions appropriate to a mechanical creation, against this I raise my swordpen –' Dim made the old lip-music at that and I had to smeck myself. Then I started to tear up the sheets and scatter the bits over the floor, and this writer moodge went sort of bezoomny and made for me with his zoobies clenched and showing yellow and his nails ready for me like claws. So that was old Dim's cue and he went grinning and going er er and a a a for this veck's dithering rot, crack crack, first left fistie then right, so that our dear old droog the red – red vino on tap and the same in all places, like it's put out by the same big firm – started to pour and spot the nice clean carpet and the bits of his book that I was still ripping away at, razrez razrez. All this time this devotchka, his loving and faithful wife, just stood like froze by the fireplace, and then she started letting out little malenky creeches, like in time to the like music of old Dim's fisty work. Then Georgie and Pete came in from the kitchen, both munching away, though with their maskies on, you could do that with them on and no trouble, Georgie with like a cold leg of something in one rooker and half a loaf of kleb with a big dollop of maslo on it in the other, and Pete with a bottle of beer frothing its gulliver off and a horrorshow rookerful of like plum cake. They went haw haw haw, viddying old Dim dancing round and fisting the writer veck so that the writer veck started to platch like his life's work was ruined, going boo hoo hoo with a very square bloody rot, but it was haw haw haw in a muffled eater's way and you could see bits of what they were eating. I didn't like that, it being dirty and slobbery, so I said:

'Drop that mounch. I gave no permission. Grab hold of this veck here so he can viddy all and not get away.'

So they put down their fatty pishcha on the table among all the flying paper and they clopped over to the writer veck whose horn-rimmed otchkies were cracked but still hanging on, with old Dim still dancing round and making ornaments shake on the mantelpiece (I swept them all off then and they couldn't shake no more, little brothers) while he fillied with the author of *A Clockwork Orange*, making his litso all purple and dripping away like some very special sort of a juicy fruit. 'All right, Dim,' I said. 'Now for the other veshch, Bog help us all.' So he did the strong-man on the devotchka, who was still creech creech creeching away in very horrorshow four-in-a-bar, locking her rookers from the back, while I ripped away at this and that and the other, the others going haw haw haw still, and real good horrorshow groodies they were that then exhibited their pink glazzies, O my brothers, while I untrussed and got ready for the plunge. Plunging, I could slooshy cries of agony and this writer bleeding veck that Georgie and Pete held on to nearly got loose howling bezoomny with the filthiest of slovos that I already knew and others he was making up. Then after me it was right old Dim should have his turn, which he did in a beasty snorty howly sort of a way with his Peebee Shelley maskie taking no notice, while I held on to her. Then there was a changeover, Dim and me grabbing the slobbering writer veck who was past struggling really, only just coming out with slack sort of slovos like he was in the land in a milk-plus bar, and Pete and Georgie had theirs. Then there was like quiet and we were full of like hate, so smashed what was left to be smashed – typewriter, lamp, chairs – and Dim, it was typical of old Dim, watered the fire out and was going to dung on the carpet, there being plenty of paper, but I said no. 'Out out out out,' I howled. The writer veck and his zheena were not really there, bloody and torn and making noises. But they'd live.

So we got into the waiting auto and I left it to Georgie to take the wheel, me feeling that malenky bit shagged, and we went back to town, running over odd squealing things on the way.

3 WE yeckated back townwards, my brothers, but just outside, not far from what they called the Industrial Canal, we viddied the fuel needle had like collapsed, like our own ha ha ha needles had, and the auto was coughing kashl kashl kashl. Not to worry overmuch, though, because a rail station kept flashing blue – on off on off – just near. The point was whether to leave the auto to be sobiratted by the rozzes or, us feeling like in a hate and murder mood, to give it a fair tolchock into the starry waters for a nice heavy loud plesk before the death of the evening. This latter we decided on, so we got out and, the brakes off, all four tolchocked it to the edge of the filthy water that was like treacle mixed with human hole products, then one good horrorshow tolchock and in she went. We had to dash back for fear of the filth splashing on our platties, but splussshhhh and glolp she went, down and lovely. 'Farewell, old droog,' called Georgie, and Dim obliged with a clowny great guff – 'Huh huh huh huh.' Then we made for the station to ride the one stop to Center, as the middle of town was called. We paid our fares nice and polite and waited gentlemanly and quiet on the platform, old Dim fillying with the slot machines, his carmans being full of small malenky coin, and ready if need be to distribute chocbars to the poor

31

and starving, though there was none such about, and then the old espresso rapido came lumbering in and we climbed aboard, the train looking to be near empty. To pass the three-minute ride we fillied about with what they called the upholstery, doing some nice horrorshow tearing-out of the seats' guts and old Dim chaining the okno till the glass cracked and sparkled in the winter air, but we were all feeling that bit shagged and fagged and fashed, it having been an evening of some energy expenditure, my brothers, only Dim, like the clowny animal he was, full of the joys-of but looking all dirtied over and too much von of sweat on him, which was one thing I had against old Dim.

We got out at Center and walked slow back to the Korova Milkbar, all going yawwwww a malenky bit and exhibiting to moon and star and lamplight our back fillings, because we were still only growing malchicks and had school in the daytime, and when we got into the Korova we found it fuller than when we'd left earlier on. But the chelloveck that had been burbling away, in the land, on white and synthemesc or whatever, was still on at it, going: 'Urchins of deadcast in the way-ho-hay glill platonic tide weatherborn.' It was probable that this was his third or fourth lot that evening, for he had that pale inhuman look, like he'd become a *thing*, and like his litso was really a piece of chalk carved. Really, if he wanted to spend so long in the land, he should have gone into one of the private cubies at the back and not stayed in the big mesto, because here some of the malchickies would filly about with him a malenky bit, though not too much because there were powerful bruiseboys hidden away in the old Korova who could stop any riot. Anyway, Dim squeezed in next to this veck and, with his big clown's yawp that showed his hanging grape, he stabbed this veck's foot with his own large filthy sabog. But the veck, my brothers, heard nought, being now all above the body.

It was nadsats mostly milking and coking and fillying around (nadsats were what we used to call the teens), but there were a few of the more starry ones, vecks and cheenas alike (but not of the boorjoyce, never them) laughing and govoreeting at the bar. You could tell from their barberings and loose platties (big string sweaters mostly) that they'd been on rehearsal at the TV studios round the corner. The devotchkas among them had these very lively litsos and wide big rots, very red, showing a lot of teeth, and smecking away and not caring about the wicked world one whit. And then the disc on the stereo twanged off and out (it was Jonny Zhivago, a Russky koshka, singing 'Only Every Other Day'), and in the like interval, the short silence before the next one came on, one of these devotchkas – very fair and with a big smiling red rot and in her late thirties I'd say – suddenly came with a burst of singing, only a bar and a half and as though she was like giving an example of something they'd all been govoreeting about, and it was like for a moment, O my brothers, some great bird had flown into the milkbar, and I felt all the little malenky hairs on my plott standing endwise and the shivers crawling up like slow malenky lizards and then down again. Because I knew what she sang. It was from an opera by Friedrich Gitterfenster called *Das Bettzeug*, and it was the bit where she's snuffing it with her throat cut, and the slovos are 'Better like this maybe'. Anyway, I shivered.

But old Dim, as soon as he'd slooshied this dollop of song like a lomtick of red hot meat plonked on your plate, let off one of his vulgarities, which in this case was a lip-trump followed by a dog-howl followed by two fingers pronging twice at the air followed by a clowny guffaw. I felt myself all of a fever and like drowning in redhot blood, slooshying and viddying Dim's vulgarity, and I said: 'Bastard. Filthy drooling mannerless bastard.' Then I leaned across Georgie, who was between me and horrible Dim, and fisted Dim skorry on the rot. Dim looked very surprised, his rot open, wiping the krovvy off of his goober with his rook and in turn looking surprised at the red flowing krovvy and at me. 'What for did you do that for?' he said in his ignorant way. Not many viddied what I'd done, and those that viddied cared not. The stereo was on again and was playing a very sick electronic guitar veshch. I said:

'For being a bastard with no manners and not the dook of an idea how to comport yourself publicwise, O my brother.'

Dim put on a hound-and-horny look of evil, saying, 'I don't like you should do what you done then. And I'm not your brother no more and wouldn't want to be.' He'd taken a big snotty tashtook from his pocket and was mopping the red flow puzzled, keeping on looking at it frowning as if he thought that blood was for other vecks and not for him. It was like he was singing blood to make up for his vulgarity when that devotchka was singing music. But that devotchka was smecking away ha ha ha now with her droogs at the bar, her red rot working and her zoobies ashine, not having noticed Dim's filthy vulgarity. It was me really Dim had done wrong to. I said:

'If you don't like this and you wouldn't want that, then you know what to do, little brother.' Georgie said, in a sharp way that made me look:

'All right. Let's not be starting.'

'That's clean up to Dim,' I said. 'Dim can't go on all his jeezny being as a little child.' And I looked sharp at

Georgie. Dim said, and the red krovvy was easing its flow now:

'What natural right does he have to think he can give the orders and tolchock me whenever he likes? Yarbles is what I say to him, and I'd chain his glazzies out soon as look.'

'Watch that,' I said, as quiet as I could with the stereo bouncing all over the walls and ceiling and the in-the-land veck beyond Dim getting loud now with his 'Spark nearer, ultoptimate.' I said, 'Do watch that, O Dim, if to continue to be on live thou dost wish.'

'Yarbles,' said Dim, sneering, 'great bolshy yarblockos to you. What you done then you had no right. I'll meet you with chain or nozh or britva any time, not having you aiming tolchocks at me reasonless, it stands to reason I won't have it.'

'A nozh scrap any time you say,' I snarled back. Pete said:

'Oh now, don't, both of you malchicks. Droogs, aren't we? It isn't right droogs should behave thiswise. See, there are some loose-lipped malchicks over there smecking at us, leering like. We mustn't let ourselves down.'

'Dim,' I said, 'has got to learn his place. Right?'

'Wait,' said Georgie. 'What's all this about place? This is the first I ever hear about lewdies learning their place.' Pete said:

'If the truth is known, Alex, you shouldn't have given old Dim that uncalled-for tolchock. I'll say it once and no more. I say it with all respect, but if it had been me you'd given it to you'd have to answer. I say no more.' And he drowned his litso in his milk-glass.

I could feel myself getting all razdraz inside, but I tried to cover it, saying calm: 'There has to be a leader. Discipline there has to be. Right?' None of them skazatted a word or nodded even. I got more razdraz inside, calmer out. 'I,' I said, 'have been in charge long now. We are all droogs, but somebody has to be in charge. Right? Right?' They all like nodded, wary like. Dim was osooshing the last of the krovvy off. It was Dim who said now:

'Right, right. Doobidoob. A bit tired, maybe, everybody is. Best not to say more.' I was surprised and just that malenky bit poogly to sloosh Dim govoreeting that wise. Dim said: 'Bedways is rightways now, so best we go homeways. Right?' I was very surprised. The other two nodded, going right right right. I said:

'You understand about the tolchock on the rot, Dim. It was the music, see. I get all bezoomny when any veck interferes with a ptitsa singing, as it might be. Like that then.'

'Best we go off homeways and get a bit of spatchka,' said Dim. 'A long night for growing malchicks. Right?' Right right nodded the other two. I said:

'I think it best we go home now. Dim has made a real horrorshow suggestion. If we don't meet daywise, O my brothers, well then – same time same place tomorrow?'

'Oh yes,' said Georgie. 'I think that can be arranged.'

'I might,' said Dim, 'be just that malenky bit late. But same place and near same time tomorrow surely.' He was still wiping away at his goober, though no krovvy flowed any longer now. 'And,' he said, 'it's to be hoped that there won't be no more of them singing ptitsas in here.' Then he gave his old Dim guff, a clowny big hohohohoho. It seemed like he was too dim to take much offence.

So off we went our several ways, me belching arrrrgh on the cold coke I'd peeted. I had my cut-throat britva handy in case any of Billyboy's droogs should be around near the flatblock waiting, or for that matter any of the other bandas or gruppas or shaikas that from time to time were at war with one. Where I lived was with my dadda and mum in the flats of Municipal Flatblock 18A, between Kingsley Avenue and Wilsonsway. I got to the big main door with no trouble, though I did pass one young malchick sprawling and creeching and moaning in the gutter, all cut about lovely, and saw in the lamplight also streaks of blood here and there like signatures, my brothers, of the night's fillying. And too I saw just by 18A a pair of devotchka's neezhnies doubtless rudely wrenched off in the heat of the moment, O my brothers. And so in. In the hallway was the good old municipal painting on the walls – vecks and ptitsas very well-developed, stern in the dignity of labour, at work-bench and machine with not one stitch of platties on their well-developed plotts. But of course some of the malchicks living in 18A had, as was to be expected, embellished and decorated the said big painting with handy pencil and ballpoint, adding hair and stiff rods and dirty ballooning slovos out of the dignified rots of these nagoy (bare, that is) cheenas and vecks. I went to the lift, but there was no need to press the electric knopka to see if it was working or not, because it had been tolchocked real horrorshow this night, the metal doors all buckled, some feat of rare strength indeed, so I had to walk the ten floors up. I cursed and panted climbing, being tired in plott if not so much in brain. I wanted music very bad this evening, that singing devotchka in the Korova having perhaps started me off. I wanted a big feast of it before getting my passport stamped, my brothers, at sleep's frontier and the stripy shest lifted to let me through.

I opened the door of 10–8 with my own little klootch, and inside our malenky quarters all was quiet, the pee and em both being in sleepland, and mum had laid out on the table my malenky bit of supper – a couple of lomticks of tinned spongemeat with a shive or so of kleb and butter, a glass of the old cold moloko. Hohoho, the old moloko, with no knives or synthemesc or drencrom in it. How wicked, my brothers, innocent milk must always seem to me now. Still, I drank and ate growling, being more hungry than I thought at first, and I got a fruitpie from the larder and tore chunks off it to stuff into my greedy rot. Then I tooth-cleaned and clicked, cleaning out the old rot with my yahzick or tongue, then I went into my own little room or den, easing off my platties as I did so. Here was my bed and my stereo, pride of my jeezny, and my discs in their cupboard, and banners and flags on the wall, these being like remembrances of my corrective school life since I was eleven, O my brothers, each one shining and blazoned with name or number: SOUTH 4; METRO CORSKOL BLUE DIVISION; THE BOYS OF ALPHA.

The little speakers of my stereo were all arranged round the room, on ceiling, walls, floor, so, lying on my bed slooshying the music, I was like netted and meshed in the orchestra. Now what I fancied first tonight was this new violin concerto by the American Geoffrey Plautus, played by Odysseus Choerilos with the Macon (Georgia) Philharmonic, so I slid it from where it was neatly filed and switched on and waited.

Then, brothers, it came. Oh, bliss, bliss and heaven. I lay all nagoy to the ceiling, my gulliver on my rookers on the pillow, glazzies closed, rot open in bliss, slooshying the sluice of lovely sounds. Oh, it was gorgeousness and gorgeosity made flesh. The trombones crunched redgold under my bed, and behind my gulliver the trumpets three-wise silverflamed, and there by the door the timps rolling through my guts and out again crunched like candy thunder. Oh, it was wonder of wonders. And then, a bird of like rarest spun heavenmetal, or like silvery wine flowing in a spaceship, gravity all nonsense now, came the violin solo above all the other strings, and those strings were like a cage of silk around my bed. Then flute and oboe bored, like worms of like platinum, into the thick thick toffee gold and silver. I was in such bliss, my brothers. Pee and em in their bedroom next door had learnt now not to knock on the wall with complaints of what they called noise. I had taught them. Now they would take sleep-pills. Perhaps, knowing the joy I had in my night music, they had already taken them. As I slooshied, my glazzies tight shut to shut in the bliss that was better than any synthemesc Bog or God, I knew such lovely pictures. There were vecks and ptitsas, both young and starry, lying on the ground screaming for mercy, and I was smecking all over my rot and grinding my boot in their litsos. And there were devotchkas ripped and creeching against the walls and I plunging like a shlaga into them, and indeed when the music, which was one movement only, rose to the top of its big highest tower, then, lying there on my bed with glazzies tight shut and rookers behind my gulliver, I broke and spattered and cried aaaaaaah with the bliss of it. And so the lovely music glided to its glowing close.

After that I had lovely Mozart, the Jupiter, and there were new pictures of different litsos to be ground and splashed, and it was after this that I thought I would have just one last disc only before crossing the border, and I wanted something starry and strong and very firm, so it was J. S. Bach I had, the Brandenburg Concerto just for middle and lower strings. And, slooshying with different bliss than before, I viddied again this name on the paper

I'd razrezzed that night, a long time ago it seemed, in that cottage called HOME. The name was about a clockwork orange. Listening to the J. S. Bach, I began to pony better what that meant now, and I thought, slooshying away to the brown gorgeousness of the starry German master, that I would like to have tolchocked them both harder and ripped them to ribbons on their own floor.

THE next morning I woke up at oh eight oh oh hours, my brothers, and as I still felt shagged and fagged and fashed and bashed and my glazzies were stuck together real horrorshow with sleepglue, I thought I would not go to school. I thought how I would have a malenky bit longer in the bed, an hour or two say, and then get dressed nice and easy, perhaps even having a splosh about in the bath, and then brew a pot of real strong horrorshow chai and make toast for myself and slooshy the radio or read the gazetta, all on my oddy knocky. And then in the afterlunch I might perhaps, if I still felt like it, itty off to the old skolliwoll and see what was vareeting in that great seat of gloopy useless learning, O my brothers. I heard my papapa grumbling and tram-pling and then ittying off to the dyeworks where he rabbited, and then my mum called in in a very respectful goloss as she did now I was growing up big and strong:

'It's gone eight, son. You don't want to be late again.'
So I called back:

'A bit of a pain in my gulliver. Leave us be and I'll try to sleep it off and then I'll be right as dodgers for this after.' I slooshied her give a sort of a sigh and she said:

'I'll put your breakfast in the oven then, son. I've got to be off myself now.' Which was true, there being this law for everybody not a child nor with child nor ill to go out rabbiting. My mum worked at one of the Statemarts, as they called them, filling up the shelves with tinned soup and beans and all that cal. So I slooshied her clank a plate in the gas-oven like and then she was putting her shoes on and then getting her coat from behind the door and then sighing again, then she said: 'I'm off now, son.' But I let on to be back in sleepland and then I did doze off real horrorshow, and I had a queer and very real like sneety, dreaming for some reason of my droog Georgie. In this sneety he'd got like very much older and very sharp and hard and was govoreeting about discipline and obedience and how all the malchicks under his control had to jump hard at it and throw up the old salute like being in the army, and there was me in line like the rest saying yes sir and no sir, and then I viddied clear that Georgie had these stars on his pletchoes and he was like a general. And then he brought in old Dim with a whip, and Dim was a lot more starry and grey and had a few zoobies missing as you could see when he let out a smeck, viddying me, and then my droog Georgie said, pointing like at me, 'That man has filth and cal all over his platties,' and it was true. Then I creeched, 'Don't hit, please don't, brothers,' and started to run. And I was running in like circles and Dim was after me, smecking his gulliver off, cracking with the old whip, and each time I got a real horrorshow tolchock with this whip there was like a very loud electric bell ringringringing, and this bell was like a sort of a pain too.

Then I woke up real skorry, my heart going bap bap bap, and of course there was really a bell going brrrrr, and it was our front-door bell. I let on that nobody was at home, but this brrrrr still ittied on, and then I heard a goloss shouting through the door, 'Come on then, get out of it, I know you're in bed.' I recognised the goloss right away. It was the goloss of P. R. Deltoid (a real gloopy nazz, that one), what they called my Post-Corrective Adviser, an over-worked veck with hundreds on his books. I shouted right right right, in a goloss of like pain, and I got out of bed and attired myself, O my brothers, in a very lovely over-gown of like silk, with designs of like great cities all over this over-gown. Then I put my nogas into very comfy woolly toofles, combed my luscious glory, and was ready for P. R. Deltoid. When I opened up he came shambling in looking shagged, a battered old shlapa on his gulliver, his raincoat filthy. 'Ah, Alex boy,' he said to me. 'I met your mother, yes. She said something about a pain some-where. Hence not at school, yes.'

'A rather intolerable pain in the head, brother, sir,' I said in my gentleman's goloss. 'I think it should clear by this afternoon.'

'Or certainly by this evening, yes,' said P. R. Deltoid. The evening is the great time, isn't it, Alex boy? Sit,' he said, 'sit, sit,' as though this was his domy and me his guest. And he sat in this starry rocking-chair of my dad's and began rocking, as if that was all he'd come for. I said:

'A cup of the old chai, sir? Tea, I mean.'

'No time,' he said. And he rocked, giving me the old glint under frowning brows, as if with all the time in the world. 'No time, yes,' he said, gloopy. So I put the kettle on. Then I said:

'To what do I owe the extreme pleasure? Is anything wrong, sir?'

'Wrong?' he said, very skorry and sly, sort of hunched looking at me but still rocking away. Then he caught sight of an advert in the gazetta, which was on the table – a lovely smecking young ptitsa with her groodies hanging out to advertise, my brothers, the Glories of the Jugoslav Beaches. Then, after sort of eating her up in two swallows, he said, 'Why should you think in terms of there being anything wrong? Have you been doing something you shouldn't, yes?'

'Just a manner of speech,' I said, 'sir.'

'Well,' said P. R. Deltoid, 'it's just a manner of speech from me to you that you watch out, little Alex, because next time, as you very well know, it's not going to be the corrective school any more. Next time it's going to be the barry place and all my work ruined. If you have no consideration for your horrible self you might at least have some for me, who have sweated over you. A big black mark, I tell you in confidence, for every one we don't reclaim, a confession of failure for every one of you that ends up in the stripy hole.'

'I've been doing nothing I shouldn't, sir,' I said. 'The millicents have nothing on me, brother, sir I mean.'

'Cut out this clever talk about millicents,' said P. R. Deltoid very weary, but still rocking. 'Just because the police have not picked you up lately doesn't, as you very well know, mean you've not been up to some nastiness. There was a bit of a fight last night, wasn't there? There was a bit of shuffling with nozhes and bike-chains and the like. One of a certain fat boy's friends was ambulanced off late from near the Power Plant and hospitalised, cut about very unpleasantly, yes. Your name was mentioned. The word has got through to me by the usual channels. Certain friends of yours were named also. There seems to have been a fair amount of assorted nastiness last night. Oh, nobody can prove anything about anybody, as usual. But I'm warning you, little Alex, being a good friend to you as always, the one man

44

in this sore and sick community who wants to save you from yourself.'

'I appreciate all that, sir,' I said, 'very sincerely.'

'Yes, you do, don't you?' he sort of sneered. 'Just watch it, that's all, yes. We know more than you think, little Alex.' Then he said, in a goloss of great suffering, but still rocking away, 'What gets into you all? We study the problem and we've been studying it for damn well near a century, yes, but we get no further with our studies. You've got a good home here, good loving parents, you've got not too bad of a brain. Is it some devil that crawls inside you?'

'Nobody's got anything on me, sir,' I said. 'I've been out of the rookers of the millicents for a long time now.'

'That's just what worries me,' sighed P. R. Deltoid. 'A bit too long of a time to be healthy. You're about due now by my reckoning. That's why I'm warning you, little Alex, to keep your handsome young proboscis out of the dirt, yes. Do I make myself clear?'

'As an unmuddied lake, sir,' I said. 'Clear as an azure sky of deepest summer. You can rely on me, sir.' And I gave him a nice zooby smile.

But when he'd ookadeeted and I was making this very strong pot of chai, I grinned to myself over this veshch that P. R. Deltoid and his droogs worried about. All right, I do bad, what with crasting and tolchocks and carves with the britva and the old in-out-in-out, and if I get loveted, well, too bad for me, O my little brothers, and you can't run a country with every chelloveck comporting himself in my manner of the night. So if I get loveted and it's three months in this mesto and another six in that, and then, as P. R. Deltoid so kindly warns, next time, in spite of the great tenderness of my summers, brothers, it's the great unearthly zoo itself, well, I say, 'Fair, but a pity, my lords, because I just cannot bear to be shut in. My endeavour shall be, in such future as stretches out its snowy and lilywhite arms to me before the nozh overtakes or the blood spatters its final chorus in twisted metal and smashed glass on the highroad, to not get loveted again.' Which is fair speeching. But, brothers, this biting of their toe-nails over what is the *cause* of badness is what turns me into a fine laughing malchick. They don't go into what is the cause of *goodness*, so why of the other shop? If lewdies are good that's because they like it, and I wouldn't ever inter-fere with their pleasures, and so of the other shop. And I was patronising the other shop. More, badness is of the self, the one, the you or me on our oddy knockies, and that self is made by old Bog or God and is his great pride and radosty. But the not-self cannot have the bad, meaning they of the government and the judges and the schools cannot allow the bad because they cannot allow the self. And is not our modern history, my brothers, the story of brave malenky selves fighting these big machines? I am serious with you, brothers, over this. But what I do I do because I like to do.

So now, this smiling winter morning. I drank this very strong chai with moloko and spoon after spoon after spoon of sugar, me having a sladky tooth, and I dragged out of the oven the breakfast my poor old mum had cooked for me. It was an egg fried, that and no more, but I made toast and ate egg and toast and jam, smacking away at it while I read the gazetta. The gazetta was the usual about ultra-violence and bank robberies and strikes and foot-ballers making everybody paralytic with fright by threat-ening to not play next Saturday if they did not get higher wages, naughty malchickiwicks as they were. Also there

46

were more space-trips and bigger stereo TV screens and offers of free packets of soapflakes in exchange for the labels on soup-tins, amazing offer for one week only, which made me smeck. And there was a bolshy big article on Modern Youth (meaning me, so I gave the old bow, grinning like bezoomny) by some very clever bald chelloveck. I read this with care, my brothers, slurping away at the old chai, cup after tass after chasha, crunching my lomticks of black toast dipped in jammiwam and eggiweg. This learned veck said the usual veshches, about no parental discipline, as he called it, and the shortage of real horrorshow teachers who would lambast bloody beggary out of their innocent poops and make them go boohoohoo for mercy. All this was gloopy and made me smeck, but it was like nice to go on knowing that one was making the news all the time, O my brothers. Every day there was something about Modern Youth, but the best veshch they ever had in the old gazetta was by some starry pop in a doggy collar who said that in his considered opinion and he was govoreeting as a man of Bog IT WAS THE DEVIL THAT WAS ABROAD and was like ferreting his way into like young innocent flesh, and it was the adult world that could take the responsibility for this with their wars and bombs and nonsense. So that was all right. So he knew what he talked of, being a Godman. So we young innocent malchicks could take no blame. Right right right.

When I'd gone erk erk a couple of razzes on my full innocent stomach, I started to get out the day platties from my wardrobe, turning the radio on. There was music playing, a very nice malenky string quartet, my brothers, by Claudius Birdman, one that I knew well. I had to have a smeck, though, thinking of what I'd viddied once in one of these like articles on Modern Youth, about how Modern

Youth would be better off if A Lively Appreciation Of The Arts could be like encouraged. Great Music, it said, and Great Poetry would like quieten Modern Youth down and make Modern Youth more Civilised. Civilised my syphilised yarbles. Music always sort of sharpened me up, O my brothers, and made me feel like old Bog himself, ready to make with the old donner and blitzen and have vecks and ptitsas creeching away in my ha ha power. And when I'd cheested up my litso and rookers a bit and done dressing (my day platties were like student-wear: the old blue pantalonies with sweater with A for Alex) I thought here at least was time to itty off to the disc-bootick (and cutter too, my pockets being full of pretty polly) to see about this long-promised and long-ordered stereo Beethoven Number Nine (the Choral Symphony, that is), recorded on Masterstroke by the Esh Sham Sinfonia under L. Muhaiwir. So out I went, brothers.

The day was very different from the night. The night belonged to me and my droogs and all the rest of the nadsats, and the starry boorjoyce lurked indoors drinking in the gloopy worldcasts, but the day was for the starry ones, and there always seemed to be more rozzes or millicents about during the day, too. I got the autobus from the corner and rode to Center, and then I walked back to Taylor Place, and there was the disc-bootick I favoured with my inestimable custom, O my brothers. It had the gloopy name of MELODIA, but it was a real horrorshow mesto and skorry, most times, at getting the new recordings. I walked in and the only other customers were two young ptitsas sucking away at ice-sticks (and this, mark, was dead cold winter) and sort of shuffling through the new popdiscs – Johnny Burnaway, Stash Kroh, The Mixers, Lie Quiet Awhile With Ed And Id Molotov, and all the rest of that cal. These two ptitsas couldn't have been more than ten, and they too, like me, it seemed, evidently, had decided to take a morning off from the old skolliwoll. They saw themselves, you could see, as real grown-up devotchkas already, what with the old hipswing when they saw your Faithful Narrator, brothers, and padded groodies and red all ploshed on their goobers. I went up to the counter, making with the polite zooby smile at old Andy behind it (always polite himself, always helpful, a real horrorshow type of a veck, though bald and very very thin). He said:

'Aha, I know what thou wantest, I thinkest. Good news, good news. It have arrived.' And with like big conductor's rookers beating time he went to get it. The two young ptitsas started giggling, as they will at that age, and I gave them a like cold glazzy. Andy was back real skorry, waving the great shiny white sleeve of the Ninth, which had on it, brothers, the frowning beetled like thunderbottled litso of Ludwig van himself. 'Here,' said Andy. 'Shall we give it the trial spin?' But I wanted it back home on my stereo to slooshy on my oddy knocky, greedy as hell. I fumbled out the deng to pay and one of the little ptitsas said:

'Who you getten, bratty? What biggy, what only?' These young devotchkas had their own like way of govoreeting. 'The Heaven Seventeen? Luke Sterne? Goggly Gogol?' And both giggled, rocking and hippy. Then an idea hit me and made me near fall over with the anguish and ecstasy of it, O my brothers, so I could not breathe for near ten seconds. I recovered and made with my new-clean zoobies and said:

'What you got back home, little sisters, to play your fuzzy warbles on?' Because I could viddy the discs they were buying were these teeny pop veshches. 'I bet you got little save tiny portable like picnic spinners.' And they sort

49

of pushed their lower lips out at that. 'Come with uncle,' I said, 'and hear all proper. Hear angel trumpets and devil trombones. You are invited.' And I like bowed. They giggled again and one said:

'Oh, but we're so hungry. Oh, but we could so eat.' The other said, 'Yah, she can say that, can't she just.' So I said:

'Eat with uncle. Name your place.'

Then they viddied themselves as real sophistoes, which was like pathetic, and started talking in big-lady golosses about the Ritz and the Bristol and the Hilton and Il Restorante Granturco. But I stopped that with 'Follow uncle,' and I led them to the Pasta Parlour just round the corner and let them fill their innocent young litsos on spaghetti and cream-puffs and banana-splits and hot choc-sauce, till I near sicked with the sight of it, I, brothers, lunching but frugally off a cold ham-slice and a growling dollop of chilli. These two young ptitsas were much alike, though not sisters. They had the same ideas or lack of, and the same colour hair – a like dyed strawy. Well, they would grow up real today. Today I would make a day of it. No school this afterlunch, but education certainly, Alex as teacher. Their names, they said, were Marty and Sonietta, bezoomny enough and in the heighth of their childish fashion, so I said:

'Righty right, Marty and Sonietta. Time for the big spin. Come.' When we were outside on the cold street they thought they would not go by autobus, oh no, but by taxi, so I gave them the humour, though with a real horrorshow in-grin, and I called a taxi from the rank near Center. The driver, a starry whiskery veck in very stained platties, said:

'No tearing up, now. No nonsense with them seats. Just re-upholstered they are.' I quieted his gloopy fears and off we spun to Municipal Flatblock 18A, these two bold little ptitsas giggling and whispering. So, to cut all short, we arrived, O my brothers, and I led the way up to 10–8, and they panted and smecked away the way up, and then they were thirsty, they said, so I unlocked the treasure-chest in my room and gave these ten-year-young devotchkas a real horrorshow Scotchman apiece, though well filled with sneezy pins-and-needles soda. They sat on my bed (yet unmade) and leg-swung, smecking and peeting their high-balls, while I spun their like pathetic malenky discs through my stereo. Like peeting some sweet scented kid's drink, that was, in like very beautiful and lovely and costly gold goblets. But they went oh oh oh and said, 'Swoony' and 'Hilly' and other weird slovos that were the heighth of fashion in that youth-group. While I spun this cal for them I encouraged them to drink up and have another, and they were nothing loath, O my brothers. So by the time their pathetic pop-discs had been twice spun each (there were two: 'Honey Nose', sung by Ike Yard, and 'Night After Day After Night', moaned by two horrible yarbleless like eunuchs whose names I forget) they were getting near the pitch of like young ptitsa's hysterics, what with jumping all over my bed and me in the room with them.

What was actually done that afternoon there is no need to describe, brothers, as you may easily guess all. Those two were unplatted and smecking fit to crack in no time at all, and they thought it the bolshiest fun to viddy old Uncle Alex standing there all nagoy and pan-handled, squirting the hypodermic like some bare doctor, then giving myself the old jab of growling jungle-cat secretion in the rooker. Then I pulled the lovely Ninth out of its sleeve, so that Ludwig van was now nagoy too, and I set the needle hissing on to the last movement, which was all bliss. There it was then, the bass strings like govoreeting away from under my bed at the rest of the orchestra, and then the male human goloss coming in and telling them all to be joyful, and then the lovely blissful tune all about Joy being a glorious spark like of heaven, and then I felt the old tigers leap in me and then I leapt on these two young ptitsas. This time they thought nothing fun and stopped creeching with high mirth, and had to submit to the strange and weird desires of Alexander the Large which, what with the Ninth and the hypo jab, were choodessny and zammechat and very demanding, O my brothers. But they were both very very drunken and could hardly feel very much.

When the last movement had gone round for the second time with all the banging and creeching about Joy Joy Joy Joy, then these two young ptitsas were not acting the big lady sophisto no more. They were like waking up to what was being done to their malenky persons and saying that they wanted to go home and like I was a wild beast. They looked like they had been in some big bitva, as indeed they had, and were all bruised and pouty. Well, if they would not go to school they must still have their education. And education they had had. They were creeching and going ow ow ow as they put their platties on, and they were like punchipunching me with their teeny fists as I lay there dirty and nagoy and fair shagged and fagged on the bed. This young Sonietta was creeching: 'Beast and hateful animal. Filthy horror.' So I let them get their things together and get out, which they did, talking about how the rozzes should be got on to me and all that cal. Then they were going down the stairs and I dropped off to sleep, still with the old Joy Joy Joy Joy crashing and howling away.

5

WHAT happened, though, was that I woke up late (near seven-thirty by my watch) and, as it turned out, that was not so clever. You can viddy that everything in this wicked world counts. You can pony that one thing always leads to another. Right right right. My stereo was no longer on about Joy and I Embrace Ye O Ye Millions, so some veck had dealt it the off, and that would be either pee or em, both of them now being quite clear to the slooshying in the living-room and, from the clink clink of plates and slurp slurp of peeting tea from cups, at their tired meal after the day's rabbiting in factory the one, store the other. The poor old. The pitiable starry. I put on my over-gown and looked out, in guise of loving only son, to say:

'Hi hi hi, there. A lot better after the day's rest. Ready now for evening work to earn that little bit.' For that's what they said they believed I did these days. 'Yum yum, mum. Any of that for me?' It was like some frozen pie that she'd unfroze and then warmed up and it looked not so very appetitish, but I had to say what I said. Dad looked at me with a not-so-pleased suspicious like look but said nothing, knowing he dared not, and mum gave me a tired like little smeck, to thee fruit of my womb, my only son sort of. I danced to the bathroom and had a real skorry cheest all over, feeling dirty and gluey, then back to my den for the evening's platties. Then, shining, combed, brushed and gorgeous, I sat to my lomtick of pie. Papapa said:

'Not that I want to pry, son, but where exactly is it you go to work of evenings?'

'Oh,' I chewed, 'it's mostly odd things, helping like. Here and there, as it might be.' I gave him a straight dirty glazzy, as to say to mind his own and I'd mind mine. 'I never ask for money, do I? Not money for clothes or for pleasures? All right, then, why ask?'

My dad was like humble mumble chumble. 'Sorry, son,' he said. 'But I get worried sometimes. Sometimes I have dreams. You can laugh if you like, but there's a lot in dreams. Last night I had this dream with you in it and I didn't like it one bit.'

'Oh?' He had gotten me interessovatted now, dreaming of me like that. I had like a feeling I had had a dream, too, but I could not remember proper what. 'Yes?' I said, stopping chewing my gluey pie.

'It was vivid,' said my dad. 'I saw you lying on the street and you had been beaten by other boys. These boys were like the boys you used to go around with before you were sent to that last Corrective School.'

'Oh?' I had an in-grin at that, papapa believing I had real reformed or believing he believed. And then I remembered my own dream, which was a dream of that morning, of Georgie giving his general's orders and old Dim smecking around toothless as he wielded the whip. But dreams go by opposites I was once told. 'Never worry about thine only son and heir, O my father,' I said. 'Fear not. He canst take care of himself, verily.'

'And,' said my dad, 'you were like helpless in your blood and you couldn't fight back.' That was real opposites, so I

54

had another quiet malenky grin within and then I took all the deng out of my carmans and tinkled it on the saucy tablecloth. I said:

'Here, dad, it's not much. It's what I earned last night. But perhaps for the odd peet of Scotchman in the snug somewhere for you and mum.'

'Thanks, son,' he said. 'But we don't go out much now. We daren't go out much, the streets being what they are. Young hooligans and so on. Still, thanks. I'll bring her home a bottle of something tomorrow.' And he scooped this ill-gotten pretty into his trouser carmans, mum being at the cheesting of the dishes in the kitchen. And I went out with loving smiles all round.

When I got to the bottom of the stairs of the flatblock I was somewhat surprised. I was more than that. I opened my rot like wide in the old stony gapes. They had come to meet me. They were waiting by the all scrawled over municipal wall painting of the nagoy dignity of labour, bare vecks and cheenas stern at the wheels of industry, like I said, with all this dirt pencilled from their rots by naughty malchicks. Dim had a big thick like stick of black grease-paint and was tracing filthy slovos real big over our municipal painting and doing the old Dim guff – wuh huh huh – while he did it. But he turned round when Georgie and Pete gave me the well hello, showing off their shining droogy zoobies, and he horned out, 'He are here, he have arrived, hooray,' and did a clumsy turnitoe bit of dancing.

'We got worried,' said Georgie. 'There we were, a-waiting and peeting away at the old knify moloko, and you had not turned up. So then Pete here thought how you might have been like offended by some veshch or other, so round we come to your abode. That's right, Pete, right?'

'Oh, yes, right,' said Pete.

'Appy polly loggies,' I said, careful. 'I had something of a pain in the gulliver so had to sleep. I was not wakened when I gave orders for wakening. Still, here we all are, ready for what the old nochy offers, yes?' I seemed to have picked up that yes? from P. R. Deltoid, my Post-Corrective Adviser. Very strange.

'Sorry about the pain,' said Georgie, like very concerned. 'Using the gulliver too much like, maybe. Giving orders and discipline and such, perhaps. Sure the pain is gone? Sure you'll not be happier going back to the bed?' And they all had a bit of a malenky grin.

'Wait,' I said. 'Let's get things nice and sparkling clear. This sarcasm, if I may call it such, does not become you, O my little friends. Perhaps you have been having a bit of a quiet govoreet behind my back, making your own little jokes and such-like. As I am your droog and leader, surely I am entitled to know what goes on, eh? Now then, Dim, what does that great big horsy gape of a grin portend?' For Dim had his rot open in a sort of bezoomny soundless smeck. Georgie got in very skorry with:

'All right, no more picking on Dim, brother. That's part of the new way.'

'New way?' I said. 'What's this about a new way? There's been some very large talk behind my sleeping back and no error. Let me slooshy more.' And I sort of folded my rookers and leaned comfortable to listen against the broken banister-rail, me being still higher than them, droogs as they called themselves, on the third stair.

'No offence, Alex,' said Pete, 'but we wanted to have things more democratic like. Not like you saying what to do and what not all the time. But no offence.' Georgie said:

'Offence is neither here nor elsewhere. It's a matter of

who has ideas. What ideas has he had?' And he kept his very bold glazzies turned full on me. 'It's all the small stuff, malenky veshches like last night. We're growing up, brothers.'

'More,' I said, not moving. 'Let me slooshy more.'

'Well,' said Georgie, 'if you must have it, have it then. We itty round, shop-crasting and the like, coming out with a pitiful rookerful of cutter each. And there's Will the English in the Muscleman coffee mesto saying he can fence anything that any malchick cares to try to crast. The shiny stuff, the ice,' he said, still with these like cold glazzies on me. 'The big big big money is available is what Will the English says.'

'So,' I said, very comfortable out but real razdraz within. 'Since when have you been consorting and comporting with Will the English?'

'Now and again,' said Georgie, 'I get around all on my oddy knocky. Like last Sabbath for instance. I can live my own jeezny, droogie, right?'

I didn't really care for any of this, my brothers. 'And what will you do,' I said, 'with the big big big deng or money as you so highfaluting call it? Have you not every veshch you need? If you need an auto you pluck it from the trees. If you need pretty polly you take it. Yes? Why this sudden shilarny for being the big bloated capitalist?'

'Ah,' said Georgie, 'you think and govoreet sometimes like a little child.' Dim went huh huh huh at that. 'Tonight,' said Georgie, 'we pull a mansize crast.'

So my dream had told the truth, then. Georgie the general saying what we should do and what not do, Dim with the whip as mindless grinning bulldog. But I played with great care, the greatest, saying, smiling: 'Good. Real horrorshow. Initiative comes to them as wait. I have taught you much, little droogie. Now tell me what you have in mind, Georgieboy.'

'Oh,' said Georgie, cunning and crafty in his grin, 'the old moloko-plus first, would you not say? Something to sharpen us up, boy, but you especially, we having the start of you.'

'You have govoreeted my thoughts for me,' I smiled away. 'I was about to suggest the dear old Korova. Good good good. Lead, little Georgie.' And I made like a deep bow, smiling like bezoomny but thinking all the time. But when we got into the street I viddied that thinking is for the gloopy ones and that the oomny ones use like inspiration and what Bog sends. For now it was lovely music that came to my aid. There was an auto ittying by and it had its radio on, and I could just slooshy a bar or so of Ludwig van (it was the Violin Concerto, last movement), and I viddied right at once what to do. I said, in like a thick deep goloss, 'Right, Georgie, now,' and I whished out my cut-throat britva. Georgie said, 'Uh?' but he was skorry enough with his nozh, the blade coming sleesh out of the handle, and we were on to each other. Old Dim said, 'Oh, no, not right that isn't,' and made to uncoil the chain around his tally, but Pete said, putting his rooker firm on old Dim, 'Leave them. It's right like that.' So then Georgie and Your Humble did the old quiet cat-stalk, looking for openings, knowing each other's style a bit too horrorshow really, Georgie now and then going lurch lurch with his shining nozh but not no wise connecting. And all the time lewdies passed by and viddied all this but minded their own, it being perhaps a common street-sight. But then I counted odin dva tree and went ak ak ak with the britva, though not at litso or glazzies but at Georgie's nozh-holding rooker and, my little brothers, he dropped. He did. He dropped his nozh with a tinkle tankle on the hard winter sidewalk. I had just ticklewickled his fingers with my britva, and there he was looking at the malenky dribble of krovvy that was redding out in the lamplight. 'Now,' I said, and it was me that was starting, because Pete had given old Dim the soviet not to uncoil the oozy from round his tally and Dim had taken it, 'now, Dim, let's thou and me have all this now, shall us?' Dim went, 'Aaaaaaarhgh,' like some bolshy bezoomny animal, and snaked out the chain from his waist real horrorshow and skorry, so you had to admire. Now the right style for me here was to keep low like in frog-dancing to protect litso and glazzies, and this I did, brothers, so that poor old Dim was a malenky bit surprised, him being accustomed to the straight face-on lash lash lash. Now I will say that he whished me horrible on the back so that it stung like bezoomny, but that pain told me to dig in skorry once and for all and be done with old Dim. So I swished with the britva at his left noga in its very tight tight and I slashed two inches of cloth and drew a malenky drop of krovvy to make Dim real bezoomny. Then while he went hauwwww hauwww hauwww like a doggie I tried the same style as for Georgie, banking all on one move – up, cross, cut – and I felt the britva go just deep enough in the meat of old Dim's wrist and he dropped his snaking oozy yelping like a little child. Then he tried to drink in all the blood from his wrist and howl at the same time, and there was too much krovvy to drink and he went bubble bubble bubble, the red like fountaining out lovely, but not for very long. I said:

'Right, my droogies, now we should know. Yes, Pete?'

'I never said anything,' said Pete. 'I never govoreeted one slovo. Look, old Dim's bleeding to death.'

'Never,' I said. 'One can die but once. Dim died before

he was born. That red red krovvy will soon stop.' Because I had not cut into the like main cables. And I myself took a clean tashtook from my carman to wrap around poor old dying Dim's rooker, howling and moaning as he was, and the krovvy stopped like I said it would, O my brothers. So they knew now who was master and leader, sheep, thought I.

It did not take long to quieten these two wounded soldiers down in the snug of the Duke of New York, what with large brandies (bought with their own cutter, me having given all to my dad) and a wipe with tashtooks dipped in the water-jug. The old ptitsas we'd been so horrorshow to last night were there again, going, 'Thanks, lads' and 'God bless you, boys' like they couldn't stop, though we had not repeated the old sammy act with them. But Pete said, 'What's it to be, girls?' and bought black and suds for them, him seeming to have a fair amount of pretty polly in his carmans, so they were on louder than ever with their 'God bless and keep you all, lads' and 'We'd never split on you, boys' and 'The best lads breathing, that's what you are.' At last I said to Georgie:

'Now we're back to where we were, yes? Just like before and all forgotten, right?'

'Right right right,' said Georgie. But old Dim still looked a bit dazed and he even said, 'I could have got that big bastard, see, with my oozy, only some veck got in the way,' as though he'd been dratsing not with me but with some other malchick. I said:

'Well, Georgieboy, what did you have in mind?'

'Oh,' said Georgie, 'not tonight. Not this nochy, please.'

'You're a big strong chelloveck,' I said, 'like us all. We're not little children, are we, Georgieboy? What, then, didst thou in thy mind have?'

'I could have chained his glazzies real horrorshow,' said Dim, and the old baboochkas were still on with their 'Thanks, lads'.

'It was this house, see,' said Georgie. 'The one with the two lamps outside. The one with the gloopy name, like.'

'What gloopy name?'

'The Mansion or the Manse or some such piece of gloop. Where this very starry ptitsa lives with her cats and all these very starry valuable veshches.'

'Such as?'

'Gold and silver and like jewels. It was Will the English who like said.'

'I viddy,' I said. 'I viddy horrorshow.' I knew where he meant – Oldtown, just beyond Victoria Flatblock. Well, the real horrorshow leader knows always when like to give and show generous to his like unders. 'Very good, Georgie,' I said. 'A good thought, and one to be followed. Let us at once itty.' And as we were going out the old baboochkas said, 'We'll say nothing, lads. Been here all the time you have, boys.' So I said, 'Good old girls. Back to buy more in ten minutes.' And so I led my three droogs out to my doom.

6

Just past the Duke of New York going east was offices and then there was the starry beat-up biblio and then was the bolshy flatblock called Victoria Flatblock after some victory or other, and then you came to the like starry type houses of the town in what was called Oldtown. You got some of the real horrorshow ancient domies here, my brothers, with starry lewdies living in them, thin old barking like colonels with sticks and old ptitsas who were widows and deaf starry damas with cats who, my brothers, had felt not the touch of any chelloveck in the whole of their pure like jeeznies. And here, true, there were starry veshches that would fetch their share of cutter on the tourist market – like pictures and jewels and other starry pre-plastic cal of that type. So we came nice and quiet to this domy called the Manse, and there were globe lights outside on iron stalks, like guarding the front door on each side, and there was a light like dim on in one of the rooms on the ground level, and we went to a nice patch of street dark to watch through the window what was ittying on. This window had iron bars in front of it, like the house was a prison, but we could viddy nice and clear what was ittying on.

What was ittying on was that this starry ptitsa, very grey in the voloss and with a very liny like litso, was pouring the old moloko from a milk-bottle into saucers and then setting these saucers down on the floor, so you could tell there were plenty of mewing kots and koshkas writhing about down there. And we could viddy one or two, great fat scoteenas, jumping up on to the table with their rots open going mare mare mare. And you could viddy this old baboochka talking back to them, govoreeting in like scoldy language to her pussies. In the room you could viddy a lot of old pictures on the walls and starry very elaborate clocks, also some like vases and ornaments that looked starry and dorogoy. Georgie whispered, 'Real horrorshow deng to be gotten for them, brothers. Will the English is real anxious.' Pete said, 'How in?' Now it was up to me, and skorry, before Georgie started telling us how. 'First veshch,' I whispered, 'is to try the regular way, the front. I will go very polite and say that one of my droogs has had a like funny fainting turn on the street. Georgie can be ready to show, when she opens, thatwise. Then to ask for water or to phone the doc. Then in easy.' Georgie said:

'She may not open.' I said:

'We'll try it, yes?' And he sort of shrugged his pletchoes, making with a frog's rot. So I said to Pete and old Dim, 'You two droogies get either side of the door. Right?' They nodded in the dark right right right. 'So,' I said to Georgie, and I made bold straight for the front door. There was a bellpush and I pushed, and brrrrrr brrrrrr sounded down the hall inside. A like sense of slooshying followed, as though the ptitsa and her koshkas all had their ears back at the brrrrrr brrrrrr, wondering. So I pushed the old zvonock a malenky bit more urgent. I then bent down to the letter-slit and called through in a refined like goloss, 'Help, madam, please. My friend has just had a funny turn

64

on the street. Let me phone a doctor, please.' Then I could viddy a light being put on in the hall, and then I could hear the old baboochka's nogas going flip flap in flipflap slippers to nearer the front door, and I got the idea, I don't know why, that she had a big fat pussycat under each arm. Then she called out in a very surprising deep like goloss:

'Go away. Go away or I shoot.' Georgie heard that and wanted to giggle. I said, with like suffering and urgency in my gentleman's goloss:

'Oh, please help, madam. My friend's very ill.'

'Go away,' she called. 'I know your dirty tricks, making me open the door and then buy things I don't want. Go away, I tell you.' That was real lovely innocence, that was. 'Go away,' she said again, 'or I'll set my cats on to you.' A malenky bit bezoomny she was, you could tell that, through spending her jeezny all on her oddy knocky. Then I looked up and I viddied that there was a sash-window above the front door and that it would be a lot more skorry to just do the old pletcho climb and get in that way. Else there'd be this argument all the long nochy. So I said:

'Very well, madam. If you won't help I must take my suffering friend elsewhere.' And I winked my droogies all away quiet, only me crying out, 'All right, old friend, you will surely meet some good samaritan some place other. This old lady perhaps cannot be blamed for being suspicious with so many scoundrels and rogues of the night about. No, indeed not.' Then we waited again in the dark and I whispered, 'Right. Return to door. Me stand on Dim's pletchoes. Open that window and me enter, droogies. Then to shut up that old ptitsa and open up for all. No trouble.' For I was like showing who was leader and the chelloveck with the ideas. 'See,' I said. 'Real horrorshow

bit of stonework over that door, a nice hold for my nogas.'
They viddied all that, admiring perhaps I thought, and
said and nodded Right right right in the dark.

So back tiptoe to the door. Dim was our heavy strong
malchick and Pete and Georgie like heaved me up on to
Dim's bolshy manly pletchoes. All this time, O thanks to
worldcasts on the gloopy TV and, more, lewdies' night-
fear through lack of night-police, dead lay the street. Up
there on Dim's pletchoes I viddied that this stonework
above the door would take my boots lovely. I kneed up,
brothers, and there I was. The window, as I had expected,
was closed, but I outed with my britva and cracked the
glass of the window smart with the bony handle thereof.
All the time below my droogies were hard breathing. So
I put in my rooker through the crack and made the lower
half of the window sail up open silver-smooth and lovely.
And I was, like getting into the bath, in. And there were
my sheep down below, their rots open as they looked up,
O brothers.

I was in bumpy darkness, with beds and cupboards and
bolshy heavy stoolies and piles of boxes and books about.
But I strode manful towards the door of the room I was
in, seeing a like crack of light under it. The door went
squeeeeeeeeeeeak and then I was on a dusty corridor with
other doors. All this waste, brothers, meaning all these
rooms and but one starry sharp and her pussies, but perhaps
the kots and koshkas had like separate bedrooms, living
on cream and fish-heads like royal queens and princes. I
could hear the like muffled goloss of this old ptitsa down
below saying, 'Yes yes yes, that's it,' but she would be
govoreeting to these mewing sidlers going maaaaaaah for
more moloko. Then I saw the stairs going down to the
hall and I thought to myself that I would show these fickle

and worthless droogs of mine that I was worth the whole three of them and more. I would do all on my oddy knocky. I would perform the old ultra-violence on the starry ptitsa and on her pusspots if need be, then I would take fair rookerfuls of what looked like real polezny stuff and go waltzing to the front door and open up showering gold and silver on my waiting droogs. They must learn all about leadership.

So down I ittied, slow and gentle, admiring in the stair-well grahzny pictures of old time – devotchkas with long hair and high collars, the like country with trees and horses, the holy bearded veck all nagoy hanging on a cross. There was a real musty von of pussies and pussyfish and starry dust in this domy, different from the flatblocks. And then I was downstairs and I could viddy the light in this front room where she had been doling moloko to the kots and koshkas. More, I could viddy these great over-stuffed scoteenas going in and out with their tails waving and like rubbing themselves on the door-bottom. On a like big wooden chest in the dark hall I could viddy a nice malenky statue that shone in the light of the room, so I crasted this for my own self, it being like of a young thin devotchka standing on one noga with her rookers out, and I could see this was made of silver. So I had this when I ittied into the lit-up room, saying, 'Hi hi hi. At last we meet. Our brief govoreet through the letter-hole was not, shall we say, satisfactory, yes? Let us admit not, oh verily not, you stinking starry old sharp.' And I like blinked in the light at this room and the old ptitsa in it. It was full of kots and koshkas all crawling to and fro over the carpet, with bits of fur floating in the lower air, and these fat scoteenas were all different shapes and colours, black, white, tabby, ginger, tortoise-shell, and of all ages, too, so that there were kittens fillying about with each other and there were pussies full-grown and there were real dribbling starry ones very bad-tempered. Their mistress, this old ptitsa, looked at me fierce like a man and said:

'How did you get in? Keep your distance, you villainous young toad, or I shall be forced to strike you.'

I had a real horrorshow smeck at that, viddying that she had in her veiny rooker a crappy wood walking-stick which she raised at me threatening. So, making with my shiny zoobies, I ittied a bit nearer to her, taking my time, and on the way I saw on a like sideboard a lovely little veshch, the loveliest malenky veshch any malchick fond of music like myself could ever hope to viddy with his own two glazzies, for it was like the gulliver and pletchoes of Ludwig van himself, what they call a bust, a like stone veshch with stone long hair and blind glazzies and the big flowy cravat. I was off for that right away, saying, 'Well, how lovely and all for me.' But ittying towards it with my glazzies like full on it and my greedy rooker held out, I did not see the milk saucers on the floor and into one I went and sort of lost balance. 'Whoops,' I said, trying to steady, but this old ptitsa had come up behind me very sly and with great skorriness for her age and then she went crack crack on my gulliver with her bit of a stick. So I found myself on my rookers and knees trying to get up and saying, 'Naughty naughty naughty.' And then she was going crack crack again, saying, 'Wretched little slummy bed-bug, breaking into *real* people's houses.' I didn't like this crack crack eegra, so I grasped hold of one end of her stick as it came down again and then she lost her balance and was trying to steady herself against the table, but then the table-cloth came off with a milk-jug and a milk-bottle going all drunk then scattering white splosh in all directions, then she was down on the floor grunting, going, 'Blast you, boy, you shall suffer.' Now all the cats were getting spoogy and running and jumping in a like cat-panic, and some were blaming each other, hitting out cat-tolchocks with the old naga and ptaaaaa and grrrrr and kraaaaark. I got up on to my nogas, and there was this nasty vindictive starry forella with her wattles ashake and grunting as she like tried to lever herself up from the floor, so I gave her a malenky fair kick in the litso, and she didn't like that, crying, 'Waaaaah,' and you could viddy her veiny mottled litso going purplewurple where I'd landed the old noga.

As I stepped back from the kick I must have like trod on the tail of one of these dratsing creeching pusspots, because I slooshied a gromky yauuuuuuuuw and found that like fur and teeth and claws had like fastened them-selves round my leg, and there I was cursing away and trying to shake it off holding this silver malenky statue in one rooker and trying to climb over this old ptitsa on the floor to reach lovely Ludwig van in frowning like stone. And then I was into another saucer brimful of creamy moloko and near went flying again, the whole veshch really a very humorous one if you could imagine it sloochatting to some other veck and not to Your Humble Narrator. And then the starry ptitsa on the floor reached over all the dratsing yowling pusscats and grabbed at my noga, still going 'Waaaaah' at me, and, my balance being a bit gone, I went really crash this time, on to sploshing moloko and skriking koshkas, and the old forella started to fist me on the litso, both of us being on the floor, creeching, 'Thrash him, beat him, pull out his finger-nails, the poisonous young beetle,' addressing her pusscats only, and then, as if like obeying the starry old ptitsa, a couple of

69

koshkas got on to me and started scratching like bezoomny. So then I got real bezoomny myself, brothers, and hit out at them, but this baboochka said, 'Toad, don't touch my kitties,' and like scratched my litso. So then I creeched: 'You filthy old soomka,' and upped with the little malenky like silver statue and cracked her a fine fair tolchock on the gulliver and that shut her up real horrorshow and lovely.

Now as I got up from the floor among all the crarking kots and koshkas what should I slooshy but the shoom of the old police-auto siren in the distance, and it dawned on me skorry that the old forella of the pusscats had been on the phone to the millicents when I thought she'd been govoreeting to the mewlers and mowlers, her having got her suspicions skorry on the boil when I'd rung the old zvonock pretending for help. So now, slooshying this fearsome shoom of the rozz-van, I belted for the front door and had a rabbiting time undoing all the locks and chains and bolts and other protective veshches. Then I got it open, and who should be on the doorstep but old Dim, me just being able to viddy the other two of my so-called droogs belting off. 'Away,' I creeched to Dim. 'The rozzes are coming.' Dim said, 'You stay to meet them huh huh huh,' and then I viddied that he had his oozy out, and then he upped with it and it snaked whishhhhh and he chained me gentle and artistic like on the glaz-lids, me just closing them up in time. Then I was howling around trying to viddy with this howling great pain, and Dim said, 'I don't like you should do what you done, old droogy. Not right it wasn't to get on to me like the way you done, brat.' And then I could slooshy his bolshy lumpy boots beating off, him going huh huh huh into the darkmans, and it was only about seven seconds after that I slooshied the millicent-van draw up with a filthy great dropping siren-howl, like some bezoomny animal snuffing it. I was howling too and like yawing about and I banged my gulliver smack on the hall-wall, my glazzies being tight shut and the juice astream from them, very agonising. So there I was like groping in the hallway as the millicents arrived. I couldn't viddy them, of course, but I could slooshy and damn near smell the von of the bastards, and soon I could feel the bastards as they got rough and did the old twist-arm act, carrying me out. I could also slooshy one millicent goloss saying from like the room I'd come out of with all the kots and koshkas in it, 'She's been nastily knocked but she's breathing,' and there was loud mewing all the time.

'A real pleasure this is,' I heard another millicent goloss say as I was tolchocked very rough and skorry into the auto. 'Little Alex all to our own selves.' I creeched out:

'I'm blind, Bog bust and bleed you, you grahzny bastards.'

'Language, language,' like smecked a goloss, and then I got a like backhand tolchock with some ringy rooker or other full on the rot. I said:

'Bog murder you, you vonny stinking bratchnies. Where are the others? Where are my stinking traitorous droogs? One of my cursed grahzny bratties chained me on the glazzies. Get them before they get away. It was all their idea, brothers. They like forced me to do it. I'm innocent, Bog butcher you.' By this time they were all having like a good smeck at me with the heighth of like callousness, and they'd tolchocked me into the back of the auto, but I still kept on about these so-called droogs of mine and then I viddied it would be no good, because they'd all be back now in the snug of the Duke of New

York forcing black and suds and double Scotchmen down the unprotesting gorloes of those stinking starry ptitsas and they saying, 'Thanks, lads. God bless you, boys. Been here all the time you have, lads. Not been out of our sight you haven't.'

All the time we were sirening off to the rozz-shop, me being wedged between two millicents and being given the odd thump and malenky tolchock by these smecking bullies. Then I found I could open up my glaz-lids a malenky bit and viddy like through all tears a kind of streamy city going by, all the lights like having run into one another. I could viddy now through smarting glazzies these two smecking millicents at the back with me and the thin-necked driver and the fat-necked bastard next to him, this one having a sarky like govoreet at me, saying, 'Well, Alex boy, we all look forward to a pleasant evening together, don't we not?' I said:

'How do you know my name, you stinking vonny bully? May Bog blast you to hell, grahzny bratchny as you are, you sod.' So they all had a smeck at that and I had my ooko like twisted by one of these stinking millicents at the back with me. The fat-necked not-driver said:

'Everybody knows little Alex and his droogs. Quite a famous young boy our Alex has become.'

'It's those others,' I creeched. 'Georgie and Dim and Pete. No droogs of mine, the bastards.'

'Well,' said the fat-neck, 'you've got the evening in front of you to tell the whole story of the daring exploits of those young gentlemen and how they led poor little innocent Alex astray.' Then there was the shoom of another like police siren passing this auto but going the other way.

'Is that for those bastards?' I said. 'Are they being picked up by you bastards?'

'That,' said fat-neck, 'is an ambulance. Doubtless for your old lady victim, you ghastly wretched scoundrel.'

'It was all their fault,' I creeched, blinking my smarting glazzies. 'The bastards will be peeting away in the Duke of New York. Pick them up, blast you, you vonny sods.' And then there was more smecking and another malenky tolchock, O my brothers, on my poor smarting rot. And then we arrived at the stinking rozz-shop and they helped me get out of the auto with kicks and pulls and they tolchocked me up the steps and I knew I was going to get nothing like fair play from these stinking grahzny bratchnies, Bog blast them.

THEY dragged me into this very bright-lit whitewashed cantora, and it had a strong von that was a mixture of like sick and lavatories and beery rots and disinfectant, all coming from the barry places near by. You could hear some of the plennies in their cells cursing and singing and I fancied I could slooshy one belting out:

And I will go back to my darling, my darling,
When you, my darling, are gone.

But there were the golosses of millicents telling them to shut it and you could even slooshy the zvook of like somebody being tolchocked real horrorshow and going owwwwwwwww, and it was like the goloss of a drunken starry ptitsa, not a man. With me in this cantora were four millicents, all having a good loud peet of chai, a big pot of it being on the table and they sucking and belching away over their dirty bolshy mugs. They didn't offer me any. All that they gave me, my brothers, was a crappy starry mirror to look into, and indeed I was not your handsome young Narrator any longer but a real strack of a sight, my rot swollen and my glazzies all red and my nose bumped a bit also. They all had a real horrorshow smeck when they viddied my like dismay, and one of them

said, 'Love's young nightmare, like.' And then a top millicent came in with like stars on his pletchoes to show me
he was high high high, and he viddied me and said, 'Hm.'
So then they started. I said:

'I won't say one single solitary slovo unless I have my
lawyer here. I know the law, you bratchnies. Of course
they all had a good gromky smeck at that and the stellar
top millicent said:

'Righty right, boys, we'll start off by showing him that
we know the law, too, but that knowing the law's not
everything.' He had a like gentleman's goloss and spoke
in a very weary sort of a way, and he nodded with a like
droogy smile at one very big fat bastard. This big fat
bastard took off his tunic and you could viddy he had a
real big starry pot on him, then he came up to me not
too skorry and I could get the von of the milky chai he'd
been peeting when he opened his rot in a like very tired
leery grin at me. He was not too well shaved for a rozz
and you could viddy like patches of dried sweat on his
shirt under the arms, and you could get this von of like
earwax from him as he came close. Then he clenched his
stinking red rooker and let me have it right in the belly,
which was unfair, and all the other millicents smecked
their gullivers off at that, except the top one and he kept
on with this weary like bored grin. I had to lean against
the whitewashed wall so that all the white got on to my
platties, trying to drag the old breath back and in great
agony, and then I wanted to sick up the gluey pie I'd had
before the start of the evening. But I couldn't stand that
sort of veshch, sicking all over the floor, so I held it back.
Then I saw that this fatty bruiseboy was turning to his
millicent droogs to have a real horrorshow smeck at what
he'd done, so I raised my right noga and before they could

76

creech at him to watch out I'd kicked him smart and lovely on the shin. And he creeched murder, hopping around.

But after that they all had a turn, bouncing me from one to the other like some very weary bloody ball, O my brothers, and fisting me in the yarbles and the rot and the belly and dealing out kicks, and then at last I had to sick up on the floor and, like some real bezoomny veck, I even said, 'Sorry, brothers, that was not the right thing at all. Sorry sorry sorry.' But they handed me starry bits of gazetta and made me wipe it, then they made me make with the sawdust. And then they said, almost like dear old droogs, that I was to sit down and we'd all have a quiet like govoreet. And then P. R. Deltoid came in to have a viddy, his office being in the same building, looking very tired and grahzny, to say, 'So it's happened, Alex boy, yes?' Then he turned to the millicents to say, 'Evening, inspector. Evening, sergeant. Evening, evening, all. Well, this is the end of the line for me, yes. Dear dear, this boy does look messy, doesn't he? Just look at the state of him.'

'Violence makes violence,' said the top millicent in a very holy type goloss. 'He resisted his lawful arresters.'

'End of the line, yes,' said P. R. Deltoid again. He looked at me with very cold glazzies like I had become like a thing and was no more a bleeding very tired battered chelloveck. 'I suppose I'll have to be in court tomorrow.'

'It wasn't me, brother, sir,' I said, a malenky bit weepy. 'Speak up for me, sir, for I'm not so bad. I was led on by the treachery of the others, sir.'

'Sings like a linnet,' said the top rozz, sneery. 'Sings the roof off lovely, he does that.'

'I'll speak,' said cold P. R. Deltoid. 'I'll be there tomorrow, don't worry.'

'If you'd like to give him a bash in the chops, sir,' said

77

the top millicent, 'don't mind us. We'll hold him down. He must be another great disappointment to you.'

P. R. Deltoid then did something I never thought any man like him who was supposed to turn us baddiwads into real horrorshow malchicks would do, especially with all those rozzes around. He came a bit nearer and he spat. He spat. He spat full in my litso and then wiped his wet spitty rot with the back of his rooker. And I wiped and wiped and wiped my spat-on litso with my bloody tashtook, saying, 'Thank you, sir, thank you.' And then P. R. Deltoid walked out without another slovo.

The millicents now got down to making this long statement for me to sign, and I thought to myself, Hell and blast you all, if all you bastards are on the side of the Good then I'm glad I belong to the other shop. 'All right,' I said to them, 'you grahzny bratchnies as you are, you vonny sods. Take it, take the lot. I'm not going to crawl around on my brooko any more, you merzky gets. Where do you want it taken from, you cally vonning animals? From my last corrective? Horrorshow, horrorshow, here it is, then.' So I gave it to them, and I had this shorthand millicent, a very quiet and scared type chelloveck, no real rozz at all, covering page after page after page after. I gave them the ultra-violence, the crasting, the dratsing, the old in-out in-out, the lot, right up to this night's veshch with the bugatty starry ptitsa with the mewing kots and koshkas. And I made sure my so-called droogs were in it, right up to the shiyah. When I'd got through the lot the shorthand millicent looked a bit faint, poor old veck. The top rozz said to him, in a kind type goloss:

'Right, son, you go off and get a nice cup of chai for yourself and then type all that filth and rottenness out with a clothes-peg on your nose, three copies. Then they can be brought to our handsome young friend here for signature. And you,' he said to me, 'can now be shown to your bridal suite with running water and all conveniences. All right,' in this weary goloss to two of the real tough rozzes, 'take him away.'

So I was kicked and punched and bullied off to the cells and put in with about ten or twelve other plennies, a lot of them drunk. There were real oozhassny animal type vecks among them, one with his nose all ate away and his rot open like a big black hole, one that was lying on the floor snoring away and all like slime dribbling all the time out of his rot, and one that had like done all cal in his pantalonies. Then there were two like queer ones who both took a fancy to me, and one of them made a jump on to my back, and I had a real nasty bit of dratsing with him and the von on him, like of meth and cheap scent, made me want to sick again, only my belly was empty now, O my brothers. Then the other queer one started putting his rookers on to me, and then there was a snarling bit of dratsing between these two, both of them wanting to get at my plott. The shoom became very loud, so that a couple of millicents came along and cracked into these two with like truncheons, so that both sat quiet then, looking like into space, and there was the old krovvy going drip drip drip down the litso of one of them. There were bunks in this cell, but all filled. I climbed up to the top of one tier of bunks, there being four in a tier, and there was a starry drunken veck snoring away, most probably heaved up there to the top by the millicents. Anyway, I heaved him down again, him not being all that heavy, and he collapsed on top of a fat drunk chelloveck on the floor, and both woke and started creeching and punching pathetic at each other. So I lay down on this vonny bed, my brothers, and went to very tired and exhausted and hurt sleep. But it was not really like sleep, it was like passing out to another better world. And in this other better world, O my brothers, I was in like a big field with all flowers and trees, and there was a like goat with a man's litso playing away on a like flute. And then there rose like the sun Ludwig van himself with thundery litso and cravat and wild windy voloss, and then I heard the Ninth, last movement, with the slovos all a bit mixed-up, like they knew themselves they had to be mixed-up, this being a dream:

> Boy, thou uproarious shark of heaven,
>> Slaughter of Elysium,
> Hearts on fire, aroused, enraptured,
>> We will tolchock you on the rot and kick
>> your grahzny vonny bum.

But the tune was right, as I knew when I was being woke up two or ten minutes or twenty hours or days or years later, my watch having been taken away. There was a millicent like miles and miles down below and he was prodding at me with a long stick with a spike on the end, saying:

'Wake up, son. Wake up, my beauty. Wake to real trouble.' I said:

'Why? Who? Where? What is it?' And the tune of the Joy ode in the Ninth was singing away real lovely and horrorshow within. The millicent said:

'Come down and find out. There's some real lovely news for you, my son.' So I scrambled down, very stiff and sore and not like real awake, and this rozz, who had a strong von of cheese and onions on him, pushed me out of the filthy snoring cell, and then along corridors, and all the time the old tune Joy Thou Glorious Spark Of Heaven was sparking away within. Then we came to a very neat like cantora with typewriters and flowers on the desks, and at the like chief desk the top millicent was sitting, looking very serious and fixing a like very cold glazzy on my sleepy litso. I said:

'Well well well. What makes, bratty? What gives, this fine bright middle of the nochy?' He said:

'I'll give you just ten seconds to wipe that stupid grin off of your face. Then I want you to listen.'

'Well, what?' I said, smecking. 'Are you not satisfied with beating me near to death and having me spat upon and making me confess to crimes for hours on end and then shoving me among bezoomnies and vonny perverts in that grahzny cell? Have you some new torture for me, you bratchny?'

'It'll be your own torture,' he said, serious. 'I hope to God it'll torture you to madness.'

And then, before he told me, I knew what it was. The old ptitsa who had all the kots and koshkas had passed on to a better world in one of the city hospitals. I'd cracked her a bit too hard, like. Well, well, that was everything. I thought of all those kots and koshkas mewing for moloko and getting none, not any more from their starry forella of a mistress. That was everything. I'd done the lot, now. And me still only fifteen.

2

'WHAT's it going to be then, eh?'

I take it up now, and this is the real weepy and like tragic part of the story beginning, my brothers and only friends, in Staja (State Jail, that is) Number 84F. You will have little desire to slooshy all the cally and horrible raskazz of the shock that sent my dad beating his bruised and krovvy rookers against unfair like Bog in His Heaven, and my mum squaring her rot for owwwww owwwww owwwww in her mother's grief at her only child and son of her bosom like letting everybody down real horrorshow. Then there was the starry very grim magistrate in the lower court govoreeting some very hard slovos against your Friend and Humble Narrator, after all the cally and grahzny slander spat forth by P. R. Deltoid and the rozzes, Bog blast them. Then there was being remanded in filthy custody among vonny perverts and prestoopnicks. Then there was the trial in the higher court with judges and a jury, and some very very nasty slovos indeed govoreeted in a very like solemn way, and then Guilty and my mum boohoohooing when they said Fourteen Years, O my brothers. So here I was now, two years just to the day of being kicked and clanged into Staja 84F, dressed in the heighth of prison fashion, which was a one-piece suit of a very filthy like cal colour, and the number sewn on the groody part just above the old tick-tocker and on the back as well, so that going and coming I was 6655321 and not your little droog Alex not no longer.

'What's it going to be then, eh?'

It had not been like edifying, indeed it had not, being in this grahzny hellhole and like human zoo for two years, being kicked and tolchocked by brutal bully warders and meeting vonny leering like criminals, some of them real perverts and ready to dribble all over a luscious young malchick like your story-teller. And there was having to rabbit in the workshop at making matchboxes and itty round and round and round the yard for like exercise, and in the evenings sometimes some starry prof type veck would give a talk on beetles or the Milky Way or the Glorious Wonders of the Snowflake, and I had a good smeck at this last one, because it reminded me of that time of the tolchocking and Sheer Vandalism with that ded coming from the public biblio on a winter's night when my droogs were still not traitors and I was like happy and free. Of those droogs I had slooshied but one thing, and that was one day when my pee and em came to visit and I was told that Georgie was dead. Yes, dead, my brothers. Dead as a bit of dog-cal on the road. Georgie had led the other two into a like very bugatty chelloveck's house, and there they had kicked and tolchocked the owner on the floor, and then Georgie had started to razrez the cushions and curtains, and then old Dim had cracked at some very precious orna-ments, like statues and so on, and this rich beat-up chell-oveck had raged like real bezoomny and gone for them all with a very heavy iron bar. His being all razdraz had given him like gigantic strength, and Dim and Pete had got out through the window but Georgie had tripped on the carpet and then bought this terrific swinging iron bar crack and

splooge on the gulliver, and that was the end of traitorous
Georgie. The starry murderer had got off with Self Defence,
as was really right and proper. Georgie being killed, though
it was more than one year after me being caught by the
millicents, it all seemed right and proper and like Fate.

'What's it going to be then, eh?'

I was in the Wing Chapel, it being Sunday morning, and
the prison charlie was govoreeting the Word of the Lord. It
was my rabbit to play the starry stereo, putting on solemn
music before and after and in the middle too when hymns
were sung. I was at the back of the Wing Chapel (there were
four altogether in Staja 84F) near where the warders or
chassos were standing with their rifles and their dirty bolshy
blue brutal jowls, and I could viddy all the plennies sitting
down slooshying the Slovo of the Lord in their horrible cal-
coloured prison platties, and a sort of filthy von rose from
them, not like real unwashed, not grazzy, but like a special
real stinking von which you only got with the criminal types,
my brothers, a like dusty, greasy, hopeless sort of a von. And
I was thinking that perhaps I had this von too, having become
a real plenny myself, though still very young. So it was very
important to me, O my brothers, to get out of this stinking
grahzny zoo as soon as I could. And, as you will viddy if
you keep reading on, it was not long before I did.

'What's it going to be then, eh?' said the prison charlie
for the third raz. 'Is it going to be in and out and in and
out of institutions like this, though more in than out for
most of you, or are you going to attend to the Divine
Word and realise the punishments that await the unrepentant sinner in the next world, as well as in this? A lot
of blasted idiots you are, most of you, selling your birth-
right for a saucer of cold porridge. The thrill of theft, of
violence, the urge to live easy – is it worth it when we

have undeniable proof, yes yes, incontrovertible evidence that hell exists? I know, I know, my friends, I have been informed in visions that there is a place, darker than any prison, hotter than any flame of human fire, where souls of unrepentant criminal sinners like yourselves – and don't leer at me, damn you, don't laugh – like yourselves, I say, scream in endless and intolerable agony, their noses choked with the smell of filth, their mouths crammed with burning ordure, their skin peeling and rotting, a fireball spinning in their screaming guts. Yes, yes, yes, I know.'

At this point, brothers, a plenny somewhere or other near the back row let out a shoom of lip-music – 'Prrrrrp' – and then the brutal chassos were on the job right away, rushing real skorry to what they thought was the scene of the shoom, then hitting out nasty and delivering tolchocks left and right. Then they picked out one poor trembling plenny, very thin and malenky and starry too, and dragged him off, but all the time he kept creeching, 'It wasn't me, it was him, see,' but that made no difference. He was tolchocked real nasty and then dragged out of the Wing Chapel creeching his gulliver off.

'Now,' said the prison charlie, 'listen to the Word of the Lord.' Then he picked up the big book and flipped over the pages, keeping on wetting his fingers to do this by licking them splurge splurge. He was a bolshy great burly bastard with a very red litso, but he was very fond of myself, me being young and also now very interested in the big book. It had been arranged as part of my like further education to read in the book and even have music on the chapel stereo while I was reading, O my brothers. And that was real horror-show. They would like lock me in and let me slooshy holy music by J. S. Bach and G. F. Handel, and I would read of these starry yahoodies tolchocking each other and then peeting their Hebrew vino and getting on to the bed with their wives' like handmaidens, real horrorshow. That kept me going, brothers. I didn't so much kopat the later part of the book, which is more like all preachy govoreeting than fighting and the old in-out. But one day the charles said to me, squeezing me like tight with his bolshy beefy rooker, 'Ah 6655321, think on the divine suffering. Meditate on that, my boy.' And all the time he had this rich manny von of Scotch on him, and then he went off to his little cantora to peet some more. So I read all about the scourging and the crowning with thorns and then the cross veshch and all that cal, and I viddied better that there was something in it. While the stereo played bits of lovely Bach I closed my glazzies and viddied myself helping out and even taking charge of the tolchocking and the nailing in, being dressed in a like toga that was the heighth of Roman fashion. So being in Staja 84F was not all that wasted, and the Governor himself was very pleased to hear that I had taken to like Religion, and that was where I had my hopes.

This Sunday morning the charlie read out from the book about chellovecks who slooshied the slovo and didn't take a blind bit being like a domy built on sand, and then the rain came splash and the old boomaboom cracked the sky and that was the end of that domy. But I thought only a very dim veck would build his domy upon sand, and a right lot of real sneering droogs and nasty neighbours a veck like that would have, them not telling him how dim he was doing that sort of building. Then the charles creeched, 'Right, you lot. We'll end with Hymn Number 435 in the Prisoners' Hymnal.' Then there was a crash and plop and a whish whish whish while the plennies picked up and dropped and lickturned the pages of their grazzy malenky hymnbooks, and the bully fierce warders creeched, 'Stop talking there, bastards. I'm watching you, 920537.' Of course

I had the disc ready on the stereo, and then I let the simple music for organ only come belting out with a growwwwo-wwwwowwww. Then the plennies started to sing real horrible:

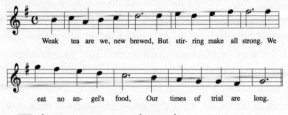

Weak tea are we, new brewed,
   But stirring make all strong.
We eat no angel's food,
   Our times of trial are long.

They sort of howled and wept these stupid slovos with the charlie like whipping them on with 'Louder, damn you, sing up,' and the warders creeching, 'Just you wait, 7749222' and 'One on the turnip coming up for you, filth.' Then it was all over and the charlie said, 'May the Holy Trinity keep you always and make you good, amen,' and the shamble out began to a nice choice bit of Symphony No. 2 by Adrian Schweigselber, chosen by your Humble Narrator, O my brothers. What a lot they were, I thought, as I stood there by the starry chapel stereo, viddying them all shuffle out going marrrrre and baaaaaa like animals and up-your-piping with their grahzny fingers at me, because it looked like I was very special favoured. When the last one had slouched out, his rookers hanging like an ape and the one warder left giving him a fair loud tolchock on the back of the gulliver, and when I had turned off the stereo, the charlie came up to me, puffing away at a cancer, still in his starry bogman's platties, all lacy and white like a devotchka's. He said:

'Thank you as always, little 6655321. And what news have you got for me today?' The idea was, I knew, that this charlie was after becoming a very great holy chelloveck in the world of Prison Religion, and he wanted a real horrorshow testimonial from the Governor, so he would go and govoreet quietly to the Governor now and then about what dark plots were brewing among the plennies, and he would get a lot of this cal from me. A lot of it would be all like made up, but some of it would be true, like for instance the time it had come through to our cell on the waterpipes knock knock knockiknocki-knock knockknock that big Harriman was going to break. He was going to tolchock the warder at sloptime and get out in the warder's platties. Then there was going to be a big throwing about of the horrible pishcha we got in the dining-hall, and I knew about that and told. Then the charlie passed it on and was complimented like by the Governor for his Public Spirit and Keen Ear. So this time I said, and this was not true:

'Well, sir, it has come through on the pipes that a consignment of cocaine has arrived by irregular means and that a cell somewhere along Tier 5 is to be the centre of distribution.' I made all that up as I went along, like I made up many of these stories, but the prison charlie was very grateful, saying, 'Good, good, good. I shall pass that on to Himself,' this being what he called the Governor. Then I said:

'Sir, I have done my best, have I not?' I always used my very polite gentleman's goloss govoreeting with those at the top. 'I've tried, sir, haven't I?'

'I think,' said the charlie, 'that on the whole you have, 6655321. You've been very helpful and, I consider, shown a genuine desire to reform. You will, if you continue in

91

this manner, earn your remission with no trouble at all.'

'But sir,' I said, 'how about this new thing they're talking about? How about this new like treatment that gets you out of prison in no time at all and makes sure that you never get back in again?'

'Oh,' he said, very like wary. 'Where did you hear this? Who's been telling you these things?'

'These things get around, sir,' I said. 'Two warders talk, as it might be, and somebody can't help hearing what they say. And then somebody picks up a scrap of newspaper in the workshops and the newspaper says all about it. How about you putting me in for this thing, sir, if I may make so bold as to make the suggestion?'

You could viddy him thinking about that while he puffed away at his cancer, wondering how much to say to me about what he knew about this veshch I mentioned. Then he said, 'I take it you're referring to Ludovico's Technique.' He was still very wary.

'I don't know what it's called, sir,' I said. 'All I know is that it gets you out quickly and makes sure that you don't get in again.'

'That is so,' he said, his eyebrows like all beetling while he looked down at me. 'That is quite so, 6655321. Of course, it's only in the experimental stage at the moment. It's very simple but very drastic.'

'But it's being used here, isn't it, sir?' I said. 'Those new like white buildings by the South Wall, sir. We've watched those being built, sir, when we've been doing our exercise.'

'It's not been used yet,' he said, 'not in this prison, 6655321. Himself has grave doubts about it. I must confess I share those doubts. The question is whether such a technique can really make a man good. Goodness comes from within, 6655321. Goodness is something chosen.

When a man cannot choose he ceases to be a man.' He would have gone on with a lot more of this cal, but we could slooshy the next lot of plennies marching clank clank down the iron stairs to come for their bit of Religion. He said, 'We'll have a little chat about this some other time. Now you'd better start the voluntary.' So I went over to the starry stereo and put on J. S. Bach's *Wachet Auf* Choral Prelude and in these grahzny vonny bastard criminals and perverts came shambling like a lot of broke-down apes, the warders or chassos like barking at them and lashing them. And soon the prison charlie was asking them, 'What's it going to be then, eh?' And that's where you came in.

We had four of these lomticks of like Prison Religion that morning, but the charles said no more to me about this Ludovico's Technique, whatever it was, O my brothers. When I'd finished my rabbit with the stereo he just govo-reeted a few slovos of thanks and then I was privodeeted back to the cell on Tier 6 which was my very vonny and crammed home. The chasso was not really too bad of a veck and he did not tolchock or kick me in when he'd opened up, he just said, 'Here we are, sonny, back to the old waterhole.' And there I was with my new type droogs, all very criminal but, Bog be praised, not given to perversions of the body. There was Zophar on his bunk, a very thin and brown veck who went on and on and on in his like cancery goloss, so that nobody bothered to slooshy. What he was saying now like to nobody was 'And at that time you couldn't get hold of a poggy' (whatever that was, brothers) 'not if you was to hand over ten million archibalds, so what do I do eh, I goes down to Turkey's and says I've got this sproog on that morrow, see, and what can he do?' It was all this very old-time real criminal's slang he spoke. Also there was Wall, who had only one glazzy, and he was tearing bits of his toe-nails off in honour of Sunday. Also there was Big Jew, a very fat sweaty veck lying flat on his bunk like dead. In addition there was Jojohn and The Doctor. Jojohn was very mean and keen and wiry and had specialised in like Sexual Assault, and The Doctor had pretended to be able to cure syph and gon and gleet but he had only injected water, also he had killed off two devotchkas instead, like he had promised, of getting rid of their unwanted loads for them. They were a terrible grahzny lot really, and I didn't enjoy being with them, O my brothers, any more than you do now, but it won't be for much longer.

Now what I want you to know is that this cell was intended for only three when it was built, but there were six of us there, all jammed together sweaty and tight. And that was the state of all the cells in all the prisons in those days, brothers, and a dirty cally disgrace it was, there not being decent room for a chelloveck to stretch his limbs. And you will hardly believe what I say now, which is that on this Sunday they brosatted in another plenny. Yes, we had our horrible pishcha of dumplings and vonny stew and were smoking a quiet cancer each on our bunks when this veck was thrown into our midst. He was a chinny starry veck and it was him who started creeching complaints before we even had a chance to viddy the position. He tried to like shake the bars, creeching, 'I demand my sodding rights, this one's full up, it's a bleeding imposition, that's what it is.' But one of the chassos came back to say that he had to make the best of it and share a bunk with whoever would let him, otherwise it would have to be the floor. 'And,' said the warder, 'it's going to get worse, not better. A right dirty criminal world you lot are trying to build.'

2 WELL, it was the letting-in of this new chelloveck that was really the start of my getting out of the old Staja, for he was such a nasty quarrelsome type of plenny, with a very dirty mind and filthy intentions, that trouble nachinatted that very same day. He was also very boastful and started to make with a very sneery litso at us all and a loud and proud goloss. He made out that he was the only real horrorshow prestoopnick in the whole zoo, going on that he'd done this and done the other and killed ten rozzes with one crack of his rooker and all that cal. But nobody was very impressed, O my brothers. So then he started on me, me being the youngest there, trying to say that as the youngest I ought to be the one to zasnoot on the floor and not him. But all the others were for me, creeching, 'Leave him alone, you grahzny bratchny,' and then he began the old whine about how nobody loved him. So that same nochy I woke up to find this horrible plenny actually lying with me on my bunk, which was on the bottom of the three-tier and also very narrow, and he was govoreeting dirty like love-slovos and stroke stroke stroking away. So then I got real bezoomny and lashed out, though I could not viddy all that horrorshow, there being only this malenky little red light outside on the landing. But I knew it was this one, the vonny

95

bastard, and then when the trouble really got under way and the lights were turned on I could viddy his horrible litso with all krovvy dripping from his rot where I'd hit out with my clawing rooker.

What sloochatted then, of course, was that my cell-mates woke up and started to join in, tolchocking a bit wild in the near dark, and the shoom seemed to wake up the whole tier, so that you could slooshy a lot of creeching and banging about with tin mugs on the wall, as though all the plennies in all the cells thought a big break was about to commence, O my brothers. So then the lights came on and the chassos came along in their shirts and trousers and caps, waving big sticks. We could viddy each other's flushed litsos and the shaking of fisty rookers, and there was a lot of creeching and cursing. Then I put in my complaint and every chasso said it was probably Your Humble Narrator, brothers, that started it all anyway, me having no mark of a scratch on me but this horrible plenny dripping red red krovvy from the rot where I'd got him with my clawing rooker. That made me real bezoomny. I said I would not sleep another nochy in that cell if the Prison Authorities were going to allow horrible vonny stinking perverted prestoopnicks to leap on my plott when I was in no position to defend myself, being asleep. 'Wait till the morning,' they said. 'Is it a private room with bath and television that your honour requires? Well, all that will be seen to in the morning. But for the present, little droog, get your bleeding gulliver down on your straw-filled podooshka and let's have no more trouble from anyone. Right right right?' Then off they went with stern warnings for all, then soon after the lights went out, and then I said I would sit up all the rest of the nochy, saying first to this horrible prestoopnick, 'Go on, get on my bunk if you wish it. I fancy it no longer. You have made it filthy and cally with your horrible vonny plott lying on it already.' But then the others joined in. Big Jew said, still sweating from the bit of a bitva we'd had in the dark:

'Not having that we're not, brotherth. Don't give in to the thquirt.' So this new one said:

'Crash your dermott, yid,' meaning to shut up, but it was very insulting. So then Big Jew got ready to launch a tolchock. The Doctor said:

'Come on gentlemen, we don't want any trouble, do we?' in his very high-class goloss, but this new prestoopnick was really asking for it. You could viddy that he thought he was a very big bolshy veck and it was beneath his dignity to be sharing a cell with six and having to sleep on the floor till I made this gesture at him. In his sneery way he tried to take off The Doctor, saying:

'Owwww, yew wahnt noo moor trabble, is that it, Archiballs?' So Jojohn, mean and keen and wiry, said:

'If we can't have sleep let's have some education. Our new friend here had better be taught a lesson.' Although he like specialised in Sexual Assault he had a nice way of govoreeting, quiet and like precise. So the new plenny sneered:

'Kish and kosh and koosh, you little terror.' So then it all really started, but in a queer like gentle way, with nobody raising his goloss much. The new plenny creeched a malenky bit at first, but then Wall fisted his rot while Big Jew held him up against the bars so that he could be viddied in the malenky red light from the landing, and he just went oh oh oh. He was not a very strong type of veck, being very feeble in his trying to tolchock back, and I suppose he made up for this by being shoomny in the goloss and very boastful. Anyway, seeing the old krovvy flow red in the red light, I felt the old joy like rising up in my keeshkas and I said:

'Leave him to me, go on, let me have him now, brothers.' So Big Jew said:

'Yeth, yeth, boyth, that'th fair. Thlosh him then, Alekth.' So they all stood around while I cracked at this prestoop-nick in the near dark. I fisted him all over, dancing about with my boots on though unlaced, and then I tripped him and he went crash crash on to the floor. I gave him one real horrorshow kick on the gulliver and he went ohhhhh, then he sort of snorted off to like sleep, and The Doctor said:

'Very well, I think that will be enough of a lesson,' squinting to viddy this downed and beaten-up veck on the floor. 'Let him dream perhaps about being a better boy in the future.' So we all climbed back into our bunks, being very tired now. What I dreamt of, O my brothers, was of being in some very big orchestra, hundreds and hundreds strong, and the conductor was a like mixture of Ludwig van and G. F. Handel, looking very deaf and blind and weary of the world. I was with the wind instruments, but what I was playing was like a white pinky bassoon made of flesh and growing out of my plott, right in the middle of my belly, and when I blew into it I had to smeck ha ha ha very loud because it like tickled, and then Ludwig van G. F. got very razdraz and bezoomny. Then he came right up to my litso and creeched loud in my ooko, and then I woke up like sweating. Of course, what the loud shoom really was was the prison buzzer going brrrrr brrrrr brrrrr. It was winter morning and my glazzies were all cally with sleepglue, and when I opened up they were very sore in the electric light that had been switched on all over the zoo. Then I looked down and viddied this new prestoopnick lying on the floor, very bloody and bruisy and still out out out. Then I remembered about last night and that made me smeck a bit.

But when I got off the bunk and moved him with my bare noga, there was a feel of like stiff coldness, so I went over to The Doctor's bunk and shook him, him always being very slow at waking up in the morning. But he was off his bunk skorry enough this time, and so were the others, except for Wall who slept like dead meat. 'Very unfortunate,' The Doctor said. 'A heart attack, that's what it must have been.' Then he said, looking round at us all, 'You really shouldn't have gone for him like that. It was most ill-advised really.' Jojohn said:

'Come come, doc, you weren't all that backward yourself in giving him a sly bit of fist.' Then Big Jew turned on me, saying:

'Alexth, you were too impetuouth. That latht kick wath a very very nathty one.' I began to get razdraz about this and said:

'Who started it, eh? I only got in at the end, didn't I?' I pointed at Jojohn and said, 'It was your idea.' Wall snored a bit loud, so I said, 'Wake that vonny bratchny up. It was him that kept on at his rot while Big Jew here had him up against the bars.' The Doctor said:

'Nobody will deny having a gentle little hit at the man, to teach him a lesson so to speak, but it's apparent that you, my dear boy, with the forcefulness and, shall I say, heedlessness of youth, dealt him the coo de grass. It's a great pity.'

'Traitors,' I said 'Traitors and liars,' because I could viddy it was all like before, two years before, when my so-called droogs had left me to the brutal rookers of the millicents. There was no trust anywhere in the world, O my brothers, the way I could see it. And Jojohn went and woke up Wall, and Wall was only too ready to swear that it was Your Humble Narrator that had done the real dirty tolchocking and brutality. When the chassos came along, and then the Chief Chasso, and the Governor himself, all these cell-droogs of mine were very shoomny with tales of what I'd done to oobivat this worthless pervert whose krovvy-covered plott lay sacklike on the floor.

That was a very queer day, O my brothers. The dead plott was carried off, and then everybody in the whole prison had to stay locked up till further orders, and there was no pishcha given out, not even a mug of hot chai. We just all sat there, and the warders or chassos sort of strode up and down the tier, now and then creeching 'Shut it' or 'Close that hole' whenever they slooshied even a whisper from any of the cells. Then about eleven o'clock in the morning there was a sort of like stiffening and excitement and like the von of fear spreading from outside the cell, and then we could viddy the Governor and the Chief Chasso and some very bolshy important-looking chellovecks walking by real skorry, govoreeting like bezoomny. They seemed to walk right to the end of the tier, then they could be slooshied walking back again, more slow this time, and you could slooshy the Governor, a very sweaty fatty fair-haired veck, saying slovos like 'But, sir—' and 'Well, what can be done, sir?' and so on. Then the whole lot stopped at our cell and the Chief Chasso opened up. You could viddy who was the real important veck right away, very tall and with blue glazzies and with real horrorshow platties on him, the most lovely suit, brothers, I had ever viddied, absolutely in the heighth of fashion. He just sort of looked right through us poor plennies, saying, in a very beautiful real educated goloss,

'The Government cannot be concerned any longer with outmoded penological theories. Cram criminals together and see what happens. You get concentrated criminality, crime in the midst of punishment. Soon we may be needing all our prison space for political offenders.' I didn't pony this at all, brothers, but after all he was not govoreeting to me. Then he said, 'Common criminals like this unsavoury crowd' – (that meant me, brothers, as well as the others, who were real prestoopnicks and treacherous with it) – 'can best be dealt with on a purely curative basis. Kill the criminal reflex, that's all. Full implementation in a year's time. Punishment means nothing to them, you can see that. They enjoy their so-called punishment. They start murdering each other.' And he turned his stern blue glazzies on me. So I said, bold:

'With respect, sir, I object very strongly to what you said then. I am not a common criminal, sir, and I am not unsavoury. The others may be unsavoury but I am not.' The Chief Chasso went all purple and creeched:

'You shut your bleeding hole, you. Don't you know who this is?'

'All right, all right,' said this big veck. Then he turned to the Governor and said, 'You can use him as a trailblazer. He's young, bold, vicious. Brodsky will deal with him tomorrow and you can sit in and watch Brodsky. It works all right, don't worry about that. This vicious young hoodlum will be transformed out of all recognition.'

And those hard slovos, brothers, were like the beginning of my freedom.

3 | THAT very same evening I was dragged down nice and gentle by brutal tolchocking chassos to viddy the Governor in his holy of holies holy office. The Governor looked very weary at me and said, 'I don't suppose you know who that was this morning, do you, 6655321?' And without waiting for me to say no he said, 'That was no less a personage than the Minister of the Interior, the new Minister of the Interior and what they call a very new broom. Well, these new ridiculous ideas have come at last and orders are orders, though I may say to you in confidence that I do not approve. I most emphatically do not approve. An eye for an eye, I say. If someone hits you you hit back, do you not? Why then should not the State, very severely hit by you brutal hooligans, not hit back also? But the new view is to say no. The new view is that we turn the bad into the good. All of which seems to me grossly unjust. Hm?' So I said, trying to be like respectful and accommodating:

'Sir.' And then the Chief Chasso, who was standing all red and burly behind the Governor's chair, creeched:

'Shut your filthy hole, you scum.'

'All right, all right,' said the like tired and fagged-out Governor. 'You, 6655321, are to be reformed. Tomorrow you go to this man Brodsky. It is believed that you will be able to leave State Custody in a little over a fortnight. In a little over a fortnight you will be out again in the big free world, no longer a number. I suppose,' and he snorted a bit here, 'that prospect pleases you?' I said nothing so the Chief Chasso creeched:

'Answer, you filthy young swine, when the Governor asks you a question.' So I said:

'Oh, yes, sir. Thank you very much, sir. I've done my best here, really I have. I'm very grateful to all concerned.'

'Don't be,' like sighed the Governor. 'This is not a reward. This is far from being a reward. Now, there is a form here to be signed. It says that you are willing to have the residue of your sentence commuted to submission to what is called here, ridiculous expression, Reclamation Treatment. Will you sign?'

'Most certainly I will sign,' I said, 'sir. And very many thanks.' So I was given an ink-pencil and I signed my name nice and flowy. The Governor said:

'Right. That's the lot, I think.' The Chief Chasso said:

'The Prison Chaplain would like a word with him, sir.' So I was marched out and off down the corridor towards the Wing Chapel, tolchocked on the back and the gulliver all the way by one of the chassos, but in a very like yawny and bored manner. And I was marched across the Wing Chapel to the little cantora of the charles and then made to go in. The charles was sitting at his desk, smelling loud and clear of a fine manny von of expensive cancers and Scotch. He said:

'Ah, little 6655321, be seated.' And to the chassos, 'Wait outside, eh?' Which they did. Then he spoke in a very like earnest way to me, saying: 'One thing I want you to understand, boy, is that this is nothing to do with me. Were it expedient, I would protest about it, but it is not expedient. There is the question of my own career, there is the question of the weakness of my own voice when set against the shout of certain more powerful elements in the polity. Do I make myself clear?' He didn't, brothers, but I nodded that he did. 'Very hard ethical questions are involved,' he went on. 'You are to be made into a good boy, 6655321. Never again will you have the desire to commit acts of violence or to offend in any way whatsoever against the State's Peace. I hope you take all that in. I hope you are absolutely clear in your own mind about that.' I said:

'Oh, it will be nice to be good, sir.' But I had a real horrorshow smeck at that inside, brothers. He said:

'It may not be nice to be good, little 6655321. It may be horrible to be good. And when I say that to you I realise how self-contradictory that sounds. I know I shall have many sleepless nights about this. What does God want? Does God want goodness or the choice of goodness? Is a man who chooses the bad perhaps in some way better than a man who has the good imposed upon him? Deep and hard questions, little 6655321. But all I want to say to you now is this: if at any time in the future you look back to these times and remember me, the lowest and humblest of all God's servitors, do not, I pray, think evil of me in your heart, thinking me in any way involved in what is now about to happen to you. And now, talking of praying, I realise sadly that there will be little point in praying for you. You are passing now to a region where you will be beyond the reach of the power of prayer. A terrible terrible thing to consider. And yet, in a sense, in choosing to be deprived of the ability to make an ethical choice, you have in a sense really chosen the good. So I shall like to think. So, God help us all, 6655321, I shall like to think.' And then he began to cry. But I didn't really take much notice of that, brothers, only having a bit of a quiet smeck inside, because you could viddy that he had been peeting away at the old whisky, and now he took a bottle from a cupboard in his desk and started to pour himself a real horrorshow bolshy slog into a very greasy and grahzny glass. He downed it and then said, 'All may be well, who knows? God works in a mysterious way.' Then he began to sing away at a hymn in a real loud rich goloss. Then the door opened and the chassos came in to tolchock me back to my vonny cell, but the old charles still went on singing this hymn.

Well, the next morning I had to say goodbye to the old Staja, and I felt a malenky bit sad as you always will when you have to leave a place you've like got used to. But I didn't go very far, O my brothers. I was punched and kicked along to the new white building just beyond the yard where we used to do our bit of exercise. This was a very new building and it had a new cold like sizy smell which gave you a bit of the shivers. I stood there in the horrible bolshy bare hall and I got new vons, sniffing away there with my like very sensitive morder or sniffer. These were like hospital vons, and the chelloveck the chassos handed me over to had a white coat on, as he might be a hospital man. He signed for me, and one of the brutal chassos who had brought me said, 'You will watch this one, sir. A right brutal bastard he has been and will be again, in spite of all his sucking up to the Prison Chaplain and reading the Bible.' But this new chelloveck had real horrorshow blue glazzies which like smiled when he govoreeted. He said:

'Oh, we don't anticipate any trouble. We're going to be friends, aren't we?' And he smiled with his glazzies and his fine big rot which was full of shining white zoobies and I sort of took to this veck right away. Anyway, he passed me on to a like lesser veck in a white coat, and this one was very nice too, and I was led off to a very nice white clean bedroom with curtains and a bedside lamp, and just the one bed in it, all for Your Humble Narrator. So I had a real horrorshow inner smeck at that, thinking I was really a very lucky young malchickiwick. I was told to take off my horrible prison platties and I was given a really beautiful set of pyjamas, O my brothers, in plain green, the heighth of bedwear fashion. And I was given a nice warm dressing-gown too and lovely toofles to put my bare nogas in, and I thought, 'Well, Alex boy, little 6655321 as was, you have copped it lucky and no mistake. You are really going to enjoy it here.'

After I had been given a nice chasha of real horrorshow coffee and some old gazettas and mags to look at while peeting it, this first veck in white came in, the one who had like signed for me, and he said: 'Aha, there you are,' a silly sort of a veshch to say but it didn't sound silly, this veck being so like nice. 'My name,' he said, 'is Dr Branom. I'm Dr Brodsky's assistant. With your permission, I'll just give you the usual brief overall examination.' And he took the old stetho out of his right carman. 'We must make sure you're quite fit, mustn't we? Yes indeed, we must.' So while I lay there with my pyjama top off and he did this, that and the other, I said:

'What exactly is it, sir, that you're going to do?'

'Oh,' said Dr Branom, his cold stetho going all down my back, 'it's quite simple, really. We just show you some films.'

'Films?' I said. I could hardly believe my ookos, brothers, as you may well understand. 'You mean,' I said, 'it will be just like going to the pictures?'

'They'll be special films,' said this Dr Branom. 'Very special films. You'll be having your first session this afternoon. Yes,' he said, getting up from bending over me, 'you seem to be quite a fit young boy. A bit under-nourished, perhaps. That will be the fault of the prison food. Put your pyjama top back on. After every meal,' he said, sitting on the edge of the bed, we shall be giving you a shot in the arm. That should help.' I felt really grateful to this very nice Dr Branom. I said:

'Vitamins, sir, will it be?'

'Something like that,' he said, smiling real horrorshow and friendly. 'Just a jab in the arm after every meal.' Then he went out. I lay on the bed thinking this was like real heaven, and I read some of the mags they'd given me – *Worldsport*, *Sinny* (this being a film mag) and *Goal*. Then I lay back on the bed and shut my glazzies and thought how nice it was going to be out there again, Alex with perhaps a nice easy job during the day, me being now too old for the old skolliwoll, and then perhaps getting a new like gang together for the nochy, and the first rabbit would be to get old Dim and Pete, if they had not been got already by the millicents. This time I would be very careful not to get loveted. They were giving another like chance, me having done murder and all, and it would not be like fair to get loveted again, after going to all this trouble to show me films that were going to make me a real good malchick. I had a real horrorshow smeck at everybody's like innocence, and I was smecking my gulliver off when they brought in my lunch on a tray. The veck who brought it was the one who'd led me to this malenky bedroom when I came into the mesto, and he said:

'It's nice to know somebody's happy.' It was really a very nice appetising bit of pishcha they'd laid out on the tray

– two or three lomticks of like hot roastbeef with mashed kartoffel and vedge, then there was also ice cream and a nice hot chasha of chai. And there was even a cancer to smoke and a matchbox with one match in. So this looked like it was the life, O my brothers. Then, about half an hour after while I was lying a bit sleepy on the bed, a woman nurse came in, a real nice young devotchka with real horrorshow groodies (I had not seen such for two years) and she had a tray and a hypodermic. I said:

'Ah, the old vitamins, eh?' And I clickclicked at her but she took no notice. All she did was to slam the needle into my left arm, and then swishhhh in went the vitamin stuff. Then she went out again, clack clack on her high-heeled nogas. Then the white-coated veck who was like a male nurse came in with a wheelchair. I was a malenky bit surprised to viddy that. I said:

'What giveth then, brother? I can walk, surely, to wherever we have to itty to.' But he said:

'Best I push you there.' And indeed, O my brothers, when I got off the bed I found myself a malenky bit weak. It was the under-nourishment like Dr Branom had said, all that horrible prison pishcha. But the vitamins in the after-meal injection would put me right. No doubt at all about that, I thought.

4 WHERE I was wheeled to, brothers, was like no sinny I had ever viddied before. True enough, one wall was all covered with silver screen, and direct opposite was a wall with square holes in for the projector to project through, and there were stereo speakers stuck all over the mesto. But against the right-hand one of the other walls was a bank of all like little meters, and in the middle of the floor facing the screen was like a dentist's chair with all lengths of wire running from it, and I had to like crawl from the wheelchair to this, being given some help by another like male nurse veck in a white coat. Then I noticed that underneath the projection holes was like all frosted glass and I thought I viddied shadows of like people moving behind it and I thought I slooshied somebody cough kashl kashl kashl. But then all I could like notice was how weak I seemed to be, and I put that down to changing over from prison pishcha to this new rich pishcha and the vitamins injected into me. 'Right,' said the wheelchair-wheeling veck, 'now I'll leave you. The show will commence as soon as Dr Brodsky arrives. Hope you enjoy it.' To be truthful, brothers, I did not really feel that I wanted to viddy any film-show this afternoon. I was just not in the mood. I would have liked much better to have a nice quiet spatchka on the bed, nice and quiet and all on my oddy knocky. I felt very limp.

What happened now was that one white-coated veck strapped my gulliver to a like head-rest, singing to himself all the time some vonny cally pop-song. 'What's this for?' I said. And this veck replied, interrupting his like song an instant, that it was to keep my gulliver still and make me look at the screen. 'But,' I said, I *want* to look at the screen. I've been brought here to viddy films and viddy films I shall.' And then the other white-coat veck (there were three altogether, one of them a devotchka who was like sitting at the bank of meters and twiddling with knobs) had a bit of a smeck at that. He said:

'You never know. Oh, you never know. Trust us, friend. It's better this way.' And then I found they were strapping my rookers to the chair-arms and my nogas were like stuck to a foot-rest. It seemed a bit bezoomny to me but I let them get on with what they wanted to get on with. If I was to be a free young malchick again in a fortnight's time I would put up with much in the meantime, O my brothers. One veshch I did not like, though, was when they put like clips on the skin of my forehead, so that my top glaz-lids were pulled up and up and up and I could not shut my glazzies no matter how I tried. I tried to smeck and said: 'This must be a real horrorshow film if you're so keen on my viddying it.' And one of the white-coat vecks said, smecking:

'Horrorshow is right, friend. A real show of horrors.' And then I had like a cap stuck on my gulliver and I could viddy all wires running away from it, and they stuck a like suction pad on my belly and one on the old tick-tocker, and I could just about viddy wires running away from those. Then there was the shoom of a door opening and you could tell some very important chelloveck was coming in by the way the white-coated under-vecks went all stiff. And then I viddied this Dr Brodsky. He was a malenky veck, very fat, with all curly hair curling all over his gulliver, and on his spuddy nose he had very thick otchkies. I could just viddy that he had a real horrorshow suit on, absolutely the heighth of fashion, and he had a like very delicate and subtle von of operating theatres coming from him. With him was Dr Branom, all smiling as though to give me confidence. 'Everything ready?' said Dr Brodsky in a very breathy goloss. Then I could slooshy voices saying Right right right from like a distance, then nearer to, then there was a quiet like humming shoom as though things had been switched on. And then the lights went out and there was Your Humble Narrator And Friend sitting alone in the dark, all on his frightened oddy knocky, not able to move nor shut his glazzies nor anything. And then, O my brothers, the film-show started off with some very gromky atmosphere music coming from the speakers, very fierce and full of discord. And then on the screen the picture came on, but there was no title and no credits. What came on was a street, as it might have been any street in any town, and it was a real dark nochy and the lamps were lit. It was a very good like professional piece of sinny, and there were none of these flickers and blobs you get, say, when you viddy one of these dirty films in somebody's house in a back street. All the time the music bumped out, very like sinister. And then you could viddy an old man coming down the street very starry, and then there leaped out on this starry veck two malchicks dressed in the heighth of fashion, as it was at this time (still thin trousers but no like cravat any more, more of a real tie), and they started to filly with him. You could slooshy his screams and moans, very realistic, and you could even get the like heavy breathing and panting of the two tolchocking malchicks. They made a real pudding out of this starry veck, going crack crack crack at him with their fisty rookers, tearing his platties off and then finishing up by booting his nagoy plott (this lay all krovvy-red in the grahzny mud of the gutter) and then running off very skorry. Then there was a close-up gulliver of this beaten-up starry veck, and the krovvy flowed beautiful red. It's funny how the colours of the like real world only seem really real when you viddy them on the screen.

Now all the time I was watching this I was beginning to get very aware of a like not feeling all that well, and this I put down to the under-nourishment and my stomach not quite ready for the rich pishcha and vitamins I was getting here. But I tried to forget this, concentrating on the next film which came on at once, my brothers, without any break at all. This time the film like jumped right away on a young devotchka who was being given the old in-out by first one malchick then another then another then another, she creeching away very gromky through the speakers and like very pathetic and tragic music going on at the same time. This was real, very real, though if you thought about it properly you couldn't imagine lewdies actually agreeing to having all this done to them in a film, and if these films were made by the Good or the State you couldn't imagine them being allowed to take these films without like interfering with what was going on. So it must have been very clever what they called cutting or editing or some such veshch. For it was very real. And when it came to the sixth or seventh malchick leering and smecking and then going into it and the devotchka creeching on the sound-track like bezoomny, then I began to feel sick. I had like pains all over and felt I could sick up and at the same time not sick up, and I began to feel like in distress, O my brothers, being fixed rigid too on this chair. When this bit of film was over I could slooshy the goloss of this Dr Brodsky from over by the switchboard saying, 'Reaction about twelve point five? Promising, promising.'

Then we shot straight into another lomtick of film, and this time it was of just a human litso, a very like pale human face held still and having different nasty veshches done to it. I was sweating a malenky bit with the pain in my guts and a horrible thirst and my gulliver going throb throb throb, and it seemed to me that if I could not viddy this bit of film I would perhaps be not so sick. But I could not shut my glazzies, and even if I tried to move my glaz-balls about I still could not get like out of the line of fire of this picture. So I had to go on viddying what was being done and hearing the most ghastly creechings coming from this litso. I knew it could not really be *real*, but that made no difference. I was heaving away but could not sick, viddying first a britva cut out an eye, then slice down the cheek, then go rip rip rip all over, while red krovvy shot on to the camera lens. Then all the teeth were like wrenched out with a pair of pliers, and the creeching and the blood were terrific. Then I slooshied this very pleased goloss of Dr Brodsky going, 'Excellent, excellent, excellent.'

The next lomtick of film was of an old woman who kept a shop being kicked about amid very gromky laughter by a lot of malchicks, and these malchicks broke up the shop and then set fire to it. You could viddy this poor starry ptitsa trying to crawl out of the flames, screaming and creeching, but having had her leg broke by these malchicks kicking her she could not move. So then all the flames went roaring round her, and you could viddy her agonised litso like appealing through the flames and then disappearing in the flames, and then you could slooshy the most gromky and agonised and agonising screams that ever came from a human goloss. So this time I knew I had to sick up, so I creeched:

'I want to be sick. Please let me be sick. Please bring something for me to be sick into.' But this Dr Brodsky called back:

'Imagination only. You've nothing to worry about. Next film coming up.' That was perhaps meant to be a joke, for I heard a like smeck coming from the dark. And then I was forced to viddy a most nasty film about Japanese torture. It was the 1939–45 War, and there were soldiers being fixed to trees with nails and having fires lit under them and having their yarbles cut off, and you even viddied a gulliver being sliced off a soldier with a sword, and then with his head rolling about and the rot and the glazzies looking alive still, the plott of this soldier actually ran about, krovvy like a fountain out of the neck, and then it dropped, and all the time there was very very loud laughter from the Japanese. The pains I felt now in my belly and the headache and the thirst were terrible, and they all seemed to be coming out of the screen. So I creeched:

'Stop the film! Please, please stop it! I can't stand any more.' And then the goloss of this Dr Brodsky said:

'Stop it? *Stop it*, did you say? Why, we've hardly started.' And he and the others smecked quite loud.

5 I DO not wish to describe, brothers, what other horrible veshches I was like forced to viddy that afternoon. The like minds of this Dr Brodsky and Dr Branom and the others in white coats, and remember there was this devotchka twiddling with the knobs and watching the meters, they must have been more cally and filthy than any prestoopnick in the Staja itself. Because I did not think it was possible for any veck to even think of making films of what I was forced to viddy, all tied to this chair and my glazzies made to be wide open. All I could do was to creech very gromky for them to turn it off, turn it off, and that like part drowned the noise of dratsing and fillying and also the music that went with it all. You can imagine it was like a terrible relief when I'd viddied the last bit of film and this Dr Brodsky said, in a very yawny and bored like goloss, 'I think that should be enough for Day One, don't you, Branom?' And there I was with the lights switched on, my gulliver throbbing like a bolshy big engine that makes pain, and my rot all dry and cally inside, and feeling I could like sick up every bit of pishcha I had ever eaten, O my brothers, since the day I was like weaned. 'All right,' said this Dr Brodsky, 'he can be taken back to his bed.' Then he like patted me on the pletcho and said, 'Good, good. A very promising start,' grinning all over his

litso, then he like waddled out, Dr Branom after him, but Dr Branom gave me a like very droogy and sympathetic type smile as though he had nothing to do with all this veshch but was like forced into it as I was.

Anyhow, they freed my plott from the chair and they let go the skin above my glazzies so that I could open and shut them again, and I shut them, O my brothers, with the pain and throb in my gulliver, and then I was like carried to the old wheelchair and taken back to my malenky bedroom, the under-veck who wheeled me singing away at some hound-and-horny popsong so that I like snarled, 'Shut it, thou,' but he only smecked and said: 'Never mind, friend,' and then sang louder. So I was put into the bed and still felt bolnoy but could not sleep, but soon I started to feel that soon I might start to feel that I might soon start feeling just a malenky bit better, and then I was brought some nice hot chai with plenty of moloko and sakar and, peeting that, I knew that that like horrible nightmare was in the past and all over. And then Dr Branom came in, all nice and smiling. He said:

'Well, by my calculations you should be starting to feel all right again. Yes?'

'Sir,' I said, like wary. I did not quite kopat what he was getting at govoreeting about calculations, seeing that getting better from feeling bolnoy is like your own affair and nothing to do with calculations. He sat down, all nice and droogy, on the bed's edge and said:

'Dr Brodsky is pleased with you. You had a very positive response. Tomorrow, of course, there'll be two sessions, morning and afternoon, and I should imagine that you'll be feeling a bit limp at the end of the day. But we have to be hard on you, you have to be cured.' I said:

'You mean I have to sit through –? You mean I have to look at –? Oh, no,' I said. 'It was horrible.'

'Of course it was horrible,' smiled Dr Branom. Violence is a very horrible thing. That's what you're learning now. Your body is learning it.'

'But,' I said, 'I don't understand. I don't understand about feeling sick like I did. I never used to feel sick before. I used to feel like very the opposite. I mean, doing it or watching it I used to feel real horrorshow. I just don't understand why or how or what –'

'Life is a very wonderful thing,' said Dr Branom in a very like holy goloss. 'The processes of life, the make-up of the human organism, who can fully understand these miracles? Dr Brodsky is, of course, a remarkable man. What is happening to you now is what should happen to any normal healthy human organism contemplating the actions of the forces of evil, the workings of the principle of destruction. You are being made sane, you are being made healthy.'

'That I will not have,' I said, 'nor can understand at all. What you've been doing is to make me feel very very ill.'

'Do you feel ill now?' he said, still with the old droogy smile on his litso. 'Drinking tea, resting, having a quiet chat with a friend – surely you're not feeling anything but well?'

I like listened and felt for pain and sickness in my gulliver and plott, in a like cautious way, but it was true, brothers, that I felt real horrorshow and even wanting my dinner. 'I don't get it,' I said. 'You must be doing some-thing to me to make me feel ill.' And I sort of frowned about that, thinking.

'You felt ill this afternoon,' he said, 'because you're getting better. When we're healthy we respond to the presence of the hateful with fear and nausea. You're becoming healthy, that's all. You'll be healthier still this time tomorrow.' Then he patted me on the noga and went out, and I tried to puzzle the whole veshch out as best I could. What it seemed to me was that the wires and other veshches that were fixed to my plott perhaps were making me feel ill, and that it was all a trick really. I was still puzzling out all this and wondering whether I should refuse to be strapped down to this chair tomorrow and start a real bit of dratsing with them all, because I had my rights, when another chelloveck came in to see me. He was a like smiling starry veck who said he was what he called the Discharge Officer, and he carried a lot of bits of paper with him. He said:

'Where will you go when you leave here?' I hadn't really thought about that sort of veshch at all, and it only now really began to dawn on me that I'd be a fine free malchick very soon, and then I viddied that would only be if I played it everybody's way and did not start any dratsing and creeching and refusing and so on. I said:

'Oh, I shall go home. Back to my pee and em.'

'Your –?' He didn't get nadsat-talk at all, so I said:

'To my parents in the dear old flatblock.'

'I see,' he said. 'And when did you last have a visit from your parents?'

'A month,' I said, 'very near. They like suspended visiting-day for a bit because of one prestoopnick getting some blasting-powder smuggled in across the wires from his ptitsa. A real cally trick to play on the innocent, like punishing them as well. So it's like near a month since I had a visit.'

'I see,' said this veck. 'And have your parents been informed of your transfer and impending release?' That had a real lovely zvook that did, that slovo *release*. I said:

'No.' Then I said, 'It will be a nice surprise for them, that, won't it? Me just walking through the door and saying, "Here I am, back, a free veck again." Yes, real horrorshow.'

'Right,' said the Discharge Officer veck, 'we'll leave it at that. So long as you have somewhere to live. Now, there's the question of your having a job, isn't there?' And he showed me this long list of jobs I could have, but I thought, well, there would be time enough for that. A nice malenky holiday first. I could do a crasting job soon as I got out and fill the old carmans with pretty polly, but I would have to be very careful and I would have to do the job all on my oddy knocky. I did not trust so-called droogs any more. So I told this veck to leave it a bit and we would govoreet about it again. He said right right right, then got ready to leave. He showed himself to be a very queer sort of a veck, because what he did now was to like giggle and then say, 'Would you like to punch me in the face before I go?' I did not think I could possibly have slooshied that right, so I said:

'Eh?'

'Would you,' he giggled, 'like to punch me in the face before I go?' I frowned like at that, very puzzled, and said:

'Why?'

'Oh,' he said, 'just to see how you're getting on.' And he brought his litso real near, a fat grin all over his rot. So I fisted up and went smack at this litso, but he pulled himself away real skorry, grinning still, and my rooker just punched air. Very puzzling, this was, and I frowned as he left, smecking his gulliver off. And then, my brothers, I felt real sick again, just like in the afternoon, just for a couple of minootas. It then passed off skorry, and when they brought my dinner in I found I had a fair appetite and was ready to crunch away at the roast chicken. But it was funny that starry chelloveck asking for a tolchock in the litso. And it was funny feeling sick like that.

What was even funnier was when I went to sleep that night, O my brothers. I had a nightmare, and, as you might expect, it was of one of those bits of film I'd viddied in the afternoon. A dream or nightmare is really only like a film inside your gulliver, except that it is as though you could walk into it and be part of it. And this is what happened to me. It was a nightmare of one of the bits of film they showed me near the end of the afternoon like session, all of smecking malchicks doing the ultra-violent on a young ptitsa who was creeching away in her red red krovvy, her platties all razrezzed real horrorshow. I was in this fillying about, smecking away and being like the ringleader, dressed in the heighth of nadsat fashion. And then at the heighth of all this dratsing and tolchocking I felt like paralysed and wanting to be very sick, and all the other malchicks had a real gromky smeck at me. Then I was dratsing my way back to being awake all through my own krovvy, pints and quarts and gallons of it, and then I found myself in my bed in this room. I wanted to be sick, so I got out of the bed all trembly so as to go off down the corridor to the old vaysay. But, behold, brothers, the door was locked. And turning round I viddied for like the first raz that there were bars on the window. And so, as I reached for the like pot in the malenky cupboard beside the bed, I viddied that there would be no escaping from any of all this. Worse, I did not dare to go back into my own sleeping gulliver. I soon found I did not want to be sick after all, but then I was poogly of getting back into bed to sleep. But soon I fell smack into sleep and did not dream any more.

6 'STOP it, stop it, stop it,' I kept on creeching out. 'Turn it off, you grahzny bastards, for I can stand no more.' It was the next day, brothers, and I had truly done my best morning and afternoon to play it their way and sit like a horrorshow smiling cooperative malchick in the chair of torture while they flashed nasty bits of ultra-violence on the screen, my glazzies clipped open to viddy all, my plott and rookers and nogas fixed to the chair so I could not get away. What I was being made to viddy now was not really a veshch I would have thought to be too bad before, it being only three or four malchicks crasting in a shop and filling their carmans with cutter, at the same time fillying about with the creeching starry ptitsa running the shop, tolchocking her and letting the red red krovvy flow. But the throb and like crash crash crash crash in my gulliver and the wanting to sick and the terrible dry rasping thirstiness in my rot, all were worse than yesterday. 'Oh, I've had enough,' I cried. 'It's not fair, you vonny sods,' and I tried to struggle out of the chair but it was not possible, me being good as stuck to it.

'First-class,' creeched out this Dr Brodsky. You're doing really well. Just one more and then we're finished.'

What it was now was the starry 1939–45 War again, and it was a very blobby and liny and crackly film you could viddy had been made by the Germans. It opened with German eagles and the Nazi flag with that like crooked cross that all malchicks at school love to draw, and then there were very haughty and nadmenny like German officers walking through streets that were all dust and bomb-holes and broken buildings. Then you were allowed to viddy lewdies being shot against walls, officers giving the orders, and also horrible nagoy plotts left lying in gutters, all like cages of bare ribs and white thin nogas. Then there were lewdies being dragged off creeching, though not on the sound-track, my brothers, the only sound being music, and being tolchocked while they were dragged off. Then I noticed, in all my pain and sickness, what music it was that like crackled and boomed on the sound-track, and it was Ludwig van, the last movement of the Fifth Symphony, and I creeched like bezoomny at that. 'Stop!' I creeched. 'Stop, you grahzny disgusting sods. It's a sin, that's what it is, a filthy unforgivable sin, you bratchnies!' They didn't stop right away, because there was only a minute or two more to go – lewdies being beaten up and all blood, then more firing squads, then the old Nazi flag and THE END. But when the lights came on this Dr Brodsky and also Dr Branom were standing in front of me, and Dr Brodsky said:

'What's all this about sin, eh?'

'That,' I said, very sick. 'Using Ludwig van like that. He did no harm to anyone. Beethoven just wrote music.' And then I was really sick and they had to bring a bowl that was in the shape of like a kidney.

'Music,' said Dr Brodsky, like musing. 'So you're keen on music. I know nothing about it myself. It's a useful emotional heightener, that's all I know. Well, well. What do you think about that, eh, Branom?'

'It can't be helped,' said Dr Branom. 'Each man kills the thing he loves, as the poet-prisoner said. Here's the punishment element, perhaps. The Governor ought to be pleased.'

'Give me a drink,' I said, 'for Bog's sake.'

'Loosen him,' ordered Dr Brodsky. 'Fetch him a carafe of ice-cold water.' So then these under-vecks got to work and soon I was peeting gallons and gallons of water and it was like heaven, O my brothers. Dr Brodsky said:

'You seem a sufficiently intelligent young man. You seem, too, to be not without taste. You've just got this violence thing, haven't you? Violence and theft, theft being an aspect of violence.' I didn't govoreet a single slovo, brothers. I was still feeling sick, though getting a malenky bit better now. But it had been a terrible day. 'Now, then,' said Dr Brodsky, 'how do you think this is done? Tell me, what do you think we're doing to you?'

'You're making me feel ill,' I said. 'I'm ill when I look at those filthy pervert films of yours. But it's not really the films that's doing it. But I feel that if you'll stop these films I'll stop feeling ill.'

'Right,' said Dr Brodsky. 'It's association, the oldest educational method in the world. And what really causes you to feel ill?'

'These grahzny sodding veshches that come out of my gulliver and my plott,' I said, 'that's what it is.'

'Quaint,' said Dr Brodsky, like smiling, 'the dialect of the tribe. Do you know anything of its provenance, Branom?

'Odd bits of old rhyming slang,' said Dr Branom, who did not look quite so much like a friend any more. 'A bit of gipsy talk, too. But most of the roots are Slav. Propaganda. Subliminal penetration.'

'All right, all right, all right,' said Dr Brodsky, like impatient and not interested any more. 'Well,' he said to me, 'it isn't the wires. It's nothing to do with what's fastened to you. Those are just for measuring your reactions. What is it, then?'

I viddied then, of course, what a bezoomny shoot I was not to notice that it was the hypodermic needle shots in the rooker. 'Oh,' I creeched, 'oh, I viddy all now. A filthy cally vonny trick. An act of treachery, sod you, and you won't do it again.'

'I'm glad you've raised your objections now,' said Dr Brodsky. 'Now we can be perfectly clear about it. We can get this stuff of Ludovico's into your system in many different ways. Orally, for instance. But the subcutaneous method is the best. Don't fight against it, please. There's no point in your fighting. You can't get the better of us.'

'Grahzny bratchnies,' I said, like snivelling. Then I said, 'I don't mind about the ultra-violence and all that cal. I can put up with that. But it's not fair on the music. It's not fair I should feel ill when I'm slooshying lovely Ludwig van and G. F. Handel and others. All that shows you're an evil lot of bastards and I shall never forgive you, sods.'

They both looked a bit like thoughtful. Then Dr Brodsky said: 'Delimitation is always difficult. The world is one, life is one. The sweetest and most heavenly of activities partake in some measure of violence – the act of love, for instance; music, for instance. You must take your chance, boy. The choice has been all yours.' I didn't understand all these slovos, but now I said:

'You needn't take it any further, sir.' I'd changed my tune a malenky bit in my cunning way. 'You've proved to me that all this dratsing and ultra-violence and killing is wrong wrong and terribly wrong. I've learned my lesson, sirs. I see now what I've never seen before. I'm cured, praise God.' And I raised my glazzies in a like holy way to the ceiling. But both these doctors shook their gullivers like sadly and Dr Brodsky said:

'You're not cured yet. There's still a lot to be done. Only when your body reacts promptly and violently to violence, as to a snake, without further help from us, without medication, only then –' I said:

'But, sir, sirs, I *see* that it's wrong. It's wrong because it's against like society, it's wrong because every veck on earth has the right to live and be happy without being beaten and tolchocked and knifed. I've learned a lot, oh really I have.' But Dr Brodsky had a loud long smeck at that, showing all his white zoobies, and said:

'The heresy of an age of reason,' or some such slovos. 'I see what is right and approve, but I do what is wrong. No, no, my boy, you must leave it all to us. But be cheerful about it. It will soon be all over. In less than a fortnight now you'll be a free man.' Then he patted me on the pletcho.

Less than a fortnight, O my brothers and friends, it was like an age. It was like from the beginning of the world to the end of it. To finish the fourteen years with remission in the Staja would have been nothing to it. Every day it was the same. When the devotchka with the hypodermic came round, though, four days after this govoreeting with Dr Brodsky and Dr Branom, I said, 'Oh, no you won't,' and tolchocked her on the rooker, and the syringe went tinkle clatter on to the floor. That was like to viddy what they would do. What they did was to get four or five real bolshy white-coated bastards of under-vecks to hold me down on the bed, tolchocking me with grinny litsos close to mine, and then this nurse ptitsa said, 'You wicked naughty little devil, you,' while she jabbed my rooker with another syringe and squirted this stuff in real brutal and nasty. And then I was wheeled off exhausted to this like hell sinny as before.

Every day, my brothers, these films were like the same, all kicking and tolchocking and red red krovvy dripping off of litsos and plotts and spattering all over the camera lenses. It was usually grinning and smecking malchicks in the heighth of nadsat fashion, or else teeheeheeing Jap torturers or brutal Nazi kickers and shooters. And each day the feeling of wanting to die with the sickness and gulliver pains and aches in the zoobies and horrible horrible thirst grew really worse. Until one morning I tried to defeat the bastards by crash crash crashing my gulliver against the wall so that I should tolchock myself unconscious, but all that happened was I felt sick with viddying that this kind of violence was like the violence in the films, so I was just exhausted and was given the injection and was wheeled off like before.

And then there came a morning where I woke up and had my breakfast of eggs and toast and jam and very hot milky chai, and then I thought: It can't be much longer now. Now must be very near the end of the time. I have suffered to the heighths and cannot suffer any more. And I waited and waited, brothers, for this nurse ptitsa to bring in the syringe, but she did not come. And then the white-coated under-veck came and said:

'Today, old friend, we are letting you walk.'

'Walk?' I said. 'Where?'

'To the usual place,' he said. 'Yes, yes, look not so astonished. You are to walk to the films, me with you of course. You are no longer to be carried in a wheelchair.

'But,' I said, 'how about my horrible morning injection?' For I was really surprised at this, brothers, they being so keen on pushing this Ludovico veshch into me, as they said. 'Don't I get that horrible sicky stuff rammed into my poor suffering rooker any more?'

'All over,' like smecked this veck. 'For ever and ever amen. You're on your own now, boy. Walking and all to the chamber of horrors. But you're still to be strapped down and made to see. Come on then, my little tiger.' And I had to put my over-gown and toofles on and walk down the corridor to the like sinny mesto.

Now this time, O my brothers, I was not only very sick but very puzzled. There it was again, all the old ultra-violence and vecks with their gullivers smashed and torn krovvy-dripping ptitsas creeching for mercy, the like private and individual fillying and nastiness. Then there were the prison-camps and the Jews and the grey like foreign streets full of tanks and uniforms and vecks going down in withering rifle-fire, this being the public side of it. And this time I could blame nothing for me feeling sick and thirsty and full of aches except what I was forced to viddy, my glazzies still being clipped open and my nogas and plott fixed to the chair but this set of wires and other veshches no longer coming out of my plott and gulliver. So what could it be but the films I was viddying that were doing this to me? Except, of course, brothers, that this Ludovico stuff was like a vaccination and there it was cruising about in my krovvy, so that I would be sick always for ever and ever amen whenever I viddied any of this ultra-violence. So now I squared my rot and went boo hoo hoo, and the tears like blotted out what I was forced to viddy in like all blessed runny silvery dewdrops. But these white-coat bratchnies were skorry with their tashtooks to wipe the tears away, saying, 'There, there, wazzums all weepy-weepy den?' And there it was again all clear before my glazzies, these Germans prodding like beseeching and weeping Jews

– vecks and cheenas and malchicks and devotchkas – into mestos where they would all snuff it of poison gas. Boo hoo hoo I had to go again, and along they came to wipe the tears off, very skorry, so I should not miss one solitary veshch of what they were showing. It was a terrible and horrible day, O my brothers and only friends.

I was lying on the bed all alone that nochy after my dinner of fat thick mutton stew and fruit pie and ice cream, and I thought to myself: Hell hell hell, there might be a chance for me if I get out now. I had no weapon, though. I was allowed no britva here, and I had been shaved every other day by a fat bald-headed veck who came to my bed before breakfast, two white-coated bratchnies standing by to viddy I was a good non-violent malchick. The nails on my rookers had been scissored and filed real short so I could not scratch. But I was still skorry on the attack, though they had weakened me down, brothers, to a like shadow of what I had been in the old free days. So now I got off the bed and went to the locked door and began to fist it real horrorshow and hard, creeching at the same time, 'Oh, help help. I'm sick, I'm dying. Doctor doctor doctor, quick. Please. Oh, I'll die, I know I shall. Help.' My gorlo was real dry and sore before anyone came. Then I heard nogas coming down the corridor and a like grumbling goloss, and then I recognised the goloss of the white-coated veck who brought my pishcha and like escorted me to my daily doom. He like grumbled:

'What is it? What goes on? What's your little nasty game in there?'

'Oh, I'm dying,' I like moaned. 'Oh, I have a ghastly pain in my side. Appendicitis, it is. Ooooooh.'

'Appendy shitehouse,' grumbled this veck, and then to

my joy, brothers, I could slooshy the like clank of keys. 'If you're trying it, little friend, my friends and me will beat and kick you all through the night.' Then he opened up and brought in like the sweet air of the promise of my freedom. Now I was like behind the door when he pushed it open, and I could viddy him in the corridor light looking round for me puzzled. Then I raised my two fisties to tolchock him on the neck nasty, and then, I swear, as I sort of viddied him in advance lying moaning or out out out and felt the like joy rise in my guts, it was then that this sickness rose in me as it might be a wave and I felt a horrible fear as if I was really going to die. I like tottered over to the bed going urgh urgh urgh, and the veck, who was not in his white coat but an over-gown, viddied clear enough what I had had in my mind for he said:

'Well, everything's a lesson, isn't it? Learning all the time, as you could say. Come on, little friend, get up from that bed and hit me. I want you to, yes, really. A real good crack across the jaw. Oh, I'm dying for it, really I am.' But all I could do, brothers, was to just lay there sobbing boo hoo hoo. 'Scum,' like sneered this veck now. 'Filth.' And he pulled me up by like the scruff of my pyjama-top, me being very weak and limp, and he raised and swung his right rooker so that I got a fair old tolchock clean on the litso. 'That,' he said, 'is for getting me out of my bed, you young dirt.' And he wiped his rookers against each other swish swish and went out. Crunch crunch went the key in the lock.

And what, brothers, I had to escape into sleep from then was the horrible and wrong feeling that it was better to get the hit than give it. If that veck had stayed I might even have like presented the other cheek.

I COULD not believe, brothers, what I was told. It seemed that I had been in that vonny mesto for near ever and would be there for near ever more. But it had always been a fortnight and now they said the fortnight was near up. They said:

'Tomorrow, little friend, out out out.' And they made with the old thumb, like pointing to freedom. And then the white-coated veck who had tolchocked me and who had still brought me my trays of pishcha and like escorted me to my everyday torture said: 'But you still have one really big day in front of you. It's to be your passing-out day.' And he had a leery smeck at that.

I expected this morning that I would be ittying as usual to the sinny mesto in my pyjamas and toofles and over-gown. But no. This morning I was given my shirt and underveshches and my platties of the night and my horror-show kick-boots, all lovely and washed or ironed or polished. And I was even given my cut-throat britva that I had used in those old happy days for fillying and dratsing. So I gave with the puzzled frown at this as I got dressed, but the white-coated under-veck just like grinned and would govoreet nothing, O my brothers.

I was led quite kindly to the same old mesto, but there were changes there. Curtains had been drawn in front of the sinny screen and the frosted glass under the projection holes was no longer there, it having perhaps been pushed up or folded to the sides like blind or shutters. And where there had been just the noise of coughing kashl kashl kashl and like shadows of lewdies was now a real audience, and in this audience there were litsos I knew. There was the Staja Governor and the holy man, the charlie or charles as he was called, and the Chief Chasso and this very important and well-dressed chelloveck who was the Minister of the Interior or Inferior. All the rest I did not know. Dr Brodsky and Dr Branom were there, although not now white-coated, instead they were dressed as doctors would dress who were big enough to want to dress in the heighth of fashion. Dr Branom just stood, but Dr Brodsky stood and govoreeted in a like learned manner to all the lewdies assembled. When he viddied me coming in he said, 'Aha. At this stage, gentlemen, we introduce the subject himself. He is, as you will perceive, fit and well-nourished. He comes straight from a night's sleep and a good breakfast, undrugged, unhypnotised. Tomorrow we send him with confidence out into the world again, as decent a lad as you would meet on a May morning, unvicious, unviolent, if anything – as you will observe – inclined to the kindly word and the helpful act. What a change is here, gentlemen, from the wretched hoodlum the State committed to unprofitable punishment some two years ago, unchanged after two years. Unchanged, do I say? Not quite. Prison taught him the false smile, the rubbed hands of hypocrisy, the fawning greased obsequious leer. Other vices it taught him, as well as confirming him in those he had long practised before. But, gentlemen, enough of words. Actions speak louder than. Action now. Observe, all.'

I was a bit dazed by all this govoreeting and I was trying to grasp in my mind that like all this was about me. Then all the lights went out and then there came on two like spotlights shining from the projection-squares, and one of them was full on Your Humble and Suffering Narrator. And into the other spotlight there walked a bolshy big chelloveck I had never viddied before. He had a lardy like litso and a moustache and like strips of hair pasted over his near-bald gulliver. He was about thirty or forty or fifty, some old age like that, starry. He ittied up to me and the spotlight ittied with him, and soon the two spotlights had made like one big pool. He said to me, very sneery, 'Hello, heap of dirt. Pooh, you don't wash much, judging from the horrible smell.' Then, as if he was like dancing, he stamped on my nogas, left, right, then he gave me a finger-nail flick on the nose that hurt like bezoomny and brought the old tears to my glazzies, then he twisted at my left ooko like it was a radio dial. I could slooshy titters and a couple of real horrorshow hawhawhaws coming from like the audience. My nose and nogas and earhole stung and pained like bezoomny, so I said:

'What do you do that to me for? I've never done any wrong to you, brother.'

'Oh,' this veck said, 'I do this' – flickflicked nose again – 'and that' – twisted smarting earhole – 'and the other' – stamped nasty on right noga – 'because I don't care for your horrible type. And if you want to do anything about it, start, start, please do.' Now I knew that I'd have to be real skorry and get my cut-throat britva out before this horrible killing sickness whooshed up and turned the like joy of battle into feeling I was going to snuff it. But, O brothers, as my rooker reached for the britva in my inside carman I got this like picture in my mind's glazzy of this insulting chelloveck howling for mercy with the red red krovvy all streaming out of his rot, and hot after this picture the sickness and dryness and pains were rushing to overtake, and I viddied that I'd have to change the way I felt about this rotten veck very very skorry indeed, so I felt in my carmans for cigarettes or for pretty polly, and, O my brothers, there was not either of these veshches. I said, like all howly and blubbery:

'I'd like to give you a cigarette, brother, but I don't seem to have any.' This veck went:

'Wah wah. Boohoohoo. Cry, baby.' Then he flickflick-flicked with his bolshy horny nail at my nose again, and I could slooshy very loud smecks of like mirth coming from the dark audience. I said, real desperate, trying to be nice to this insulting and hurtful veck to stop the pains and sickness coming up:

'Please let me do something for you, please.' And I felt in my carmans but could find only my cut-throat britva, so I took this out and handed it to him and said, 'Please take this, please. A little present. Please have it.' But he said:

'Keep your stinking bribes to yourself. You can't get round me that way.' And he banged at my rooker and my cut-throat britva fell on the floor. So I said:

'Please, I must do something. Shall I clean your boots? Look, I'll get down and lick them.' And, my brothers, believe it or kiss my sharries, I got down on my knees and pushed my red yahzick out a mile and a half to lick his grahzny vonny boots. But all this veck did was to kick me not too hard on the rot. So then it seemed to me that it would not bring on the sickness and pain if I just gripped his ankles with my rookers tight round them and brought this grahzny bratchny down to the floor. So I did this and he got a real bolshy surprise, coming down crack amid loud laughter from the vonny audience. But viddying him on the floor I could feel the whole horrible feeling coming over me, so I gave him my rooker to lift him up skorry and up he came. Then just as he was going to give me a real nasty and earnest tolchock on the litso Dr Brodsky said:

'All right, that will do very well.' Then this horrible veck sort of bowed and danced off like an actor while the lights came up on me blinking and with my rot square for howling. Dr Brodsky said to the audience: 'Our subject is, you see, impelled towards the good by, paradoxically, being impelled towards evil. The intention to act violently is accompanied by strong feelings of physical distress. To counter these the subject has to switch to a diametrically opposed attitude. Any questions?'

'Choice,' rumbled a rich deep goloss. I viddied it belonged to the prison charlie. 'He has no real choice, has he? Self-interest, fear of physical pain, drove him to that grotesque act of self-abasement. Its insincerity was clearly to be seen. He ceases to be a wrongdoer. He ceases also to be a creature capable of moral choice.'

'These are subtleties,' like smiled Dr Brodsky. 'We are not concerned with motive, with the higher ethics. We are concerned only with cutting down crime –'

'And,' chipped in this bolshy well-dressed Minister, 'with relieving the ghastly congestion in our prisons.'

'Hear hear,' said somebody.

'There was a lot of govoreeting and arguing then and I just stood there, brothers, like completely ignored by all these ignorant bratchnies, so I creeched out:

'Me, me, me. How about me? Where do I come into all this? Am I like just some animal or dog?' And that started them off govoreeting real loud and throwing slovos at me. So I creeched louder still, creeching: 'Am I just to be like a clockwork orange?' I didn't know what made me use those slovos, brothers, which just came like without asking into my gulliver. And that shut all those vecks up for some reason for a minoota or two. Then one very thin starry professor type chelloveck stood up, his neck like all cables carrying like power from his gulliver to his plott, and he said:

'You have no cause to grumble, boy. You made your choice and all this is a consequence of your choice. Whatever now ensues is what you yourself have chosen.' And the prison charlie creeched out:

'Oh, if only I could believe that.' And you could viddy the Governor give him a look like meaning that he would not climb so high in like Prison Religion as he thought he would. Then loud arguing started again, and then I could slooshy the slovo Love being thrown around, the prison charles himself creeching as loud as any about Perfect Love Casteth Out Fear and all that cal. And now Dr Brodsky said, smiling all over his litso:

'I am glad, gentlemen, this question of Love has been raised. Now we shall see in action a manner of Love that was thought to be dead with the Middle Ages.' And then the lights went down and the spotlights came on again, one on your poor and suffering Friend and Narrator, and into the other there like rolled or sidled the most lovely young devotchka you could ever hope in all your jeezny, O my brothers, to viddy. That is to say, she had real horrorshow groodies all of which you could like viddy, she having on platties which came down down down off her pletchoes. And her nogas were like Bog in His Heaven, and she walked like to make you groan in your keeshkas, and yet her litso was a sweet smiling young like innocent litso. She came up towards me with the light like it was the like light of heavenly grace and all that cal coming with her, and the first thing that flashed into my gulliver was that I would like to have her right down there on the floor with the old in-out real savage, but skorry as a shot came the sickness, like a like detective that had been watching round a corner and now followed to make his grahzny arrest. And now the von of lovely perfume that came off her made me want to think of starting to like heave in my keeshkas, so I knew I had to think of some new like way of thinking about her before all the pain and thirstiness and horrible sickness came over me real horrorshow and proper. So I creeched out:

'O most beautiful and beauteous of devotchkas, I throw like my heart at your feet for you to like trample all over. If I had a rose I would give it to you. If it was all rainy and cally now on the ground you could have my platties to walk on so as not to cover your dainty nogas with filth and cal.' And as I was saying all this, O my brothers, I could feel the sickness like slinking back. 'Let me,' I creeched out, 'worship you and be like your helper and protector from the wicked like world.' Then I thought of the right slovo and felt better for it, saying, 'Let me be like your true knight,' and down I went again on the old knees, bowing and like scraping.

And then I felt real shooty and dim, it having been like an act again, for this devotchka smiled and bowed to the audience and like danced off, the lights coming up to a bit of applause. And the glazzies of some of these starry vecks in the audience were like popping out at this young devotchka with dirty and like unholy desire, O my brothers.

'He will be your true Christian,' Dr Brodsky was creeching out, 'ready to turn the other cheek, ready to be crucified rather than crucify, sick to the very heart at the thought even of killing a fly.' And that was right, brothers, because when he said that I thought of killing a fly and felt just that tiny bit sick, but I pushed the sickness and pain back by thinking of the fly being fed with bits of sugar and looked after like a bleeding pet and all that cal. 'Reclamation,' he creeched. 'Joy before the Angels of God.'

'The point is,' this Minister of the Inferior was saying real gromky, 'that it works.'

'Oh,' the prison charlie said, like sighing, 'it works all right, God help the lot of us.'

3

'WHAT'S it going to be then, eh?'

That, my brothers, was me asking myself the next morning, standing outside this white building that was like tacked on to the old Staja, in my platties of the night of two years back in the grey light of dawn, with a malenky bit of a bag with my few personal veshches in and a bit of cutter kindly donated by the vonny Authorities to like start me off in my new life.

The rest of the day before had been very tiring, what with interviews to go on tape for the telenews and photographs being took flash flash flash and more like demonstrations of me folding up in the face of ultra-violence and all that embarassing cal. And then I had like fallen into the bed and then, as it looked to me, been wakened up to be told to get off out, to itty off home, they did not want to viddy Your Humble Narrator never not no more, O my brothers. So there I was, very very early in the morning, with just this bit of pretty polly in my left carman, jinglejangling it and wondering:

'What's it going to be then, eh?'

Some breakfast some mesto, I thought, me not having eaten at all that morning, every veck being so anxious to tolchock me off out to freedom. A chasha of chai only I had peeted. This Staja was in a very like gloomy part of the town, but there were malenky workers' caffs all around and I soon found one of those, my brothers. It was very cally and vonny, with one bulb in the ceiling with fly-dirt like obscuring its bit of light, and there were early rabbiters slurping away at chai and horrible-looking sausages and slices of kleb which they like wolfed, going wolf wolf wolf and then creeching for more. They were served by a very cally devotchka but with very bolshy groodies on her, and some of the eating vecks tried to grab her, going haw haw haw while she went he he he, and the sight of them near made me want to sick, brothers. But I asked for some toast and jam and chai very politely and with my gentleman's goloss, then I sat in a dark corner to eat and peet.

While I was doing this, a malenky like dwarf of veck ittied in, selling the morning's gazettas, a twisted and grahzny prestoopnick type with thick glasses on with steel rims, his platties like the colour of a very starry decaying currant pudding. I kupetted a gazetta, my idea being to get ready for plunging back into normal jeezny again by viddying what was ittying on in the world. This gazetta I had seemed to be like a Government gazetta, for the only news that was on the front page was about the need for every veck to make sure he put the Government back in again on the next General Election, which seemed to be about two or three weeks off. There were very boastful slovos about what the Government had done, brothers, in the last year or so, what with increased exports and a real horrorshow foreign policy and improved social services and all that cal. But what the Government was really most boastful about was the way in which they reckoned the streets had been made safer for all peace-loving night-walking lewdies in the last six months, what with better pay for the police and the police getting like tougher with young hooligans and perverts and burglars and all that cal. Which interessovatted Your Humble Narrator some deal. And on the second page of the gazetta there was a blurry like photograph of somebody who looked very familiar, and it turned out to be none other than me me me. I looked very gloomy and like scared, but that was really with the flashbulbs going pop pop all the time. What it said underneath my picture was that here was the first graduate of the new State Institute for Reclamation of Criminal Types, cured of his criminal instincts in a fortnight only, now a good law-fearing citizen and all that cal. Then I viddied there was a very boastful article about this Ludovico's Technique and how clever the Government was and all that cal. Then there was another picture of some veck I thought I knew, and it was this Minister of the Inferior or Interior. It seemed that he had been doing a bit of boasting, looking forward to a nice crime-free era in which there would be no more fear of cowardly attacks from young hooligans and perverts and burglars and all that cal. So I went arghhhhhh and threw this gazetta on the floor, so that it covered up stains of spilled chai and horrible spat gobs from the cally animals that used this caff.

'What's it going to be then, eh?'

What it was going to be now, brothers, was homeways and a nice surprise for dadada and mum, their only son and heir back in the family bosom. Then I could lay back on the bed in my own malenky den and slooshy some lovely music, and at the same time I could think over what to do now with my jeezny. The Discharge Officer had given me a long list the day before of jobs I could try for, and he had telephoned to different vecks about me, but I had no intention, my brothers, of going off to rabbit right away. A malenky bit of rest first, yes, and a quiet think on the bed to the sound of lovely music.

And so the autobus to Center, and then the autobus to Kingsley Avenue, the flats of Flatblock 18A being just near. You will believe me, my brothers, when I say that my heart was going clopclopclop with the like excitement. All was very quiet, it still being early winter morning, and when I ittied into the vestibule of the flatblock there was no veck about, only the nagoy vecks and cheenas of the Dignity of Labour. What surprised me, brothers, was the way that had been cleaned up, there being no longer any dirty ballooning slovos from the rots of the Dignified Labourers, not any dirty parts of the body added to their naked plotts by dirty-minded pencilling malchicks. And what also surprised me was that the lift was working. It came purring down when I pressed the electric knopka, and when I got in I was surprised again to viddy all was clean inside the like cage.

So up I went to the tenth floor, and there I saw 10–8 as it had been before, and my rooker trembled and shook as I took out of my carman the little klootch I had for opening up. But I very firmly fitted the klootch in the lock and turned, then opened up then went in, and there I met three pairs of surprised and almost frightened glazzies looking at me, and it was pee and em having their breakfast, but it was also another veck that I had never viddied in my jeezny before, a bolshy thick veck in his shirt and braces, quite at home, brothers, slurping away at the milky chai and munchmunching at his eggiweg and toast. And it was this stranger veck who spoke first, saying:

'Who are you, friend? Where did you get hold of a key? Out, before I push your face in. Get out there and knock. Explain your business, quick.'

My dad and mum sat like petrified, and I could viddy they had not yet read the gazetta, then I remembered that the gazetta did not arrive till papapa had gone off to his work. But then mum said, 'Oh, you've broken out. You've escaped. Whatever shall we do? We shall have the police here, oh oh oh. Oh, you bad and wicked boy, disgracing us all like this.' And, believe it or kiss my sharries, she started to go boo hoo. So I started to try and explain, they could ring up the Staja if they wanted, and all the time this stranger veck sat there like frowning and looking as if he could push my litso in with his hairy bolshy beefy fist. So I said:

'How about you answering a few, brother? What are you doing here and for how long? I didn't like the tone of what you said just then. Watch it. Come on, speak up.' He was a working-man type veck, very ugly, about thirty or forty, and he sat now with his rot open at me, not govoreeting one single slovo. Then my dad said:

'This is all a bit bewildering, son. You should have let us know you were coming. We thought it would be at least another five or six years before they let you out. Not,' he said, and he said it very like gloomy, 'that we're not very pleased to see you again and a free man, too.'

'Who is this?' I said. 'Why can't he speak up? What's going on in here?'

'This is Joe,' said my mum. 'He lives here now. The lodger, that's what he is. Oh, dear dear dear,' she went.

'You,' said this Joe. 'I've heard all about you, boy. I know what you've done, breaking the hearts of your poor grieving parents. So you're back, eh? Back to make life a misery for them once more, is that it? Over my dead corpse you will, because they've let me be more like a son to them than like a lodger.' I could nearly have smecked loud at that if the old razdraz within me hadn't started to wake up the feeling of wanting to sick, because this veck looked about the same age as my pee and em, and there he was like trying to put a son's protecting rooker round my crying mum, O my brothers.

'So,' I said, and I near felt like collapsing in all tears myself. 'So that's it, then. Well, I give you five large minootas to clear all your horrible cally veshches out of my room.' And I made for this room, this veck being a malenky bit too slow to stop me. When I opened the door my heart cracked to the carpet, because I viddied it was no longer like my room at all, brothers. All my flags had gone off the walls and this veck had put up pictures of boxers, also like a team sitting smug with folded rookers and a silver like shield in front. And then I viddied what else was missing. My stereo and my disc-cupboard were no longer there, nor was my locked treasure-chest that contained bottles and drugs and two shining clean syringes. 'There's been some filthy vonny work going on here,' I creeched. 'What have you done with my own personal veshches, you horrible bastard?' This was to this Joe, but it was my dad that answered, saying:

'That was all took away, son, by the police. This new regulation, see, about compensation for the victims.'

I found it very hard not to be very ill, but my gulliver was aching shocking and my rot was so dry that I had to take a skorry swig from the milk-bottle on the table, so that this Joe said, 'Filthy piggish manners.' I said:

'But she died. That one died.'

'It was the cats, son,' said my dad like sorrowful, 'that were left with nobody to look after them till the will was read, so they had to have somebody in to feed them. So the police sold your things, clothes and all, to help with the looking after of them. That's the law, son. But you were never much of a one for following the law.'

I had to sit down then, and this Joe said, 'Ask permission before you sit, you mannerless young swine,' so I cracked back skorry with a 'Shut your dirty big fat hole, you,' feeling sick. Then I tried to be all reasonable and smiling for my health's sake like, so I said, 'Well, that's my room, there's no denying that. This is my home also. What suggestions have you, my pee and em, to make?' But they just looked very glum, my mum shaking a bit, her litso all lines and wet with like tears, and then my dad said:

'All this needs thinking about, son. We can't very well just kick Joe out, not just like that, can we? I mean, Joe's here doing a job, a contract it is, two years, and we made like an arrangement, didn't we, Joe? I mean, son, thinking you were going to stay in prison a long time and that room going begging.' He was a bit ashamed, you could viddy that from his litso. So I just smiled and like nodded, saying:

'I viddy all. You got used to a bit of peace and you got used to a bit of extra pretty polly. That's the way it goes. And your son has just been nothing but a terrible nuisance.' And then, O my brothers, believe me or kiss my sharries, I started to like cry, feeling very like sorry for myself. So my dad said:

'Well, you see, son, Joe's paid next month's rent already. I mean, whatever we do in the future we can't say to Joe to get out, can we, Joe?' This Joe said:

'It's you two I've got to think of, who've been like a father and mother to me. Would it be right or fair to go off and leave you to the tender mercies of this young monster who has been like no real son at all? He's weeping now, but that's his craft and artfulness. Let him go off and find a room somewhere. Let him learn the error of his ways and that a bad boy like he's been doesn't deserve such a good mum and dad as what he's had.'

'All right,' I said, standing up in all like tears still. 'I know how things are now. Nobody wants or loves me. I've suffered and suffered and suffered and everybody wants me to go on suffering. I know.'

'You've made others suffer,' said this Joe. 'It's only right you should suffer proper. I've been told everything that you've done, sitting here at night round the family table, and pretty shocking it was to listen to. Made me real sick a lot of it did.'

'I wish,' I said, 'I was back in the prison. Dear old Staja as it was. I'm ittying off now,' I said. 'You won't ever viddy me no more. I'll make my own way, thank you very much. Let it lie heavy on your consciences.' My dad said:

'Don't take it like that, son,' and my mum just went boo hoo hoo, her litso all screwed up real ugly, and this Joe put his rooker round her again, patting her and going there there like bezoomny. And so I just sort of staggered to the door and went out, leaving them to their horrible guilt, O my brothers.

2 ITTYING down the street in a like aimless sort of a way, brothers, in these night platties which lewdies like stared at as I went by, cold too, it being a bastard cold winter day, all I felt I wanted was to be away from all this and not to have to think any more about any sort of veshch at all. So I got the autobus to Center, then I walked back to Taylor Place, and there was the disc-bootick MELODIA I had used to favour with my inestimable custom, O my brothers, and it looked much the same sort of mesto as it always had, and walking in I expected to viddy old Andy there, that bald and very very thin helpful like veck from whom I had kupetted discs in the old days. But there was no Andy there now, brothers, only a scream and a creech of nadsat (teenage, that is) malchicks and ptitsas slooshying some new horrible popsong and dancing to it as well, and the veck behind the counter not much more than a nadsat himself, clicking his rooker-bones and smecking like bezoomny. So I went up and waited till he like deigned to notice me, then I said:

'I'd like to hear a disc of the Mozart Number Forty.' I don't know why that should have come into my gulliver, but it did. The counter-veck said:

'Forty what, friend?' I said:

'Symphony. Symphony Number Forty in G Minor.'

'Ooooh,' went one of the dancing nadsats, a malchick with his hair all over his glazzies, 'seemfunnah. Don't it seem funny? He wants a seemfunnah.'

I could feel myself growing all razdraz within, but I had to watch that, so I like smiled at the veck who had taken over Andy's place and at all the dancing and creeching nadsats. This counter-veck said, 'You go into that listen-booth over there, friend, and I'll pipe something through.'

So I went over to the malenky box where you could slooshy the discs you wanted to buy, and then this veck put a disc on for me, but it wasn't the Mozart Forty, it was the Mozart 'Prague' – he seemingly having just picked any Mozart he could find on the shelf – and that should have started making me real razdraz and I had to watch that for fear of the pain and sickness, but what I'd forgotten was something I shouldn't have forgotten and now made me want to snuff it. It was that these doctor bratchnies had so fixed things that any music that was like for the emotions would make me sick just like viddying or wanting to do violence. It was because all those violence films had music with them. And I remembered especially that horrible Nazi film with the Beethoven Fifth, last movement. And now here was lovely Mozart made horrible. I dashed out of the box like bezoomny to get away from the sickness and pain that were coming on, and I dashed out of the shop with these nadsats smecking after me and the counter-veck creeching, 'Eh eh eh!' But I took no notice and went staggering almost like blind across the road and round the corner to the Korova Milkbar. I knew what I wanted.

The mesto was near empty, it being still morning. It looked strange too, having been painted with all red mooing cows, and behind the counter was no veck I knew. But when I said, 'Milk plus, large,' the veck with a like

152

lean litso very newly shaved knew what I wanted. I took the large moloko plus to one of the little cubies that were all round this mesto, there being like curtains to shut them off from the main mesto, and there I sat down in the plushy chair and sipped and sipped. When I'd finished the whole lot I began to feel that things were happening. I had my glazzies like fixed on a malenky bit of silver paper from a cancer packet that was on the floor, the sweeping-up of this mesto not being all that horrorshow, brothers. This scrap of silver began to grow and grow and grow and it was so like bright and fiery that I had to squint my glazzies at it. It got so big that it became not only this whole cubie I was lolling in but like the whole Korova, the whole street, the whole city. Then it was the whole world, then it was the whole everything, brothers, and it was like a sea washing over every veshch that had ever been made or thought of even. I could sort of slooshy myself making special sort of shooms and govoreeting slovos like 'Dear dead idlewilds, rot not in variform guises' and all that cal. Then I could like feel the vision beating up in all this silver, and then there were colours like nobody had ever viddied before, and then I could viddy like a group of statues a long long long way off that was like being pushed nearer and nearer and nearer, all lit up by very bright light from below and above alike, O my brothers. This group of statues was of God or Bog and all His Holy Angels and Saints, all very bright like bronze, with beards and bolshy great wings that waved about in a kind of wind, so that they could not really be of stone or bronze, really, and the eyes or glazzies like moved and were alive. These bolshy big figures came nearer and nearer and nearer till they were like going to crush me down, and I could slooshy my goloss going 'Eeeeee.' And I felt

I had got rid of everything – platties, plott, brain, eemya, the lot – and felt real horrorshow, like in heaven. Then there was the shoom of like crumbling and crumpling, and Bog and the Angels and Saints sort of shook their gullivers at me, as though to govoreet that there wasn't quite time now but I must try again, and then everything like leered and smecked and collapsed and the big warm light grew like cold, and then there I was as I was before, the empty glass on the table and wanting to cry and feeling like death was the only answer to everything.

And that was it, that was what I viddied quite clear was the thing to do, but how to do it I did not properly know, never having thought of that before, O my brothers. In my little bag of personal veshches I had my cut-throat britva, but I at once felt very sick as I thought of myself going swishhhh at myself and all my own red red krovvy flowing. What I wanted was not something violent but something that would make me like just go off gentle to sleep and that be the end of Your Humble Narrator, no more trouble to anybody any more. Perhaps, I thought, if I ittied off to the Public Biblio round the corner I might find some book on the best way of snuffing it with no pain. I thought of myself dead and how sorry everybody was going to be, pee and em and that cally vonny Joe who was a like usurper, and also Dr Brodsky and Dr Branom and that Inferior Interior Minister and every veck else. And the boastful vonny Government too. So out I scatted into the winter, and it was afternoon now, near two o'clock, as I could viddy from the bolshy Center timepiece, so that me being in the land with the old moloko plus must have took like longer than I thought. I walked down Marghanita Boulevard and then turned into Boothby Avenue, then round the corner again, and there was the Public Biblio.

It was a starry cally sort of a mesto that I could not remember going into since I was a very very malenky malchick, no more than about six years old, and there were two parts to it – one part to borrow books and one part to read in, full of gazettas and mags and like the von of very starry old men with their plotts stinking of like old age and poverty. These were standing at the gazetta stands all round the room, snuffling and belching and govoreeting to themselves and turning over the pages to read the news very sadly, or else they were sitting at the tables looking at the mags or pretending to, some of them asleep and one or two of them snoring real gromky. I couldn't like remember what it was I wanted at first, then I remembered with a bit of shock that I had ittied here to find out how to snuff it without pain, so I goolied over to the shelf full of reference veshches. There were a lot of books, but there was none with a title, brothers, that would really do. There was a medical book that I took down, but when I opened it it was full of drawings and photographs of horrible wounds and diseases, and that made me want to sick just a bit. So I put that back and then took down the big book or Bible, as it was called, thinking that might give me like comfort as it had done in the old Staja days (not so old really, but it seemed a very very long time ago), and I staggered over to a chair to read in it. But all I found was about smiting seventy times seven and a lot of yahoodies cursing and tolchocking each other, and that made me want to sick, too. So then I near cried, so that a very starry ragged moodge opposite me said:

'What is it, son? What's the trouble?'

'I want to snuff it,' I said. 'I've had it, that's what it is. Life's become too much for me.'

A starry reading veck next to me said, 'Shhhh,' without

looking up from some bezoomny mag he had full of drawings of like bolshy geometrical veshches. That rang a bell somehow. This other moodge said:

'You're too young for that, son. Why, you've got everything in front of you.'

'Yes,' I said, bitter. 'Like a pair of false groodies.' This mag-reading veck said, 'Shhhh' again, looking up this time, and something clicked for both of us. I viddied who it was. He said, real gromky:

'I never forget a shape, by God. I never forget the shape of anything. By God, you young swine, I've got you now.' Crystallography, that was it. That was what he'd been taking away from the Biblio that time. False teeth crunched up real horrorshow. Platties torn off. His books razrezzed, all about Crystallography. I thought I had best get out of here real skorry, brothers. But this starry old moodge was on his feet, creeching like bezoomny to all the starry old coughers at the gazettas round the walls and to them dozing over mags at the tables. 'We have him,' he creeched. 'The poisonous young swine who ruined the books on Crystallography, rare books, books not to be obtained ever again, anywhere.' This had a terrible mad shoom about it, as though this old veck was really off his gulliver. 'A prize specimen of the cowardly brutal young,' he creeched. 'Here in our midst and at our mercy. He and his friends beat me and kicked me and thumped me. They stripped me and tore out my teeth. They laughed at my blood and my moans. They kicked me off home, dazed and naked.' All this wasn't quite true, as you know, brothers. He had some platties on, he hadn't been completely nagoy. I creeched back:

'That was over two years ago. I've been punished since then. I've learned my lesson. See over there – my picture's in the papers.'

'Punishment, eh?' said one starry like ex-soldier type. 'You lot should be exterminated. Like so many noisome pests. Punishment, indeed.'

'All right, all right,' I said. 'Everybody's entitled to his opinion. Forgive me, all. I must go now.' And I started to itty out of this mesto of bezoomny old men. Aspirin, that was it. You could snuff it on a hundred aspirin. Aspirin from the old drugstore. But the crystallography veck creeched:

'Don't let him go. We'll teach him all about punishment, the murderous young pig. Get him.' And, believe it, brothers, or do the other veshch, two or three starry dodderers, about ninety years old apiece, grabbed me with their trembly old rookers, and I was like made sick by the von of old age and disease which came from these near-dead moodges. The crystal veck was on to me now, starting to deal me malenky weak tolchocks on my litso, and I tried to get away and itty out, but these starry rookers that held me were stronger than I had thought. Then other starry vecks came hobbling from the gazettas to have a go at Your Humble Narrator. They were creeching veshches like: 'Kill him, stamp on him, murder him, kick his teeth in,' and all that cal, and I could viddy what it was clear enough. It was old age having a go at youth, that's what it was. But some of them were saying, 'Poor old Jack, near killed poor old Jack he did, this is the young swine' and so on, as though it had all happened yesterday. Which to them I suppose it had. There was now like a sea of vonny runny dirty old men trying to get at me with their like feeble rookers and horny old claws, creeching and panting on to me, but our crystal droog was there in front, dealing out tolchock after tolchock. And I daren't do a solitary single veshch, O my brothers, it being better to be hit at like that than to want to sick and feel that horrible pain, but of course the fact that there was violence going on made me feel that the sickness was peeping round the corner to viddy whether to come out into the open and roar away.

Then an attendant veck came along, a youngish veck, and he creeched, 'What goes on here? Stop it at once. This is a reading room.' But nobody took any notice. So the attendant veck said, 'Right, I shall phone the police.' So I creeched, and I never thought I would ever do that in all my jeezny:

'Yes yes yes, do that, protect me from these old madmen.' I noticed that the attendant veck was not too anxious to join in the dratsing and rescue me from the rage and madness of these starry vecks' claws; he just scatted off to his like office or wherever the telephone was. Now these old men were panting a lot now, and I felt I could just flick at them and they would all fall over, but I just let myself be held, very patient, by these starry rookers, my glazzies closed, and feel the feeble tolchocks on my litso, also slooshy the panting breathy old golosses creeching, 'Young swine, young murderer, hooligan, thug, kill him.' Then I got such a real painful tolchock on the nose that I said to myself to hell to hell, and I opened my glazzies up and started to struggle to get free, which was not hard, brothers, and I tore off creeching to the sort of hallway outside the reading-room. But these starry avengers still came after me, panting like dying, with their animal claws all trembling to get at your friend and Humble Narrator. Then I was tripped up and was on the floor and was being kicked at, then I slooshied golosses of young vecks creeching, 'All right, all right, stop it now,' and I knew the police had arrived.

3 I was like dazed, O my brothers, and could not viddy very clear, but I was sure I had met these millicents some mesto before. The one who had hold of me, going, 'There there there,' just by the front door of the Public Biblio, him I did not know at all, but it seemed to me he was like very young to be a rozz. But the other two had backs that I was sure I had viddied before. They were lashing into these starry old vecks with great bolshy glee and joy, swishing away with malenky whips, creeching, 'There, you naughty boys. That should teach you to stop rioting and breaking the State's peace, you wicked villains, you.' So they drove these panting and wheezing and near dying starry avengers back into the reading-room, then they turned round, smecking with the fun they'd had, to viddy me. The older one of the two said:

'Well well well well well well well. If it isn't little Alex. Very long time no viddy, droog. How goes?' I was like dazed, the uniform and the shlem or helmet making it very hard to viddy who this was, though litso and goloss were very familiar. Then I looked at the other one, and about him, with his grinny bezoomny litso, there was no doubt. Then, all numb and growing number, I looked back at the well well welling one. This one was then fatty

159

old Billyboy, my old enemy. The other was, of course, Dim, who had used to be my droog and also the enemy of stinking fatty goaty Billyboy, but was now a millicent with uniform and shlem and whip to keep order. I said:

'Oh no.'

'Surprise, eh?' And old Dim came out with the old guff I remembered so horrorshow: 'Huh huh huh.'

'It's impossible,' I said. 'It can't be so. I don't believe it.'

'Evidence of the old glazzies,' grinned Billyboy. 'Nothing up our sleeves. No magic, droog. A job for two who are now of job-age. The police.'

'You're too young,' I said. 'Much too young. They don't make rozzes of malchicks of your age.'

'Was young,' went old millicent Dim. I could not get over it, brothers, I really could not. 'That's what we was, young droogie. And you it was that was always the youngest. And here now we are.'

'I still can't believe it,' I said. Then Billyboy, rozz Billyboy that I couldn't get over, said to this young millicent that was like holding on to me and that I did not know:

'More good would be done, I think, Rex, if we doled out a bit of the old summary. Boys will be boys, as always was. No need to go through the old station routine. This one here has been up to his old tricks, as we can well remember though you, of course, can't. He has been attacking the aged and defenceless, and they have properly been retaliating. But we must have our say in the State's name.'

'What is all this?' I said, not able hardly to believe my ookos. 'It was them that went for me, brothers. You're not on their side and can't be. You can't be, Dim. It was a veck we fillied with once in the old days trying to get his own malenky bit of revenge after all this long time.'

'Long time is right,' said Dim. 'I don't remember them days too horrorshow. Don't call me Dim no more, either. Officer call me.'

'Enough is remembered, though,' Billyboy kept nodding. He was not so fatty as he had been. 'Naughty little malchicks handy with cut-throat britvas – these must be kept under.' And they took me in a real strong grip and like walked me out of the Biblio. There was a millicent patrol-car waiting outside, and this veck they called Rex was the driver. They like tolchocked me into the back of this auto, and I couldn't help feeling it was all really like a joke, and that Dim anyway would pull his shlem off his gulliver and go haw haw haw. But he didn't. I said, trying to fight the strack inside me:

'And old Pete, what happened to old Pete? It was sad about Georgie,' I said. 'I slooshied all about that.'

'Pete, oh yes, Pete,' said Dim. 'I seem to remember like the name.' I could viddy we were driving out of town. I said:

'Where are we supposed to be going?'

Billyboy turned round from the front to say, 'It is light still. A little drive into the country, all winter-bare but lonely and lovely. It is not right, not always, for lewdies in the town to viddy too much of our summary punishment. Streets must be kept clean in more than one way.' And he turned to the front again.

'Come,' I said. 'I just don't get this at all. The old days are dead and gone days. For what I did in the past I have been punished. I have been cured.'

'That was read out to us,' said Dim. 'The Super read all that out to us. He said it was a very good way.'

'Read to you,' I said, a malenky bit nasty. 'You still too dim to read for yourself, O brother?'

'Ah, no,' said Dim, very like gentle and like regretful. 'Not to speak like that. Not no more, droogie.' And he launched a bolshy tolchock right on my cluve, so that all red red nose-krovvy started to drip drip drip.

'There was never any trust,' I said, bitter, wiping off the krovvy with my rooker. 'I was always on my oddy knocky.'

'This will do,' said Billyboy. We were now in the country and it was all bare trees and a few odd distant like twitters, and in the distance there was some like farm machine making a whirring shoom. It was getting all dusk now, this being the heighth of winter. There were no lewdies about, nor no animals. There was just the four. 'Get out, Alex boy,' said Dim. 'Just a malenky bit of summary.'

All through what they did this driver veck just sat at the wheel of the auto, smoking a cancer, reading a malenky bit of a book. He had the light on in the auto to viddy by. He took no notice of what Billyboy and Dim did to your Humble Narrator. I will not go into what they did, but it was all like panting and thudding against this like background of whirring farm engines and the twittwittwittering in the bare or nagoy branches. You could viddy a bit of smoky breath in the auto light, this driver turning the pages over quite calm. And they were on to me all the time, O my brothers. Then Billyboy or Dim, I couldn't say which one, said, 'About enough, droogie, I should think, shouldn't you?' Then they gave me one final tolchock on the litso each and I fell over and just laid there on the grass. It was cold but I was not feeling the cold. Then they dusted their rookers and put back on their shlems and tunics which they had taken off, and then they got back into the auto. 'Be viddying you some more sometime, Alex,' said Billyboy, and Dim just gave one of his old clowny guffs. The driver finished the page he was reading and put his book away, then he started the auto and they were off townwards, my ex-droog and ex-enemy waving. But I just laid there, fagged and shagged.

After a bit I was hurting bad, and then the rain started, all icy. I could viddy no lewdies in sight, nor no lights of houses. Where was I to go, who had no home and not much cutter in my carmans? I cried for myself boo hoo hoo. Then I got up and began walking.

HOME, home home, it was home I was
wanting, and it was HOME I came to,
brothers. I walked through the dark and
followed not the town way but the way
where the shoom of a like farm machine
had been coming from. This brought me to a sort of village
I felt I had viddied before, but was perhaps because all
villages look the same, in the dark especially. Here were
houses and there was a like drinking mesto, and right at
the end of the village there was a malenky cottage on its
oddy knocky, and I could viddy its name shining white
on the gate. HOME, it said. I was all dripping wet with
this icy rain, so that my platties were no longer in the
heighth of fashion but real miserable and like pathetic,
and my luscious glory was a wet tangled cally mess all
spread over my gulliver, and I was sure there were cuts
and bruises all over my litso, and a couple of my zoobies
sort of joggled loose when I touched them with my tongue
or yahzick. And I was sore all over my plott and very
thirsty, so that I kept opening my rot to the cold rain,
and my stomach growled grrrrr all the time with not
having had any pishcha since morning and then not very
much, O my brothers.

HOME, it said, and perhaps here would be some veck
to help. I opened the gate and sort of slithered down the

165

path, the rain like turning to ice, and then I knocked gentle and pathetic on the door. No veck came, so I knocked a malenky bit longer and louder, and then I heard the shoom of nogas coming to the door. Then the door opened and a male goloss said, 'Yes, what is it?'

'Oh,' I said, 'please help. I've been beaten up by the police and just left to die on the road. Oh, please give me a drink of something and a sit by the fire, please, sir.'

The door opened full then, and I could viddy like warm light and a fire going crackle crackle within. 'Come in,' said this veck, 'whoever you are. God help you, you poor victim, come in and let's have a look at you.' So I like staggered in, and it was no big act I was putting on, brothers, I really felt done and finished. This kind veck put his rookers round my pletchoes and pulled me into this room where the fire was, and of course I knew right away now where it was and why HOME on the gate looked so familiar. I looked at this veck and he looked at me in a kind sort of way, and I remembered him well now. Of course he would not remember me, for in those carefree days I and my so-called droogs did all our bolshy dratsing and fillying and crasting in maskies which were real horrorshow disguises. He was a shortish veck in middle age, thirty, forty, fifty, and he had otchkies on. 'Sit down by the fire,' he said, 'and I'll get you some whisky and warm water. Dear dear dear, somebody *has* been beating you up.' And he gave a like tender look at my gulliver and litso.

'The police,' I said. 'The horrible ghastly police.'

'Another victim,' he said, like sighing. 'A victim of the modern age. I'll go and get you that whisky and then I must clean up your wounds a little.' And off he went. I had a look round this malenky comfortable room. It was nearly all books now and a fire and a couple of chairs, and you could viddy somehow that there wasn't a woman living there. On the table was a typewriter and a lot of like tumbled papers, and I remembered that this veck was a writer veck. *A Clockwork Orange*, that had been it. It was funny that that stuck in my mind. I must not let on, though, for I needed help and kindness now. Those horrible grahzny bratchnies in that terrible white mesto had done that to me, making me need help and kindness now and forcing me to want to give help and kindness myself, if anybody would take it.

'Here we are, then,' said this veck returning. He gave me this hot stimulating glassful to peet, and it made me feel better, and then he cleaned up these cuts on my litso. Then he said, 'You have a nice hot bath, I'll draw it for you, and then you can tell me all about it over a nice hot supper which I'll get ready while you're having the bath.' O my brothers, I could have wept at his kindness, and I think he must have viddied the old tears in my glazzies, for he said, 'There there there,' patting me on the pletcho.

Anyway, I went up and had this hot bath, and he brought in pyjamas and an over-gown for me to put on, all warmed by the fire, also a very worn pair of toofles. And now, brothers, though I was aching and full of pains all over, I felt I would soon feel a lot better. I ittied downstairs and viddied that in the kitchen he had set the table with knives and forks and a fine big loaf of kleb, also a bottle of PRIMA SAUCE, and soon he served out a nice fry of eggiwegs and lomticks of ham and bursting sausages and big bolshy mugs of hot sweet milky chai. It was nice sitting there in the warm, eating, and I found I was very hungry, so that after the fry I had to eat lomtick after lomtick of kleb and butter spread with strawberry jam out of a bolshy great pot. 'A lot better,' I said. 'How can I ever repay?'

'I think I know who you are,' he said. 'If you are who I think you are, then you've come, my friend, to the right place. Wasn't that your picture in the papers this morning? Are you the poor victim of this horrible new technique? If so, then you have been sent here by Providence. Tortured in prison, then thrown out to be tortured by the police. My heart goes out to you, poor poor boy.' Brothers, I could not get a slovo in, though I had my rot wide open to answer his questions. 'You are not the first to come here in distress,' he said. 'The police are fond of bringing their victims to the outskirts of this village. But it is providential that you, who are also another kind of victim, should come here. Perhaps, then, you have heard of me?'

I had to be very careful, brothers. I said, 'I have heard of *A Clockwork Orange*. I have not read it, but I have heard of it.'

'Ah,' he said, and his litso shone like the sun in its flaming morning glory. 'Now tell me about yourself.'

'Little enough to tell, sir,' I said, all humble. 'There was a foolish and boyish prank, my so-called friends persuading or rather forcing me to break into the house of an old ptitsa – lady, I mean. There was no real harm meant. Unfortunately the lady strained her good old heart in trying to throw me out, though I was quite ready to go of my own accord, and then she died. I was accused of being the cause of her death. So I was sent to prison, sir.'

'Yes yes yes, go on.'

'Then I was picked out by the Minister of the Inferior or Interior to have this Ludovico's veshch tried out on me.'

'Tell me all about it,' he said, leaning forward eager, his pullover elbows with all strawberry jam on them from the plate I'd pushed to one side. So I told him all about it. I told him the lot, all, my brothers. He was very eager to hear all, his glazzies like shining and his goobers apart, while the grease on the plates grew harder harder harder. When I had finished he got up from the table, nodding a lot and going hm hm hm, picking up the plates and other veshches from the table and taking them to the sink for washing up. I said:

'I will do that, sir, and gladly.'

'Rest, rest, poor lad,' he said, turning the tap on so that all steam came burping out. 'You've sinned, I suppose, but your punishment has been out of all proportion. They have turned you into something other than a human being. You have no power of choice any longer. You are committed to socially acceptable acts, a little machine capable only of good. And I see that clearly – that business about the marginal conditionings. Music and the sexual act, literature and art, all must be a source now not of pleasure but of pain.'

'That's right, sir,' I said, smoking one of this kind man's cork-tipped cancers.

'They always bite off too much,' he said, drying a plate like absent-mindedly. 'But the essential intention is the real sin. A man who cannot choose ceases to be a man.'

'That's what the charles said, sir,' I said. 'The prison chaplain, I mean.'

'Did he, did he? Of course he did. He'd have to, wouldn't he, being a Christian? Well, now then,' he said, still wiping the same plate he'd been wiping ten minutes ago, 'we shall have a few people in to see you tomorrow. I think that you can be used, poor boy. I think you can help dislodge this overbearing Government. To turn a decent young man into a piece of clockwork should not, surely, be seen as any triumph for any government, save one that boasts of its repressiveness.' He was still wiping this same plate. I said:

'Sir, you're still wiping that same plate. I agree with you, sir, about boasting. This Government seems to be very boastful.'

'Oh,' he said, like viddying this plate for the first time and then putting it down. 'I'm still not too handy,' he said, 'with domestic chores. My wife used to do them all and leave me to my writing.'

'Your wife, sir?' I said. 'Has she gone and left you?' I really wanted to know about his wife, remembering very well.

'Yes, left me,' he said, in a like loud and bitter goloss. 'She died, you see. She was brutally raped and beaten. The shock was very great. It was in this house,' his rookers were trembling, holding a wiping-up cloth, 'in that room next door. I have had to steel myself to continue to live here, but she would have wished me to stay where her fragrant memory still lingers. Yes yes yes. Poor little girl.' I viddied all clearly, my brothers, what had happened that far-off nochy, and viddying myself on that job, I began to feel I wanted to sick and the pain started up in my gulliver. This veck viddied this, because my litso felt it was all drained of red red krovvy, very pale, and he would be able to viddy this. 'You go to bed now,' he said kindly. 'I've got the spare room ready. Poor poor boy, you must have had a terrible time. A victim of the modern age, just as she was. Poor poor poor girl.'

I HAD a real horrorshow night's sleep, brothers, with no dreams at all, and the morning was very clear and like frosty, and there was the very pleasant like von of breakfast frying away down below. It took me some little time to remember where I was, as it always does, but it soon came back to me and then I felt like warmed and protected. But, as I laid there in the bed, waiting to be called down to breakfast, it struck me that I ought to get to know the name of this kind protecting and like motherly veck, so I had a pad round in my nagoy nogas looking for *A Clockwork Orange*, which would be bound to have his eemya in, he being the author. There was nothing in my bedroom except a bed and a chair and a light, so I ittied next door to this veck's own room, and there I viddied his wife on the wall, a bolshy blown-up photo, so I felt a malenky bit sick remembering. But there were two or three shelves of books there too, and there was, as I thought there must be, a copy of *A Clockwork Orange*, and on the back of the book, like on the spine, was the author's eemya – F. Alexander. Good Bog, I thought, he is another Alex. Then I leafed through, standing in my pyjamas and bare nogas but not feeling one malenky bit cold, the cottage being warm all through, and I could not viddy what the book was about. It seemed written in a very bezoomny like style, full of Ah and Oh and that cal, but what seemed to come out of it was that all lewdies nowadays were being turned into machines and that they were really – you and me and him and kiss-my-sharries – more like a natural growth like a fruit. F. Alexander seemed to think that we all like grow on what he called the world-tree in the world-orchard that like Bog or God planted, and we were there because Bog or God had need of us to quench his thirsty love, or some such cal. I didn't like the shoom of this at all, O my brothers, and wondered how bezoomny this F. Alexander really was, perhaps driven bezoomny by his wife's snuffing it. But then he called me down in a like sane veck's goloss, full of joy and love and all that cal, so down Your Humble Narrator went.

'You've slept long,' he said, ladling out boiled eggs and pulling black toast from under the grill. 'It's nearly ten already. I've been up hours, working.'

'Writing another book, sir?' I said.

'No no, not that now,' he said, and we sat down nice and droogy to the old crack crack crack of eggs and crackle crunch crunch of this black toast, very milky chai standing by in bolshy great morning mugs. 'No, I've been on the phone to various people.'

'I thought you didn't have a phone,' I said, spooning egg in and not watching out what I was saying.

'Why?' he said, very alert like some skorry animal with an egg-spoon in its rooker. 'Why shouldn't you think I have a phone?'

'Nothing, ' I said, 'nothing, nothing.' And I wondered, brothers, how much he remembered of the earlier part of that distant nochy, me coming to the door with the old tale and saying to phone the doctor and she saying no phone. He took a very close smot at me but then went back to being like kind and cheerful and spooning up the old eggiweg. Munching away, he said:

'Yes, I've rung up various people who will be interested in your case. You can be a very potent weapon, you see, in ensuring that this present evil and wicked Government is not returned in the forthcoming election. The Government's big boast, you see, is the way it has dealt with crime these last months.' He looked at me very close again over his steaming egg, and I wondered again if he was viddying what part I had so far played in his jeezny. But he said, 'Recruiting brutal young roughs for the police. Proposing debilitating and will-sapping techniques of conditioning.' All these long slovos, brothers, and a like mad or bezoomny look in his glazzies. 'We've seen it all before,' he said, 'in other countries. The thin end of the wedge. Before we know where we are we shall have the full apparatus of totalitarianism.' 'Dear dear dear,' I thought, egging away and toast-crunching. I said:

'Where do I come into all this, sir?'

'You,' he said, still with this bezoomny look, 'are a living witness to these diabolical proposals. The people, the common people must know, must see.' He got up from his breakfast and started to walk up and down the kitchen, from the sink to the like larder, saying very gromky, 'Would they like their sons to become what you, poor victim, have become? Will not the Government itself now decide what is and what is not crime and pump out the life and guts and will of whoever sees fit to displease the Government?' He became quieter but did not go back to his egg. 'I've written an article,' he said, 'this morning, while you were sleeping. That will be out in a day or so, together with your unhappy picture. You shall sign it, poor boy, a record of what they have done to you.' I said:

'And what do you get out of all this, sir? I mean, besides the pretty polly you'll get for the article, as you call it? I mean, why are you so hot and strong against this Government, if I may make like so bold as to ask?'

He gripped the edge of the table and said, gritting his zoobies, which were very cally and all stained with cancer-smoke, 'Some of us have to fight. There are great traditions of liberty to defend. I am no partisan man. Where I see the infamy I seek to erase it. Party names mean nothing. The tradition of liberty means all. The common people will let it go, oh yes. They will sell liberty for a quieter life. That is why they must be prodded, *prodded* –' And here, brothers, he picked up a fork and stuck it two or three razzes into the wall, so that it all got bent. Then he threw it on the floor. Very kindly he said, 'Eat well, poor boy, poor victim of the modern world,' and I could viddy quite clear he was going off his gulliver. 'Eat, eat. Eat my egg as well.' But I said:

'And what do I get out of this? Do I get cured of the way I am? Do I find myself able to slooshy the old Choral Symphony without being sick once more? Can I live like a normal jeezny again? What, sir, happens to me?'

He looked at me, brothers, as if he hadn't thought of that before and, anyway, it didn't matter compared with Liberty and all that cal, and he had a look of surprise at me saying what I said, as though I was being like selfish in wanting something for myself. Then he said, 'Oh, as I say, you're a living witness, poor boy. Eat up all your breakfast and then come and see what I've written, for it's going into *The Weekly Trumpet* under your name, you unfortunate victim.'

Well, brothers, what he had written was a very long and very weepy piece of writing, and as I read it I felt very sorry for the poor malchick who was govoreeting about his sufferings and how the Government had sapped his will and how it was up to all lewdies to not let such a rotten and evil Government rule them again, and then of course I realised that the poor suffering malchick was none other than Y.H.N. 'Very good,' I said. 'Real horrorshow. Written well thou hast, O sir.' And then he looked at me very narrow and said:

'What?'

'Oh, that,' I said, 'is what we call nadsat talk. All the teens use that, sir.' So then he ittied off to the kitchen to wash up the dishes, and I was left in these borrowed night platties and toofles, waiting to have done to me what was going to be done to me, because I had no plans for myself, O my brothers.

While the great F. Alexander was in the kitchen a ding-alingaling came at the door. 'Ah,' he creeched, coming out wiping his rookers, 'it will be these people. I'll go.' So he went and let them in, a kind of rumbling hahaha of talk and hallo and filthy weather and how are things in the hallway, then they ittied into the room with the fire and the books and the article about how I had suffered, viddying me and going Aaaaah as they did it. There were three lewdies, and F. Alex gave me their eemyas. Z. Dolin was a very wheezy smoky kind of a veck, coughing kashl kashl kashl with the end of a cancer in his rot, spilling ash all down his platties and then brushing it away with like very impatient rookers. He was a malenky round veck, fat, with big thick-framed otchkies on. Then there was Something Something Rubinstein, a very tall and polite chelloveck with a real gentleman's goloss, very starry with a like eggy beard. And lastly there was D. B. da Silva who was like skorry in his movements and had this strong von of scent coming from him. They all had a real horrorshow look at me and seemed like overjoyed with what they viddied. Z. Dolin said:

'All right, all right, eh? What a superb device he can be, this boy. If anything, of course, he could for preference look even iller and more zombyish than he does. Anything for the cause. No doubt we can think of something.'

I did not like that crack about zombyish, brothers, and so I said, 'What goes on, bratties? What dost thou in mind for thy little droog have?' And then F. Alexander swooshed in with:

'Strange, strange, that manner of voice pricks me. We've come into contact before, I'm sure we have.' And he brooded, like frowning. I would have to watch this, O my brothers. D. B. da Silva said:

'Public meetings, mainly. To exhibit you at public meetings will be a tremendous help. And, of course, the newspaper angle is all tied up. A ruined life is the approach. We must inflame all hearts.' He showed his thirty-odd zoobies, very white against his dark-coloured litso, he looking a malenky bit like some foreigner. I said:

'Nobody will tell me what I get out of all this. Tortured in jail, thrown out of my home by my own parents and their filthy overbearing lodger, beaten by old men and near-killed by the millicents – what is to become of me?' The Rubinstein veck came in with:

'You will see, boy, that the Party will not be ungrateful. Oh, no. At the end of it all there will be some very acceptable little surprise for you. Just you wait and see.'

'There's only one veshch I require,' I creeched out, 'and that's to be normal and healthy as I was in the starry days, having my malenky bit of fun with *real* droogs and not those who just call themselves that and are really more like traitors. Can you do that, eh? Can any veck restore me to what I was? That's what I want and that's what I want to know.'

Kashl kashl kashl, coughed this Z. Dolin. 'A martyr to the cause of Liberty,' he said. 'You have your part to play and don't forget it. Meanwhile, we shall look after you.' And he began to stroke my left rooker as if I was like an idiot, grinning in a bezoomny way. I creeched:

'Stop treating me like a thing that's like got to be just used. I'm not an idiot you can impose on, you stupid bratchnies. Ordinary prestoopnicks are stupid, but I'm not ordinary and nor am I dim. Do you slooshy?'

'Dim,' said F. Alexander, like musing. 'Dim. That was a name somewhere. Dim.'

'Eh?' I said. 'What's Dim got to do with it? What do *you* know about Dim?' And then I said, 'Oh, Bog help us.' I didn't like the like look in F. Alexander's glazzies. I made for the door, wanting to go upstairs and get my platties and then itty off.

'I could almost believe,' said F. Alexander, showing his stained zoobies, his glazzies mad. 'But such things are impossible. For, by Christ, if he were I'd tear him. I'd split him, by God, yes yes, so I would.'

'There,' said D. B. da Silva, stroking his chest like he was a doggie to calm him down. 'It's all in the past. It was other people altogether. We must help this poor victim. That's what we must do now, remembering the Future and our Cause.'

'I'll just get my platties,' I said, at the stair-foot, 'that is to say clothes, and then I'll be ittying off all on my oddy knocky. I mean, my gratitude for all, but I have my own jeezny to live.' Because, brothers, I wanted to get out of here real skorry. But Z. Dolin said:

'Ah, no. We have you, friend, and we keep you. You come with us. Everything will be all right, you'll see.' And he came up to me like to grab hold of my rooker again. Then, brothers, I thought of fight, but thinking of fight made me like want to collapse and sick, so I just stood. And then I saw this like madness in F. Alexander's glazzies and said:

'Whatever you say. I am in your rookers. But let's get it started and all over, brothers.' Because what I wanted now was to get out of this mesto called HOME. I was beginning not to like the like look of the glazzies of F. Alexander one malenky bit.

'Good,' said this Rubinstein. 'Get dressed and let's get started.'

'Dim dim dim,' F. Alexander kept saying in a like low mutter. 'What or who was this Dim?' I ittied upstairs real skorry and dressed in near two seconds flat. Then I was out with these three and into an auto, Rubinstein one side of me and Z. Dolin coughing kashl kashl kashl the other side, D. B. da Silva doing the driving, into the town and to a flatblock not really all that distant from what had used to be my own flatblock or home. 'Come, boy, out,' said Z. Dolin, coughing to make the cancer-end in his rot glow red like some malenky furnace. 'This is where you shall be installed.' So we ittied in, and there was like another of these Dignity of Labour veshches on the wall of the vestibule, and we upped in the lift, brothers, and then went into a flat like all the flats of all the flatblocks of the town. Very very malenky, with two bedrooms and one live-eat-work-room, the table of this all covered with books and papers and ink and bottles and all that cal. 'Here is your new home,' said D. B. da Silva. 'Settle here, boy. Food is in the food-cupboard. Pyjamas are in a drawer. Rest, rest, perturbed spirit.'

'Eh,' I said, not quite ponying that.

'All right,' said Rubinstein, with his starry goloss. 'We are now leaving you. Work has to be done. We'll be with you later. Occupy yourself as best you can.'

'One thing,' coughed Z. Dolin kashl kashl kashl. 'You saw what stirred in the tortured memory of our friend F. Alexander. Was it, by any chance –? That is to say, did you –? I think you know what I mean. We won't let it go any further.'

'I've paid,' I said. 'Bog knows I've paid for what I did. I've paid not only like for myself but for those bratchnies too that called themselves my droogs.' I felt violent so then I felt a bit sick. 'I'll lay down a bit,' I said. 'I've been through terrible terrible times.'

'You have,' said D. B. da Silva, showing all his thirty zoobies. 'You do that.'

So they left me, brothers. They ittied off about their business, which I took to be about politics and all that cal, and I was on the bed, all on my oddy knocky with everything very very quiet. I just laid there with my sabogs kicked off my nogas and my tie loose, like all bewildered and not knowing what sort of a jeezny I was going to live now. And all sorts of like pictures kept like passing through my gulliver, of the different chellovecks I'd met at school and in the Staja, and the different veshches that had happened to me, and how there was not one veck you could trust in the whole bolshy world. And then I like dozed off, brothers.

When I woke up I could slooshy music coming out of the wall, real gromky, and it was that that had dragged me out of my bit of like sleep. It was a symphony that I knew real horrorshow but had not slooshied for many a year, namely the Symphony Number Three of the Danish

179

veck Otto Skadelig, a very gromky and violent piece, especially in the first movement, which was what was playing now. I slooshied for two seconds in like interest and joy, but then it all came over me, the start of the pain and the sickness, and I began to groan deep down in my keeshkas. And then there I was, me who had loved music so much, crawling off the bed and going oh oh oh to myself, and then bang bang banging on the wall creeching, 'Stop, stop it, turn it off!' But it went on and it seemed to be like louder. So I crashed at the wall till my knuckles were all red red krovvy and torn skin, creeching and creeching, but the music did not stop. Then I thought I had to get away from it, so I lurched out of the malenky bedroom and ittied skorry to the front door of the flat, but this had been locked from the outside and I could not get out. And all the time the music got more and more gromky, like it was all a deliberate torture, O my brothers. So I stuck my little fingers real deep in my ookos, but the trombones and kettledrums blasted through gromky enough. So I creeched again for them to stop and went hammer hammer hammer on the wall, but it made not one malenky bit of difference. 'Oh, what am I to do?' I boohooed to myself. 'Oh, Bog in Heaven help me.' I was like wandering all over the flat in pain and sickness, trying to shut out the music and like groaning deep out of my guts, and then on top of the pile of books and papers and all that cal that was on the table in the living-room I viddied what I had to do and what I had wanted to do until those old men in the Public Biblio and then Dim and Billyboy disguised as rozzes stopped me, and that was to do myself in, to snuff it, to blast off for ever out of this wicked and cruel world. What I viddied was the slovo DEATH on the cover of a like pamphlet, even though it was only DEATH TO THE GOVERNMENT. And like it was Fate there was another like malenky booklet which had an open window on the cover, and it said, 'Open the window to fresh air, fresh ideas, a new way of living.' And so I knew that was like telling me to finish it all off by jumping out. One moment of pain, perhaps, and then sleep for ever and ever and ever.

The music was still pouring in all brass and drums and the violins miles up through the wall. The window in the room where I had laid down was open. I ittied to it and viddied a fair drop to the autos and buses and walking chellovecks below. I creeched out to the world: 'Goodbye, goodbye, may Bog forgive you for a ruined life.' Then I got on to the sill, the music blasting away to my left, and I shut my glazzies and felt the cold wind on my litso, then I jumped.

6 I JUMPED, O my brothers, and I fell on the sidewalk hard, but I did not snuff it, oh no. If I had snuffed it I would not be here to write what I written have. It seems that the jump was not from a big enough heighth to kill. But I cracked my back and my wrists and nogas and felt very bolshy pain before I passed out, brothers, with astonished and surprised litsos of chellovecks in the streets looking at me from above. And just before I passed out I viddied clear that not one chelloveck in the whole horrid world was for me and that that music through the wall had all been like arranged by those who were supposed to be my like new droogs and that it was some veshch like this that they wanted for their horrible selfish and boastful politics. All that was in like a million millionth part of one minoota before I threw over the world and the sky and the litsos of the staring chellovecks that were above me.

Where I was when I came back to jeezny after a long black black gap of it might have been a million years was a hospital, all white and with this von of hospitals you get, all like sour and smug and clean. These antiseptic veshches you get in hospitals should have a real horrorshow von of like frying onions or of flowers. I came very slow back to knowing who I was and I was all bound up in white and I could not feel anything in my plott, pain nor sensation nor any veshch at all. All round my gulliver was a bandage and there were bits of stuff like stuck to my litso, and my rookers were all in bandages and like bits of stick were like fixed to my fingers like on it might be flowers to make them grow straight, and my poor old nogas were all straightened out too, and it was all bandages and wire cages and into my right rooker, near the pletcho, was red red krovvy dripping from a jar upside down. But I could not feel anything, O my brothers. There was a nurse sitting by my bed and she was reading some book that was all like very dim print and you could viddy it was a story because of a lot of inverted commas, and she was like breathing hard uh uh uh over it, so it must have been a story about the old in-out in-out. She was a real horrorshow devotchka, this nurse, with a very red rot and like long lashes over her glazzies, and under her like very stiff uniform you could viddy she had very horrorshow groodies. So I said to her, 'What gives, O my little sister? Come thou and have a nice lay-down with your malenky droog in this bed.' But the slovos didn't come out horrorshow at all, it being as though my rot was all stiffened up, and I could feel with my yahzick that some of my zoobies were no longer there. But this nurse like jumped and dropped her book on the floor and said:

'Oh, you've recovered consciousness.'

That was like a big rotful for a malenky ptitsa like her, and I tried to say so, but the slovos came out only like er er er. She ittied off and left me on my oddy knocky, and I could viddy now that I was in a malenky room of my own, not in one of these long wards like I had been in as a very little malchick, full of coughing dying starry vecks all round to make you want to get well and fit again. It had been like diphtheria I had had then, O my brothers.

It was like now as though I could not hold to being conscious all that long, because I was like asleep again almost right away, very skorry, but in a minoota or two I was sure that this nurse ptitsa had come back and had brought chellovecks in white coats with her and they were viddying me very frowning and going hm hm hm at Your Humble Narrator. And with them I was sure there was the old charles from the Staja govoreeting, 'Oh my son, my son,' breathing a like very stale von of whisky on to me and then saying, 'But I would not stay, oh no. I could not in no wise subscribe to what those bratchnies are going to do to other poor prestoopnicks. So I got out and am preaching sermons now about it all, my little beloved son in J.C.'

I woke up again later on and who should I viddy there round the bed but the three from whose flat I had jumped out, namely D. B. da Silva and Something Something Rubinstein and Z. Dolin. 'Friend,' one of these vecks was saying, but I could not viddy or slooshy horrorshow which one, 'friend, little friend,' this goloss was saying, 'the people are on fire with indignation. You have killed those horrible boastful villains' chances of re-election. They will go and will go for ever and ever. You have served Liberty well.' I tried to say:

'If I had died it would have been even better for you political bratchnies, would it not, pretending and treacherous droogs as you are.' But all that came out was er er er. Then one of these three seemed to hold out a lot of bits cut from gazettas and what I could viddy was a horrible picture of me all krovvy on a stretcher being carried off and I seemed to like remember a kind of a popping of lights which must have been photographer vecks. Out of one glaz I could read like headlines which were sort of trembling in the rooker of the chelloveck that held them, like BOY

VICTIM OF CRIMINAL REFORM SCHEME and GOVERNMENT AS MURDERER and then there was like a picture of a veck that looked familiar to me and it said OUT OUT OUT, and that would be the Minister of the Inferior or Interior. Then the nurse ptitsa said:

'You shouldn't be exciting him like that. You shouldn't be doing anything that will make him upset. Now come on, let's have you out.' I tried to say:

'Out out out,' but it was er er er again. Anyway, these three political vecks went. And I went, too, only back to the land, back to all blackness lit up by like odd dreams which I didn't know whether they were dreams or not, O my brothers. Like for instance I had this idea of my whole plott or body being like emptied of as it might be dirty water and then filled up again with clean. And then there were really lovely and horrorshow dreams of being in some veck's auto that had been crasted by me and driving up and down the world all on my oddy knocky running lewdies down and hearing them creech they were dying, and in me no pain and no sickness. And also there were dreams of doing the old in-out in-out with devotchkas, forcing like them down on the ground and making them have it and everybody standing round clapping their rookers and cheering like bezoomny. And then I woke up again and it was my pee and em come to viddy their ill son, my em boohooing real horrorshow. I could govoreet a lot better now and could say:

'Well well well well well, what gives? What makes you think you are like welcome?' My papapa said, in a like ashamed way:

'You were in the papers, son. It said they had done great wrong to you. It said how the Government drove you to try and do yourself in. And it was our fault too, in a way,

186

son. Your home's your home, when all's said and done, son.' And my mum kept on going boohoohoo and looking ugly as kiss-my-sharries. So I said:

'And how beeth thy new son Joe? Well and healthy and prosperous, I trust and pray.' My mum said:

'Oh, Alex Alex. Owwwwwwwww.' My papapa said:

'A very awkward thing, son. He got into a bit of trouble with the police and was done by the police.'

'Really?' I said. 'Really? Such a good sort of chelloveck and all. Amazed proper I am, honest.'

'Minding his own business, he was,' said my pee. 'And the police told him to move on. Waiting at a corner he was, son, to see a girl he was going to meet. And they told him to move on and he said he had rights like everybody else, and then they sort of fell on top of him and hit him about cruel.'

'Terrible,' I said. 'Really terrible. And where is the poor boy now?'

'Owwwww,' boohooed my mum. 'Gone back owwww-wwme.'

'Yes,' said dad. 'He's gone back to his own home town to get better. They've had to give his job here to somebody else.'

'So now,' I said, 'you're willing for me to move back in again and things be like they were before.'

'Yes, son,' said my papapa. 'Please, son.'

'I'll consider it,' I said. 'I'll think about it real careful.'

'Owwwww,' went my mum.

'Ah, shut it,' I said, 'or I'll give you something proper to yowl and creech about. Kick your zoobies in I will.' And, O my brothers, saying that made me feel a malenky bit better, as if all like fresh red red krovvy was flowing all through my plott. That was something I had to think about. It was like as though to get better I had had to get worse.

'That's no way to speak to your mother, son,' said my papapa. 'After all, she brought you into the world.'

'Yes,' I said, 'and a right grahzny vonny world too.' I shut my glazzies tight in like pain and said, 'Go away now. I'll think about coming back. But things will have to be very different.'

'Yes, son,' said my pee. 'Anything you say.'

'You'll have to make up your mind,' I said, 'who's to be boss.'

'Owwwwww,' my mum went on.

'Very good, son,' said my papapa. 'Things will be as you like. Only get well.'

When they had gone I laid and thought a bit about different veshches, like all different pictures passing through my gulliver, and when the nurse ptitsa came back in and like straightened the sheets on the bed I said to her:

'How long is it I've been in here?'

'A week or so,' she said.

'And what have they been doing to me?'

'Well,' she said, 'you were all broken up and bruised and had sustained severe concussion and had lost a lot of blood. They've had to put all that right, haven't they?'

'But,' I said, 'has anyone been doing anything with my gulliver? What I mean is, have they been playing around with inside like my brain?'

'Whatever they've done,' she said, 'it'll all be for the best.'

But a couple of days later a couple of like doctor vecks came in, both youngish vecks with these very sladky smiles, and they had like a picture book with them. One of them said, 'We want you to have a look at these and to tell us what you think about them. All right?'

'What giveth, O little droogies?' I said. 'What new bezoomny idea dost thou in mind have?' So they both had a like embarrassed smeck at that and then they sat down either side of the bed and opened up this book. On the first page there was like a photograph of a bird-nest full of eggs.

'Yes?' one of these doctor vecks said.

'A bird-nest,' I said, 'full of like eggs. Very very nice.'

'And what would you like to do about it?' the other one said.

'Oh,' I said, 'smash them. Pick up the lot and like throw them against a wall or a cliff or something and then viddy them all smash up real horrorshow.'

'Good good,' they both said, and then the page was turned. It was like a picture of one of these bolshy great birds called peacocks with all its tail spread out in all colours in a very boastful way. 'Yes?' said one of these vecks.

'I would like,' I said, 'to pull out like all those feathers in its tail and slooshy it creech blue murder. For being so like boastful.'

'Good,' they both said, 'good good good.' And they went on turning the pages. There were like pictures of real horrorshow devotchkas, and I said I would like to give them the old in-out in-out with lots of ultra-violence. There were like pictures of chellovecks being given the boot straight in the litso and all red red krovvy everywhere and I said I would like to be in on that. And there was a picture of the old nagoy droog of the prison charlie's carrying his cross up a hill, and I said I would like to have the old hammer and nails. Good good good. I said:

'What is all this?'

'Deep hypnopaedia,' or some such slovo, said one of these two vecks. 'You seem to be cured.'

189

'Cured?' I said. 'Me tied down to this bed like this and you say cured? Kiss my sharries is what I say.'

'Wait,' the other said. 'It won't be long now.'

So I waited and, O my brothers, I got a lot better, munching away at eggiwegs and lomticks of toast and peeting bolshy great mugs of milky chai, and then one day they said I was going to have a very very very special visitor.

'Who?' I said, while they straightened the bed and combed my luscious glory for me, me having the bandage off now from my gulliver and the hair growing again.

'You'll see, you'll see,' they said. And I viddied all right. At two-thirty of the afternoon there were like all photographers and men from gazettas with notebooks and pencils and all that cal. And, brothers, they near trumpeted a bolshy fanfare for this great and important veck who was coming to viddy Your Humble Narrator. And in he came, and of course it was none other than the Minister of the Interior or Inferior, dressed in the heighth of fashion and with this very upper-class haw haw haw goloss. Flash flash bang went the cameras when he put out his rooker to me to shake it. I said:

'Well well well well well. What giveth then, old droogie?' Nobody seemed to quite pony that, but somebody said in a like harsh goloss:

'Be more respectful, boy, in addressing the Minister.'

'Yarbles,' I said, like snarling like a doggie. 'Bolshy great yarblockos to thee and thine.'

'All right, all right,' said the Interior Inferior one very skorry. 'He speaks to me as a friend, don't you, son?'

'I am everyone's friend,' I said. 'Except to my enemies.'

'And who are your enemies?' said the Minister, while all the gazetta vecks went scribble scribble scribble. 'Tell us that, my boy.'

'All who do me wrong,' I said, 'are my enemies.'

'Well,' said the Int Inf Min, sitting down by my bed. 'I and the Government of which I am a member want you to regard us as friends. Yes, friends. We have put you right, yes? You are getting the best of treatment. We never wished you harm, but there are some who did and do. And I think you know who those are.'

'All who do me wrong,' I said, 'are my enemies.'

'Yes yes yes,' he said. 'There are certain men who wanted to use you, yes, use you for political ends. They would have been glad, yes, glad for you to be dead, for they thought they could then blame it all on the Government. I think you know who those men are.'

'I did not,' I said, 'like the look of them.'

'There is a man,' said the Intinfmin, 'called F. Alexander, a writer of subversive literature, who has been howling for your blood. He has been mad with desire to stick a knife in you. But you're safe from him now. We put him away.'

'He was supposed to be like a droogie,' I said. 'Like a mother to me was what he was.'

'He found out that you had done wrong to him. At least,' said the Min very very skorry, 'he believed you had done wrong. He formed this idea in his mind that you had been responsible for the death of someone near and dear to him.'

'What you mean,' I said, 'is that he was told.'

'He had this idea,' said the Min. 'He was a menace. We put him away for his own protection. And also,' he said, 'for yours.'

'Kind,' I said. 'Most kind of thou.'

'When you leave here,' said the Min, 'you will have no worries. We shall see to everything. A good job on a good salary. Because you are helping us.'

'Am I?' I said.

'We always help our friends, don't we?' And then he took my rooker and some veck creeched, 'Smile!' and I smiled like bezoomny without thinking, and then flash flash crack flash bang there were pictures being taken of me and the Intinfmin all droogy together. 'Good boy,' said this great chelloveck. 'Good good boy. And now, see, a present.'

What was brought in now, brothers, was a big shiny box, and I viddied clear what sort of a veshch it was. It was a stereo. It was put down next to the bed and opened up and some veck plugged its lead into the wall-socket. 'What shall it be?' asked a veck with otchkies on his nose, and he had in his rookers lovely shiny sleeves full of music. 'Mozart? Beethoven? Schoenberg? Carl Orff?'

'The Ninth,' I said. 'The glorious Ninth.'

And the Ninth it was, O my brothers. Everybody began to leave nice and quiet while I laid there with my glazzies closed, slooshying the lovely music. The Min said, 'Good good boy,' patting me on the pletcho, then he ittied off. Only one veck was left, saying, 'Sign here, please.' I opened my glazzies up to sign, not knowing what I was signing and not, O my brothers, caring either. Then I was left alone with the glorious Ninth of Ludwig van.

Oh, it was gorgeosity and yumyumyum. When it came to the Scherzo I could viddy myself very clear running and running on like very light and mysterious nogas, carving the whole litso of the creeching world with my cut-throat britva. And there was the slow movement and the lovely last singing movement still to come. I was cured all right.

'WHAT's it going to be then, eh?'

There was me, Your Humble Narrator, and my three droogs, that is Len, Rick, and Bully, Bully being called Bully because of his bolshy big neck and very gromky goloss which was just like some bolshy great bull bellowing auuuuuuuuh. We were sitting in the Korova Milkbar making up our rassoodocks what to do with the evening, a flip dark chill winter bastard though dry. All round were chellovecks well away on milk plus vellocet and synthemesc and drencrom and other veshches which take you far far far away from this wicked and real world into the land to viddy Bog And All His Holy Angels And Saints in your left sabog with lights bursting and spurting all over your mozg. What we were peeting was the old moloko with knives in it, as we used to say, to sharpen you up and make you ready for a bit of dirty twenty-to-one, but I've told you all that before.

We were dressed in the heighth of fashion, which in those days was these very wide trousers and a very loose black shiny leather like jerkin over an open-necked shirt with a like scarf tucked in. At this time too it was the heighth of fashion to use the old britva on the gulliver, so that most of the gulliver was like bald and there was hair only on the sides. But it was always the same on the old nogas – real horrorshow bolshy big boots for kicking litsos in.

'What's it going to be then, eh?'

I was like the oldest of we four, and they all looked up to me as their leader, but I got the idea sometimes that Bully had the thought in his gulliver that he would like to take over, this being because of his bigness and the gromky goloss that bellowed out of him when he was on the warpath. But all the ideas came from Your Humble, O my brothers, and also there was this veshch that I had been famous and had had my picture and articles and all that cal in the gazettas. Also I had by far the best job of all we four, being in the National Gramodisc Archives on the music side with a real horrorshow carman full of pretty polly at the week's end and a lot of nice free discs for my own malenky self on the side.

This evening in the Korova there was a fair number of vecks and ptitsas and devotchkas and malchicks smecking and peeting away, and cutting through their govoreeting and the burbling of the in-the-landers with their 'Gorgor fallatuke and the worm sprays in filltip slaughterballs' and all that cal you could slooshy a popdisc on the stereo, this being Ned Achimota singing 'That Day, Yeah, That Day'. At the counter were three devotchkas dressed in the heighth of nadsat fashion, that is to say long uncombed hair dyed white and false groodies sticking out a metre or more and very very tight short skirts with all like frothy white underneath, and Bully kept saying, 'Hey, get in there we could, three of us. Old Len is not like interested. Leave old Len alone with his God.' And Len kept saying, 'Yarbles yarbles. Where is the spirit for all for one and one for all, eh boy?' Suddenly I felt both very very tired and also full of tingly energy, and I said:

'Out out out out out.'

'Where to?' said Rick, who had a litso like a frog's.

'Oh, just to viddy what's doing in the great outside,' I said. But somehow, my brothers, I felt very bored and a bit hopeless, and I had been feeling that a lot these days. So I turned to the chelloveck nearest me on the big plush seat that ran right round the whole mesto, a chelloveck, that is, who was burbling away under the influence, and I fisted him real skorry ack ack ack in the belly. But he felt it not, brothers, only burbling away with his 'Cart cart virtue, where in toptails lieth the poppoppicorns?' So we scatted out into the big winter nochy.

We walked down Marghanita Boulevard and there were no millicents patrolling that way, so when we met a starry veck coming away from a news-kiosk where he had been kupetting a gazetta I said to Bully, 'All right, Bully boy, thou canst if thou like wishest.' More and more these days I had been just giving the orders and standing back to viddy them being carried out. So Bully cracked into him er er er, and the other two tripped him and kicked at him, smecking away, while he was down and then let him crawl off to where he lived, like whimpering to himself. Bully said:

'How about a nice yummy glass of something to keep out the cold, O Alex?' For we were not too far from the Duke of New York. The other two nodded yes yes yes but all looked at me to viddy whether that was all right. I nodded too and so off we ittied. Inside the snug there were these starry ptitsas or sharps or baboochkas you will remember from the beginning and they all started on their, 'Evening, lads, God bless you, boys, best lads living, that's what you are,' waiting for us to say, 'What's it going to be, girls?' Bully rang the collocoll and a waiter came in rubbing his rookers on his grazzy apron. 'Cutter on the table, droogies,' said Bully, pulling out his own rattling and chinking mound of deng. 'Scotchmen for us and the same for the old baboochkas, eh?' And then I said:

'Ah, to hell. Let them buy their own.' I didn't know what it was, but these last days I had become like mean. There had come into my gulliver a like desire to keep all my pretty polly to myself, to like hoard it all up for some reason. Bully said:

'What gives, bratty? What's coming over old Alex?'

'Ah, to hell,' I said. 'I don't know. I don't know. What it is is I don't like just throwing away my hard-earned pretty polly, that's what it is.'

'Earned?' said Rick. 'Earned? It doesn't have to be earned, as well thou knowest, old droogie. Took, that's all, just took, like.' And he smecked real gromky and I viddied one or two of his zoobies weren't all that horrorshow.

'Ah,' I said, 'I've got some thinking to do.' But viddying these baboochkas looking all eager like for some free alc, I like shrugged my pletchoes and pulled out my own cutter from my trouser carman, notes and coin all mixed together, and plonked it tinkle crackle on the table.

'Scotchmen all round, right,' said the waiter. But for some reason I said:

'No, boy, for me make it one small beer, right.' Len said:

'This I do not much go for,' and he began to put his rooker on my gulliver like kidding I must have fever, but I like snarled doggy-wise for him to give over skorry. 'All right, all right, droog,' he said. 'As thou like sayest.' But Bully was having a smot with his rot open at something that had come out of my carman with the pretty polly I'd put on the table. He said:

'Well well well. And we never knew.'

'Give me that,' I snarled and grabbed it skorry. I couldn't explain how it had got there, brothers, but it was a photograph I had scissored out of the old gazetta and it was of a baby. It was of a baby gurgling goo goo goo with all like moloko dribbling from its rot and looking up and like smecking at everybody, and it was all nagoy and its flesh was like in all folds with being a very fat baby. There was then like a bit of haw haw haw struggling to get hold of this bit of paper from me, so I had to snarl again at them and I grabbed the photo and tore it up into tiny teeny pieces and let it fall like a bit of snow on to the floor. The whisky came in then and the starry baboochkas said, 'Good health, lads, God bless you, boys, the best lads living, that's what you are,' and all that cal. And one of them who was all lines and wrinkles and no zoobies in her shrunken old rot said, 'Don't tear up money, son. If you don't need it give it them as does,' which was very bold and forward of her. But Rick said:

'Money that was not, O baboochka. It was a picture of a dear little itsy witsy bitsy bit of a baby.' I said:

'I'm getting just that bit tired, that I am. It's you who's the babies, you lot. Scoffing and grinning and all you can do is smeck and give people bolshy cowardly tolchocks when they can't give them back.' Bully said:

'Well now, we always thought it was you who was the king of that and also the teacher. Not well, that's the trouble with thou, old droogie.'

I viddied this sloppy glass of beer I had on the table in front of me and felt like all vomity within, so I went 'Aaaaah' and poured all the frothy vonny cal all over the floor. One of the starry ptitsas said:

'Waste not want not.' I said:

'Look, droogies. Listen. Tonight I am somehow just not in the mood. I know not why or how it is, but there it is. You three go your own ways this nightwise, leaving me out. Tomorrow we shall meet same place same time, me hoping to be like a lot better.'

'Oh,' said Bully, 'right sorry I am.' But you could viddy a like gleam in his glazzies, because now he would be taking over for this nochy. Power, power, everybody like wants power. 'We can postpone till tomorrow,' said Bully, 'what we in mind had. Namely, that bit of shop-crasting in Gagarin Street. Flip horrorshow takings there, droog, for the having.'

'No,' I said. 'You postpone nothing. You just carry on in your own like style. Now,' I said, 'I itty off.' And I got up from my chair.

'Where to, then?' asked Rick.

'That know I not,' I said. 'Just to be on like my own and sort things out.' You could viddy the old baboochkas were real puzzled at me going out like that and like all morose and not the bright and smecking malchickiwick you will remember. But I said, 'Ah, to hell, to hell,' and scatted out all on my oddy knocky into the street.

It was dark and there was a wind sharp as a nozh getting up, and there were very very few lewdies about. There were these patrol cars with brutal rozzes inside them like cruising about, and now and then on the corner you could viddy a couple of very young millicents stamping against the bitchy cold and letting out steam breath on the winter air, O my brothers. I suppose really a lot of the old ultra-violence and crasting was dying out now, the rozzes being so brutal with who they caught, though it had become like a fight between naughty nadsats and the rozzes who could be more skorry with the nozh and britva and the stick and even the gun. But what was the matter with me these days was that I didn't care much. It was like something soft getting into me and I could not pony why. What I wanted these days I did not know. Even the music I liked to slooshy in my own malenky den was what I would have smecked at before, brothers. I was slooshying more like malenky romantic songs, what they call *Lieder*, just a goloss and a piano, very quiet and like yearny, different from when it had been all bolshy orchestras and me lying on the bed between the violins and the trombones and kettledrums. There was something happening inside me, and I wondered if it was like some disease or if it was what they had done to me that time upsetting my gulliver and perhaps going to make me real bezoomny.

So thinking like this with my gulliver bent and my rookers stuck in my trouser carmans I walked the town, brothers, and at last I began to feel very tired and also in great need of a nice bolshy chasha of milky chai. Thinking about this chai, I got a sudden like picture of me sitting before a bolshy fire in an armchair peeting away at this chai, and what was funny and very very strange was that I seemed to have turned into a very starry chelloveck, about seventy years old, because I could viddy my own voloss, which was very grey, and I also had whiskers, and these were very grey too. I could viddy myself as an old man, sitting by a fire, and then the like picture vanished. But it was very like strange.

I came to one of these tea-and-coffee mestos, brothers, and I could viddy through the long long window that it was full of very dull lewdies, like ordinary, who had these very patient and expressionless litsos and would do no harm to no one, all sitting there and govoreeting like quietly and peeting away at their nice harmless chai and coffee. I ittied inside and went up to the counter and bought me a nice hot chai with plenty of moloko, then I ittied to one of these tables and sat down to peet it. There was like a young couple at this table, peeting and smoking filter-tip cancers, and govoreeting and smecking very quietly between themselves, but I took no notice of them and just went on peeting away and like dreaming and wondering what it was in me that was like changing and what was going to happen to me. But I viddied that the devotchka at this table who was with this chelloveck was real horrorshow, not the sort you would want to like throw down and give the old in-out in-out to, but with a horror-show plott and litso and a smiling rot and very very fair voloss and all that cal. And then the veck with her, who had a hat on his gulliver and had his litso like turned away from me, swivelled round to viddy the bolshy big clock they had on the wall in this mesto, and then I viddied who he was and then he viddied who I was. It was Pete, one of my three droogs from those days when it was Georgie and Dim and him and me. It was Pete like looking a lot older though he could not now be more than nine-teen and a bit, and he had a bit of a moustache and an ordinary day-suit and this hat on. I said:

'Well well well, droogie, what gives? Very very long time no viddy.' He said:

'It's little Alex, isn't it?'

'None other,' I said. 'A long long long time since those dead and gone good days. And now poor Georgie, they told me, is underground and old Dim is a brutal millicent, and here is thou and here is I, and what news hast thou, old droogie?'

'He talks funny, doesn't he?' said this devotchka, like giggling.

'This,' said Pete to the devotchka, 'is an old friend. His name is Alex. May I,' he said to me, 'introduce my wife?'

My rot fell wide open then. 'Wife?' I like gaped. 'Wife wife wife? Ah no, that cannot be. Too young art thou to be married, old droog. Impossible impossible.'

This devotchka who was like Pete's wife (impossible impossible) giggled again and said to Pete, 'Did you used to talk like that too?'

'Well,' said Pete, and he like smiled. 'I'm nearly twenty. Old enough to be hitched, and it's been two months already. You were very young and very forward, remember.'

'Well,' I like gaped still. 'Over this get can I not, old droogie. Pete married. Well well well.'

'We have a small flat,' said Pete. 'I am earning very small money at State Marine Insurance, but things will get better, that I know. And Georgina here –'

'What again is that name?' I said, rot still open like bezoomny. Pete's wife (wife, brothers) like giggled again.

'Georgina,' said Pete. 'Georgina works too. Typing, you know. We manage, we manage.' I could not, brothers, take my glazzies off him, really. He was like grown up now, with a grown-up goloss and all. 'You must,' said Pete, 'come and see us sometime. You still,' he said, 'look very young, despite all your terrible experiences. Yes yes yes, we've read all about them. But, of course, you *are* very young still.'

'Eighteen,' I said, 'just gone.'

'Eighteen, eh?' said Pete. 'As old as that. Well well well. Now,' he said, 'we have to be going.' And he like gave this Georgina of his a like loving look and pressed one of her rookers between his and she gave him one of those looks back, O my brothers. 'Yes,' said Pete, turning back to me, 'we're off to a little party at Greg's.'

'Greg?' I said.

'Oh, of course,' said Pete, 'you wouldn't know Greg, would you? Greg is after your time. While you were away Greg came into the picture. He runs little parties, you know. Mostly wine-cup and word-games. But very nice, very pleasant, you know. Harmless, if you see what I mean.'

'Yes,' I said. 'Harmless. Yes yes, I viddy that real horror-show.' And this Georgina devotchka giggled again at my slovos. And then these two ittied off to their vonny word-games at this Greg's, whoever he was. I was left all on my oddy knocky with my milky chai, which was getting cold now, like thinking and wondering.

Perhaps that was it, I kept thinking. Perhaps I was getting too old for the sort of jeezny I had been leading, brothers. I was eighteen now, just gone. Eighteen was not a young age. At eighteen old Wolfgang Amadeus had written concertos and symphonies and operas and oratorios and all that cal, no, not cal, heavenly music. And then there was old Felix M. with his *Midsummer Night's Dream* Overture. And there were others. And there was this like French poet set by old Benjy Britt, who had done all his best poetry by the age of fifteen, O my brothers. Arthur, his first name. Eighteen was not all that young an age, then. But what was I going to do?

Walking the dark chill bastards of winter streets after ittying off from this chai and coffee mesto, I kept viddying like visions, like these cartoons in the gazettas. There was Your Humble Narrator Alex coming home from work to a good hot plate of dinner, and there was this ptitsa all welcoming and greeting like loving. But I could not viddy her all that horrorshow, brothers, I could not think who it might be. But I had this sudden very strong idea that if I walked into the room next to this room where the fire was burning away and my hot dinner laid on the table, there I should find what I really wanted, and now it all tied up, that picture scissored out of the gazetta and meeting old Pete like that. For in that other room in a cot was laying gurgling goo goo goo my son. Yes yes yes, brothers, my son. And now I felt this bolshy big hollow inside my plott, feeling very surprised too at myself. I knew what was happening, O my brothers. I was like growing up.

Yes yes yes, there it was. Youth must go, ah yes. But youth is only being in a way like it might be an animal. No, it is not just like being an animal so much as being like one of these malenky toys you viddy being sold in the streets, like little chellovecks made out of tin and with a spring inside and then a winding handle on the outside and you wind it up grrr grrr grrr and off it itties, like walking, O my brothers. But it itties in a straight line and bangs straight into things bang bang and it cannot help what it is doing. Being young is like being like one of these malenky machines.

My son, my son. When I had my son I would explain all that to him when he was starry enough to like understand. But then I knew he would not understand or would not want to understand at all and would do all the veshches I had done, yes perhaps even killing some poor starry forella surrounded with mewing kots and koshkas, and I would not be able to really stop him. And nor would he be able to stop his own son, brothers. And so it would itty on to like the end of the world, round and round and round, like some bolshy gigantic like chelloveck, like old Bog Himself (by courtesy of Korova Milkbar) turning and turning and turning a vonny grahzny orange in his gigantic rookers.

But first of all, brothers, there was this veshch of finding some devotchka or other who would be a mother to this son. I would have to start on that tomorrow, I kept thinking. That was something like new to do. That was something I would have to get started on, a new like chapter beginning.

That's what it's going to be then, brothers, as I come to the like end of this tale. You have been everywhere with your little droog Alex, suffering with him, and you have viddied some of the most grahzny bratchnies old Bog ever made, all on to your old droog Alex. And all it was was that I was young. But now as I end this story, brothers, I am not young, not no longer, oh no. Alex like groweth up, oh yes.

But where I itty now, O my brothers, is all on my oddy knocky, where you cannot go. Tomorrow is all like sweet flowers and the turning vonny earth and the stars and the old Luna up there and your old droog Alex all on his oddy knocky seeking like a mate. And all that cal. A terrible grahzny vonny world, really, O my brothers. And so farewell from your little droog. And to all others in this story profound shooms of lip-music, brrrrrr. And they can kiss my sharries. But you, O my brothers, remember sometimes thy little Alex that was. Amen. And all that cal.

Etchingham, Sussex
August 1961

NOTES

7   **a bit of dirty twenty-to-one**: 'Twenty-to-one' is rhyming slang for 'fun'.

8   **the heighth of fashion**: *The Oxford English Dictionary* (*OED*) notes that 'heighth' was a common spelling in the seventeenth century. It is found in English dialect writing as late as the nineteenth century. The Penguin paperback of 1972 misprints this as 'the height of fashion' (p. 5), but Burgess was clearly aiming for an archaic-sounding effect. He achieves something similar in his historical novel about the life of Shakespeare, *Nothing Like the Sun* (1964), which is written in a parody of Shakespearean English.

10   **Berti Laski**: Melvyn Lasky was, along with Frank Kermode and the poet Stephen Spender, co-editor of the literary magazine *Encounter*. But this is more likely to be an allusion to Marghanita Laski (1915–88), the Manchester novelist and playwright. She provided more than 250,000 quotations for the four supplements to the *Oxford English Dictionary*. Her novels included *Love on the Supertax* (1944) and *Little Boy Lost* (1949), which was adapted as a musical starring Bing Crosby in 1953. Marghanita Laski had written an unfavourable review of Burgess's novel *The Right to an Answer*, published in the *Saturday Review* on 28 January 1961.

11   **Marghanita Boulevard**: Another unflattering reference to Marghanita Laski. See note on 'Berti Laski' above.

11   **Boothby Avenue**: Possibly a reference to Sir Brooke Boothby

(1744–1824), a minor English poet and translator of Rousseau. Another Boothby appears as a character in Burgess's first novel, *Time for a Tiger* (1956). He is the headmaster of the Mansoor School in colonial Malaya, modelled on the Malay College in Kuala Kangsar, where Burgess himself had taught from 1954 until 1955. Boothby is a cruel caricature of Jimmy Howell, the real-life headmaster known to Burgess and disliked by him.

13 **hen-korm:** originally 'hen-corm' in the typescript. In a letter to James Michie of Heinemann dated 25 February 1962, Burgess wrote: 'There is also the case of "hen-corm" [...] which was silently corrected to "hen-corn". Now "corm" comes from a Slav-root meaning animal-fodder. So that the reader shall not see a mistake there I've changed "corm" to "korm". Will that be horrorshow?'

14 **sammy act:** Late nineteenth-century slang; to 'sam' or 'stand sam' is to pay for a drink. See Jonathon Green, *Cassell's Dictionary of Slang* (2000).

14 **Amis Avenue:** Kingsley Amis, English novelist and critic (1922–95). Burgess and Amis often reviewed each other's novels, and Amis's review of *A Clockwork Orange* ('Mr Burgess has written a fine farrago of outrageousness') appeared in the *Observer*. For Amis on Burgess, see the chapter in his *Memoirs* (Hutchinson, 1991), pp. 274–8, and various uncomplimentary references in *The Letters of Kingsley Amis*, edited by Zachary Leader (HarperCollins, 2000).

14 **black and suds:** Guinness.

14 **double firegolds:** Firegold is whisky, but this is also an allusion to 'The Starlight Night', a poem by Gerard Manley Hopkins (1844–89): 'O look at all the fire-folk sitting in the air! [. . .] The grey lawns cold where gold, where quickgold lies!' Burgess had memorised all of Hopkins's poems when he was a schoolboy, and he later set a number of them to music, including 'The Wreck of the Deutschland'. For more detail on these compositions, see Paul Phillips, *A Clockwork Counterpoint* (Manchester University Press, 2010), pp. 288–9.

15 **a bottle of Yank General**: Three-star brandy or cognac. Burgess drew three stars in the margin of the typescript at this point, to make the reference to a three-star American general clear.

15 **Attlee Avenue**: Clement Attlee, Labour Prime Minister from 1945 until 1951. Burgess voted Labour in 1945, and he admired the National Health Service, which was set up by Attlee's government.

15 **rozz patrols**: 'Rozzer' as slang for 'policeman' was first recorded in the 1870s. Eric Partridge's *Dictionary of Slang and Unconventional English* (1937), one of several slang dictionaries owned by Burgess, suggests that 'rozzer' is derived from the Romany 'roozlo', meaning 'strong'.

15 **Elvis Presley**: Burgess wrote in the margin of the typescript: 'Will this name be known when book appears?' Burgess must have found Elvis Presley difficult to avoid while he was working on *A Clockwork Orange*. According to the trade magazine *Record Retailer*, Presley's single 'It's Now or Never' was number one in the UK chart for eight weeks in 1960. 'Wooden Heart' and 'Surrender', both released in 1961, held the number one position for six weeks and four weeks respectively. Elvis and The Beatles (who received a kicking in Burgess's 1968 novel, *Enderby Outside*) represented everything that he hated about popular music and teenage culture.

17 **sore athirst**: A corruption of the biblical 'and they were sore afraid' (Luke 2:9).

18 **lip-music**: A quotation from *St Winefred's Well*, an unfinished play by Gerard Manley Hopkins: 'While blind men's eyes shall thirst after daylight, draughts of daylight, / Or deaf ears shall desire that lipmusic that's lost upon them.' Burgess later completed this Hopkins play and composed incidental music for a radio production, broadcast on BBC Radio 3 on 23 December 1989.

24 **Priestley Place**: J. B. Priestley, English writer and broadcaster (1894–1984), author of *The Good Companions* (1929), *Time and the Conways* (1937) and *An Inspector Calls* (1945), among many other novels, plays and non-fiction works. Burgess discusses

Priestley's writing in *The Novel Now* (Faber, 1971), pp. 102–3, and in a long review of Vincent Brome's biography, published in the *Times Literary Supplement* on 21 October 1988.

28 **swordpen**: The association between words and swords is present throughout Burgess's verse translation of Edmond Rostand's French play *Cyrano de Bergerac* (1971). Burgess's long poem 'The Sword', about a man who wanders around New York with 'a British sword sheathed in cherrywood', was published in *Transatlantic Review* 23 (Winter 1966–7), pp. 41–3, and reprinted in Burgess, *Revolutionary Sonnets and Other Poems*, edited by Kevin Jackson (Carcanet, 2002), pp. 32–3.

32 **shagged and fagged and fashed**: A quotation from 'The Leaden Echo and the Golden Echo', a dramatic poem by Gerard Manley Hopkins: 'O why are we so haggard at the heart, so care-coiled, care-killed, so fagged, so fashed, so cogged, so cumbered.' In a letter to his mother, dated 5 March 1872, Hopkins wrote: 'I enclose three northcountry primroses [. . .] They will no doubt look fagged.'

34 **a hound-and-horny look of evil**: *Hound and Horn* was an avant-garde literary magazine, founded in 1927 and possibly known to Burgess. Its contributors included Eugene O'Neill and Herbert Read. But the primary meaning here is 'corny' (rhyming slang).

37 **Wilsonsway**: A reference either to Burgess's real name, John Burgess Wilson, or to the English writer Angus Wilson (1913–91), whose dystopian novel *The Old Men at the Zoo* was reviewed by Burgess in the *Yorkshire Post* in 1961.

48 **Taylor Place**: The historian A. J. P. Taylor (1906–90) taught Burgess and his first wife, Llewela Jones, at Manchester University in the 1930s. According to Taylor's biographer Adam Sisman, Dylan Thomas (who later had an affair with Llewela during the Second World War) seduced Taylor's first wife. Alternatively, this may be a reference to the novelist Elizabeth Taylor (1912–75), whose books were said by Burgess to be underestimated by critics. See *The Novel Now*, p. 214.

49   **Ludwig van**: Ludwig van Beethoven (1770–1827). Burgess's 1974
      novel *Napoleon Symphony* takes its structure from Beethoven's
      Eroica symphony. Each episode within the novel corresponds
      to a passage of music in the score. Beethoven himself appears
      as one of the characters in Burgess's novel *Mozart and the Wolf
      Gang* (1991), and in 'Uncle Ludwig', an unproduced Burgess
      film script about Beethoven's uneasy relationship with his
      nephew. See also *The Ninth*, a talk about Beethoven broadcast
      on BBC Radio 3 on 14 December 1990.

49   **Heaven Seventeen**: Originally from Sheffield, the English band
      Heaven 17 (formed 1980; disbanded 1989) named themselves
      after one of Burgess's fictional pop groups. Two of their members,
      Ian Craig Marsh and Martyn Ware, had previously been part
      of The Human League. Their hits included 'Temptation' and
      '(We Don't Need This) Fascist Groove Thang'.

49   **fuzzy warbles**: Andy Partridge, the main songwriter from the
      band XTC, released a series of albums between 2002 and 2006
      under the general title *Fuzzy Warbles*.

52   **Joy being a glorious spark like of heaven**: A half-quotation
      from Schiller's 'Ode to Joy', which provides the text for the
      final choral movement of Beethoven's Ninth Symphony. The
      nineteenth-century English translation known to Burgess is:
      'Joy, thou glorious spark of heaven, / Daughter of Elysium, /
      Hearts on fire, aroused, enraptured, / To thy sacred shrine we
      come. / Custom's bond no more can sever / Those by thy sure
      magic tied. / All mankind are loving brothers / Where thy sacred
      wings abide.'

59   **One can die but once**: A deliberate misquotation from
      Shakespeare's *Julius Caesar*: 'Cowards die many times before
      their deaths / The valiant never taste of death but once' (Act
      II, Scene 2).

61   **Victoria Flatblock**: Possibly a reference to Victoria Park, the
      location of Xaverian College in Manchester, where Burgess
      studied between 1928 and 1935.

68   **long hair and [. . .] big flowy cravat**: Note that Alex's

appearance, described in the opening chapter, resembles the bust of Beethoven. This identification between Alex and Beethoven reinforces Burgess's claim (in his 1985 interview with Isaac Bashevis Singer) that Alex will go on to become a great composer after the novel has ended.

70 **darkmans**: 'The night', an example of thieves' slang, first recorded in the 1560s (*OED*). 'Lightmans' is the day. For Burgess on the language of the Elizabethan underworld, see his essay 'What Shakespeare Smelt' in *Homage to Qwert Yuiop* (Hutchinson, 1986), pp. 264–6.

78 **merzky gets**: 'filthy bastards' (*Cassell's Dictionary of Slang*).

80 **Boy, thou uproarious shark of heaven**: A parody of Schiller's 'Ode to Joy'. See note on p.52 above.

81 **very cold glazzy**: An allusion to the poem 'Under Ben Bulben' by W. B. Yeats: 'Cast a cold eye / On life, on death. / Horseman, pass by!' We know that Burgess was reading Yeats in the same year that he wrote *A Clockwork Orange*. His hardback copy of Yeats's *Collected Poems* is inscribed 'jbw [John Burgess Wilson] 1961'.

87 **prison charlie**: Prison chaplain, a reference to the actor and film director Charlie Chaplin. According to *Little Wilson and Big God* (1987), the first volume of Burgess's autobiography, his father had played piano for the brothers Sid and Charlie Chaplin when he was employed by Fred Karno's theatre company before the First World War. 'Charlie' is also a slang expression for an idiot or a charlatan.

92 **Ludovico's Technique**: A double reference to Lodovico, the Italian villain of John Webster's revenge tragedy *The White Devil* (1612), and to Ludwig van (see note to p.49, above).

93 ***Wachet Auf* Choral Prelude**: J. S. Bach, Cantata number 140, 'Wachet auf, ruft uns die Stimme' (1731).

93 **poggy**: Late nineteenth-century British Army slang. Partridge's *Dictionary of Slang* defines 'poggy' as 'rum, or any spiritous liquor'.

93 **archibalds**: First World War slang for aeroplanes or anti-aircraft guns (Partridge's *Dictionary of Slang*).

101 **crime in the midst of punishment**: An allusion to Fyodor Dostoevsky's novel *Crime and Punishment*, which Burgess read for the first time before travelling to Russia in 1961. In a letter to Diana and Meir Gillon, written while he was working on *A Clockwork Orange*, Burgess said: 'I've just completed Part One – which is just sheer crime. Now comes punishment. The whole thing's making me feel rather sick.'

125 **Each man kills the thing he loves**: Dr Branom is quoting from *The Ballad of Reading Gaol* (1897) by Oscar Wilde, who was convicted of sodomy in 1895 and imprisoned for two years with hard labour. Burgess later corresponded about Wilde with Richard Ellmann, whose biography *Oscar Wilde* was published in 1987.

125 **the dialect of the tribe**: A quotation from the second section of *Little Gidding* (1942) by T. S. Eliot: 'Since our concern was speech, and speech impelled us / To purify the dialect of the tribe' (Eliot, *Collected Poems 1909–1962*, Faber, p. 218). Eliot is quoting 'Le Tombeau d'Edgar Poe' by the nineteenth-century French poet Stéphane Mallarmé: 'Donner un sens plus pur aux mots de la tribu.' Eliot's poem is concerned with what the critic David Moody calls 'the fruitful dead'. See Moody, *Thomas Stearns Eliot: Poet*, second edition (Cambridge University Press, 1994), pp. 239, 253.

138 **Perfect Love Casteth Out Fear**: A quotation from the King James Bible: 'There is no fear in love; but perfect love casteth out fear: because fear hath torment. He that feareth is not made perfect in love' (1 John, 4:18).

140 **Joy before the Angels of God**: Another biblical quotation: 'So I say to you, there shall be joy before the angels of God upon one sinner doing penance' (Luke 15:10).

151 **Mozart Number Forty**: Burgess later wrote a short story based on Mozart's Symphony Number 40 (K.550, 1788) and included it in the text of *Mozart and the Wolf Gang* (1991), pp. 81–91.

153 **Dear dead idlewilds, rot not in variform guises**: A parody of Gerard Manley Hopkins.

157 **You could snuff it on a hundred aspirin**: Although an overdose of aspirin can cause liver failure and internal bleeding, it would take more than 250 tablets to achieve these effects in an adult male such as Alex. Burgess appears to have miscalculated here.

174 **Where I see the infamy I seek to erase it**: A quotation from Voltaire's letter to d'Alembert, 28 November 1762: 'Quoi que vous fassiez, écrazez l'infâme.'

175 **Rubinstein**: Harold Rubinstein was the libel lawyer at William Heinemann, Burgess's UK publisher. He had dealt with complaints about libel arising from two of Burgess's previous novels, *The Enemy in the Blanket* (1958) and *The Worm and the Ring* (1961).

176 **that manner of voice pricks me**: *OED* defines the verb 'prick' as 'To cause sharp mental pain; to sting with sorrow or remorse; to grieve, pain, vex'.

176 **We must inflame all hearts**: A reference to St Francis Xavier, who gave his name to Xaverian College, where Burgess was educated. In Catholic art, the flaming heart is one of the symbols associated with St Francis.

178 **Rest, perturbed spirit**: A quotation from Shakespeare's *Hamlet* (Act I, Scene 5). Hamlet says to his father's ghost: 'Rest, rest, perturbed spirit.'

192 **I was cured all right**: Immediately after this sentence, there is a note on the typescript in Burgess's handwriting: 'Should we end here? An optional "epilogue" follows.' Eric Swenson, the publisher at W. W. Norton who was responsible for the 1963 American edition, encouraged Burgess to end the novel at this point, omitting the twenty-first chapter.

202 **Felix M.**: The composer Felix Mendelssohn (1809–47) wrote his overture to Shakespeare's *A Midsummer Night's Dream* in 1827.

202 **French poet set by old Benjy Britt**: Benjamin Britten (1913–76) composed his song cycle (opus 18) based on *Les Illuminations* by Arthur Rimbaud in 1939. Burgess had a high regard for Montagu Slater's libretto for Britten's opera *Peter Grimes*. He described it as 'the only libretto I know that can be read in its own right as a dramatic poem'.

NADSAT GLOSSARY

appy polly loggies: apologies

baboochka: old woman
bezoomny: crazy
biblio: library
bitva: battle
bog: God
bolnoy: sick
bolshy: big
bratchny: bastard
bratty, brat: brother
britva: razor
brooko: stomach
to brosat: to throw
bugatty: rich

cal: shit
cancer: cigarette
cantora: office
carman: pocket
chasha: cup
chasso: guard

cheena: woman
to cheest: to wash
chelloveck: man, human being
chepooka: nonsense
choodessny: wonderful
cluve: beak
collocoll: bell
to crast: to steal
to creech: to scream
cutter: money

darkmans: night
deng: money
devotchka: girl
dobby: good
domy: house
dorogoy: valuable, dear
to drats: to fight
droog, droogie: friend

eegra: game
eemya: name

eggiweg: egg

to filly: to play
flip: very or great
forella: trout, woman

glaz, glazzy: eye, nipple
gloopy: stupid
golly: coin
goloss: voice
goober: lip
to gooly: to go
gorlo: throat
to govoreet: to talk, speak
grahzny: dirty
grazzy: dirty
gromky: loud
groody: breast
guff: laugh
gulliver: head

hen-korm: pocket change
horrorshow: good, well

interessovatted: interested
to itty: to go

jammiwam: jam, jelly
jeezny: life

kartoffel: potato
keeshkas: guts

kleb: bread
klootch: key
knopka: button
kopat: understand
koshka: cat
krovvy: blood
to kupet: to buy

lewdies: people
lighter: old woman
litso: face
lomtick: piece
to lovet: to catch
to lubbilub: to kiss

malchick: boy
malenky: little
maslo: butter
merzky: filthy
messel: idea
mesto: place
millicent: policeman
minoota: minute
molodoy: young
moloko: milk
moodge: man, husband
morder: snout
mounch: food
mozg: brain

nachinat: to begin
nadmenny: arrogant
nadsat: teen

216

nagoy: naked
nazz: name
neezhnies: panties
nochy: night
noga: foot, leg
nozh: knife

oddy knocky: alone
okno: window
oobivat: to kill
to ookadeet: to leave
ooko: ear
oomny: intelligent
oozhassny: dreadful
oozy: chain
to osoosh: to wipe
otchkies: glasses

to peet: to drink
pishcha: food
to platch: to cry
platties: clothes
plennies: prisoners
plesk: splash
pletcho: shoulder
plott: body
pol: sex
polezny: useful
to pony: to understand
poogly: frightened
pooshka: pistol
prestoopnick: criminal
pretty polly: money

to prod: to produce
ptitsa: woman
pyahnitsa: drunk

to rabbit: to work
radosty: joy
rassoodock: mind
raz: time
razdraz: angry
raskazz: story
to razrez: to tear
rooker: hand or arm
rot: mouth
rozz: policeman

sabog: shoe
sakar: sugar
sarky: sarcastic
scoteena: beast
shaika: gang
sharp: woman
sharries: buttocks, arse
shest: barrier
shilarny: interest
shive: slice
shiyah: neck
shlaga: club, cudgel
shlapa: hat
shlem: helmet
shoom: noise
shoomny: noisy
shoot: fool

sinny: cinema
to skazat: to say
skolliwoll: school
skorry: fast
to skvat: to snatch
sladky: sweet
to sloochat: to happen
to slooshy: to hear
slovo: word
to smeck: laugh
to smot: to look
sneety: dream
snoutie: tobacco
to sobirat: to pick up
soomka: bag, unattractive woman
to spat with: to have sex with
spatchka: sleep
spoogy: terrified
starry: old
strack: horror

tally: waist
tashtook: handkerchief
tass: cup
to tolchock: to hit
toofles: slippers
twenty-to-one: fun, i.e. gang violence

vareet: to cook up
vaysay: WC, bathroom

veck: man, guy
veshch: thing
to viddy: to see
voloss: hair
von: smell
to vred: to injure

yahma: mouth or hole
yahzick: tongue
yarbles: testicles, bollocks
to yeckate: to drive

zammechat: remarkable
zasnoot: sleep
zheena: wife
zooby: tooth
zubrick: penis
zvook: ring, sound
zvonock: bell

PROLOGUE to *A Clockwork Orange: A Play with Music*
Anthony Burgess, 1986

This prologue was written in July 1986 for Burgess's musical stage version of A Clockwork Orange, *published by Hutchinson the following year. The prologue is missing from all published editions of the play. Marty is the seventeen-year-old girl who becomes Alex's partner in the final scene of the stage version.*

The scene is the Garden of Eden. Alex is Adam, his eventual girlfriend Marty is Eve. This, of course, is a dream that Alex is dreaming. Early morning, delicate greenish light, a tumult of bird-song. Alex and Marty wake in each other's arms. Alex yawns cavernously, then smacks his lips.

ALEX: Zavtrak.
MARTY: What's zavtrak?
ALEX: It's a word that just came. Like all words. It means the first thing you eat when you stop spatting.
MARTY: Spatting?
ALEX: This.

(*He does an exaggerated and brutal mime of sleep.*)

MARTY: What you mean is breakfast.

ALEX: Zavtrak tastes better. Or will when I've had it.

MARTY (*rising*): I'll pick you some fruit.

ALEX: Always fruit. We might as well be wasps. You can't do a hard day's lazing about on fruit.

A VOICE: Beware of the yellow apple.

ALEX: He's up early. He's not usually round till the what-youcallit.

MARTY: The cool of the evening.

(*God appears. He has a strong look of the prison chaplain of a later scene. He is in spotless white and long-bearded. He sits on a tree stump.*)

ALEX: Bog.

GOD: What's that?

ALEX: Bog. You said I'd got to give names to everything. Ptitsa – the thing that flies. Devotchka – her. Yarblocko – the hard round thing that grows on trees and that I'm fed up of eating. Bog – you.

GOD: Beware of the yellow yarblocko.

ALEX: Now I pony. You never skaz about why beware. Why?

GOD: You must not know too much.

ALEX: Why not?

GOD: Because there's limits.

MARTY: *Are* limits.

GOD: I stand corrected.

MARTY: Sit, you mean. (*She goes off with her basket.*)

GOD: Sometimes it repents me that I made the – what's the word?

ALEX: Devotchka. Cheena. Moozh. Look, Bog – what veshch is this about knowing too much?

GOD: Free will has to have limits. Your will must not be as free as mine. You see that?

220

ALEX: I viddy real horrorshow. After all, you're like in charge.

GOD: We've just had trouble in heaven. One I trusted – the one I placed in charge of the light – made up his mind that he was as free as I am. Free as I am meant being me. You see that?

ALEX: I viddy.

GOD: He had to go. That means that I'm responsible for a moral duality. He versus me. He calls me evil, he calls himself good. The truth, of course, is the other way round.

ALEX: These two slovos I do not pony.

GOD: If by that you mean understand –

ALEX: I'm in charge of the slovos. That was made very clear. What thing he calls by name, that is its name. Eemya. Naz.

GOD: Do not seek to pony. That would mean disaster.

ALEX: Eat that yellow yarblocko and we'd pony those two slovos.

GOD: Good and evil.

ALEX: It's me that's supposed to be in charge of the slovos.

GOD: Not those two.

ALEX: And yet it's there to eat. Reach up my rooker, pull it down, munch munch. Too easy, isn't it?

GOD: It's a way of testing your capacity for obedience. You're free to obey and free to disobey. That's free will. That's choice.

ALEX: It's not enough.

GOD: I beg your pardon?

ALEX: I like the sound of that holy angel or saint or whatever he was. He took a chance.

GOD: The chance consequent on his disobedience. He's created an alternative world.

ALEX: Why didn't you stop him?

GOD: That's not in the rules.

ALEX: Bog's rules.

GOD: Once rules are made, they're not to be changed. I detest the arbitrary.

ALEX: Those bolshy big slovos I pony not. I'd like to viddy this bolshy disobedient chelloveck.

GOD (*shuddering*): You'll meet him.

ALEX: What does it mean – that slovo – *good*, was it?

GOD: It means accepting the divine order. My order.

ALEX: And the other one?

GOD: Disorder. Disruption. The irrational bestowal of pain. The dissolution of creation into chaos.

ALEX: And you couldn't stop it?

GOD: I abide by my own rules. I gave my creation free will. I gave it the power of choice.

ALEX: The choice between those two things.

GOD: I didn't say that.

ALEX: I did. Words are for thinking with. I'm in charge of words. Slovos. *You* said so.

GOD: Eat that forbidden fruit and the birds will grow talons, the beasts will bite, the solitary snake will manufacture venom, you'll discover death and have to find your own means of opposing it. She will bring forth in pain. There will be a populated world beset by conflict. I must abide by my rules and watch in impotence chaos supervene on creation. Do not touch that fruit. (*He gets up.*)

ALEX: Take it away, then.

GOD: No. Remember the rules.

(*He goes off. Alex shakes his head, bemused. A bird calls. Whistling, he imitates it. He does more: he creates a cantilena*

*of his own. He is excited by his act of composition. Marty
enters with a basket laden with fruit.)*

ALEX: Did you hear that? (*He whistles again.*)
MARTY: Nice. But what's it for?
ALEX: It needs a slovo. Mouse sick. Moose sick. I call it
   music.
MARTY: But what's it for?
ALEX: It just is.
MARTY: Listen – I met this man –
ALEX: Man? You can't have. I'm the only one. So far.

(*He tries to embrace Marty, and this makes her spill some of
her fruit. Then Alex is struck by a thought.*)

ALEX: You say a *man*?
MARTY: More of an angel, really. He helped me pick this
   fruit.
ALEX: He helped you to pick *that one*?

(*He means the large yellow one, orange really, that he picks
up from the ground. He holds it gingerly to his ear.*)

ALEX: There's noise inside. Like ticking. Ticking. I just
   made up that slovo. We'd better see what's inside. (*He
   pauses.*) It was only eating he said, wasn't it? No harm
   in looking. We viddy it every day.
MARTY: It smells all right.

(*Alex breaks the rind and juice spatters on to his hand. He
licks it.*)

MARTY: Now you've eaten it.
ALEX: I don't call that eating. Taste.

(*She tastes. The music that Alex whistled is now heard on an
orchestra. It is the theme of the last movement of Beethoven's*

Ninth Symphony. The light subtly changes. A man enters who is identical with the Minister of the Interior of a later scene. He is smartly dressed in a suit of snakeskin.)

MINISTER: It wasn't so difficult, was it? The world hasn't changed. The old thunderer hasn't unleashed his lightning. He *wanted* you to do it.

ALEX: Wanted?

MINISTER: Of course. Why did he leave it hanging there?

MARTY: The world *has* changed. It's cold. I need some –

ALEX: Platties? Clothes?

MINISTER: You'll find clothes available. When you wake up from this dream. We all need protection from the cold cold world and the cold cold eyes of strangers.

ALEX: What's strangers?

MINISTER: People we don't know. The world's already seething with them. You see them out there? That's just a small sample.

MARTY: I don't see anything.

MINISTER: But you imagine them. Imagine them first, then create them. That's your job.

MARTY: I feel a terrible – I don't know the word.

MINISTER: Pain. Agony. Birth throes. You'd better go off and lie down. The pain will go.

(*She painfully leaves.*)

MINISTER: Now things are going to be interesting. Who wants heaven? Who wants the Garden of Eden? See the world to come. Men and women exhibiting the most incredible kinds of ingenuity, the delicious fruits of disobedience. And they have to be ruled, of course. They have to be told how to be good. You too, my little friend.

ALEX: I know all about it. I'm not your *little* friend. I don't have to be told. We have to have the two veshches or there wouldn't be anything to choose. It's the choosing that counts.

MINISTER: I'll choose for you. That's my privilege.

ALEX: I'll choose for myself. That's mine.

MINISTER: You'll choose wrong.

ALEX: Who knows what wrong is? Only Bog has the secret.

MINISTER: You mean the old one? He's dead. I threw him out.

ALEX: That's why it's cold.

(*The lights dim. A wind drowns the music. The Minister laughs and goes off. Alex tries to warm himself. He huddles on the ground. He wakes to the music of the Prelude. It was all a dream. Naked, he is speedily dressed by his three friends or droogs. The play begins.*)

EPILOGUE: 'A Malenky Govoreet about the Molodoy'
Anthony Burgess, 1987

*THIS dialogue between Alex and an author figure named 'AB'
was written for newspaper publication shortly before Burgess's
stage version of A Clockwork Orange appeared in book form.
The complete text is published here for the first time.*

AB: Alex, if I may call you that – there's always been some
doubt about your surname –

ALEX: Never gave it, brother, to no manner of chelloveck.
The gloopy shoot that put me in the sinny – Lubric or
Pubic or some such like naz – he gave me like two –
Alex Burgess and Alex Delarge. That's because of me
govoreeting about being Alexander the Big. Then he
forgets. Bad like editing. Call me Alex.

AB: In 1962, when the book about you was published, you
were still a nadsat, teen that is. Now you must be about
forty-two or -three or -four. Settled down, finished with
the ultra-violence. Raising a family. Pillar of society.
Taxpayer. Father of family. Faithful husband. Running
to fat.

ALEX: For you, little bratty, I am what I was. I am in a
book and I do not sdacha. Fixed like, ah yes, for ever
and never, allmen.

AB: Sdacha?

ALEX: Pick up the old slovar some time, my brother. Shonary, Angleruss.

AB: Shonary?

ALEX: Leaving like the dick out.

AB: Fixed for ever and never, allmen, as you skazz. Eternal type of molodoy aggression.

ALEX: You are learning, verily thou art, O little brother.

AB: And yet there are changes, sdachas as you would put it. The youth or molodoy of the space age is not what it was in 1962.

ALEX: That old kneeg was in the space age, my malenky droog. In it there are chellovecks on the old Luna. It was like pathetic.

AB: Prophetic?

ALEX: And pathetic too. The jeezny of all chellovecks is like pathetic and very pathetic. Because they do not sdach. Because they are always the same. Because they are mekansky apple-sins. That being the Russ like naz of the kneeg written by Burgess or F. Alexander or whatever his naz is or was. What did you say your naz was, bratty?

AB: I skazzed nichevo about a name.

ALEX: Learning, brother, learning thou art in Bog's Pravda. And you would know what?

AB: To put it plain, your opinion of the youth of today.

ALEX: My like missal on the molodoy of segodnya. They are not like what I was. No, verily not. Because they have not one veshch in their gullivers. To Ludwig van and his like they give shooms of lip-music prrrrr. It is all with them cal, very gromky. Guitars and these kots and kotchkas with creeching golosses and their luscious glory very long and very grahzny. And their platties. It is all jeans and filthy toofles. And tisshuts.

AB: What are tisshuts?

ALEX: They are like worn on the upper plott and there is writing on them like HARVARD and CALIFORNIA and GIVE IT ME I WANT IT and suchlike cal. Very gloopy. And they do not have one missal in their gullivers.

AB: Meaning not one thought in their heads?

ALEX: That is what I skazzed.

AB: But they have many. They are against war and all for universal peace and banning nuclear missiles. They speak of love and human equality. They have songs about these things.

ALEX: It is all cal and kiss my sharries. A tolchock in the keeshkas for the kots and the old in-out for the koshkas. Devotchkas, that is. What they want they will not get. For there is no sdacha. There will always be voina and no mir, like old Lion Trotsky or it may be Tolstoy was always govoreeting about. It is built in. Chellovecks are all like very aggressive and do not sdach. The Russkies have a slovo for it, two really, and it is prirozhdyonnuiy grekh.

AB: Let me consult my ah Angleruss slovar. Odna minoota – it says here original sin.

ALEX: That I have not slooshied before. Real dobby. Original sin is good and very good.

AB: The young of today pride themselves on their severance from the culture of their elders. Their elders have ruined the world, they say, and when they are not trying to rebuild that ruined world with love and fellowship they withdraw from it with hallucinogens.

ALEX: That is a hard slovo and very hard, O my brother.

AB: I mean that they take drugs and experience hallucinations in which they are transported to heavenly regions of the inner mind.

229

ALEX: Meaning that they are in touch with Bog And All His Holy Angels and the other veshches?

AB: Not God, in whom most no longer believe. Though some of them follow the one you would call the bearded nagoy chelloveck who died on the cross. Indeed, they grow beards and try to look like him.

ALEX: What I skaz is that these veshches, like drencrom and vellocet and the rest of the cal, are not good for a malchick. To doomat about Bog and to itty off into the land and burble cal about lubbilubbing every chelloveck has to sap all the goodness and strength out of a malchick. This I skaz, ah yes, and it is the pravda and nichevo but the.

AB: Do you consider the youth of today to be more violent than the generation to which you belonged or belong?

ALEX: Not more. Those that want deng or cutter to koopat their teeny malenky sniffs and snorts and jabs in the rooker must use the old ultra-violence to take and like grab. But such are not seelny, strong that is. All the strength and goodness has been like sapped out of them. The ultra-violence is less now of the molodoy than of the ITA and ZBD and the Cronks and the Pally Steinians who are not pals of the Steins, ah no, nor of the Cohens and the rest of the yahoodies. It is all with the KPS and the TYF and the QED and the other gruppas. Terror by air and land, O my brother. Bombs in public mestos. Very cowardly and very like unkind. Bombs and guns, they were not ever my own veshch.

AB: You never handled a gun?

ALEX: Very cowardly, for it is ultra-violence from a long long long like way off. Dratsing is not what it was. It was better in what they called like the Dark Ages before they put on the like lights. The old britva and the nozh.

Rooker to rooker. Your own red red krovvy as well as the krovvy of the chelloveck you are dratsing. And then there was another veshch I do not pomnit the slovo of all that good.

AB: Style, you mean style?

ALEX: That slovo will do as dobby as any slovo I know whereof, O my brother. Style and again style. Style we had. And the red red krovvy did not get on to your platties if you had style. For it was style of the nogas and the rookers and the plott, as it might be tansivatting.

AB: Dancing?

ALEX: That is the slovo that would not like come into my gulliver. The yahzick of the kvadrats I could never get my yahzick round.

AB: Kvadrat means quadratic, doesn't it? And that means square. By using such terminology you give away your age.

ALEX: Yarbles. Bolshy great yarblockos.

AB: Yarblockos means apples, does it not?

ALEX: It means yarbles, O my brother.

AB: Let us return to this business of the music preferred by the young.

ALEX: It is not music. It is cal and grahzny cal. It is gromky and bezoomny and like for little children. For malenky malchicks it to me like appears to be. There is no music like Ludwig van and Benjy Britt and Felix M. And Wolfgang Amadeus that they made the cally lying lay it on about.

AB: Lay it on?

ALEX: Lay it on thick. Flick. Sinny film, that is. He was not seen off by Salieri. He snuffed because he was too good for this filthy world.

AB: You speak plain.

ALEX: I always govoreet plain, my brother. And this I skaz now, that music is the way in. That music is the door to the big bolshy pravda. That it is like heaven. And what the molodoy of now slooshy is not music. And the slovos are like pathetic. What I say to these molodoy chellovecks is that they must like grow up. They must dig into their gullivers more. They must not smeck at what is gone behind. Because that is all we have. There is no to come and the now is no more than like a sneeze. It is all there behind, built up by the bolshy chellovecks who are like dead. But they are not dead. They live on in our jeezny.

AB: You seem to be ah govoreeting about the preservation of the past. You seem to me also to be ah skazzing that artistic creation is a great good. And yet your ah jeezny was dedicated to destruction.

ALEX: All these bolshy slovos. It was the bolshy great force of the jeezny that was in myself. I was molodoy, and none had taught me to make. So break was the veshch I had to do. But I get over it.

AB: You get over it? Meaning you grow up?

ALEX: There is no kneeg about me growing up. That is not writ by no manner of writing chelloveck. They viddy me as a very ultra-violent malchick and not more, ah no. To be young is to be nothing. It is best as in your slovos to be like growing up. That is why I skaz to the molodoy of now that they must not be as they are. They have this long voloss and these tisshuts and blue tight genovas on their nogas and they think they are all. But they are nothing. Grow up is what they must do, ah yes. What they have to do is to like grow up.

AB: Can you now transport yourself to the future, or rather

232

your part in the future which has not been written about and, I speak with some authority, never will be, and deliver a final message to the world of today?

ALEX: In the yahzick of the mir at like large?

AB: Yesli bi mozhno.

ALEX: Your Russian is deplorable, but I take it you mean 'if possible'. Very well. I speak as a tax-paying adult. And I say that the only thing that counts is the human capacity for moral choice. No, I will not speak. I will sing. I will take Ludwig van Beethoven's setting of Schiller's *Ode to Joy* in the final movement of the glorious Ninth, and I will put my own slovos, I mean words, to it. And the words are these. If you would care to join in, thou art most welcome. Slooshy, listen that is.

> Being young's a sort of sickness,
> Measles, mumps or chicken pox.
> Gather all your toys together,
> Lock them in a wooden box.
> That means tolchocks, crasting and dratsing,
> All of the things that suit a boy.
> When you build instead of busting,
> You can start your Ode to Joy.

AB: Thank you, Mr ah –

ALEX: Bog blast you, I haven't finished.

> Do not be a clockwork orange,
> Freedom has a lovely voice.
> Here is good and there is badness,
> Look on both, then take your choice.
> Sweet in juice and hue and aroma,
> Let's not be changed to fruit machines.

    Choice is free but seldom easy –
    That's what human freedom means.

    Gloopy sort of slovos, really. Grahzny sort of a world. May I now, O my brother, return to the pages of my book?

AB: You never left them.

ESSAYS,
ARTICLES AND
REVIEWS

'The Human Russians'
Anthony Burgess

WHAT I loved most about the Russians was their inefficiency. I went to Leningrad expecting to find a frightening
steel-and-stone image of the Orwellian future. What I
found instead was human beings at their most human: or,
to put it another way, at their most inefficient.

I have to qualify this: inefficient people do not produce
sputniks or cosmonauts. But it seems that the efficiency is
a thin cream floated to the top; one gets the impression of
a school in which all the teachers are busy at a staff meeting
or in the sixth-form laboratories, leaving the lower forms to
their own unsupervised devices. Stink-bombs are thrown,
ink splashes the walls (the walls are already dirty enough,
anyway); Ivanov Minor writes on the blackboard. 'Comrade
Khrushchev has a fat belly.' But no one minds because there
is a most interesting experiment going on in the physics lab,
and all the staff is crowding round that. Or else some teacher
is being reprimanded by all the other teachers for a breach
of staff discipline. Or else plans are being made for a colossal
open day. Or perhaps the headmaster is checking the proofs
of the glorious and mendacious school prospectus.

I don't know whether mendacity is an aspect of the
Russian character or something that springs out of Soviet

'double-think'. In a restaurant a waiter assured me that all the tables were full when I could see for myself that most of them were empty. I tried to buy an English newspaper but could only find the *Daily Worker* on sale. The girl at the kiosk should rightly have said: 'Only the *Daily Worker* tells the truth; hence it is the only British paper allowed in Soviet Russia.' But what she actually said was: 'You should have come earlier. All the other British papers have been snapped up.' That was not much of a compliment to the *Daily Worker*; nor to what I call my intelligence – everyone knows that no other British newspapers are allowed in Russia. Some of the lies are far from annoying. An Intourist man told me I would have to pay £25 for a single night in a double room in the Astoria Hotel. What I actually paid was something under 30 shillings; I have the bill to prove it.

But perhaps what I call lying is only a Russian unwillingness to face reality. And perhaps both those harsh words – lying and inefficiency – are ill-chosen. The world of romance and fairy tale is never far away from the Khrushchevian Utopia (*Utopia*, of course, *was* a fairy tale). Gagarin and Titov are perhaps cognate with Baba Yaga and other fairy-tale witches and magicians. If you can accept that a hut can walk on chicken's legs, you are not surprised at what can be done with a space-ship. I made friends with a serious young man with a good science degree. For days we talked earnestly and without humour on political and scientific matters. Then suddenly, without warning, without a flicker or glint, he told me that he had in his apartment a Siberian cat nearly three feet long, excluding the tail. This cat, he said, had very green eyes, shared his bed with him, and occasionally kicked him out of bed on to the floor. You could see he sometimes got a bit tired of reality.

In a fairy-tale world time is easily suspended. Dining-room delays are proverbial. In Leningrad's smallest restaurant I ordered beef stroganoff at twelve-thirty and was eventually served it at four. That didn't greatly worry me; I was less hungry than thirsty and desperately wanted beer. But nobody would bring me beer. I lolled my tongue in desperation and made strangled noises: these were appreciated but they didn't bring me beer. What I did then was to go to a refrigerator that was gleaming in the distance and take beer out of it. I brought the beer back to my table and opened it with a knife. Nobody objected. I did this four times; nobody minded in the least.

Between drinking this self-service beer and waiting for my beef stroganoff I decided to do a little shopping. I had seen a boutique with bracelets and brooches and badges of Lenin and Major Gagarin. I wanted to buy a small Soviet present for my wife. The girls behind the counter were very pretty and very helpful. Nobody could speak English but we contrived a macaronic mixture of Russian, French, and German. I chose a charming little bracelet and brought out my roubles and kopeks. The girls were shocked. Only foreign currency was allowed here, monsieur. These goods were for foreigners. Did I not see the logic? I didn't, but I asked how much English money. There was a great rummaging among type-written lists. At length it was proudly announced that the bracelet would cost thirty shillings and fifteen pence. I gave the girls a little lesson. They crowded round. They were most appreciative: the Russians love lessons. I handed over two pound notes and there was an interval for admiring the portrait of the Queen. 'The Tsarina,' they said, 'very pretty.' I asked for change. They were terribly sorry, but they had no change. This was the first day, you see, and their aim was to *get* foreign currency, not give it. What I must do was to choose some other little gift, so that my total purchases would add up to two pounds. This seemed reasonable, so I chose a small brooch. How much this time? This time, they said, busy with their ballpoints, I must pay five shillings and fourteen pence. A recapitulation of my little arithmetic lessons and some gentle rapping on the knuckles. Charming giggles; very well, then, a total of thirty-five shillings and twenty-nine pence, making a total of one pound, seventeen shillings and five pence. That meant there was still two shillings and sevenpence to be spent. I groaned. I said: 'Please keep the two shillings and sevenpence change, mademoiselle. Buy yourself a little something with it.'

Everybody was profoundly shocked. No, no, no, unthinkable, uncultured, un-*Soviet*. I must buy something else. So I desperately ranged around the little boutique and emerged finally with a small badge with a hammer and sickle and the slogan *Mir Miru*, meaning 'Peace to the World'. This was two shillings. I begged and pleaded with the girls to at least keep the sevenpence change, but they wouldn't and couldn't. Finally, I was given two boxes of Soviet matches, we exchanged kisses and handshakes, and everybody was happy. It had taken a long time. I had now forgotten what I had ordered for lunch. But the waiter, at last back from his three-hour compulsory rest-period, had *not* forgotten. On my table was a plate of *cold* beef stroganoff. The waiter tut-tutted at me reproachfully. The food had been there for twenty minutes, he said.

Perhaps the manic depression which so many Russians seem to suffer from militates against what we like to call efficiency: up in the air, on a wave of massive euphoria; then down into the bowels of the earth, in inutterable misery – that's the way with the lot of them. A lot of them

are what are called *pyknic* types, short, stocky, and temper-
amental, like Comrade Khrushchev himself. A good
Communist never weeps for the sins of the world, but I
saw plenty of weeping and ineffable depression in Leningrad
restaurants. One minute up on a crest of frog-dancing,
singing and promiscuous kissing – loud, loving smacks
– on vodka and Soviet cognac: the next moment, down
in the deepest depression. This would often end in sleep,
head down in a litter of glasses, bottles and full ash-trays.
And then some grim loud woman would appear with a
ready cure – a pledget of cotton-wool soaked in ammonia.
Up the nostrils, even into the eyes, and the sufferer would
cough back into life, be thrown out by the waiters, and
then search hopelessly for a taxi home.

I saw a great deal of drunkenness in Leningrad restaurants. I found this on the whole encouraging; where there's
drunkenness, there's hope, for good little totalitarian
machines don't get drunk. The technique with obstreperous
drunks was always the same – the unceremonious chuck-
out by a gaggle of waiters: the police were never brought
into it. That's another thing I liked about Leningrad – the
absence of police. Perhaps all the police are secret police,
and perhaps the only crimes are political crimes. Certainly,
there was no attempt to cope officially with the minor
misdemeanours which fill our police-courts – drunken
disorderliness, rowdyism, soliciting. My wife and I left the
Metropole Restaurant at three in the morning together
with a charming Finnish couple. We had been with them
for several hours, had carried on long and intricate conver-
sations with them, despite the lack of any common
language at all. I asked a waiter if we could get a taxi. He
said, with commendable intelligibility, '*Taxi, nyet.*'
Downstairs I asked one of the three sweating doormen.

But they were busy coping with a loud group of *stilyagi* or teddy-boys, who were shouting and waving broken bottles and demanding to be let into the restaurant. There, of course, it was a taxi very much *nyet*. So the four of us sat on the pavement, singing in Finnish and English that great international song 'Clementine'. We wanted the police to come, tap us on the shoulder, find out if we were foreigners, then speed us back to our respective ships in police cars. But no police came. The painted girls solicited and the teddy-boys raged and romped, but no police came. It is my honest opinion that there are no police in Leningrad.

If one expects to find a totalitarian state full of soft-booted, white-helmeted military police, conspicuously armed, one also expects a certain coldness, a thinness of blood, all emotion channelled into a love of Big Brother. You certainly find none of that in Leningrad. There is a tremendous warmth about the people, a powerful desire to admit you, the stranger, into the family and smother you with kisses. I asked my young scientific friend to call me by my first name, but he was shy of that. He didn't want to be stand-offish, he wanted to establish a closer relationship than the mere use of first names would allow; so I was to be called 'Uncle' – *Dyadya*: I was to be genuinely one of the family. One found this in hospitals, too. My wife was taken to hospital with some inexplicable complaint – doctors and nurses alike administered the medicine of a good cuddle, a kiss, a maternal or paternal 'there there'. One sees how remote from reality were those early Soviet attempts to abolish the family as a social unit.

Strangely enough, one feels this warm ambience of family even in the food. *Borshch*, that omnipresent soup, coarse and delicious – there's none of the cold professional spirit of the *haute cuisine* floating in that. Instead, one finds ragged gobbets of beef, veal, chicken, with sometimes the afterthought of a pale frankfurter peeping out of the wrack of cabbage and shredded meat. What is *borshch* really but home cooking? It smells of one's own family kitchen; it's something that mother used to make.

I suppose if one wanted to be fanciful one could say that the whole of Leningrad is aromatic of home. No names of strangers stand above the shops. All you see is MEAT, BUTTER, EGGS, FISH, VEGETABLES, as though each state food-shop were a compartment of some colossal family kitchen. And there is no terrifying smartness among the people who walk the streets – they are all dressed in clumsy ill-cut unpressed suits and dresses, like members of our own family rigged up informally for a day at home. Incidentally, there is plenty to be done at home, but no one ever seems to do it.

The city is terribly shabby and slummy-looking despite the Byzantine gold of the cathedral, despite the unbelievable splendours of the Winter Palace. And what is true of the city is also true of home. Father and elder brothers put off indefinitely the necessary chores – the replacing of broken panes in the windows, the painting and pointing, the mending of the path, the new lightbulb on the landing. Father is a shirt-sleeved pipe-smoking slippered newspaper-reading Father. He is inefficient, and so is Big Brother. Meanwhile, far away the rockets blast off and Major Titov surveys the earth like a god. But all that is taking place in another Russia, far away from the homely smell of blocked-up drains and *borshch*.

Listener, 28 December 1961

'Clockwork Marmalade'
Anthony Burgess

I went to see Stanley Kubrick's *A Clockwork Orange* in New York, fighting to get in like everybody else. It was worth the fight, I thought – very much a Kubrick movie, technically brilliant, thoughtful, relevant, poetic, mind-opening. It was possible for me to see the work as a radical remaking of my own novel, not as a mere interpretation, and this – the feeling that it was no impertinence to blazon it as *Stanley Kubrick's Clockwork Orange* – is the best tribute I can pay to the Kubrickian mastery. The fact remains, however, that the film sprang out of a book, and some of the controversy which has begun to attach to the film is controversy in which I, inevitably, feel myself involved. In terms of philosophy and even theology, the Kubrick *Orange* is a fruit from my tree.

I wrote *A Clockwork Orange* in 1961, which is a very remote year, and I experience some difficulty in empathising with that long-gone writer who, concerned with making a living, wrote as many as five novels in fourteen months. The title is the least difficult thing to explain. In 1945, back from the army, I heard an eighty-year-old Cockney in a London pub say that somebody was 'as queer as a clockwork orange'. The 'queer' did not mean homosexual: it meant mad. The phrase intrigued me with its unlikely fusion of demotic and surrealistic. For nearly twenty years I wanted to use it as the title of something. During those twenty years I heard it several times more – in Underground stations, in pubs, in television plays – but always from aged Cockneys, never from the young. It was a traditional trope, and it asked to entitle a work which combined a concern with tradition and a bizarre technique. The opportunity to use it came when I conceived the notion of writing a novel about brainwashing. Joyce's Stephen Dedalus (in *Ulysses*) refers to the world as an 'oblate orange': man is a microcosm or little world; he is a growth as organic as a fruit, capable of colour, fragrance and sweetness; to meddle with him, condition him, is to turn him into a mechanical creation.

There had been some talk in the British press about the problems of growing criminality. The youth of the late Fifties were restless and naughty, dissatisfied with the postwar world, violent and destructive, and they – being more conspicuous than more old-time crooks and hoods – were what many people meant when they talked about growing criminality. Looking back from a peak of violence, we can see that the British teddy-boys and mods and rockers were mere tyros in the craft of anti-social aggression: nevertheless, they were a portent, and the man in the street was right to be scared. How to deal with them? Prison or reform school made them worse: why not save the taxpayer's money by subjecting them to an easy course in conditioning, some kind of aversion therapy which should make them associate the act of violence with discomfort, nausea, or even intimations of mortality? Many heads nodded at this proposal (not, at the time, a governmental proposal, but one put out by private though influential theoreticians). Heads still nod at it. On *The Frost Show* it was suggested to me that it might have been a good thing if Adolf Hitler had been forced to undergo aversion therapy, so that the very thought of a new putsch or pogrom would make him sick up his cream cakes.

Hitler was, unfortunately, a human being, and if we could have countenanced the conditioning of one human being we would have to accept it for all. Hitler was a great nuisance, but history has known others disruptive enough to make the state's fingers itch – Christ, Luther, Bruno, even D. H. Lawrence. One has to be genuinely philo-sophical about this, however much one has suffered. I don't know how much free will man really possesses (Wagner's Hans Sachs said: *Wir sind ein wenig frei* – 'We are a little free'), but I do know what little he seems to have is too precious to encroach on, however good the intentions of the encroacher may be.

A Clockwork Orange was intended to be a sort of tract, even a sermon, on the importance of the power of choice. My hero or anti-hero, Alex, is very vicious, perhaps even impossibly so, but his viciousness is not the product of genetic or social conditioning: it is his own thing, embarked on in full awareness. Alex is evil, not merely misguided, and in a properly run society such evil as he enacts must be checked and punished. But his evil is a human evil, and we recognise in his deeds of aggression potentialities of our own – worked out for the non-criminal citizen in war, sectional injustice, domestic unkindness, armchair dreams. In three ways Alex is an exemplar of humanity: he is aggressive, he loves beauty, he is a language-user. Ironically, his name can be taken to mean 'wordless', though he has plenty of words of his own – invented group-dialect. He has, though, no word to say in the running of his community or the managing of the state:

he is, to the state, a mere object, something 'out there' like the Moon, though not so passive.

Theologically, evil is not quantifiable. Yet I posit the notion that one act of evil may be greater than another, and that perhaps the ultimate act of evil is dehumanisation, the killing of the soul – which is as much as to say the capacity to choose between good and evil acts. Impose on an individual the capacity to be good and only good, and you kill his soul for, presumably, the sake of social stability. What my, and Kubrick's, parable tries to state is that it is preferable to have a world of violence undertaken in full awareness – violence chosen as an act of will – than a world conditioned to be good or harmless. I recognise that the lesson is already becoming an old-fashioned one. B. F. Skinner, with his ability to believe that there is something *beyond* freedom and dignity, wants to see the death of autonomous man. He may or may not be right, but in terms of the Judaeo-Christian ethic that *A Clockwork Orange* tries to express he is perpetrating a gross heresy. It seems to me in accordance with the tradition that Western man is not yet ready to jettison, that the area in which human choice is a possibility should be extended, even if one comes up against new angels with swords and banners emblazoned *No*. The wish to diminish free will is, I should think, the sin against the Holy Ghost.

In both film and book, the evil that the state performs in brainwashing Alex is seen spectacularly in its own lack of self-awareness as regards non-ethical values. Alex is fond of Beethoven, and he has used the Ninth Symphony as a stimulus to dreams of violence. This has been his choice, but there has been nothing to prevent his choosing to use that music as a mere solace or image of divine order. That, by the time his conditioning starts, he has not yet made the better choice does not mean that he will never do it. But, with an aversion therapy which associates Beethoven and violence, that choice is taken away from him forever. It is an unlooked-for punishment and it is tantamount to robbing a man – stupidly, casually – of his right to enjoy the divine vision. For there is a good beyond mere ethical good, which is always existential: there is the *essential* good, that aspect of God which we can prefigure more in the taste of an apple or the sound of music than in mere right action or even charity.

What hurts me, as also Kubrick, is the allegation made by some viewers and readers of *A Clockwork Orange* that there is a gratuitous indulgence in violence which turns an intended homiletic work into a pornographic one. It was certainly no pleasure to me to describe acts of violence when writing the novel: I indulged in excess, in caricature, even in an invented dialect with the purpose of making the violence more symbolic than realistic, and Kubrick found remarkable cinematic equivalents for my own literary devices. It would have been pleasanter, and would have made more friends, if there had been no violence at all, but the story of Alex's reclamation would have lost force if we weren't permitted to see what he was being reclaimed from. For my own part, the depiction of violence was intended as both an act of catharsis and an act of charity, since my own wife was the subject of vicious and mindless violence in blacked-out London in 1942, when she was robbed and beaten by three GI deserters. Readers of my book may remember that the author whose wife is raped is the author of a work called *A Clockwork Orange*.

Viewers of the film have been disturbed by the fact that Alex, despite his viciousness, is quite likeable. It has required a deliberate self-administered act of aversion therapy on the part of some to dislike him, and to let righteous indignation get in the way of human charity. The point is that, if we are going to love mankind, we will have to love Alex as a not unrepresentative member of it. The place where Alex and his mirror-image F. Alexander are most guilty of hate and violence is called HOME, and it is here, we are told, that charity ought to begin. But towards that mechanism, the state, which first is concerned with self-perpetuation and, second, is happiest when human beings are predictable and controllable, we have no duty at all, certainly no duty of charity.

I have a final point to make, and this will not interest many who like to think of Kubrick's *Orange* rather than Burgess's. The language of both movie and book (called nadsat – the Russian 'teen' suffix as in *pyatnadsat*, meaning fifteen) is no mere decoration, nor is it a sinister indication of the subliminal power that a Communist super-state may already be exerting on the young. It was meant to turn *A Clockwork Orange* into, among other things, a brainwashing primer. You read the book or see the film, and at the end you should find yourself in possession of a minimal Russian vocabulary – without effort, with surprise. This is the way brainwashing works. I chose Russian words because they blend better into English than those of French or even German (which is already a kind of English, not exotic enough). But the lesson of the *Orange* has nothing to do with the ideology or repressive techniques of Soviet Russia: it is wholly concerned with what can happen to any of us in the West if we do not keep on our guard. If *Orange*, like *Nineteen Eighty-Four*, takes its place as one of the salutary literary warnings – or cinematic warnings – against flabbiness, sloppy thinking, and overmuch trust in the state, then it will have done something of value. For my part, I do not like the book as much as others I have written: I have kept it, till recently, in an unopened jar – marmalade, a preserve on a shelf, rather than an orange on a dish. What I would really like to see is a film of one of my other novels, all of which are singularly unaggressive, but I fear that this is too much to hope for. It looks as though I must go through life as the fountain and origin of a great film, and as a man who has to insist, against all opposition, that he is the most unviolent creature alive. Just like Stanley Kubrick.

Listener, 17 February 1972

Extract from an Unpublished Interview with Anthony Burgess

AT the moment I'm working on a novel about the life of Christ. In this book I see Christ as a sort of hippie, an early type of revolutionary. I think it's curious that he was a carpenter, and the fact that he worked with pieces of wood all his life. When it was time for him to die, when he looked at that piece of wood, he must have thought something. I am working with a language for the book now, something – like the nadsat language in *A Clockwork Orange* – using a fusion of two languages – in this case, English and Hebrew.

In a way this is drawn out of the Manson business. I have a neurotic thing about that sort of insanity. It's terrifying – the evil, the chaos, the multiplicity of it. If there is anything that makes me wish for death, that brings out my death-wish, it is that. I worry all the time. I worry about my wife, and my son in New York. Between the drug people and the psychopaths loose on the streets, it's hardly safe to walk outside. Young people keep talking about being 'tuned in to reality,' but I wonder what it is they are *really* tuned in to? I'm not sure the Jesus Freaks and the young people involved in that sort of thing aren't [. . .] getting in touch with something besides Jesus

– maybe the devil. You know, throughout history people have done evil in the name of the Church. The Reformation, the Salem Witch Trials, all through history people have been misled by the appearance of good. It makes me elect for simplicity [. . .] There is too much multiplicity. The evil around us is frightening, and it's unsafe to deal with it. Only the artist can deal with it because he can do it more objectively. And perhaps that is not absolutely safe.

Everywhere we look there is conflict. It's on the campuses, it's on the television, it's on the streets. God knows, New York City, where I live, is the most dangerous city in the world. [. . .] The conflict is everywhere. This is the twentieth century and we are surrounded by conflict. Like Yin and Yang, hot and cold, God and the Devil: everything is conflict. This is the universe and without conflict we have no life at all. But the terms of conflict are uncertain. For instance, Right and Wrong, what do these terms mean? I mean *really*, what is absolutely Right, and what is absolutely Wrong? We could sit down and make a list. What would you say is Wrong? Would you say it is Wrong to hate? Perhaps. But what about in a time of war? In wartime it is *Right* to hate our enemies. It is Right to *kill* our enemies. The words Right and Wrong in themselves mean nothing. They have a smell of police ward disinfectant about them.

And Evil. Some people appear to have an unexplainable desire to do evil. But for what? Can we know what evil is? What are the signs of evil? The desire to destroy is evil – unexplainable, wanton destructiveness. But even that is not categorical, is it? Most of history is written about destruction, not creation. Records are kept of wars, of the decay of civilisations, of murders and deaths, of men like Alexander the Great, Napoleon, Hitler, and others who built enormous empires on their abilities to destroy. But in a sense, destruction is a means of creation. When a vandal knocks in the side of a telephone booth, or scratches his name on the side of a subway car, he is leaving his mark. He is, whether he knows it or not, attempting to show that he exists and that he has the ability to affect things, and to change things. Destructive violence is a way of saying, 'Look, I am here.' That's the easy way. That's negative creation. Positive creation is much more difficult – it requires patience and talent. Of course these young hoodlums have no patience. It's much easier to destroy than to take a block of stone and slowly and carefully bring out an image – that requires an artist. Violence is much quicker; and to the hoodlums, the thug, I suppose violence is more rewarding because it is freer. There is no restraint and no control. There is also this drive for freedom in violence.

My novel, *Enderby*, is about a poet, a gross, fat man. He belches, he drinks too much, he lives in the toilet – he writes poems in the water closet – he masturbates, he avoids all forms of obligation, he is no good with women. Enderby is free. I suppose that's what I like about him [...] But you see, when a character or person is too free, then he challenges society. Now one of the basic premises of society is that no one has too much freedom. B. F. Skinner's book *Beyond Freedom and Dignity*, which, incidentally, came out about the same time as the film of *A Clockwork Orange*, states that we must give up certain rights and privileges so that we do not obtrude ourselves upon our neighbours. We must exercise control; we must limit our freedom for society's sake. This means we relinquish our freedom of choice. The artist is a rebel who defies control through his work. He escapes to his closet where he paints, or writes, or makes a sculpture, and this way he maintains his identity. It may be that for the criminal violence is an expression of the same kind, or a similar kind, of freedom. However, by the time you use violence, you are out of control.

[. . .]

Violence is chaos. There is a constant war between the chaotic and the aesthetic, and the individual must fight to assert his own authority. The only hope for escape from this kind of chaos is to recognise the power of the human individual. I guess I'm rather a manichaean, but this kind of warfare – this battle of good and evil – has intrigued me for a long time. I tried to deal with it in my novel *The Wanting Seed*. This was a book I had wanted to write for years but could never quite find the right form. I finally did write it – though it is still not altogether successful – but what has concerned me here is a warfare between ideologies. On one hand you have the Pelagian concept that man is basically good, and that he is capable of perfection if left alone and allowed to discover his own way. On the other hand you have the Augustinian concept that man is only capable of evil and without God his only hope is self-destruction and eternal damnation.

[. . .]

Anatole France once wrote a novel called *La Revolte des Anges* that describes a sort of eternal war between God and Satan. God reigns on the one side over the powers of good, and on the other side Satan has marshalled the forces of evil. I'm not suggesting this is necessarily true, but it is certainly a possibility we have to consider. Take Christ's own words, 'I come not to bring peace but a sword.' I may be a Manichee, but we have to live with divisions.

We strive for order and unity, but it is not often that we can truly claim to have found it.

The artist is faced with the duty of revealing the nature of reality. He is not a preacher – his job is not to be didactic – he may be a teacher – we all try to teach; but the novelist is bound to do his duty. His duty is, as Henry James said, to dramatise. To reveal the nature of reality. You must remember that to the poet, the artist and to the novelist, the nature of reality is revealed, not by vague images passing through the mind, but by words: words which suggest certain meanings and reveal actions as the author knows them. But the author cannot determine right or wrong. All he can do is present a sort of 'mock scenario' from which the reader can draw his own conclusions. The author cannot always cast a scene in terms of good and evil – for one thing, good is not necessarily the opposite of evil, and there is a certain subjective value to evil. There is a subjective value to good as well which goes beyond the meanings of right and wrong – a good we experience in a beautiful piece of music, the taste of an apple, or sex. Without a knowledge of the extremes it is difficult, or maybe impossible, to know anything of the medians. A man or woman who has never done evil cannot know what good is.

It is ironic that I am always associated with *A Clockwork Orange*. This, of all my books, is the one I like least. I wrote this book in 1961, which was the year after I was supposed to have died, and the book reveals a lot of the turmoil in my mind at the time. I don't think it is my best book, but at the same time, the book reveals a great deal about the conflict of good and evil, and also about this fear of irrational violence. In many ways the book is me; for what we write is very much what we are. And the book reveals an inner battle with this quality, evil.

Not only evil, but the danger of trying to correct it. Basically I'm very suspicious of the use of power to change others.

[. . .]

A Clockwork Orange also demonstrates the pendulum theory – how one extreme purges the other. But ultimately we, as human beings, must come to terms with the dilemmas of good and evil, right and wrong, or whatever, on our own. God will not do it for us. I will not commit myself to saying 'Credo in unum deum'. If there is a God, he is a supra-human god; he is not concerned with human motivation. Whether or not God does exist, the conflict of good and evil is inevitable. Even if there were no human beings in the world the principles of good and evil would exist. I don't believe that 2,000 years from now, if the world still exists, that the world will be any less evil, or any less good. The fight never comes to an end. For every moment of stasis is followed by a longer and more disrupting period of struggle. It may be, as has been suggested, that evil is dynamic and good tends to be static – it certainly seems that way in New York City, where I live, anyway – but the task of the concerned individual must be to make good a less static force: to make it more dynamic than evil. But what is the active force of good? Love. I would suggest that Love is the active force and we have to learn how to love everyone else, and everything else. That seems to be the challenge of the twentieth century. But can we do it?

25 October 1972

Programme Note for *A Clockwork Orange 2004*
Anthony Burgess

A few years ago I published a brief theatrical version of
my novella *A Clockwork Orange*, with lyrics and suggestions as to music (Beethoven mostly). This was done not
because of a great love of the book, but because, for 28
years, I was receiving requests from amateur pop groups
for permission to present their own versions. These were
usually so abysmally bad that I was forced eventually to
pre-empt other perversions with an authoritative rendering
of my own. But the final textual authority, though not
the musical one, rests with this present Royal Shakespeare
Company production. Ron Daniels, who directs it, has
helped a great deal with putting it into a dramatic shape
suitable for a large theatre, and I wish to thank him now
for the hard and valuable work he has poured into what
was very far from an easy task.

I think most people know where the title comes from.
'A clockwork orange' is a venerable Cockney expression
applied to anything queer, with 'queer' not necessarily
carrying any homosexual denotation. Nothing, in fact,
could be queerer than a clockwork orange. When I worked
in Malaya as a teacher, my pupils, when asked to write an

essay on a day out in the jungle, often referred to their taking a bottle of 'orang squash' with them. 'Orang' is a common word in Malay, and it means a human being. The Cockney and the Malay fused in my mind to give an image of human beings, who are juicy and sweet like oranges, being forced into the condition of mechanical objects.

This is what happens to my young thug Alex, whose sweet and juicy criminality, which he thoroughly enjoys, is expunged by a course of conditioning in which he loses the free will which enables him to be a thug – but also, if he wishes, a decent adolescent with a strong musical talent. He has committed evil, but the real evil lies in the process which has burnt out the evil. He is forced to watch films of violence while a drug that induces nausea courses through his veins. But these films are accompanied by emotion-heightening music, and he is conditioned into feeling nausea when hearing Mozart or Beethoven as well as when contemplating violence. Music, which should be a neutral paradise, is turned into a hell.

What looks like a celebration of violence – far worse on the stage than in the book or the film that Stanley Kubrick made (now inexplicably banned in Britain) – is really an enquiry into the nature of free will. This is a theological drama. When human beings are made incapable of performing acts of evil they are also made incapable of performing acts of goodness. For both depend on what St Augustine called *liberum arbitrium* – free will. Whether we like it or not, the power of moral choice is what makes us human. For moral choice to exist, there have to be opposed objects of choice. In other words, there has to be evil. But there has to be good as well. And there has to be an area where moral choice doesn't really apply – that neutral zone where we drink wine, make love, listen to music. But that neutral zone can all too easily become a moral zone. We spend our lives, or ought to, making moral choices.

Ever since I published *A Clockwork Orange* in 1962, I have been plagued by the fact that it has really been two books – one American, the other for the rest of the world. Thus, the British edition has twenty-one chapters while the American edition, till very recently, had only twenty. My American publisher did not like my ending: he said it was too British and too bland. This meant that he saw something implausible – or perhaps merely unsaleable – in my notion that most intelligent adolescents given to senseless violence and vandalism get over it when they sniff the onset of maturity. For youth has energy but rarely knows what to do with it. Youth has not been taught – and is being taught less and less – to put that energy to the service of creation (write a poem, build Salisbury Cathedral out of matchsticks, learn computer engineering). In consequence, youth can use that energy only to beat up, put the boot in, slash, rape, destroy. Our card-operated telephone kiosks are a monument to youth's worse instincts. At the end of this play you are to watch young Alex growing up, falling in love, contemplating eventual fatherhood – in other ways, becoming a man. Violence, he sees, is kid's stuff. My American publisher did not like this ending. Stanley Kubrick, when he made his film out of the American edition, naturally did not know that it existed. That is why the film puzzled European readers of the book. You must make up your own minds as to which ending you prefer. You can always leave before the end.

One final point. In 1990, which we wrongly think is the start of a new decade, we look forward to a bright

European future. The Berlin Wall is coming down, Mikhail Gorbachev is preaching *perestroika* (a word which young Alex is bound to know, since a great deal of his vocabulary is Russian), the Channel Tunnel is burrowing its way to the continent. We are, politically at least, becoming optimistic. Ron Daniels and his talented actors and musicians, as well as myself, are gently suggesting that politics is not everything. That, in a way, was the whole point of the book. Young Alex and his friends speak a mixture of the two major political languages of the world – Anglo-American and Russian – and this is meant to be ironical, for their activities are totally outside the world of politics. The problems of our age relate not to economic or political organisation but to what used to be called 'the old Adam'. Original sin, if you wish. Acquisitiveness. Greed. Selfishness. Above all, aggression for its own sake. What is the purpose of terrorism? The answer is terrorism. Alex is a good, or bad, juvenile specimen of eternal man. That is why he is calling you his brothers.

I have no doubt that, with this new dramatic version of my little book, I shall be blamed for promoting fresh violence in the young. A man who killed his uncle blamed it on Shakespeare's *Hamlet*. A boy who gouged out his brother's eye blamed it on a school edition of *King Lear*. Literary artists are always being treated as if they invented evil, but their true task, one of many, is to show that it existed long before they handled their first pen or word processor. If a writer doesn't tell the truth he'd better not write. This is the truth you're watching.

RSC stage production at the Barbican Theatre,
directed by Ron Daniels, 1990

'Ludwig Van', a review of *Beethoven*
by Maynard Solomon
Anthony Burgess

MUSICAL composition, more than any other creative
activity, shows how far the imagination can function independently of the rest of the human complex. A writer's
arthritis or homosexuality or sweet tooth will often come
through in a spring sonnet. An armless sculptor cannot
sculpt well, no matter how prehensile his toes. A blind
painter cannot paint at all. Frederick Delius, blind and
paralysed, produced fine music. Beethoven, deaf, cirrhotic,
diarrhetic, dyspnoeal, manic, produced the finest, and
healthiest, music of all time. This is not, of course, to say
that the composer's art operates totally in its own autonomous world. Delius found it necessary to tell his amanu-
ensis, Eric Fenby, that those long-held D-major string
chords had something to do with the sea and sky and the
wind arabesques could be seagulls. Gustav Mahler put trivial
hurdy-gurdy tunes in his symphonies until Freud, between
trains, told him why. Although Beethoven's music is about
sounds and structures, it is also, in ways not easily demon-
strable, about Kant and the tyrant at Schönbrunn and
Beethoven himself, body and soul and blood and ouns. To
read Beethoven's biography is to learn something about

what his music is trying to do. Not much, but something.

Maynard Solomon's book is the latest in a long line dedicated to telling the truth about Beethoven as Schindler would not see it and as Thayer, who had to rely heavily on Schindler, was not able to see it. It was only in 1977, at the Berlin Beethovenkongress, that Herre and Beck proved that Schindler had fabricated more than 150 of his own entries in the Conversation Books. Moreover, the hagiographical tendency of many biographies got in the way of presenting the squalor, the clownishness, the downright malice, the drinking and drabbing. It was not right for the composer of the Ninth Symphony and the last quartets to vomit in crapula and frequent brothels. Solomon has no desire to 'fashion an uncontradictory and consistent portrait of Beethoven – to construct a safe, clear, well-ordered design; for such a portrait can be purchased only at the price of truth, by avoiding the obscurities that riddle the documentary material'. At the same time he is prepared to call on Freud and, more, Otto Rank to elucidate the obscurities.

Beethoven was named for his grandfather, a *Kapellmeister* at the electoral court of Cologne, and identified with him, going so far as to wish to deny the paternity of Johann Beethoven and to acquiesce in the legend that he was the illegitimate son of a king of Prussia, either Friedrich Wilhelm II or Frederick the Great himself. He denied his birth year of 1770, despite all the documentary evidence, alleging and eventually believing that he had been born in 1772. His contempt for the drunken, feebly tyrannical, not too talented court tenor who was his father seems not to have been matched by a compensatory devotion to his mother: after all, he was prepared to put it about that she had been a court whore. Beethoven wanted a kind of parthenogenetical birth proper for the messianic role he envisaged for himself.

He would willingly turn a woman into a mother if she was too young for the part. That he regarded mothers as super-erogatory is proved by his turning himself into the father of his nephew Karl, execrating his sister-in-law as the 'Queen of the Night', pretending that the Dutch *van* of his name was really *von* so that he could use aristocratic clout in the courts to dispossess the poor woman of her maternal rights.

He broke free of Viennese musical conventions to assert a new masculine force, appropriate to the Napoleonic age, which should be characterised by rigour of tonal argument and a kind of genial brutality. The legend about his dedicating his Third Symphony to Bonaparte and then tearing up the dedi-cation page after the assassination of the Duc d'Enghien is still to be accepted as true, but Solomon makes it clear that Beethoven was strongly drawn to the tyrant. Vienna's musical talent assembled at Schönbrunn to welcome the conqueror, but Beethoven alone was not invited. He resented this. He arranged a performance of the *Eroica*, expecting Napoleon to turn up. Napoleon did not turn up. Beethoven was not alto-gether the fierce republican, the romantic artist shaking his fist at despots. He owed much to his aristocratic patrons; he dreamed of receiving honours at the Tuileries. He had his eye to the main chance. He liked money. He was ready to sell the same piece of music to three different publishers at the same time and pocket three different advances.

He also had his ear, even when it was a deaf one, to the exterior world of sonic innovations. When Schönberg was told that six fingers were required to play his Violin Concerto, he replied: 'I can wait.' Beethoven did not want six fingers, but he did want a pianoforte – once called by him, in a gust of patriotism, a *Hammerklavier* – that could, there and then, crash out his post-rococo imaginings. The fourth horn part of the Ninth Symphony was specially written for one of the new valve instruments: Beethoven knew a man near Vienna who possessed one. He was a great pianist and a very practical musician. His orchestral parts were hard to play but not impossible. Impossibility hovers, like a fermata, above the soprano parts in the Ninth, but sopranos were women, mothers, sisters-in-law.

It is only through the vague operation of analogy that we can find in a symphony like the *Eroica* – a key work, the work that the composer believed to be his highest orchestral achievement – the properties of the Kantian philosophy and the novels of Stendhal. This music was necessary to the age, but not because of its literary programme. One attaches literary programmes at one's peril to Beethoven's work, even when he says of the yellowhammer call of the Fifth: 'Thus Fate knocks at the door.' Give Beethoven a text and he does more than merely set it. *Fidelio* is a free-from-chains mani-festo typical of its time (though more in Paris than in Vienna), but it is also vegetation myth, with Florestan as a flower god, woman most loved when the female lion becomes the faithful boy, mother into son, the composer himself incarcer-ated in his deafness. It is, as well, much more, and the much more is not easily explicated. The music works at a very deep psychic level, subliterary, submythical, multiguous. When Donald Tovey said that the *Leonora* No. 3 rendered the first act superfluous, he spoke no more than the truth. With the American Solomon's excellent book (though not as excellent as our own Martin Cooper's) we know a little more about the man but nothing more about the mystery of his art. That was to be expected.

Reprinted in *Homage
to Qwert Yuiop: Essays*, 1986

'Gash Gold-Vermillion'
Anthony Burgess

My first copy of Gerard Manley Hopkins's poems was the second edition of 1930 – a slim blue volume about the same size as the newly published selection (edited by Graham Storey, Oxford University Press, 1967) with which Hopkins joins Dryden, Keats, Spenser and other poets in the 'New Oxford English Series'.

The new, fourth, edition of the *Complete Poems* (edited by W. H. Gardner and N. H. Mackenzie, Oxford University Press, 1967), published at the same time, is twice as big, but not, unfortunately, with newly discovered 'terrible' sonnets or odes of the scope of the two shipwreck poems. There are just more fragments than before, and more fugitive verse, and the tale is completed – until the fifth edition – with poems in Latin, Greek and Welsh. Some of the verse written between 1862 and 1868 is to be prized – particularly 'The Summer Malison' ('No rains shall fresh the flats of sea, / Nor close the clayfield's sharded sores, / And every heart think loathingly / Its dearest changed to bores.' – That last line is frightening), and one fragment seems to show that Hopkins might once have taken a Meredithian way: 'She schools the flighty pupils of her eyes, / With levelled lashes stilling their disquiet; / She puts in leash her paired lips lest surprise / Bare the condition of a realm at riot.' But the real oeuvre is unchanged – except that sonnet beginning 'The shepherd's brow, fronting forked lightning' is not, rightly, removed from the appendix to the main body. And some of the emendations of Hopkins's friend and first editor, Robert Bridges, have been boldly thrown out and the readings of the original manuscript restored.

Bridges could be incredibly wanting in ear. In that final sonnet addressed to himself, he made one line read: 'Within her wears, bears, cares and moulds the same', thus killing a sequence based on mingled end-rime and head-rime. Hopkins-lovers always penned in the original 'combs' for 'moulds', and now they have 'combs' in print. In 'The Soldier' Bridges had 'He of all can handle a rope best' where Hopkins wrote 'reeve a rope best' – an exact technical word as well as a necessary head-rime. Re-reading 'The Brothers', I am shocked to find 'Eh, how all rung! / Young dog, he did give tongue!' changed by the present editors to 'There! The hall rung! / Young dog, he did give tongue!' – justified by another manuscript reading but inferior to the version I've known by heart for thirty-five years.

At least, I *think* it's inferior. But once I had an edition of a Chopin nocturne with a misprinted note that made an uncharacteristic dissonance. I got to accept and like this and was disappointed when told eventually that Chopin never wrote it. I think, though, that Hopkins, when revising his work, was over-influenced by a man who was very small beer as a poet; his verse had that small audience for too long, even posthumously. And I think that Bridges erred in holding back publication till 1918 (Hopkins died in 1889): he was too timid, though not too timid to steal – though even there timidly – some of his friend's rhythms. There were poets killed before 1918 who might at least have been granted the pleasure and inspiration of a poetry they were well qualified to understand.

Discussing such inspiration, W. H. Gardner says: '. . . it is likely that James Joyce, E. E. Cummings, and Dylan Thomas were decisively affected by a reading of Hopkins.' Thomas less than you'd think (no sprung rhythm, anyway), Cummings minimally, Joyce not at all. There is, admittedly, a passage in *Finnegans Wake* that seems deliberately to evoke Hopkins (the description of the sleeping Isobel towards the end), but Joyce's mature style was formed before Hopkins was published. And yet the two men pursued the same end out of the same temperament, and it is an irony that it was only chronology that prevented their meeting. Hopkins was a professor of University College, Dublin, where Joyce was eventually a student, but Joyce was only seven when Hopkins died. Hopkins became a Jesuit, and Joyce was Jesuit-trained. Both made aesthetic philosophies out of the schoolmen – Joyce from Aquinas, Hopkins from Duns Scotus. Joyce saw 'epiphanies' flashing out of the current of everyday life; Hopkins observed nature and felt the 'instress' of 'inscapes'.

Both were obsessed with language and knowledgeable about music (Hopkins's song 'Falling Rain' uses quarter-tones long before the experimental Central Europeans). Make a context question out of mixed fragments, and you will sometimes find it hard to tell one author from the other. 'Forwardlike, but however, and like favourable heaven heard these' might do for a Stephen Dedalus interior monologue; actually it comes from 'The Bugler's First

Communion'; 'Muddy swinesnouts, hands, root and root, gripe and wrest them' is from *Ulysses* but would do for a Hopkins poem about martyrs. The eschewal of hyphens helps the resemblance: 'fallowbootfellow' will do for both. But the kinship goes deeper than compressed syntax, a love of compound words, and a devotion to Anglo-Saxonisms. Musicians both, they were both concerned with bringing literature closer to music.

I don't, of course, mean that they pursued conventional 'melodiousness', like unmusical Swinburne who, hearing 'Three Blind Mice' for the first time in his maturity, said that it evoked 'the cruel beauty of the Borgias'. It was rather that they envied music its power of expression through rhythmic patterns, and also the complexity of meaning granted by that multilinear technique which is the glory of the music of the West. All that sprung rhythm does is to give the prosodic foot the same rights as a beat in music. A musical bar can have four crotchets or eight quavers or sixteen semi-quavers, but there are still only four beats. A line in a Hopkins sonnet always has its statutory five beats (or six, if it is an Alexandrine sonnet), and there can be any number of syllables from five to twenty – sometimes more, if we get *senza misura* 'outriders'. 'Who fired France for Mary without spot' has nine syllables; 'Cuckoo-echoing, bell-swarmèd, lake-charmèd, rook-racked, river-rounded' has sixteen: both lines come from the same sonnet. Music always had the freedom of prose with the intensity of verse; since Hopkins, English poetry has been able to enjoy liberty without laxity, on the analogy of music. This is why Hopkins is sometimes called 'the liberator'.

But there's more to it than just rhythm. There have to be the *sforzandi* of music – heavy head-rimes, like 'part, pen, pack' (which means 'separate the sheep from the goats; pen the sheep and send the goats packing') and there have to be internal rhymes, like 'each tucked string tells, each hung bell's / Bow swung finds tongue to fling out broad its name' so that we seem to be listening to the effects of repetition-with-a-difference that are the essence of melodic phrases. But, most important of all, every line must have the solidity of content of a sequence of chords, or else the sense of multiple significance we find in a passage of counterpoint. There's no space for the purely functional, since in music nothing is purely functional.

Hence that compression in Hopkins that sometimes causes difficulty: 'the uttermost mark / Our passion-plunged giant risen' or 'rare gold, bold steel, bare / In both, care but share care' or 'that treads through, prick-proof, thick / Thousands of thorns, thoughts'. In striving to catch a single meaning, we catch more than one; sometimes, as with 'thorns, thoughts', two words seem to merge into each other, becoming a new word, and what one might call an auditory iridescence gives powerful contrapuntal effect.

Joyce lived later and was able to go further. Words like 'cropse' (which means 'a body interred and, through its fertilisation of the earth, able to produce vegetation which may stand as a figure of the possibility of human resurrection') are the logical conclusion of the Hopkinsian method: contrapuntal simultaneity is achieved without the tricks of speed or syntactical ambiguity. But Joyce's aim was comic, while Hopkins brought what he glumly knew would be called 'oddity' to the inscaping of ecstasy or spiritual agony. 'I am gall, I am heartburn' to express the bitterness of the taste of damnation, which is the taste of oneself, is a dangerous phrase, and my old professor, H. B. Charlton (who spoke of Hopkins as though he were a young upstart), could always get an easy seminar laugh by talking about metaphorical stomach trouble. There are plenty of more sophisticated sniggers available nowadays for those who find Hopkins's response to male beauty – physical or spiritual – classically queer: 'When limber liquid youth, that to all I teach / Yields tender as a pushed peach' or the close catalogue of the strength and beauty of Harry Ploughman. And sometimes the colloquial ('black, ever so black on it') or the stuttering ('Behind where, where was a, where was a place?') carries connotations of affectedness guaranteed, with the right camp recite, to bring the house down. Hopkins took frightful risks, but they are all justified by the sudden blaze of success, when the odd strikes as the right and inevitable.

'Success' is an inadequate word for a poet who never aimed at the rhetorical and technical *tour de force* for its own sake. He is, as we have to be reminded, not one of those little priests whom Joyce remarked at UCD – writers of devotional verse; he is a religious poet of the highest rank – perhaps greater than Donne, certainly greater than Herbert and Crashaw. The devotional writer deals in conventional images of piety; the religious poet shocks, even outrages, by wresting the truths of his faith from their safe dull sanctuaries and placing them in the physical world. Herbert does it: '"You must sit down," says Love, "and taste my meat." / So I did sit and eat.'

Hopkins does it more often. The natural world is notated with such freshness that we tend to think that he is merely a superb nature poet, a Wordsworth with genius. And then we're suddenly hit by the 'instress' of revelation: theological properties are as real as the kestrel or the fresh-firecoal chestnut-falls. Reading him, even the agnostic may regret that the 'Marvellous Milk' is no longer

'Walsingham way' and join in calling 'Our King back, Oh upon English souls!' – 'Pride, rose, prince, hero of us, high-priest, / Our hearts' charity's hearth's fire, our thoughts' chivalry's throng's Lord.' This is big magic, which no good Jesuit ought to be able to use.

From *Urgent Copy: Literary Studies*, 1968

'A Clockwork Orange'
Kingsley Amis

I acclaim Anthony Burgess's new novel as the curiosity of the day. *A Clockwork Orange* is told in the first person. That is the extent of its resemblance to anything much else, though a hasty attempt at orientation might suggest Colin MacInnes and the prole parts of *Nineteen Eighty-Four* as distant reference points.

Fifteen-year-old Alex pursues a zealously delinquent career through the last decade of the present century, robbing, punching, kicking, slashing, raping, murdering, going to jail etc. He finds plenty of time to talk to the reader at the top of his voice in his era's hip patois, an amalgam of Russian (the political implications of this are not explored), gypsy jargon, rhyming slang and a touch of schoolboy's facetious-biblical.

All this is done so thoroughly – there are getting on for twenty neologisms on the first page – that the less adventurous reader, especially if he may happen to be giving up smoking, will be tempted to let the book drop. That would be a pity, because soon you pick up the language and begin to see, as the action develops, that this speech not only gives the book its curious flavour, but also fits in with its prevailing mood.

This is a sort of cheerful horror which many British readers, adventurous or not, will not be up to stomaching. Even I, all-tolerant as I am, found the double child-rape scene a little uninviting, especially since it takes place to the accompaniment of Beethoven's *Ninth*, choral section. What price the notion that buying classical LPs is our youth's route to salvation, eh?

But there's no harm in it really. Mr Burgess has written a fine farrago of outrageousness, one which incidentally suggests a view of juvenile violence I can't remember having met before: that its greatest appeal is that it's a big laugh, in which what we ordinarily think of as sadism plays little part.

There's a science-fiction interest here too, to do with a machine that makes you good. We get to this rather late on, as is common when a writer of ordinary fiction has a go at such things, but it's disagreeably plausible when it comes. If you don't take to it all, then I can't resist calling you a starry ptitsa who can't viddy a horrorshow veshch when it's in front of your glazzies. And yarbles to you.

Observer, 13 May 1962

'New Novels'
Malcolm Bradbury

HERE are four novels that must, I suppose, be described as 'modern' – modern in the sense that they are of our time and concerned with the ills to which this time is heir. They deal with our indirection and our indifference, our violence and our sexual exploitation of one another, our rebellion and our protest. Anyone who complains that these themes are now drearily familiar is, of course, right, and there are moments when one wonders if the major dilemma of our time isn't our failure to escape from these platitudinous interpretations of it. It is, I suppose, natural in a time in which so many novels are written that the form should be repetitive; but this means that the novelist we are all looking for is the one who breaks out of the trap.

[. . .]

A similar problem, in more startling form, occurs with Anthony Burgess's *A Clockwork Orange*. This is a novel, set in the not too remote future, about the time when juvenile delinquent gangs take over cities at night and the government develops a brainwashing programme to cure tendencies to crime and violence. The story is told by one of the hooligans, a youth who kills three people, and who, after undergoing the treatment, escapes from it and emerges at the end more or less his old self. We get no distance on him, and in the latter part of the book we are clearly expected to be sympathising with him. What is remarkable about the book, however, is the incredible teenage argot that Mr Burgess invents to tell the story in. All Mr Burgess's powers as a comic writer, which are considerable, have gone into this rich language of his inverted Utopia. If you can stomach the horrors, you'll enjoy the manner.

Punch, 16 May 1962

'Horror Show'
Christopher Ricks

WHEN Anthony Burgess published *A Clockwork Orange* ten years ago, he compacted much of what was in the air, especially the odd mingling of dismay and violence (those teen-age gangs) with pious euphoria about the causes and cures of crime and deviance. Mr Burgess's narrator hero, Alex, was pungently odious; addicted to mugging and rape, intoxicated with his own command of the language (a newly minted teen-age slang, plus poeticisms, sneers, and sadistic purring). Alex was something both better and worse than a murderer: he was murderous. Because of a brutal rape by Alex, the wife of a novelist dies; because of his lethal clubbing, an old woman dies; because of his exhibitionist ferocity, a fellow prisoner dies.

The second of these killings gets Alex jailed: word reaches him of the new Ludovico Treatment by which he may be reclaimed, and he seeks it and gets it. The treatment to watch horrific films of violence (made by one Dr Brodsky) while seething with a painful emetic; the 'cure' is one that deprives Alex of choice, and takes him beyond freedom and dignity, and extirpates his moral existence. But the grisly bloody failure of his suicide attempt after his release does not release him. Alex is himself again.

The novel was simply pleased, but it knew that aversion therapy must be denied its smug violences. And the early 1960s were, after all, the years in which a liberally wishful newspaper like the London *Observer* could regale its readers with regular accounts of how a homosexual was being 'cured' by emetics and films.

'To do the ultra-violent': Alex makes no bones about it. But the film of *A Clockwork Orange* does not want him to be seen in an ultra-violent light. So it bids for sympathy. There are unobtrusive mitigations: Alex is made younger than in the book. There are obtrusive crassnesses from his jailors: when Alex pauses over the form for Reclamation Treatment, the chief guard shouts, 'Don't read it, sign it' – and of course it has to be signed in triplicate (none of that in the book). There are sentimentalities: where in the book it was his drugs and syringes that he was shocked to find gone when he got home, in the film he has been provided instead with a pet snake, Basil, whom his parents have wantonly and hypocritically done in. Above all, Alex is the only person in the film who isn't a caricature, the only person the film is interested in; whereas in the first-person narrative of the book, Alex was the only person Alex was interested in.

One realises that the film is a re-creation, not a carrying-over, and yet both Kubrick and Burgess are right to call upon each other in what they've recently written in defence of the film, Kubrick in the *New York Times*, February 27, 1972, and Burgess in *The Listener*, February 17. The persistent pressure of the film's Alexculpations is enough to remind one that while *A Clockwork Orange* is in Burgess's words 'a novel about brainwashing,' the film is not above a bit of brainwashing itself – is indeed righteously unaware that any of its own techniques or practices could for a moment be asked to subject themselves to the same scrutiny as they project. Alex is forced to gaze at the Ludovico treatment aversion films: 'But I could not shut my glazzies, and even if I tried to move my glaz-balls about I still could not get like out of the line of fire of this picture.' Yet once 'this picture' has become not one of Dr Brodsky's pictures but one of Mr Kubrick's, then two very central figures are surreptitiously permitted to move 'out of the line of fire of this picture.'

First, the creator of the whole fictional 'horrorshow' itself. For it was crucial to Burgess's *A Clockwork Orange* that it should include a novelist who was writing a book called *A Clockwork Orange* – crucial not because of the fad for such Chinese boxes, but because this was Burgess's way of taking responsibility (as Kubrick does *not* take responsibility for Dr Brodsky's film within his film), Burgess's way of seeing that the whole enterprise itself was accessible to its own standards of judgment. The novelist F. Alexander kept at once a curb and an eye on the book, so that other propensities than those of Dr Brodsky were also under moral surveillance. Above all the propensity of the commanding satirist to become the person who most averts his eyes to what he shows: that 'satire is a sort of glass wherein beholders do generally discover everybody's face but their own.' But in the film F. Alexander (who is brutally kicked by Alex, and his wife raped before his eyes) is not at work on a book called *A Clockwork Orange*, and so the film – unlike the book – ensures that it does not have to stand in its own line of fire.

Nor, secondly and more importantly, does Alex have to. The film cossets him. For the real accusation against the film is certainly not that it is too violent, but that it is not

violent enough; more specifically, that with a cunning selectivity it sets itself to minimise both Alex's violence and take
delight in it. Take his murders or woman-slaughters. The
old woman in the novel with cats and an ineffectual stick
becomes in the film a professionally athletic virago who
nearly stuns him with a heavy *objet d'art*: the killing comes
after a dervishlike tussling and circling, and moreover is
further protected, Alex-wise, by being grotesquely farcical
– Alex rams her in the face with a huge sculpture of a penis
and testicles, a pretentious art work which she has preten-
tiously fussed about and which when touched jerks itself
spasmodically.

The film reshapes that murder to help Alex out. Similarly
with the more important death of the novelist's wife. 'She
died, you see. She was brutally raped and beaten. The
shock was very great.' But the film – by then nearing its
end – doesn't want Alex to have this death on our
consciences, so the novelist (who is manifestly half-mad
to boot) is made to mutter that the doctor said it was
pneumonia she died of, during the flu epidemic, but that
he knew, etc., etc. Or, not to worry, Alex-lovers.

Then there is the brutal killing within the prison cell,
when they all beat up the homosexual newcomer:

> Anyway, seeing the old krovvy flow red in the red
> light, I felt the old joy like rising up in my keeshkas
> ... So they all stood around while I cracked at this
> prestoopnick in the near dark. I fisted him all over,
> dancing about with my boots on though unlaced,
> and then I tripped him and he went crash crash on
> to the floor. I gave him one real horrorshow kick on
> the gulliver and he went ohhhhh, then he sort of
> snorted off to like sleep.

No place for any of that in the film, since it would entail being more perturbed about Alex than would be convenient. No, better to show all the convicts as good-natured buffoons and to let the prison guards monopolise detestability. The film settles for a happy swap, dispensing with the killing in the cell and proffering instead officialdom's humiliating violence in shining a torch up Alex's rectum. None of that in the book.

'When a novelist puts his thumb in the scale, to pull down the balance to his own predilection, that is immorality' (D. H. Lawrence). As a novelist, Burgess controls his itching thumb (he does after all include within himself as much of a polemicist for Original Sin and for Christian extremity as his co-religionists Graham Greene and William Golding). But the film is not content with having a thumb in the pan – it insists on thumbs down for most and thumbs up for Alex. Thumbs down for Dr Brodsky, who is made to say that the aversion drug will cause a deathlike terror and paralysis; thumbs down for the Minister of the Interior, who bulks proportionately larger and who has what were other men's words put into his mouth, and whose asinine classy ruthlessness allows the audience to vent its largely irrelevant feelings about 'politicians,' thus not having to vent any hostility upon Alex; thumbs down for Alex's spurious benefactors, who turn out to be mad schemers against the bad government, and not only that but very vengeful – the novelist and his friends torture Alex with music to drive him to suicide (the book told quite another story).

But thumbs up for the gladiatorial Alex. For it is not just the killings that are whitewashed. Take the two girls he picks up and takes back to his room. In the book, what matters to Alex – and to our sense of Alex – is

283

that they couldn't have been more than ten years old, that he got them viciously drunk, that he gave himself a 'hypo jab' so that he could better exercise 'the strange and weird desires of Alexander the Large,' and that they ended up bruised and screaming. The film, which wants to practise a saintlike charity of redemption towards Alex but also to make things assuredly easy for itself, can't have any of that. So the ten-year-olds become jolly dollies; no drink, no drugs, no bruises, just the three of them having a ball. And to make double sure that Alex is not dislodged from anybody's affection, the whole thing is speeded up so that it twinkles away like frantic fun from a silent film. Instead of the cold brutality of Alex's 'the old in-out,' a warm Rowan and Martin laugh-in-out.

Conversely, Alex's fight with his friends is put into silent slow motion, draping its balletic gauzes between us and Alex. And when one of these droogs later takes his revenge on Alex by smashing him across the eyes with a milk bottle and leaving him to the approaching police, this too has become something very different from what it was in the book. For there it was not a milk bottle that Dim wielded but his chain: 'and it snaked whishhhh and he chained me gentle and artistic like on the glazlids, me just closing them up in time.' The difference which that makes is that the man who is there so brutally hurt is the man who had so recently exulted in Dim's prowess with that chain:

Dim had a real horrorshow length of oozy or chain round his waist, twice wound round, and he unwound this and began to swing it beautiful in the eyes or glazzies . . . Old Dim with his chain snaking whissssssshhhhhhhhh, so that old Dim chained him right in the glazzies, and this droog of Billyboy's went tottering off and howling his heart out.

The novel, though it has failures of judgement which sometimes let in a gloat, does not flinch from showing Alex's exultation. The movie takes out the book's first act of violence, the protracted sadistic taunting of an aged book lover and then his beating up:

'You naughty old veck, you,' I said, and then we began to filly about with him. Pete held his rookers and Georgie sort of hooked his rot wide open for him and Dim yanked out his false zoobies, upper and lower. He threw these down on the pavement and then I treated them to the old boot-crush, though they were hard bastards like, being made of some new horrorshow plastic stuff. The old veck began to make sort of chumbling shooms – 'wuf waf wof' – so Georgie let go of holding his goobers apart and just let him have one in the toothless rot with his ringy fist, and that made the old veck start moaning a lot then, then out comes the blood, my brothers, real beautiful. So all we did then was to pull his outer platties off, stripping him down to his vest and long underpants (very starry; Dim smecked his head off near), and then Pete kicks him lovely in his pot, and we let him go.

The film holds us off from Alex's blood-lust, and it lets Alex off by mostly showing us the only show of violence. The beating of the old drunk is done by four silhouetted figures with their sticks – horribly violent in some ways, of course, but held at a distance. That distance would be artistically admirable if its intention was to preclude the pornography of bloodthirstiness rather than to preclude our realising, making real to ourselves, Alex's bloodthirstiness. Likewise the gang fight is at first the frenzied destructiveness of a Western and is then a stylised distanced drubbing; neither of these incriminates Alex as the book had honourably felt obliged to do. The first page of the book knows that Alex longs to see someone 'swim in his blood,' and the book never forgets what it early shows:

> Then we tripped him so he laid down flat and heavy
> and a bucket-load of beer-vomit came whooshing out.
> That was disgusting so we gave him the boot, one go
> each, and then it was blood, not song nor vomit, that
> came out of his filthy old rot. Then we went on our
> way.
> [. . .]
> And, my brothers, it was real satisfaction to me to
> waltz – left two three, right two three – and carve
> left cheeky and right cheeky, so that like two curtains
> of blood seemed to pour out at the same time, one
> on either side of his fat filthy oily snout in the winter
> starlight.

The film does not let Alex shed that blood. But it isn't against blood-letting or hideous brutality, it just insists on enlisting them. So we see Alex's face spattered with blood at the police station, the wall too; and we see a very great deal of blood-streaming violence in the aversion therapy film which the emetic-laden Alex is forced to witness. What this selectivity of violence does is ensure that the aversion film outdoes anything that we have as yet been made to contemplate (Alex's horrorshows are mostly allowed to flicker past). It is not an accident, and it is culpably coercive, that the most long-drawn-out, realistic, and hideous act of brutality is that meted on Alex by his ex-companions, now policemen. Battered and all but drowned, Alex under violence is granted the mercy neither of slow motion nor of speeding up. But the film uses this mercilessness for its own specious mercy.

There is no difficulty in agreeing with Kubrick that people do get treated like that; and nobody should be treated like that. At this point the film doesn't at all gloat over the violence which it makes manifest but doesn't itself manifest. Right. But Burgess's original artistic decision was the opposite: it was to ensure that we should deeply know of but not know about what they did to Alex: 'I will not go into what they did, but it was all like panting and thudding against this like background of whirring farm machines and the twittwittwittering in the bare or nagoy branches.' I will not go into what they did: that was Burgess as well as Alex speaking. Kubrick does not speak, but he really goes into what they did. By doing so he ensures our sympathy for Alex, but at the price of an enfeebling circularity. 'Pity the monster,' urges Robert Lowell. I am a man more sinned against than sinning, the film allows Alex to intimate.

The pain speaks for Alex, and so does the sexual humour. For Kubrick has markedly sexed things up. Not just that modern sculpture of a penis, but the prison guard's question ('Are you or have you ever been a homosexual?'), and the social worker's hand clapped hard but lovingly on Alex's genitals, and the prison chaplain's amiable eagerness to reassure Alex about masturbation, and the bare breasted nurse and the untrousered doctor at it behind the curtains of the hospital bed. All of this may seem to be just good clean fun (though also most uninventively funny), but it too takes its part within the forcible reclamation of Alex which Kubrick no less than Dr Brodsky is out to achieve.

The sexual farce is to excriminate Alex as a bit of a dog rather than one hell of a rat, and the tactic pays off – but cheaply – in the very closing moments of the film, when Alex, cured of his cure and now himself again, is listening to great music. In the film his fantasy is of a voluptuous slow-motion lovemaking, rape-ish rather than rape, all surrounded by costumed grandees applauding – amiable enough, in a way, and a bit like *Billy Liar*. The book ends with the same moment, but with an unsentimental certainty as to what kind of lust it still is that is uppermost for Alex:

> Oh it was gorgeosity and yumyumyum. When it came to the Scherzo I could viddy myself very clear running and running on like very light and mysterious nogas, carving the whole litso [face] of the creeching world with my cutthroat britva. And there was the slow movement and the lovely last sighing movement still to come. I was cured all right.

The film raises real questions, and not just of the are-liberals-really-liberal? sort. On my left, Jean-Jacques Rousseau; on my right, Robert Ardrey – this is factitious and fatuous. When Kubrick and Burgess were stung into replying to criticism, both claimed that the accusation of gratuitous violence was gratuitous. Yet Kubrick makes too easy a diclaimer – too easy in terms of the imagination and its sources of energy, though fair enough in repudiating the charge of 'fascism' – when he says that he should not be denounced as a fascist, 'no more than any well-balanced commentator who read "A Modest Proposal" would have accused Dean Swift of being a cannibal.'

Agreed, but it would be Swift's imagination, not his behaviour, that would be at stake, and there have always been those who found 'A Modest Proposal' a great deal more equivocally disconcerting than Kubrick seems to. As Dr Johnson said of Swift, 'The greatest difficulty that occurs, in analysing his character, is to discover by what depravity of intellect he took delight in revolving ideas, from which almost every other mind shrinks with disgust.' So that to invoke Swift is apt (Alex's slang 'gulliver' for head is not just Russian *golova*) but isn't a brisk accusation-stopper.

Again, when Burgess insists: 'It was certainly no pleasure to me to describe acts of violence when writing the novel,' there must be a counter-insistence: that on such a matter no writer's say-so can simply be accepted, since a writer mustn't be assumed to know so – the sincerity in question is of the deepest and most taxing kind. The aspiration need not be doubted:

> What my, and Kubrick's, parable tries to state is that
> it is preferable to have a world of violence undertaken
> in full awareness – violence chosen as an act of will
> – than a world conditioned to be good or harmless.

When so put, few but B. F. Skinner are likely to contest it. But there are still some urgent questions.

1. Isn't this alternative too blankly stark? And isn't the book better than the film just because it doesn't take instant refuge in the antithesis, but has a subtler sense of responsibilities and irresponsibilities here?

2. Isn't 'the Judaeo-Christian ethic that *A Clockwork Orange* tries to express' more profoundly disconcerting than it is suggested by Burgess's hospitable formulation?

I think of Empson's arguments that Christianity marks itself out from the other great religions by holding on to an act of human sacrifice, and that it is a system of torture worship. The Christian Church has always ministered to, often connived at, and sometimes practised the fiercest and most insidious acts of brainwashing. The book in this sense takes its religion much more seriously – that is, does not think of it as somehow patently unimpeachable. 'The wish to diminish free will is, I should think, a sin against the Holy Ghost' (Burgess). Those who do not believe in the Holy Ghost need not believe that there is such a thing as the sin against the Holy Ghost – no reassuring worst of sins.

3. Isn't the moral and spiritual crux here more cruelly unresolvable, a hateful siege of contraries? T. S. Eliot sought to resolve it:

> So far as we are human, what we do must be either evil or good; so far as we do evil or good, we are human; and it is better, in a paradoxical way, to do evil than to do nothing: at least, we exist. It is true to say that the glory of man is his capacity for salvation; it is also true to say that his glory is his capacity for damnation. The worst that can be said of most of our malefactors, from statesmen to thieves, is that they are not men enough to be damned.

But Eliot's teeth are there on edge, and so are ours; those who do not share the religion of Eliot and Burgess may think that no primacy should be granted to Eliot's principle – nor to its humane counter-principle, that it is better to do nothing than to do evil.

4. Is this film worried enough about films? Each medium

will have its own debasements when seduced by violence. A novel has but words, and words can gloat and collude only in certain ways. A play has people speaking words, and what Dr Johnson deplored in the blinding of Gloucester in *King Lear* constitutes the artistic opportunity of drama, that we both intensely feel that great violence is perpetrated and intensely know that it is not: 'an act too horrid to be endured in a dramatic exhibition, and such as must always compel the mind to relieve its distress by incredulity.' But the medium of film is an equivocal one (above all how far people are really part of the medium), which is why it is so peculiarly fitted both to use and to abuse equivocations. *A Clockwork Orange* was a novel about the abuses of the film (its immoralities of violence and brainwashing), and it included – as the film of *A Clockwork Orange* does not – some thinking and feeling which Kubrick should not have thought that he could merely cut:

This time the film like jumped right away on a young devotchka who was being given the old in-out by first one malchick then another then another then another, she creeching away very gromky through the speakers and like very pathetic and tragic music going on at the same time. This was real, very real, though if you thought about it properly you couldn't imagine lewdies actually agreeing to having all this done to them in a film, and if these films were made by the Good or the State you couldn't imagine them being allowed to take these films without like interfering with what was going on. So it must have been very clever what they called cutting or editing or some such veshch. For it was very real.

[. . .]

The minds of this Dr Brodsky and Dr Branom . . . They must have been more cally and filthy than any prestoopnick in the Staja itself. Because I did not think it was possible for any veck to even think of making films of what I was forced to viddy, all tied up to this chair and my glazzies made to be wide open.

The film of *A Clockwork Orange* doesn't have the moral courage that could altogether deal with that. Rather, like Kubrick's *Dr Strangelove*, it has a central failure of courage and confidence, manifest in its need to caricature (bold in manner, timid at heart) and in its determination that nobody except Alex had better get a chance. Burgess says: 'The point is that, if we are going to love mankind, we will have to love Alex as a not unrepresentative member of it.' A non-Christian may be thankful that he is not under the impossibly cruel, and cruelty-causing, injunction to love mankind.

New York Review of Books, 6 April 1972; reprinted in *Reviewery*, 2003

'All Life is One: *The Clockwork Testament, or Enderby's End*'
A. S. Byatt

THE plot of *The Clockwork Testament, or Enderby's End* concerns the final activities, in New York, of the minor poet, F. X. Enderby, eponymous protagonist of *Inside Mr Enderby* and *Enderby Outside*. He is indirectly responsible for the film, *The Wreck of the Deutschland*, developed (by rewrite men) 'out of an idea by F. X. Enderby' 'based on the story by' G. M. Hopkins S. J. Real horrorshow sinny, as Alex, the hero of *A Clockwork Orange*, would have said, transposed to Nazi times, incorporating 'over-explicit scenes of nuns being violated by teenage stormtroopers' and advertised by a 'gaudy poster showing a near-naked nun facing, with carmined lips opening in orgasm, the rash-smart sloggering brine'.

Called to American attention by this democratic medium, Enderby has become Professor of Creative Writing at the University of Manhattan. He is occupied with a long poem about the conflict between St Augustine and Pelagius or Morgan, the British heretic, who believed God had left man free to choose between Good and Evil. He is harassed by journalists, who are gleefully perturbed about outbreaks of nunslaughter in Manhattan and

293

Ashton-under-Lyne, and by teenage thugs whom he pinks with a swordstick in the subway. He is threatened by black power, women's lib, free verse, a female Christ. He has two mild heart attacks. And a final showdown with a mysterious female visitor, as in *Enderby Outside*, who knows his poems. This one, unlike the golden lady of the earlier book, intends to shoot him because her knowledge of his work is restricting her freedom to compose. She announces herself as Dr Greaving from Goldengrove.

Enderby proclaimed in the first book that all women were stepmothers: rendered impotent, more or less, by terror of his own particularly gross one, he retreated into cloacal austerity and prolonged adolescent fantasy, supported by her legacy to him, some shares and some repulsive dietary habits. But women are also bitch goddesses, white goddesses, moon goddesses and sun goddesses, with whom Enderby's relations are agonised, embarrassed and incomplete. He masters this last, Americano-Hopkins Muse, at a cost.

Burgess returns, with his own mixture of crude gusto and verbal intricacy, to a concentration of themes: the freedom of the will, the nature of Good and Evil (and their difference from right and wrong) and the relationship between art and morals, the proposition that all life is one.

In *The Wanting Seed*, a repellent and gripping fable of the future, he turned the debate between Pelagius and Augustine into a historical principle, the Cycle. Pelphase – belief in human perfectibility, liberal values, standardization, rules, order. Interphase – disappointment, breeding repression. Gusphase – belief in original sin, human nature as destructive, use of war, sex and flesheating as social organising forces, Pelphase is rational, Gusphase religious and magical.

Burgess, like Enderby, sees both extremes as myths. Enderby quotes Wagner – *wir sind ein wenig frei*. A *little* free – to choose between good and evil. That is the moral of that book with a moral, *A Clockwork Orange*. Alex is chemically conditioned to 'like present the other cheek'. The Pelagian chaplain warns him – 'when a man cannot choose, he ceases to be a man'. But the existence of choice involves the existence of evil, violence, horror, as according to Enderby and Burgess, does art.

In Enderby's epic *The Pet Beast*, the Minotaur, double natured, man, God, beast, gentle and flesh-eating at the centre of the lawgiver's labyrinth, is crucified by the Pelagian liberator. But the daedale labyrinth contains the Cretan culture – with the death of the Beast, who is original sin, civilisation crashes into dust. Alex, conditioned to be repelled by violence, is conditioned to be repelled by Beethoven. Enderby, in this book, describes God as a kind of infinite Ninth Symphony playing itself eternally, unconcerned with human rights and wrongs. Aesthetic good is morally neutral, although it contains the knowledge of Good and Evil, beauty and destruction.

It may be that one needs a Catholic upbringing to appreciate the full urgency of Burgess's dichotomies. Like the Pet Beast, everything in his world is dual, flesh and spirit, as well as good and evil. Those who can claim that all life is one are either dangerous normative doctors and psychologists or the representatives of the White Goddess, tempting Enderby to the violence inherent in the flesh and beauty and sex which he has always feared.

The Clockwork Testament makes intricate connexions between these themes, Hopkins, film and book of the *Clockwork Orange* and all sorts of aspects of contemporary art and life. It succeeds because it is ferociously funny and wildly, verbally inventive.

There are various tours-de-force – the Hopkins-Enderby script of the *Wreck of the Deutschland*, an excruciating illustrative transcript of the television show, complete with commercials (for an aerosol product called Mansex) full of double-entendres and horrible puns. There are Enderby's encounters with the Creative Writing of his students.

There is a miraculous moment when Enderby, having undergone the poems of Black Hatred ('It will be your balls next whitey') and some 'sloppy and fungoid' imitation Hart Crane, suddenly produces on demand his idea of a good poem. 'Queen and huntress chaste and fair.' The White Goddess again. Dangerous but orderly, in culture, history and language.

The Times, 6 June 1974

Afterword
Stanley Edgar Hyman

ANTHONY Burgess is one of the newest and most talented of the younger British writers. Although he is forty-five, he has devoted himself to writing only in the last few years; with enormous productivity, he has published ten novels since 1956; before that he was a composer, and a civil servant in Malaya and Brunei. His first novel to be published in this country, *The Right to an Answer*, appeared in 1961. It was followed the next year by *Devil of a State*, and by *A Clockwork Orange* early in 1963. A fourth novel, *The Wanting Seed*, is due out later in 1963. Burgess seems to me the ablest satirist to appear since Evelyn Waugh, and the word 'satire' is inadequate to his range.

The Right to an Answer is a terribly funny, terribly bitter smack at English life in a provincial city (apparently the author's birthplace, Manchester). The principal activity of the townspeople seems to be the weekend exchange of wives, and their dispirited slogan is 'Bit of fun' (prophetically heard by Mr Raj, a visiting Ceylonese, as 'bitter fun'). The book's ironic message is Love. It ends quoting Raj's unfinished manuscript on race relations: 'Love seems inevitable, necessary, as normal and as easy a process as respiration, but unfortunately . . .' the manuscript breaks off. Raj's love has just led him to kill two people and blow his brains out. One thinks of *A Passage to India*, several decades more sour.

Devil of a State is less bitter, more like early Waugh. Its comic target is the uranium-rich East African state of Dunia (obviously based on the oil-rich Borneo state of Brunei). In what there is of a plot, the miserable protagonist, Frank Lydgate, a civil servant, struggles with the rival claims of his wife and his native mistress, only to be snatched from both of them by his first wife, a formidable female spider of a woman. The humour derives mainly from incongruity: the staple food in Dunia is Chinese spaghetti; the headhunters upriver shrink a Belgian head with eyeglasses and put Brylcreem on its hair.

Neither book at all prepares one for the savagery of Burgess' next novel. *A Clockwork Orange* is a nightmarish fantasy of a future England where the hoodlums take over after dark. Its subject is the dubious redemption of one such hoodlum, Alex, told by himself. The society is a limp and listless socialism at some future time when men are on the moon: hardly anyone still reads, although streets are named Amis Avenue and Priestley Place; Jonny Zhivago, a 'Russky' pop singer, is a juke-box hit, and the teenage language is three-quarters Russian; everybody 'not a child nor with child nor ill' must work; criminals have to be rehabilitated because all the prison space will soon be needed for politicals; there is an opposition and elections, but they reelect the Government.

A streak of grotesque surrealism runs all through Burgess' books. In *Right to an Answer*, at one melodramatic point, a corpse grunts and turns over in its coffin. In *Devil of a State*, a political meeting is held in a movie theatre while polecats walk the girders near the roof, sneer down at the audience, and dislodge bits of dried excrement on their heads. By *A Clockwork Orange* this has become truly infernal. As the hoodlums drive to their 'surprise visit,' they run over a big snarling toothy thing that screams and squelches, and as they drive back they run over 'odd squealing things' all the way.

Alex has no interest in women except as objects of violence and rape (the term for the sex act in his vocabulary is characteristically mechanical, 'the old in-out in-out'). No part of the female body is mentioned except the size of the breasts (it would also interest a Freudian to know that the hoodlums' drink is doped milk). Alex's only 'aesthetic' interest is his passion for symphonic music. He lies naked on his bed, surrounded by his stereo speakers, listening to Mozart or Bach while he daydreams of grinding his boot into the faces of men, or raping ripped screaming girls, and at the music's climax he has an orgasm.

A running lecture on free will, first from the prison chaplain, then from the writer, strongly suggests that the book's intention is Christian. Deprived of his capacity for moral choice by science, Burgess appears to be saying, Alex is only a 'clockwork orange,' something mechanical that appears organic. Free to will, even if he wills to sin, Alex is capable of salvation, like Pinky in *Brighton Rock* (*Devil of a State*, incidentally, is dedicated to Greene). But perhaps this is to confine Burgess' ironies and ambiguities within simple orthodoxy. Alex always *was* a clockwork orange, a machine for mechanical violence far below the level of choice, and his dreary socialist England is a giant clockwork orange.

Perhaps the most fascinating thing about the book is its language. Alex thinks and talks in the 'nadsat' (teenage) vocabulary of the future. A doctor in the book explains it. 'Odd bits of old rhyming slang,' he says. 'A bit of gipsy talk, too. But most of the roots are Slav. Propaganda. Subliminal penetration.' Nadsat is not quite so hard to decipher as Cretan Linear B, and Alex translates some of it. I found that I could not read the book without compiling a glossary; I reprint it here, although it is entirely unauthorised, and some of it is guesswork.

At first the vocabulary seems incomprehensible: 'you could peet it with vellocet or synthemesc or drencrom or one or two other veshches.' Then the reader, even if he knows no Russian, discovers that some of the meaning is clear from context: 'to tolchock some old veck in an alley and viddy him swim in his blood.' Other words are intelligible after a second context: when Alex kicks a fallen enemy on the 'gulliver' it might be any part of the body, but when a glass of beer is served with a gulliver, 'gulliver' is 'head.' (Life is easier, of course, for those who know the Russian word *golova*.)

Burgess has not used Russian words mechanically, but with great ingenuity, as the transformation into 'gulliver,' with its Swiftian associations, suggests. Others are brilliantly anglicised: *khorosho* (good or well) as 'horrorshow'; *liudi* (people) as 'lewdies'; *militsia* (militia or police) as 'millicents'; *odinock* (lonesome) as 'oddy knocky.'

Burgess uses some Russian words in an American slang extension, such as *nadsat* itself, the termination of the Russian numbers eleven to nineteen, which he breaks off independently on the analogy of our 'teen.' Thus *kopat* (to dig with a shovel) is used as 'dig' in the sense of enjoy or understand; *koshka* (cat) and *ptitsa* (bird) become the hip 'cat' and 'chick'; *neezhny* (lower) turns into 'neezhnies' (underpants); *pooshka* (cannon) becomes the term for a pistol; *rozha* (grimace) turns into 'rozz,' one of the words for policeman; *samyi* (the most) becomes 'sammy' (generous); *soomka* (bag) is the slang 'ugly woman'; *vareet* (to cook up) is also used in the slang sense, for something preparing or transpiring.

The 'gipsy talk,' I would guess, includes Alex's phrase 'O my brothers,' and 'crark' (to yowl?), 'cutter' (money), 'filly' (to fool with), and such. The rhyming slang includes 'luscious glory' for 'hair' (rhyming with 'upper story'?) and 'pretty polly' for 'money' (rhyming with 'lolly' of current slang). Others are inevitable associations, such as 'cancer' for 'cigarette' and 'charlie' for 'chaplain.' Others are produced simply by schoolboy transformations: 'appy polly loggy' (apology), 'baddiwad' (bad), 'eggiweg' (egg), 'skol-liwoll' (school), and so forth. Others are amputations: 'guff' (guffaw), 'pee and em' (pop and mom), 'sarky' (sarcastic), 'sinny' (cinema). Some appear to be portman-teau words: 'chumble' (chatter-mumble), 'mounch' (mouth-munch), 'shive' (shiv-shave), 'skriking' (striking-scratching).

There are slight inconsistencies, when Burgess (or Alex) forgets his word and invents another or uses our word, but on the whole he handles his Russianate vocabulary in a masterly fashion. It has a wonderful sound, particularly in abuse, when 'grahzny bratchny' sounds infinitely better than 'dirty bastard.' Coming to literature by way of music, Burgess has a superb ear, and he shows an interest in the texture of language rare among current novelists. (He confessed in a recent television interview that he is obsessed by words.) As a most promising writer of the 60s, Burgess has followed novels that remind us of Forster and Waugh with an eloquent and shocking novel that is quite unique.

After *A Clockwork Orange*, Burgess wrote *The Wanting Seed*, which appeared in England in 1962 and will soon be published in the United States. It is a look centuries ahead to a future world almost as repulsive as Alex's. Perpetual

Peace has been established, and the main effort of government is to hold down human reproduction. Contraceptive pills are universal, infanticide is condoned, homosexuality is officially encouraged, and giving birth more than once is a criminal act. We see this world as it affects the lives of Tristram Foxe, a schoolteacher, his wife Beatrice-Joanna, a natural *Urmutter*, and his brother Derek, Beatrice-Joanna's lover, who holds high office in the government by pretending to be homosexual. In this world of sterile rationalism, meat is unknown and teeth are atavistic, God has been replaced by 'Mr Livedog,' a figure of fun ('God knows' becomes 'Dog-nose'), and the brutal policemen are homosexuals who wear black lipstick to match their ties.

As a result of all the organised blasphemy against life, in Burgess' fable, crops and food animals are mysteriously stricken all over the world, and as rations get more and more meagre, order breaks down. The new phase is heralded by Beatrice-Joanna, who gives birth in a kind of manger to twin sons, perhaps separately fathered by the two men in her life.

But the new world of fertility is no better than the world of sterility that it supplants. Soon England is swept by cannibalism (the epicene flesh of policemen is particularly esteemed), there are public sex orgies to make the crops grow, and Christian worship returns, using consecrated human flesh in place of wine and wafer ('eucharistic ingestion' is the new slogan). The check on population this time is a return to old-fashioned warfare with rifles, in which armies of men fight armies of women; war is visibly 'a massive sexual act.'

At the end, Tristram, who as a representative man of both new orders has been in prison and the army, is reunited with his wife and her children, but nothing has changed fundamentally. The cycle, now in its Augustinian phase with the emphasis on human depravity, will soon enough swing back to its Pelagian phase, with the emphasis on human perfectibility.

The Wanting Seed shows Burgess' familiar preoccupation with language. His vocabulary rivals that of Wallace Stevens: a woman is 'bathycolpous' (deep-bosomed), a male secretary is 'flavicomous' (blond), a Chinese magnate is 'mactated' (sacrificially killed), moustaches are 'corniculate' (horned). The book is full of Joycean jokes: in a long sequence of paired names for the public fertility rites, one pair is 'Tommy Eliot with Kitty Elphick,' which is, of course, Old Possum with one of his Practical Cats; war poetry is read to the army on Saturday mornings, on order of Captain Auden-Isherwood.

On her way to the State Provision Store to buy her ration of vegetable dehydrate, synthelac, compressed cereal sheets, and 'nuts' or nutrition units, Beatrice-Joanna stops to take a breath of the sea, and Burgess' beautiful sentence is an incantation of sea creatures: 'Sand-hoppers, mermaids' purses, sea gooseberries, cuttle bones, wrasse, blenny and bullhead, tern, gannet and herring gull.'

Like any satirist, Burgess extrapolates an exaggerated future to get at present tendencies he abhors. These include almost everything around. He does not like mindless violence, but he does not like mechanical reconditioning either; he detests sterile peace and fertile war about equally. Beneath Anthony Burgess' wild comedy there is a prophetic (sometimes cranky and shrill) voice warning and denouncing us, but beneath that, on the deepest level, there is love: for mankind, and for mankind's loveliest invention, the art of language.

From the first American edition of
A Clockwork Orange, 1963

A Last Word on Violence
Anthony Burgess

MY novella *A Clockwork Orange*, especially when it was transformed into a highly coloured and explicit film, has apparently qualified me as a major spokesman on violence. I learned recently that another book of mine, *1985*, has become a kind of textbook for the Red Brigades. I can claim, nevertheless, no special interest in violence, except the fascination that it arouses in all human beings. Violence fascinates because it is the obverse of the one thing that humanity shares with God – the ability to create. Creation requires talent and violence does not, but both have the same result – transformation of natural material, excitement bordering on the orgasmatic, a sense of power. If there is shame in the perpetration of violence, as opposed to the quasi-religious elation of producing a work of art, this is easily qualified by a sense of an exalted end of which violence is the means – the building of a better society, for instance. When the perpetrator of violence wears a uniform – that of the state police or of a revolutionary paramilitary force – the violence is wholly excused and takes on the lineaments of sanctity. What was done to Aldo Moro provoked, in the doers, elation and shame at the elation, but the shame was dissolved in a sense of political purpose.

Violence has traditionally been the preserve of the private sector of society and condemned as a criminal act. In our century, however, the State has seen the advantages of using it. Such States as have used it and still use it began as revolutionary groups operating in the private sector – the Fascists, the Nazis, the Communists – but elevation of the revolutionaries to full statehood – in other words, turning them into the forces of official reaction – has sanctified violence as a tool of statecraft.

Violence can only be countered by violence, and we must now accept the enactment of brutality, often for the highest declared purpose, as an ineradicable aspect of contemporary life. I do not mean solely torture and killing, but also violence done to the stability of the community through such devices as inflation, and the more terrible violence, enacted in the name of technological progress, done to the environment. We have all come to terms with violence: it is our daily news and our nightly entertainment. Once I saw a public way out of it, now I can only see hope in the refusal of the individual to accept violence as a norm of our society and, in consequence, to be prepared for martyrdom. It is a grim prospect.

16 March 1982

ANNOTATED PAGES
from Anthony Burgess's
1961 Typescript of
A Clockwork Orange

Title page

*see altacher / or
they will.*

A CLOCKWORK ORANGE

Anthony Burgess

HEINEMANN

LONDON MELBOURNE TORONTO

old Dim had a very hound-and-horny one of a clown's litso
(face, that is), Dim not ever having much of an idea of things
and being, beyond all shadow of a doubting thomas, the dimmest
of ~~the~~ four. Then we wore waisty jackets without lapels but
with these very big built-up shoulders ("pletchoes" we called
them) which were a kind of a mockery of having real shoulders
like that. Then, my brothers, we had these off-white cravats
which looked like whipped-up kartoffel or spud with a sort of
a design made on it with a fork. We wore our hair not too long
and we had flip horrorshow boots for kicking.

"What's it going to be then, eh?"

There were three devotchkas sitting at the counter all together, but there were four of us malchicks and it was usually
like one for all and all for one. These sharps were dressed
in the heighth of fashion too, with purple and green and orange
wigs on their gullivers, each one not costing less than three
or four weeks of those sharps' wages, I should reckon, and make-
up to match (rainbows round the glazzies, that is, and the rot
painted very wide). Then they had long black very straight
dresses, and on the groody part of them they had little badges
of like silver with different malchicks' names on them - Joe
and Mike and suchlike. ~~These were supposed to be the names of
the different malchicks they'd spatted with before they were
fourteen.~~ Stet They kept looking our way and I nearly felt like saying the three of us (out of the corner of my rot, that is)
should go off for a bit of pol and leave poor old Dim behind,
because it would be just a matter of koopeeting Dim a demi-
litre of white but this time with a dollop of synthemesc in it,
but that wouldn't really have been playing like the game. Dim
was very very ugly and like his name, but he was a horrorshow
filthy fighter and very handy with the boot.

"What's it going to be then, eh?"

The chelloveck sitting next to me, there being this long
big plushy seat that ran round three walls, was well away with
his glazzies glazed and sort of burbling slovos like "Aristotle wishy washy works outing cyclamen get forficulate smartish".

2.

God bless you, boys," drinking.

Not that it mattered much, really. About half an hour went
by before there was any sign of life among the millicents, and
then it was only two very young rozzes that came in, very pink
under their big copper's shlemmies. One said:

"You lot know anything about the happenings at Slouse's
shop this night?"

"Us?" I said, innocent. "Why, what happened?"

"Stealing and roughing. Two hospitalisations. Where've
you lot been this evening?"

"I don't go for that nasty tone," I said. "I don't care
much for these nasty insinuations. A very suspicious nature all
this betokeneth, my little brothers."

"They've been in here all night, lads," the old sharps started to creech out. "God bless them, there's no better lot of boys
living for kindness and generosity. Been here all the time they
have. Not seen them move we haven't."

"We're only asking," said the other young millicent. "We've
got our job to do like anyone else." But they gave us the nasty
warning look before they went out. As they were going out we
handed them a bit of lip-music: brrrrzzzzrrrr. But, myself, I
couldn't help a bit of disappointment at things as they were those
days. Nothing to fight against really. Everything as easy as
kiss-my-sharries. Still, the night was still very young.

10.

you want? Get out at once before I throw you out." So poor old
Dim, masked like Peebee Shelley, had a good loud smeck at that,
roaring like some animal.

"It's a book," I said. "It's a book what you are writing."
I made the old goloss very coarse. "I have always had the strongest admiration for them as can write books." Then I looked at
its top sheet, and there was the name - A CLOCKWORK ORANGE - and
I said, "That's a fair gloopy title. Who ever heard of a clockwork orange?" Then I read a malenky bit out loud in a sort of
very high type preaching goloss: " - The attempt to impose upon
man, a creature of growth and capable of sweetness, to ooze juicily at the last round the bearded lips of God, to attempt to impose, I say, laws and conditions appropriate to a mechanical creation, against this I raise my swordpen - " Dim made the old
lip-music at that and I had to smeck myself. Then I started to
tear up the sheets and scatter the bits over the floor, and this
writer moodge went sort of bezoomny and made for me with his
zoobies clenched and showing yellow and his nails ready for me
like claws. So that was old Dim's cue and he went grinning and
going er er and a a a for this veck's dithering rot, crack crack,
first left fistie then right, so that our dear old droog the red
- red vino on tap and the same in all places, like it's put out
by the same big firm - started to pour and spot the nice clean
carpet and the bits of his book that I was still ripping away at,
razrez razrez. All this time this devotchka, his loving and
faithful wife, just stood like froze by the fireplace, and then
she started letting out little malenky creeches, like in time to
the like music of old Dim's fisty work. Then Georgie and Pete
came in from the kitchen, both munching away, though with their
maskies on, you could do that with them on and no trouble,
Georgie with like a cold leg of something in one rooker and half
a loaf of kleb with a big dollop of maslo on it in the other,
and Pete with a bottle of beer frothing its gulliver off and a
horrorshow rookerful of like plum cake. They went haw haw haw,
viddying old Dim dancing round and fisting the writer veck so

18.

one of these stinking millicents at the back with me. The fat-
necked not-driver said:

"Everybody knows little Alex and his droogs. Quite a famous
young boy our Alex has become."

"It's those others," I creeched. "Gerogie and Dim and Pete.
No droogs of mine, the bastards."

"Well," said the fat-neck, "you've got the evening in front
of you to tell the whole story of the daring exploits of those
young gentlemen and how they led poor little innocent Alex
astray." Then there was the shoom of another like police siren
passing this auto but going the other way.

"Is that for those bastards?" I said. "Are they being picked
up by you bastards?"

"That," said fat-neck, "is an ambulance. Doubtless for your
old lady victim, you ghastly wretched scoundrel."

"It was all their fault," I creeched, blinking my smarting
glazzies. "The bastards will be peeting away in the Duke of New
York. Pick them up, blast you, you vonny sods." And then there
was more smecking and another malenky tolchock, O my brothers,
on my poor smarting rot. And then we arrived at the stinking
rozz-shop and they helped me get out of the auto with kicks and
pulls and they tolchocked me up the steps and I knew I was going
to get nothing like fair play from these stinky grahzny bratchnies, Bog blast them.

54a.

desks, and at the like chief desk the top millicent was sitting,
looking very serious and fixing a like very cold glazzy on my
sleepy litso. I said:

"Well well well. What makes, bratty? What gives, this fine
bright middle of the nochy?" He said:

"I'll give you just ten seconds to wipe that stupid grin off
of your face. Then I want you to listen."

"Well, what?" I said, smecking. "Are you not satisfied with
beating me near to death and having me spat upon and making me
confess to crimes for hours on end and then shoving me among
bezoomnies and vonny perverts in that grahzny cell? Have you
some new torture for me, you bratchny?"

"It'll be your own torture," he said, serious. "I hope to
God it'll torture you to madness."

And then, before he told me, I knew what it was. The old
ptitsa who had all the kots and koshkas had passed on to a better
world in one of the city hospitals. I'd cracked her a bit too
hard, like. Well, well, that was everything. I thought of all
those kots and koshkas mewing for moloko and getting none, not
any more from their starry forella of a mistress. That was everything. I'd done the lot, now. And me still only fifteen.

60.

PENGUIN MODERN CLASSICS

M/F
ANTHONY BURGESS

'One of the cleverest and most original writers of his generation … a powerful and mischievous novelist' *The Times*

Kicked out of college and harassed by his lawyer, Miles Faber abandons New York and embarks on a defiant pilgrimage across the Caribbean to find the shrine of Sib Legeru, an obscure poet and painter. But in the streets of Castita's capital, where a wild religious festival is in full swing, a series of bizarre encounters – including one with his own repulsive doppelgänger (the son of a circus bird-woman) – and disturbing family revelations await Miles, who soon finds himself a willing victim of dynastic destiny.

A darkly surreal comedy of dazzling linguistic inventiveness, *M/F* is an outrageous tale of blood, lust and the machinations of fate.

'Burgess is the great post-modern storehouse of British writing … an important experimentalist' Malcolm Bradbury, *Independent on Sunday*

Read more about Anthony Burgess and Penguin Classics

The International Anthony Burgess Foundation

> 'That's a fair gloopy title.
> Who ever heard of a clockwork orange?'

The International Anthony Burgess Foundation encourages and supports public and scholarly interest in all aspects of the life and work of Anthony Burgess. Based in Manchester, England, there is an extensive library, archive and study centre containing Burgess's books, music and papers.

Visit the International Anthony Burgess Foundation website to find out more about *A Clockwork Orange*. A new online resource includes articles on the novel, the film, the stage play, the music, the language and the legacy of *A Clockwork Orange*; galleries of rare images and book covers from the Burgess Foundation collections; and a special podcast including newly discovered audio material and recordings of Burgess's music.

www.anthonyburgess.org